NIGHT
SONGS

Also by Alli Dyer

Strange Folk

NIGHT SONGS

A Novel

ALLI DYER

ATRIA BOOKS

NEW YORK • AMSTERDAM/ANTWERP • LONDON
TORONTO • SYDNEY/MELBOURNE • NEW DELHI

ATRIA BOOKS

An Imprint of Simon & Schuster, LLC
1230 Avenue of the Americas
New York, NY 10020

First Atria Books hardcover edition August 2026

ATRIA BOOKS and colophon are trademarks of Simon & Schuster, LLC

Interior design by Yvonne Taylor

Manufactured in the United States of America

1 3 5 7 9 10 8 6 4 2

Library of Congress Control Number: 2025038653

ISBN 978-1-6680-4580-0
ISBN 978-1-6680-4582-4 (ebook)

For Doug and Ripley

When one life ends, another begins

NIGHT SONGS

There was a woman in town who sang so sweet
Her beauty was beyond compare
But one day a bright specter she did meet
There aft she was no longer fair
She ranted and raved and ran over town
Chased by somethin' not seen
She ran so far that she came to a cliff
And it chased her over to free'n

From *Folk Songs of the Southern United States* by Quentin C. Hermes
Title: "Untitled Folk Song #33"
Origin: Tennessee
Source and date: Unknown

PROLOGUE

Thank god for the Amtrak Quiet Car.

The moment I passed through its doorway, a calm descended. The circulated air was sweeter here, and each passenger kept to their own mind. I lurched my way down the aisle as the train swayed, finally stopping at a seat in the far corner, out of view of the security cameras.

Once settled, I absently reached into my pocket for the thin body of my phone, but instead my hand closed around the thick wedge of the burner. *6:03* glowed from the screen.

My husband wouldn't be up for another two hours. It might be fifteen or twenty more minutes before he checked my room. Then another twenty of him searching the house with his phone up to his ear, listening to my number forward to voicemail. First, he would try the most obvious places like the bathroom and the kitchen, before moving on to the strange ones—the spare room we never used, the attic with no floor, the dark hollows of the hibiscus bushes in the backyard.

Would he call my friends first, or would he go straight to the police? Months ago I would have said the former, but my sense of him has lost its dexterity.

I imagined him speaking to a detective in our living room with his hands on his hips. I used to love watching him talk to other people. I saw his self-assured posture, his thoughtful words, his calm pauses that people sometimes rushed to fill with half points and broken sentences.

Pain bled through the image, and my stomach lurched, bile crawling up my throat. I pushed it down, shifted focus. There was no vomiting allowed in the quiet car.

Regardless of what he did, it would be hours before the word spread. I had time before I needed to look over my shoulder.

I reached up and slid a lock of smooth blonde hair between my fingers. The wig looked more real than my own hair, like I'd been rendered in a higher definition.

I'd considered adding glasses, but that seemed unnecessary. I had the kind of face that people thought they'd seen before. Strangers were always narrowing their eyes in confusion, attempting to place me in their memory. The chatty ones would ask if we'd met, and I'd tell them that it happened all the time. My greatest distinction being that I lacked any distinction at all.

The conductor arrived at my seat, and I handed him the ticket I'd bought at the station with cash, my hand shaking and the wig weighing heavily on my skull. But he punched it without a look and moved on.

I loved trains. No security checks. No identification required. You were entirely anonymous in your seat, each person inhabiting their own quiet landscape.

I watched the land stream by, and I knew at any moment I could escape to its solid ground and go anywhere I wanted.

Another thing about a train was how the mind moved with it. *Train thoughts*. Different from airplane thoughts. Those were manic and giddy with altitude. Train thoughts were grounded, contemplative, moody in the best way. Something about speeding through different terrain, the constant shifting of scenery out the window—it rerouted the mind down tracks it hadn't explored in years, or perhaps ever.

That was what I needed now, more than avoiding a cramped, airless airplane or traveling under a fake name. I needed to remember where this all started, and what I had forgotten over the years, way back before I ever learned about the curse.

Not the moment everything changed, but right before, when I was still an anonymous entity, miserably unaware of where I came from.

Just a little demon child, desperate for love.

1

rhea

1995

Shelli and I sat at the edge of a rocky cliff with our legs dangling over a vast unknown. She passed me the bottle of grape Mad Dog we stole from the 7-Eleven, and I took a sip. It tasted like poisoned Halloween candy, its red glowing radioactive in the falling light.

I handed it back, and she poured some out into the still, dark waters of the quarry below. "I offer this wine to the gods, in celebration of Rhea's birth." She smiled and took another swig. "Happy Birthday." She pressed play on the boom box, and "Fade into You" by Mazzy Star wafted into the air.

I wouldn't turn eighteen until the next day, but I never celebrated on my birthday. Always the night before, and usually alone or with a friend like Shelli. I didn't want a cake or presents or to be the center of a hot, whirring celebration.

All I wanted was one moment where I would look out and feel a connection to the world that was soft and hopeful. I would know it by a sound in my throat, like a cross between a grunt and a sigh. It hadn't happened yet, but I was sure it would come. I could feel its potential in the air like downy oxygen.

The trees rustled behind us, and two boys from our high school emerged carrying a twelve-pack of Icehouse like they'd slain a bear. I had seen them before, watching from the shadows at parties as I hooked up with their more confident friends.

I grabbed the bottle from Shelli and took a large gulp.

They watched us now as they set down the beer and each took a can. One of them, Rick, had a trace of dark hair on his upper lip, and he approached first, with doughy Steve trailing behind him.

"What's up?" Rick asked, putting a bit of asshole into his voice.

I held up the bottle in explanation, and we turned wordlessly back to our celebration.

"Lesbos," Steve murmured behind us. It was the only way he could explain why we hadn't been waiting for them. Why we were content to be here alone with no one watching us.

Shelli whispered, "Let's go."

"No," I whispered back.

Rick cracked his beer and gestured toward the water. "Bet you never jumped before."

"Bet you haven't either," I answered without thinking.

He snickered. "We've done it a bunch of times."

I turned back and looked him in the eyes. They were gooey and pink like they'd smoked in the front seat of his grandma's Nissan Stanza.

"Okay, let's see it," I said.

He glanced at Steve and shook his head. "Naw. I just wanna get hammered." He took a lusty sip of beer, and a bit of it dribbled down his acne-studded chin. I couldn't imagine a more repulsive creature.

I peered over the edge. It was clear all the way down, with no outcroppings to catch on. The water was famous for its depth; a few kids had tried to swim to the bottom, but they'd never found it.

I stood up, pried my Chucks off at the heels, and tucked my socks inside. My feet were soft and pale, like new babies against the smooth, sunbaked stone. I walked up to the very tip of the ledge where it jutted out over the water like a prehistoric diving board.

"There's no way," Rick mocked.

It was my favorite time of day, just before the sun set, when the light was almost purple. The California air was so hot and dry it smelled like dust. Thick yellow-wooded pine extended for miles in the distance, and birds dove and emerged from the treetops like they were pollinating them.

I felt the soft grunt in my throat, and I knew this was the moment.

I took a few steps back, then I ran toward the ledge and jumped.

The air was slick against my body, the trees rushing up to meet me.

I entered the water like a needle sliding into a vein.

I let my body sink down until I hit a cold, silent place. Then I opened my eyes, and there was only murky dark blue, like I'd discovered a sliver of night below the water. I floated there, unmoving, just a chunk of debris.

Something smooth thumped powerfully against my ankle, and I jerked, the sudden hot movement sucking down my oxygen.

I kicked against the water and propelled myself upward, my lungs screaming and my head pulsing. I broke through the surface gasping and barely able to tread water. It seemed darker out, as if I'd been down there for hours. My limbs were nearly numb as I pulled myself up on the far bank and lay there for a while, allowing my body to return to itself.

I scanned the ledge above, and I was surprised that no one peered over. I hadn't heard a single cheer or scream. The skin on my arms prickled where it had come back to life, and I shot to my feet and moved toward the trail that led back to the ledge. My wet jean shorts rubbed against my thighs and the rocks cut into my bare feet, but the pain quickly receded as I ran up the steep incline.

When I got to the ledge, it was empty save for the twelve-pack and the bottle of Mad Dog on its side, dribbling red onto the rock. I heard murmurs in the trees, and I followed them to a cleared spot where Steve had Shelli pinned to the ground with one meaty knee. Rick stood above them with his fingers hooked in the waistband of his pants.

I charged at Rick, knocking his body down hard against the earth. We tussled, and he turned over and straddled me.

"I thought you said they were sluts," Steve said to Rick.

"I know *she* is," Rick answered, sneering down at me.

I struggled against him, but I couldn't throw off his weight. I was trapped and utterly helpless, and the claustrophobic panic I sometimes felt rose up like a toxic gas. All I wanted was for it to stop.

My body took over, and my head smashed into his, his nose bursting into a mass of lurid blood. He rolled off me clutching his face, and I crawled toward Steve, who immediately stood up and raised his hands in surrender. Shelli remained on the ground, unmoving.

I pulled her up to standing, but when I let go, her legs went limp beneath her. I crouched down and threw her tiny body over my shoulder.

As I trudged through the woods to Shelli's car, my heart slowed, and my creature instincts bristled, then receded back to their hiding place. I was a girl once more.

In my bedroom, Shelli cleaned the blood from my face with shaking hands while I inhaled In-N-Out.

"Are you okay?" I asked gently.

She nodded feebly. "Yeah, I'm fine. Nothing really happened. I was just scared."

"I would have been scared, too."

"No. You would have fought back."

I didn't know how to tell her that it wasn't me who had attacked Rick. It was this creature inside me that I couldn't control.

She picked up a bag of frozen pizza bagels and pressed it to my bruised temple. Then she wrapped an ACE bandage around my head and secured it in place. "Okay, you're all set." I looked in the mirror at the ridiculous wrap, and we both giggled.

We got into bed, and Shelli dropped off almost immediately. The clock next to me read 11:30 with its grains of demonic rice. I lay there perfectly still, listening to the white noise of Shelli's breathing, waiting for my body to shut down.

But I knew there would be no sleep tonight.

Birthdays filled me with dread. They always had, and back then, I had no idea why. When I was little, I thought it was the flu. But as I got older and noticed the sickness always dissipated the next day, I began to think of it as a premonition of the year's coming misery.

My room in that house never shook off its guest-room origins, even though I'd lived in it since I was seven. The pastel plaid bedspread and matching curtains, the white wicker furniture, and the fake flowers sprouting from their gray-pink vase all felt temporary, like I was living on the set of a sitcom that was about to get canceled. The only distinctive feature was the gold cross on the left wall, which was more like the set of *Carrie*. My aunt Lorraine's attempt to passively exorcize whatever evil lay at the center of me.

I absently traced the long purple birthmark that stretched across my collarbone like a scab that wouldn't heal. People at school gossiped that it was one sliver of an enormous tattoo or a scar from whatever killed my parents.

For me it was like a brand, marking me as the property of some distant, mysterious place, separate from everyone else.

My father died before I was born, and then my mother died when I was five. I was sent to live with my father's parents, who croaked just two years later, and then passed along to my father's sister, Lorraine, and her husband, Carl. I was like a pestilence, sowing death wherever I went. My aunt and uncle had only survived out of sheer awfulness, preserved by their meanness like cucumbers in vinegar.

They almost never talked about my parents, except to say that my father had been a good, God-fearing man until he met my mother, a "white-trash drug addict" who was apparently the devil incarnate. They didn't call her by her name, only *her* with a curving condemnation to the letters.

I didn't have any concrete memories of my mother—only a few glimmers. Some nights I would dream of being held against a warm chest, and I would feel this comfort that was almost muscular in strength, but I could never see a face. When I woke, I would be filled with this intense yearning to be touched, and I'd wish I hadn't dreamt it at all, that it was better not to know how it felt to be loved like that.

But I much preferred this dream to the nightmare I sometimes had, of squatting with my small child's body in a tight, dark space, desperate to escape, a feeling of intense, claustrophobic panic suffusing my every cell. I would wake with sweat rolling down my chest, and while it was a relief to be in my room where I could move around freely, I never quite shook the feeling of being trapped.

In lieu of a clear mental image or any physical picture of my mother, I had conjured many versions of her in my mind. But there were two main ones: a soft, fiercely loving woman like Sally Field in *Forrest Gump*, and a cold, thin-armed, tragically beautiful dope fiend like Kelly Lynch in *Drugstore Cowboy*.

Sometimes I wondered if the creature inside me, the one that filled my head with strange thoughts and impulses that didn't feel like my own, was some remnant of the early years I'd spent with my mother before she died. Some remnant of her need.

When morning broke, Shelli snuck out the window for her own bed, and I curled in a ball like a grub and prayed to the universe for the day to pass quickly.

But as much as I wanted to wallow, I knew that if I continued to lay there, at some point my uncle Carl would poke his head in and say "Feeling lazy today, are we?" hoping to catch me in my underwear. I used to lean a chair against my door in lieu of an actual lock, but that had been prohibited for the sake of "fire safety."

I dressed and walked downstairs, passing the new oil painting hanging above the mantel. It showed my cousin Dinah posing with her lustrous chestnut horse Cocoa Puff. Their manes shone equally in the play of light.

The painting looked out of place in my aunt and uncle's modest suburban house, as did the other dissonant luxuries they owned, like Carl's yellow Porsche, or Lorraine's tanning bed, which she kept in the living room for lack of space. I didn't know how they could afford these things, given Carl managed a Chili's and Lorraine worked part-time for their church, but I assumed it was something pathetic like tax evasion. Carl liked to pretend he was a red-blooded male, but at his core he was too meek to do anything truly risky.

In the kitchen, they were already eating their breakfast with Dinah. Five tiny purebred dogs surrounded them, breathing poorly, their beady eyes trained on the bacon between my aunt's fingers. As I moved about the kitchen pouring a cup of coffee and adding cream, my uncle watched me with a similar expression.

"Rhea, you're looking very mature this morning," he said.

My body suddenly felt enormous and fleshy, and impossible to hide. I glanced at my aunt to see if she was listening, but she was busy cooing to one of the dogs and feeding him bits of burned fat. When I tried to make eye contact with Dinah, she looked away.

I had learned it was better not to engage Carl. If I told him to eat shit, he'd treat me like an alley cat that needed to be tamed. He liked to watch my skin flush. It was part of the game.

I kept my face blank and leaned against the counter with my cup, preferring the physical distance. But then he continued to gaze at me from head to toe, and I moved to the table, hiding my bottom half from view.

"Happy birthday, Rhea," he leered. "It's a big one this year. *Eighteen.*"

God, I was going to be sick.

Lorraine looked up from the dog and smiled wanly. "Oh right, yes, happy birthday. Dinah?"

"Happy birthday," she said, staring down at her breakfast.

"Thanks." I cringed internally, praying that was the end of it.

The doorbell rang, and we all looked sharply toward the door.

"Are you expecting someone?" Carl asked Lorraine.

"No." She glanced at me and Dinah, and we both shrugged.

Carl grunted and went to the window that offered a view of the front stoop. He gestured at Lorraine, who joined him, and they whispered fiercely to each other before Carl muttered he wouldn't hide in his own home and opened the door.

A man in a well-tailored suit carrying a briefcase stood in the doorway, elegantly silhouetted against the suburban sunshine.

"Mr. Blau, we weren't expecting you."

"Good morning, Mr. Keller. I apologize for the intrusion, but it could not be avoided. I have made many attempts to get in touch with Miss Larsen via phone and mail, but they have all been unsuccessful." His speech was polished and polite with a slight twang.

Lorraine stepped between them and lowered her voice. "*We've* been trying to get in touch with *you*. Have you gotten any of our messages?"

His mouth flattened into a thin line. "Yes, I have." He didn't elaborate. "May I come in? I'd like to speak with Miss Larsen."

Carl stepped in front of the doorway. "No, you may not. As her legal guardians, we're not comfortable with you speaking to our daughter."

Carl liked to invoke their "guardianship" when it suited him, as if they were my fierce, loving protectors. Never mind that after eleven years, they still hadn't adopted me.

"Am I mistaken that today is Miss Larsen's eighteenth birthday? She is no longer a minor, sir, and therefore, no longer under your *jurisdiction*."

I had never seen anyone talk to Carl this way. I was stunned, and incredibly confused.

Mr. Blau craned his neck around my flustered relatives and made eye contact with me. "Miss Larsen, if your aunt and uncle aren't comfortable with me coming inside, would you care to join me on the front lawn?"

"No! No. You can come in," Carl blustered, and Lorraine ushered the man past the door before the neighbors could witness any more. They moved to sit on the couch in the living room, but Mr. Blau stopped them. "This will be a private meeting between Miss Larsen and I."

Carl swore under his breath and Lorraine scowled, but they begrudgingly trudged upstairs to their room, gesturing for Dinah to follow.

Mr. Blau trained his gaze toward the ceiling, and I watched it catch on the oil painting of Dinah and her horse. He studied it curiously until we heard two doors shut upstairs, then he took a seat and folded his hands in his lap. "Miss Larsen. My name is Anthony Blau, and I am your mother's estate lawyer. Now that you are eighteen—" He paused awkwardly. "Happy birthday, by the way."

My stomach turned at the words, and I urged him to go on.

"As I was saying, now that you are eighteen, you may assume control of your mother's estate as indicated in her will." He opened his briefcase and laid out a few papers on the coffee table.

From the picture Lorraine had painted, I'd always imagined my mother dying penniless in a dirty motel room, and my father's family being forced to take me in out of Christian guilt. I wondered what kind of "estate" she could have left behind.

He continued, "These documents describe the full contents of the estate, which includes a financial portfolio of various stocks, bonds, mutual funds, retirement accounts, and a few real estate holdings in Nashville. We've also set aside some cash that you can access right away—"

My mouth went dry. "What . . . what is this?"

"This is your mother's estate." He gestured at the papers. "Which is now being passed to you."

"How . . . how much is it worth?"

He pursed his lips. "If you liquidated right now—of course you'd pay some hefty fees, but if you wanted to take the hit . . ." He paused, calculating. "I'd say you'd have about ten million in cash. Of course it's *worth* more than that if you allow it to continue to grow." He glanced up at me for a response, but I was having a hard time breathing. "Pardon my rambling.

Do you understand the basic concept, or is there something I can explain a bit better at this juncture?"

"No, I don't understand. Where did this all come from? How did she have so much money?"

He raised an eyebrow. "Well, as you know, she was *quite* successful when she was alive, especially in the five years before her death. She was shrewd with her money, and she set it up well for you. It has grown immensely over the years."

"What do you mean, 'she was successful'? Doing what?"

He paused, collecting himself. "You don't know who your mother was?"

Shame prickled in my cheeks. "I mean . . . I know her name was Lulabelle, and she was from Tennessee. That's where I was born." I also knew she was a junkie who basically killed my father, but that didn't feel right to mention.

He scowled, and his eyes flicked back toward the ceiling. "Your mother's name was Lulabelle, yes, but she was more commonly known, at least by the public, as Belle. *Belle Powers.*"

"The country singer?"

"Yes."

The image of a woman with towering blonde hair and garish makeup entered my mind like a fever dream. My heart beat in my temples. "Is this a prank or something? I don't understand."

His mouth settled into a flat line. "Rhea, I don't know what your aunt and uncle told you, but Belle Powers was, without a doubt, your mother."

"I think you have the wrong person . . ."

He shook his head. "You and I met once before, when you were smaller. Before she died."

"But I was just a baby then. How would you even know it was me?"

Without looking down at my chest, he said, "I would know that birthmark anywhere."

Heat spread across my collarbone, where part of the mark poked out above my tank top.

"Wait—so did she die of an overdose?"

He looked taken aback. "What on earth? Is that what they told you?"

I nodded, and his shock resolved back into a scowl. "I can't believe . . ." He paused, collecting himself. "No. Your mother died in a plane crash. It actually happened a few hours from here, off the coast of Santa Barbara."

I felt a bit woozy, like my body was dissolving and pooling into the polyester of the couch. My entire existence was a lie. "And my father? Who was he? How did he die?"

Mr. Blau swallowed uncomfortably. "Your father was a notable songwriter—wrote a few songs for big acts, I believe." He smiled slightly, then went solemn again. "But he did in fact die of an overdose, I'm sorry to say."

So maybe my life wasn't a total lie. He'd OD'd. But not *her*. Her death had been some romantic tragedy. Not of weakness and negligence, but cruel fate.

And they had both been artists. Creative, glittering geniuses, and not worthless druggies fallen from grace. It struck me that I finally had something of real value, parents who were special and luminous.

And in the next moment, I'd already lost it—they were both gone.

"I know this is a lot to process," Mr. Blau said, reaching across the table and resting a gentle hand on mine. When I didn't respond, he sat back and crossed his arms over his lap. "What are your summer plans?"

I tried to remember who I'd been before this conversation. "I'm going to work full-time at the conference center." I'd cater-waited there for the last four years, and I hated every minute of it. Running around in the fake tuxedo uniform, scrubbing ranch dressing from my nail beds, fending off drunk firemen at their annual gala.

"Do you enjoy that?"

"No."

He smirked. "Well, then. What do you think about coming to Nashville for the summer? I have paperwork I need you to sign, and we could take more time to go over estate business. You can be as involved as you want, of course, but it might be good for you to get a sense of it."

I considered this. "Do I have family in Nashville?"

He sighed. "No, not exactly. I was led to believe that Belle had a few relatives where she grew up in rural Tennessee, but they've all passed."

"Oh . . . okay." Not that I was eager to meet more relatives after my track record, but perhaps her people would have been different. Maybe we would have understood each other in a way I never had with my dad's family. "What do you mean by 'not exactly'?"

"Well, she considered her friends as family more than the people she came from. And there are quite a few still living in Nashville. Do you remember any of them?"

"No, I . . . I don't even remember her."

He looked disappointed then, and something like sadness passed over his face before he shook it off. "That's a shame, but it's no matter."

I had the keen sense of missing something important, but there was that child's barrier still in the way, cutting me off from the dim, smoky layer of the world inhabited by adults.

"What was she like?" I asked suddenly, realizing this was, above all, what I yearned to know.

He smiled. "I wish I had known her better, but what I did see was . . . unexpected. She was never just one thing. I . . ." He exhaled. "I'm not very good at articulating this—I'm more of a numbers guy. It's why I like representing artists like your mother. What they do is magical to me."

I tried to conjure an image of her from these words, but all I could see were flashes of the Belle Powers I'd seen pictures of in magazines and throwback music videos. The enormous blonde wig, the heavy makeup and hot-pink lipstick, the flashy, sequined outfits. It was all shimmer and costume with no human beneath it.

"If you'd like to know more about her, coming to Nashville is a great start. I think the only way to truly know someone is to see where they spent their life."

I had never considered going to Nashville—it was only a rhinestone-studded word that I put on forms when asked for my place of birth. My limited sense of the South came from movies like *Steel Magnolias* or *Fried Green Tomatoes*, and from its bloody history. None of these were specific to Nashville.

But perhaps it was where I'd find *her* and the mysterious place I'd sprung from.

"Okay, I'd like to go. When do we leave?"

He chuckled. "Eager, are we? Well, my flight is a few hours from now, but I can delay a night or two for you to get your affairs in order."

"No, I'm good. I just need a couple minutes to pack."

He raised his eyebrows. "All right, then. I'll wait in the car outside while you ready yourself." He got up, and I followed him to the door. He put a hand on the knob, then turned back.

"In case you weren't aware, we send a sizable amount of money to your aunt and uncle every month to cover your living expenses." He looked pointedly at the oil painting of Dinah and her horse. "They've made attempts to gain access to your inheritance in the last few months, but I've put them off. As of today, the payments to them will end. Now that you control the estate, you can decide how it's distributed." He nodded politely, and then he was gone.

Carl and Lorraine were down the stairs before the door shut. "What did he say?" Lorraine hissed.

I was speechless for a moment, like those scenes in movies when a bomb goes off nearby and a person stumbles around with blood leaking from their ears.

I had never entirely believed my aunt and uncle about my parents. They were pathological liars, and even when they told the truth, I often questioned their version of reality.

But this level of deception was . . . unforgivable.

My bewilderment receded, replaced by the creature-like rage I'd felt when I saw the boys standing over Shelli's body. "Everything you told me about my mother was a lie." I clenched my fists and let it fill me up. "You had no right to keep this from me."

Lorraine looked stricken, then narrowed her eyes. "I am your guardian—I have *every* right."

"Not anymore." I charged up the stairs and into my room, barely feeling the carpet under my feet. I slammed the door behind me and wedged the chair under the knob. The door shook as Lorraine and Carl pounded on its wood.

I yanked open my backpack and frantically stuffed clothes in from the dresser. Then I tossed in my makeup case, my Discman, and my soccer cleats.

For a moment, I panicked at having to fit my entire life into this small bag, but then I looked at all my cheap, worn-out crap, and I thought, *Fuck it.* I had *money* now. I could buy whatever I needed.

I had one foot out the window when Lorraine and Carl barged in, pulling me back into the room. Lorraine stuck her finger in my face, her cheeks red. "Where do you think you're going?"

"Nashville. And I'm taking my mother's money with me."

Carl blanched. "Now hold on a minute—"

"Mr. Blau told me he's been sending you money every month."

"Well, of course. For your upkeep. It's not exactly cheap raising a teenager," Lorraine said, feigning innocence.

I stared at her in disbelief. She couldn't really believe I was that stupid. "Then you won't mind if I leave," I said as I tried to get around them, but Carl blocked the door.

"Don't you think we deserve a little *compensation* for raising you all these years?" Lorraine asked. "We could have left you on the street, but we took you in and treated you like our own."

For my entire childhood, she'd made me feel like I was the only thing keeping them from a perfect life. It's why I'd stayed out of sight, kept quiet, worked since I was fourteen—all to alleviate the weight of my existence. "Are you kidding? All you've ever done was lie to me."

"I was *protecting* you from the truth. From that *trash* who killed my poor brother."

I stared at her smug, pinched face and imagined ripping her eyes from their sockets.

"I thought if you didn't know, then maybe you wouldn't be like her," she continued, lowering her voice. "But that was naive. I see *her* in you. The way you look at my husband." She moved closer and whispered even more softly, "The devil's in you. I can feel it every time you're near. Makes my skin *crawl*."

I pushed her off hard with my shoulder, and she stumbled back against the wall in surprise. When the shock wore off, she hissed, "I want you *out* of this house."

"Don't worry. I'm gone." I slung my bag over my shoulder and headed for the door past a slack-jawed Carl. "Good luck paying for Cocoa Puff now," I called behind me as I skipped down the stairs to their stunned silence.

That evening in my roomy first-class seat, I ate white chocolate raspberry cheesecake and sipped on my fifth free Dr Pepper.

I had always thought of being rich, or more precisely, the aspiration to be rich, as pathetic and unimaginative—the provenance of my aunt and uncle and their poor taste.

But I couldn't deny that it was sort of *fun*.

The captain announced we were landing, and I watched with my face pressed up to the window as we sailed over the modest Nashville skyline with miles of fertile green spreading beyond it. I searched for some recognition of my homeland, but it still looked foreign to me. A place waiting to be discovered.

Mr. Blau leaned over and took in the view. "You know, Belle was your same age when she first came to Nashville."

"Tell me more," I demanded.

He gave me a fatherly smirk. "The story goes that in 1967, when she was eighteen, she came to Nashville on a bus from the mountains with just a cardboard suitcase and her daddy's beat-up guitar." He paused for effect. "She hopped off that bus, and just a few hours later, met a record executive at a honky-tonk." He smiled, his eyes filled with the silver reflection of the city. "The rest is history."

2

lulabelle

1967

FIFTEEN YEARS LEFT

I remember it was early morning when I stumbled onto the main road. I wiped my bloody hands in the snow and rubbed fistfuls of it against my spattered cheeks, leaving the snowbank stained a hot pink.

There was nothing that could be done about the blood on my clothes, but they were so filthy from my trek through the woods that I reckoned most would see a dirt child and move on.

I heard a rumble up ahead and stuck my thumb out, trying to look as innocent as I could. I was so lightheaded from hunger and cold that I did feel quite saintly standing there on the side of the road, bathed in the sunlight glinting off the ice. Like a holy apparition.

The truck stopped a few paces on, and I could see the driver's face in the side mirror. Middle-aged and mealy. About a 40/60 chance of him trying something, which were good enough odds for me. I felt for the kitchen knife in my coat sleeve and got in.

We wound our way out of the mountains in toasty, engine-rolling silence, and I finally began to thaw. I asked if we could listen to the radio, and he flipped a switch on the dash.

As we descended into the valley below, Mother Maybelle Carter sang about a better place waiting in the sky.

It was late afternoon when the driver dropped me on Fifth Avenue. He'd barely said a word beyond offering me half his sandwich, and I thought he must be a silent angel sent by God to get me where I needed to go.

Nashville. The promised land.

I had dreamed of this place my whole sorry life, and now here it was, solid and towering above me, the street like a narrow valley cutting through skyscrapers.

For all of my fantasizing, I wasn't sure what came next. I'd always planned to come by bus with enough money for a room, find a few gigs, get noticed. But fate had led me here, now, without a cent to my name, and I had to make the best of it.

First things first, I needed new clothes. I spotted a department store swarming with customers, and I slipped in, yanked a few items off the racks, and left through the back before anyone noticed the dirt child. In the bathroom at the drugstore, I changed and took a bird bath in the sink.

Once I was presentable, I wandered around taking in the sights. Workers stood on ladders painting billboards and on scaffolding constructing buildings, replacing the old with the new. Loew's movie theater gleamed in the winter sun.

When I came upon the Ryman, home to the Grand Ole Opry, it loomed like a fortress above me, solid and impenetrable. I stopped and ogled it from the sidewalk, imagining what was inside.

Some of my best memories were listening to the Opry broadcast with my uncle and cousins when my granddaddy went out to visit his congregation. We would put on the radio, and my uncle would pour a few inches of the whiskey he kept under the floor. I loved hearing the singers' voices coming out live and raw from the speaker; it always did something special to me that I couldn't get from records. Afterward, if he was jolly drunk, my uncle would show me a few things on the guitar. He was a genuine devil, but he did teach me how to play.

The Opry was the pinnacle. If I ever made it to that stage, I'd know I'd really done something with my time. I'd know I'd *made* it. Not arriving at a destination, but rather, an act of creation. Making my life into exactly what I wanted.

Around dinnertime, I found my way to a honky-tonk on Broadway. On the little stage in the corner, a Gene Autry wannabe played his old tunes in a high, cheap voice, and I listened politely, imagining myself up there instead, belting it for real. I scanned around the room, looking curious. I just needed one idjit cowboy to come along and buy me something. I was so hungry I'd chew their boot leather.

Sure enough, it only took five minutes or so before one sidled up and asked if he could get me a beer. I said, "Hell yeah, mister, and why don't you throw in some grub while you're at it?" I could tell he liked a little sass. Most of them do if you're small enough, and I came up to his shoulder.

I ate the fried bologna sandwich like an animal while he told me about himself. Shoe salesman downtown or some such. Lived with his mother but wouldn't admit it outright. Your average city boy with a bit of cash and no sense. When I got to the bottom of the bottle, I thanked him and headed for the door.

He followed me out, whispering sweet nothings, but when I kept walking, he went salty fast. Pushed me into the alley next to the bar and pinned me against the brick. Before he could reach for his buckle, I had my blade against his throat. That cleared things up real quick.

I walked for a long time in no particular direction, trying to keep warm. Eventually the buildings turned to houses, the windows glowing so bright in the darkness that I could almost feel their warmth. I passed scenes of families sitting around television sets and drinking cocktails in front of the fire and bickering in the kitchen.

When I could no longer feel my feet against the pavement, I searched for some kind of shelter. Back home, I could have fashioned something in the woods, but here, there was a kind of desolation I hadn't expected. Without nature, the land offered nothing.

After a while, I came upon a house with boards nailed over its windows and door. I crept around the back and tried to pry one free, but that sucker was stuck. A few more attempts failed.

In the backyard, I saw a large twisting tree that reminded me of the birthmark that took up most of my torso: the deep-purple trunk that began at my belly button and sprouted up into branches that extended to my collarbone.

Next to the tree was an old shed with a nailed door and a small hole in the roof. I climbed on the wood piled to the side and, using all the energy I had left, hoisted myself up and through the opening. It was dark and filled with God knows what critters, but it was warm. I found a tarp folded on a shelf and wrapped myself tight. Before I had another thought, I was out cold.

The next few days passed in a mad blur of searching for food and heat.

My favorite spot became the dumpster behind the Krystal Burger, where the air was warmed by grill fumes. It was sinful what people threw away in this town. Fresh golden burgers with only one lipstick-lined bite taken out. I imagined a ponytailed girl pecking at it and putting it down, trying to impress her date.

I searched the dumpster for newspapers to check for my picture, and at night, I stuffed the paper inside my tarp cocoon so I wouldn't freeze. It was an old trick from back home—we lined our walls with newspaper every winter to keep out the draft.

I asked about jobs at all the businesses I passed, no matter what they were. I'd dig graves if they'd give me a shovel. But no one wanted to hire a skinny little dirt child. They all shooed me away like a barn cat begging for scraps.

I thought about going to one of the church shelters, but I was a wanted woman now. My picture could be hanging in their office, even if it wasn't in the paper yet.

I wasn't soft. I could have lived that way for a while. But the one thing I couldn't stand, the one thing that turned me sour, was not singing.

Back home, I heard music in everything; new songs drifted in and out of my head throughout the day among the trees and creeks, sent from God above.

But now, my mind was empty of music. Even when I sang a bit of an old hymn, my voice was quiet and dry. I didn't feel the freedom to belt it like I'd done in the woods. I couldn't let go of the fear that I'd be found in the shed and locked up.

One night I went to a bar nearby to see if I could play or just listen to music, but they wouldn't even let me in the door. How was I supposed to become a country star if I couldn't sing? If I couldn't even find a job or a place to live?

There was something building up inside of me. Something that needed to get out.

At night I felt it like a cat stuffed into a sack, jerking and clawing inside my middle. When I couldn't sleep, I'd stare out the tiny shed window at the tree, and I'd think about my mother and the time I had left.

On her 33rd birthday, when she was nine months pregnant with me, she was hit by a truck and launched into a tree. While she died instantly, by some miracle and the shield of her body, I survived.

But this wasn't some freak accident.

Her mother had also died at 33. And her mother. And her mother's mother. On down the bloodline to some distant ancestor who'd made the wrong deal with the devil.

I was the latest in a long line of cursed women, destined to meet the same fate.

I had fifteen years left.

Fifteen years.

And I was no closer to getting what I wanted out of this life.

One morning, about a week after I arrived, I woke to guitar song wafting through the air. For a moment I wondered if music had returned to me. A new song floating down from above. There was something strangely appealing about it, like the melody was twisting in on itself. I closed my eyes and listened, and I realized it was outside my head, coming from somewhere nearby.

I left the shed and followed the music to a first-story window in the house next door. Through the curtained glass I could see the outline of a person playing a guitar, but nothing more. I stood there for a while not caring who saw me, soaking up the sound like cold, clear water.

I heard a gasp and the guitar stopped with a sharp pluck. My body swayed forward, wanting more. Then the curtains parted, and the window shot up.

"Excuse me, what the—" The girl stopped, eyeing me carefully. The anger drained from her face and was replaced with something like curiosity. "I'm sorry. I thought you were a Peeping Tom." She paused, cocking an eyebrow. "If you don't mind me asking, what are you doing in front of my window?"

The girl was about my age, with glossy brown hair curled like a magazine ad and a prim pink cardigan set. But these elements didn't seem a part of her. Her tall, strong body radiated a divine energy, like a goddess masquerading as a teenage girl.

In my silence, she studied me back. I imagined the dirt child she must see, and I took a step away so she couldn't get a whiff. I reached up to smooth the wild, wavy tangle of my hair.

Her gaze made its way down to the ground, where she stared at my bare feet. In my haste to sniff out the music, I had forgotten my shoes. I expected to see judgment when her eyes met mine again, but I still saw only curiosity. It released the sound in my throat.

"I heard the music. From next door."

She looked over at the boarded-up house with a frown. "The Clarks' old place? But that's been condemned for months."

"No, um, on the other side."

"The Haskins?"

"Yes, they're my cousins. I've been staying with them."

She nodded, seeming to accept it. "Well, then, I apologize for disturbing you." There was something so elegant about her speech. The way she polished each syllable and strung them together like pearls.

"No, I . . . I love music."

She exhaled. "That's a relief." Her mouth curled slightly. "If I may ask, what did you think of the song?"

"Truth is I couldn't hear it very well, so I came over to get a better listen. What song is it?"

"It's mine. I wrote it myself."

I'd never met anyone else who wrote songs. "It reminds me of something all coiled up. Like a snake, maybe."

The girl took further stock of me. "What's your name?"

"Lulabelle." I scrambled to remember the rest of the name I had crafted on the ride to Nashville. "Lulabelle *Powers*."

Her mouth curled into a full smile, and she put her hand out. "Hess Walker." I shook her solid, golden hand, and it felt like gripping a rock warmed by the sun. "Would you like to come in?" she asked, and I nodded without thinking.

She met me at the front door, and I walked carefully into the house. In the well-furnished front room, there were new-looking instruments scattered around and records stacked on shelves. So many treasures in one place.

"Is this all yours?"

"Oh, no. Most of these belong to Mom. Though I think that's Martha's bass," she said, pointing at an amber guitar leaned against the wall.

I looked at her questioningly.

"Martha's one of my roommates. This is a boardinghouse."

"Is it run by your mama?"

"Oh, ha! No. Mom owns the place, but she doesn't have children.

Everyone just calls her that. She opened her house a few years ago to give unmarried women performers a place to stay. She used to sing and play fiddle in a duo with her husband, but he passed."

I felt like I'd stumbled into some kind of dream. Who knew such a place could exist?

Hess led me back to her bedroom, which was just as beautiful as the rest of the house, with its matching floral coverlet and wallpaper and a closet full of candy-colored dresses.

While Hess tuned a gleaming blonde guitar, I waited patiently near the wall so as not to smudge anything.

"Okay, are you ready? I need your honest opinion."

I nodded, afraid I would say the wrong thing and all of this would turn to vapor.

She started the coiled-up tune I'd heard through the window. It was real tight, so that it felt like you were twisting through a narrow passage but still getting lost somehow. It conjured up how trapped I'd felt back home and in the shed, but now it was at a safe distance, allowing me to study it. A few words appeared in my head:

She sat in the room, watchin' the tree,
Waitin' for someone to set her free

I closed my eyes and hummed with the melody of the guitar, and then I quietly sang the line, which led to another, and another, like it always did when I got on a story I wanted to tell. After a few lines, I had this feeling that the music needed to crescendo, when the character feels that they can't go on. But then they get a chance at escape, and as freedom gets closer, the music gets looser, feeding air into the tight coil. I said all of this to Hess, and she built upon it as I played around with the words.

After a while, she played it through with us singing together. When it was done, she stared at me.

"My word. Where on earth did you come from?"

The front door slammed, and an older woman's voice called through the house. I jumped up from where I'd settled on the floor, suddenly aware of my surroundings. If this "Mom" woman saw me, she would certainly kick me out. "I'm sorry. I gotta go now."

Hess looked panicked. "Now?" She followed me to the door. "Will you come back? Another day?"

I wasn't sure it was wise, but I wanted to more than anything. "Yes. Just start playing the song, and I'll come."

Back in the stale air of the shed, I relived every moment of the afternoon with Hess, and I realized that my sense of time had returned. Every moment I had been in Nashville had pooled together like shit in a pit, but now there was this one crisp stretch of time that stood apart, that marked an hour gloriously spent.

Music had returned to me as well, its raw material like fairy magic swirling into different combinations in my head. Our song played over and over, and the parts I wanted to add and change glowed in the dark space of my mind. I closed my eyes and pretended I lived only in that world.

The next time I heard Hess playing, I couldn't stay away, and it was the same the next time, and the next. We met up almost every day that week, and I lived for our afternoons making music together.

I had missed the woods since I came to Nashville. It's where I wrote most of my songs, alone among the trees. Their special silence allowed me to hear the music that drifted down from above.

Now, when Hess and I harmonized, it was like walking in the woods again. Hess's voice was lower and steadier, like something made in nature. It surrounded me with its wilderness and put solid ground under my feet.

When our music-making session was over, I'd leave Hess's room, and the color and stuff of me would fade the farther I got from her, and I'd float like a spirit to my shed.

I could only hear myself, *truly* hear myself, when I was with Hess. I was only solid in her presence.

One afternoon, I noticed Hess side-eyeing me with this strange look, and after a while, I couldn't let it go on.

"Hess, just spit it out."

"What do you mean?"

"I know you got something on your mind. Come on. Out with it."

Her eyes widened. Though she never said anything, I could tell she was startled sometimes by my way of getting straight to the point. It was how I'd been raised. My family wasn't afraid of being rough with each other, for better or worse.

"Lou, I—" She stopped, took a deep breath. "I was talking to Mrs. Haskins yesterday, and I mentioned you, and she, um, she said she didn't have any cousins staying with her. She'd never heard of you."

The floor dropped away, and my body lightened.

She'd found me out.

She would tell the police, and they would lock me up, and I would never make music with her again.

She took me by the shoulders. "Lou, I don't know what your situation is, but I know it isn't good. There's an open room here, and Mom said you can have it."

I hadn't met Mom yet, but I imagined she might be singing a different tune if she saw me. "Hess, I don't have any money."

"I'll help you out," she said simply.

We never talked about it, but I knew Hess came from money. I could tell in the way she talked and her nice clothes. Though *who* she was, the *Hess* of her, was so much more than that. She didn't act like she was better than me, or make fun of me for being a hillbilly. I could tell she was someone who had made herself rather than being made, which is how I thought of me.

But that didn't mean I was going to take her money. "I can't let you do that."

"Why not?"

"I don't need your charity. I can take care of myself."

Hess leaned back from me. "So you're going to keep suffering because you're too proud?"

I didn't respond. She couldn't understand what it was like to have nothing. Taking whatever was offered had put me in this situation.

Hess lifted up my chin so my eyes met hers. "Lou, you're my friend. Friends help each other when they're in need. I'm sure you'll do the same thing for me one day. It's not about charity."

The tree on my chest rustled and sprouted little white blooms at the sound of the word "friend."

But we both knew I'd never be able to return the favor. I had nothing to give. I pulled my chin from her grasp and said, "I should go." I headed for the door, my face burning in shame.

"No, Lou, you don't have to go—"

But I was already moving through the house and walking out to the street. As I made my customary loop around the block to throw off the scent, I took the wet, salty shame and boiled it to fury, so by the time I got to the shed, I was steaming. I hurled a clay pot against the wall, shattering it.

What would I do now? Where would I go?

I resolved to leave the next morning and find another shelter, wherever that might be. But as night descended, I began to shiver uncontrollably. It wasn't a particularly chilly night, so I was a bit confused as I stuffed more and more newspaper inside my makeshift sleeping bag. My head got so hot that my eyeballs burned, and I choked up the remnants of my last Krystal burger into an old watering can.

I curled up on the ground and held myself tight until I passed into a feverish sleep.

I woke hours later with the desperate need for cold, fresh air. I wandered outside the shed and looked up at the stars. They were as bright and plentiful as they were at home.

Across the yard, shining in the starlight, was the tree like the shape of my birthmark. The same tree where my mother died.

And beneath it, like a wedge of fallen moon, was a white dog.

The dog came up and licked my hand, and I followed him to the tree, where he disappeared behind its trunk. Then another figure emerged, this one a man in a white suit as luminous as the dog's fur. I couldn't make out his face in the shadow cast by the light, but I could feel his gaze like a palm against my cheek.

The tree itself gave off a radiant, restorative energy, and I imagined how much better I would feel if I could just reach out and touch it—

The man caught my hand a few inches from the wood and held it there.

"Not yet, my dear." His voice was like fork tines scraping against my teeth.

"But why—"

"It's not your time."

I tried to protest, but the feeling traveled down my spine, and I fell to the ground, shaking beneath the tree limbs spidering across the brilliant sky.

Then the man receded into the shadows, taking his light with him, and the darkness collapsed around me.

3

lulabelle

1967

FIFTEEN YEARS LEFT

I woke to delicious softness.

The smell of soap and hot cotton. A mug of broth sat on a nightstand, still steaming.

I wondered if I was still dreaming, or if this was some kind of dirt-child heaven.

The bed was the softest I'd ever lain in, and I was wearing a clean white nightgown like a little girl from a book. A lavender housecoat I'd seen in Hess's closet was draped over a chair next to the bed, and I slipped it on.

Downstairs, I recognized the front room of Mom's house; it was quiet and dark except for a few lamps lit in the corners. A plate wrapped in plastic with a little card marked "Lulabelle" sat on the large oak dining table. There was no silverware and the food was cold, but I didn't care. I hunched over the plate and stuffed handfuls of mashed potatoes and fried chicken into my mouth, hoping that no one would walk in. I packed my gut until I was almost ill. Then I found a bathroom and washed the grease from my face and the clumps of potato from my hair.

With food in my belly, I felt a little more solid, like I might not be some lonely spirit.

But if this was real, then where was everyone? It was late, and it seemed strange for the house to be empty.

Then I heard voices, and I followed them to the back of the house where a door was propped open. I stepped through the illuminated portal to a screened porch glowing with candles.

Hess and another young woman were perched on a couch with guitars under their arms, and an older lady stood in the corner with a fiddle against her chin. A young Black woman sat in a chair with her pumps kicked off to the side, humming a melody.

She sang the first bars of Patsy Cline's "Crazy" in a low, buttery tone, and I sang the next two lines with her. All eyes went to me, lurking like a barn cat in the doorway.

The music stopped, and Hess jumped up and ushered me over to a seat on the couch next to her. The other women stared at me like a wild animal, except for the older lady, who put down her fiddle and smiled. "Looks like you're feeling better, m'dear."

"How did I get here?"

Hess eyed the other girls, then turned to me. "When you didn't show on Tuesday, I went to check on you in the shed." She paused, sharing a glance with the other guitarist. "Martha saw you going in and out of there a few times. I found you under that big tree half dead with fever, so I brought you here, and we tried to make you comfortable. You've been asleep for two days."

Another woman, this one with cherry-red hair, sat on the ground in a short yellow dress and high white boots like she was a movie star, and she put her hand on my leg. "Hess hasn't left your side."

I avoided Hess's gaze. She had seen me dirty and wrapped in garbage under that tree, then naked as a jaybird with my birthmark bared for all to see. She had seen all of that, and yet, she was still tender toward me, and the kindness was frankly overwhelming. I had never met anyone like her. I didn't know what to say.

"We should get properly acquainted," the older lady cut in. "I'm Mrs. Washburn, but everyone calls me Mom." She turned toward the other girls. "Ladies, introduce yourselves to Miss Lulabelle Powers of . . . ?" Mom looked at me curiously, and I remembered the story I'd stewed up on the drive to Nashville. It had to be as close to the truth as possible, without risking getting caught.

"Near Pigeon Forge, in a little holler."

Mom nodded and repeated, "Miss Lulabelle Powers of Pigeon Forge."

It sounded almost dignified.

The singer was named Tima, and she was from the same town in Ohio where Mom had grown up. Her parents didn't trust her living with anyone but Mom after she graduated from Fisk nearby. She worked for a lawyer over on Jefferson Street and had a college degree, so she could have had a real *career*, but she wanted to be a country star like Hess and me. I hadn't spent a lot of time around educated people, and I was immediately self-conscious about the way I spoke in front of her.

The other guitar player was Martha. She was more reserved than the others. When she failed to provide much detail about herself, Hess cut in and bragged that she was the only female session musician in Nashville. She could play guitar, bass, pedal steel, and the piano perfectly, and a slew of other instruments if a producer was in a jam. They still wouldn't book her for the good gigs, but she worked.

The stylish redhead, Phoebe, worked backstage as a seamstress at the Opry, which mostly consisted of sewing buttons on drunk cowboys and yanking tight dresses off girl singers. "Lots of crotches and girdles," she said. But it still sounded glamorous to me.

I knew Hess didn't work in the traditional sense. She came from one of the richest families in Nashville, and though they didn't approve of her living in Mom's house and playing "hillbilly music," it seemed like they still gave her heaps of money to do what she wanted.

I'd have held it against her if she wasn't the best person I'd ever met.

When they were done, I sat up in my seat. "Well, I don't know how to thank you for your generosity, but I should be going now. Do you, um, do you know where my clothes went? I didn't see them in the bedroom."

Hess looked down at the floor. "Oh, I'm sorry, Lou, but Martha burned them in the backyard."

The girls looked at me with stricken faces, but I started to laugh. "I reckon they walked into the fire on their own. Good riddance." The tension broke, and the other girls giggled with me, and for the first time since I'd sat down, I didn't feel like the barn cat who wandered in.

"But also, Lou, we want you to stay," Hess continued. I tried to interject, but she put a hand up. "I know you're concerned about *finances*," she said demurely, "but you don't have to worry about that. Phoebe says they're looking for help at Darlene's downtown."

My first instinct was to say no. But then I looked around the porch at these kind, talented women, and through the window of the house where there was heat and food and a clean bed. And I thought, *Who am I to turn down such a gift?*

I finally nodded, and Phoebe clapped her hands. "Well, all right, then!"

Martha started a new riff on the guitar, and everyone picked up their instruments, and we improvised a bit with old hymns. Tima's voice made me hungry, and Mom's had the kind of strong, clear sound that could really tell a story. The three of us harmonizing together was true magic.

After a while, Mom yawned and said that was her cue for bed.

"We should get ready anyway," Phoebe added.

"Ready for what?" I asked.

"I have a gig tonight," Tima explained casually.

"And you're all going?"

Phoebe smiled. "Of course. Want to come?"

"I don't think that's a good idea. She needs rest," Hess cautioned, but I stopped her. I'd had so much rest I felt like a limp carrot.

What I *needed* was music.

Jefferson Street was the Nashville I'd dreamed of. The music could not be contained.

People played and sang in every house and building, and when they ran out of space, they performed on the sidewalks. I'd never seen so much life compressed into one place.

Hess and I walked arm in arm behind Tima and Phoebe, who were regulars. This was a Black part of town; Fisk was just a few blocks away, and Tima's law office was somewhere in the row packed with businesses and clubs. People beeped at her from the cars backed up along the street and waved from front porches, where they shouted for chitlins and fish sandwiches at a dollar and a quarter.

Martha brought up the rear, distracted by the street players. I watched her get lost in one picker's technique, the movement of his hands mesmerizing.

We arrived at a brick building with a dark-red awning reading CLUB DEL MOROCCO and a swarm of people out front. Tima led us past the line to a man at the door who kissed her hand and let us through with a nod.

We strutted into the small, low-lit bottom level like a pack of alley cats. The place smelled of cigarillos and wood, and the tables were filled with men in suits and women with immaculate hairdos.

At the bar, Tima and Martha ordered Coca-Colas, Phoebe got something pink and fizzy, and Hess asked for a dirty martini. I'd never ordered a cocktail before, so I asked for a Manhattan like I'd seen in a movie.

The drink was cold and amber, and at first it reminded me of the syrup the holler's granny witch gave me for my stomach pains, like hickory and mountain mint coated in caramel. But then I tasted the bourbon, and I near gagged. There was that sinister sweetness, like something hiding in tall, sunlit grass. The flavor of my uncle's hot breath in my ear. I pretended to take small sips and instead held the drink as a prop.

Tima led us over to a table near the middle and disappeared backstage with Martha. A group in the corner beckoned to Phoebe, and she fluttered over in her green mini dress.

Hess and I watched as the club slowly filled with people and a bright, eager energy. I'd been to church dances back home but nothing as glamorous and unrestrained as this place.

The lights dimmed and a hush spread through the crowd.

I held my breath, waiting for the next moment, feeling each second tick by. Sometimes when I focused on each second, a bad feeling crept up on me. My heart raced, and my limbs lost feeling.

Just as I teetered on the edge, there was a beam of light. Tima stood at a microphone with Martha on pedal steel behind her and the rest of the band at the ready. She shimmered like a constellation in her silver pantsuit.

In her smooth, deep voice, she sang to us about a city girl who thought she could protect herself from fools. She was graceful and calm, but with this sense that a greater force stood behind it. You had to keep watching just to see what she would reveal.

Martha slid her fist subtly down the length of her instrument, and a hypnotic, mournful wail came in above the voice. I felt the tree's bark split a little in my chest. I realized Hess and I were holding hands, and I squeezed her palm. She squeezed back, and I knew she felt it, too.

When the final note of the song dissolved into the smoke-filled room, I was hovering above my seat, Hess's firm, dry hand the only thing keeping my butt on the wood. Tima had lifted me higher, to that golden place where I forgot where I came from, or what I'd done, or that I was ever gonna die.

I would never be like Tima. But I wondered if I could make people feel that way when I sang, too.

The next act kicked up, and people started dancing anywhere not taken up by tables. Phoebe wiggled over and offered us each a hand. We took them, and she led us to a free space in the corner so we could dance in a little circle like some kind of ritual.

I watched Phoebe and the women around me swiveling their hips with this smooth, natural rhythm. When I tried to mimic it, my moves were stiff and awkward. I looked over at Hess, who grooved in her own way, her elegance knowing not to imitate those around her.

Phoebe came up behind me like the couples we saw grinding into each other, and she took my hips and guided me into the groove. After a few beats, I finally felt it. The room twisted together, and I twisted with it.

Act after act, we moved along the sound waves.

And then it was late. Hair clung to my forehead, and sweat trickled down the back of my borrowed dress. The lights were so low that the people were only silhouettes, and the place had taken on a stumbling, breathy quality. But I wasn't afraid; there was an invisible string tying us girls together in the midst of the heavy-eyed late-night chaos. We would keep each other safe.

The house band launched into solos, each musician taking their own spotlight to fool around with a few licks. When it was the main guitarist's turn, he brought the instrument to his face, and a primal sound screeched from it.

"He's playing with his teeth," Martha said, and I looked harder at the player to see if I could get a better view. She watched him like he was a prophet, as she repeated, "He's plucking the strings with his *teeth*."

When the club cleared out, Tima took us down the block to an apartment above a beauty salon. People were making out against the walls and lounging in circles on the ground. One man danced by himself to a song nobody else could hear.

I followed Tima out to a small balcony and rested my elbows on the rail. She passed me her cigarette, and I took a polite puff. It didn't taste like the mellow, honeyed tobacco I knew from home. This had a crook in it, a raised back. Like a skunk when it got scared. I went for another drag, and she took it from me.

"One's enough. That'll do you right."

She took a hit and blew the smoke out in rings that drifted up into the midnight sky. The light from the street smoothed, then fuzzed, and my body relaxed against the railing. So often I felt like I was floating, untethered, too light to stay rooted to the ground. But now I was weighted down just enough.

"I love the way you sing," I said, and she smiled slightly. "How'd you get that gig?"

She looked out over the rows of houses that extended in both directions. "I have sang in most of the living rooms on Jefferson for nothing but a handful of peanuts." She pointed to the window of a house across the street, where a young woman sang for a single couple at a small table. "Until one night, the right person saw me and asked me to audition for the club."

I nodded, imagining people watching me up onstage and someone recognizing my face from a wanted poster. I hadn't seen one yet, but I imagined they were everywhere—in police stations, church bulletins, schools. There was still no mention of my crime in the newspaper, but maybe there would be.

"I've been trying to get on the bigger stages in town, but no one wants a Black country singer." She shook her head. "Doesn't matter. I'll make it there somehow. I always find a way." She took a puff and looked over at me. "What happened to you, girl?" she asked quietly.

Hess and the others were too polite to come out and ask, but I knew they were all wondering how I'd ended up in that shed.

And maybe I should have been more careful, considering the trouble I was in. But I knew I could trust Tima. She understood what it was to live at the margins, to watch everything you said or did for fear they would see the unvarnished version of you. She knew better than I would ever know.

"Some trouble back home."

She nodded sagely.

"I can't ever go back." I had known this, of course, but saying it out loud now, I realized it was true. I was all alone out here with no family, no money, no wilderness in which to disappear. I was suddenly gripped by a fear I could usually fight off, and I felt Tima's hand on my arm. I looked up at her.

"You are not alone. We take care of each other at Mom's."

I clutched her arm back. "Thank you," I whispered, the paranoia slowly dissipating. She patted my hand and let go of me, and we went back to looking out over the houses, my gaze traveling south where downtown glittered. "I want to be a country star, too. I want it all," I confessed.

"I meet a lot of girls out here who say the same thing." Tima took another drag. "Then they throw it all away the moment a man gives them a ring." She shook her head, disgusted.

"I'd rather chew nails than marry some man," I said.

"Lord, can you imagine?" Tima asked. "Taking care of a husband all day like some giant baby."

"Worse than death," I agreed. We met eyes and smiled.

"So are you willing to do what it takes? To make it?" she asked slyly.

"I am," I said.

She turned and gave me the eye. "All right, then. Let's make a promise to each other." She hooked her pinky in mine. "We'll put music before everything else. And if one day, we get a chance, a *real* chance, we'll take it for all it's worth."

The words resounded through me like a holy proclamation. "I promise," I said, and kissed the end of my fist.

"I promise," she agreed, and kissed hers.

A neon riff sliced through the air, and we turned to see the guitarist from the club messing around with one of those electric models through the doorway.

Tima walked over and leaned against the frame, listening for a while. Then she sang a few low, bluesy tones under the strange sound, and it melded together into a rich, blistering music.

It sounded like a new kind of weather, or the background noise of a dream.

Like the sound of revelation.

4

rhea

1995

My first morning in Nashville, I went to a cemetery.

The air was cold and lush against my cheeks, and the ground was so dewy and green that my Chucks were soaked by the time I made it to her grave.

The headstone was a single piece of marble the size of a beach towel nestled into the grass. Lipstick tubes in a spectrum of colors—onyx, jade, gold, silver—were scattered like jewels around the grave amid grocery store flowers and aging stuffed animals.

The stone read:

BELLE POWERS

MAY 16, 1949 - JULY 25, 1982

Oh, please meet me tonight in the moonlight
Please meet me tonight all alone
For I have a sad story to tell you
It's a story that's never been told

The marble was covered in kisses, all in her signature shade of pink.

I searched for a feeling that would make sense for the moment, but I couldn't find it. Maybe it was because her body wasn't actually there; it'd sunk to the bottom of the ocean after the crash. Or maybe it's impossible to truly mourn someone you don't remember.

All I could think was: I had come from a woman who inspired such devotion that strangers made out with her headstone. That had to mean something, didn't it? At the very least it meant I wasn't trash, as my aunt and some of the more sadistic kids at school had liked to imply.

I was not alone at the gravesite; about a dozen men and women hovered in the chill, clutching flowers or reverently clasping hands against their thighs. I watched them, hoping one would pull a tube of pink from their purse, apply it thickly, get to their knees, and kiss the stone in front of me. But they all remained at a respectful distance.

I made eye contact with a guy standing on the other side who'd clearly been staring at me. He gave me a nod, and I glared at him. I thought, *Don't leer at me over my mother's grave.* He, of course, didn't know she was my mother, but the stare still seemed to belie a sort of derangement.

I lingered for a while longer, waiting for the gravity of it all to sink in, but eventually I gave up.

On my way back to the entrance, I accidentally fell into step with the leerer. I tried to lag behind, but it was like he'd had a similar thought, and we slowed to the same pace.

"Do you have a lighter?" he asked, holding up a pack of Marlboro Reds. His accent had a damp sweetness like syrup, different from the dry, grassy accents of Mr. Blau and the driver he'd hired for me.

I kept my head down, refusing to make eye contact. "No. I don't smoke."

"Me neither," he said, and I raised my eyes to him.

He was sandy-haired with wily, fox-like features, and he looked about my age. He was short for a man, perhaps a few inches shorter than me, but muscular like an action figure. His lean biceps bulged from his white T-shirt.

I waited for him to elaborate about the smoking, but he stayed quiet as we walked along the path leading out of the cemetery.

"Have we met before?" he asked. "That's why I was looking at you back there. I was trying to figure it out."

"Oh, no. But I get that all the time."

"People think they've met you before?"

"Yeah, I don't know what it is. Something about my face."

"*Interesting*." He studied my features as if to discern what it might be. "Maybe you were famous in a past life."

I smiled, amused by the synchronicity of the comment. When I peered into his light-green eyes, they didn't have the same look as the other boys I often encountered, always searching my face for how they might weasel their way in. His eyes actually sparkled, as if he was in on a cosmic joke, an infinite mirth echoing deep into the recesses of his mind.

"Are you a Belle Powers fan?" I asked.

"No, not really."

"Then why are you here?"

He gestured up ahead to another grave with a small crowd. "For Johnny Cash." He paused. "But I'm not really a fan of his either."

I stayed quiet once again, clearly waiting for him to say more.

"My brother was. He always wanted to come here and visit Johnny's grave, but he never got the chance, so I told myself I would."

"Oh. I'm so sorry."

"Oh, thanks, it's fine." I could feel him wanting to say more, but instead he swallowed the words.

"What?" I asked. I was not one for engaging strangers, but I was genuinely curious.

"I haven't actually gone to see the grave yet."

"Why not?"

He took a deep breath. "I drove all night from Myrtle Beach, and now I'm here, and I feel this pressure for it to mean something. I've been wandering around this cemetery for an hour, too chickenshit to go over there."

I understood that more than he knew.

He held up the Marlboros. "Plus, I can't go until I find a lighter. I'm going to smoke one of his old cigarettes in his honor."

We kept strolling, and I spotted a white plastic lighter lying in the grass. I picked it up and pressed it into his palm. "It's a sign. Now you have to go."

He stared down at the lighter but didn't make a move.

"I'll go with you," I offered, shocked by my own friendliness.

"Really?" He gazed over at the gravesite and stuck his hands in his jeans. "Okay, you're right. It's time."

We walked in purposeful silence toward the crowd and found a small hole in which to wedge ourselves. There were two headstones laid side by side—one for "John R. Cash" and another for "June Carter Cash." A similar spread of flowers and memorabilia adorned their graves, but there were no lip prints on the marble.

We stood there side by side in the quiet, and I told myself not to look at him. I wanted him to have his privacy while he tried to feel whatever he wanted to feel.

Instead, I gazed at the twin stones and wondered why my own parents hadn't been buried in the same place. I knew there'd been five years between their deaths, but hadn't they wanted to be together? My father was buried at the family plot in Minnesota where I'd lived with my grandparents before they died.

When I could no longer resist, I snuck a glance at the leerer and saw tears running down his face. God, I envied him. He wiped them away, and then abruptly turned and walked toward a bench at the edge of the grass.

I followed and sat a few inches away while he bent over and put his face in his hands. His shoulders shook, and I wondered if I should touch him, or if he'd rather I just fuck off. I hated when people touched me when I was upset. But I didn't want to leave—the intensity of his mourning was strangely appealing, like if I stayed close enough, some of it might leak into me, too.

He took a few deep breaths and raised his head, then pulled out a cigarette from the pack. He lit the end and puffed it to life, and began violently coughing. An old woman walked by and sneered. "There's no smoking here." He tried to respond, but he choked on the words, and instead held up a hand and frantically stubbed the cigarette against the side of the bench. She muttered under her breath and walked on.

I gave him the soda I'd saved from the hired car, and he took a large sip. "Jesus, that was a terrible idea." I couldn't help but giggle, and he gave me a half smile as he rubbed his face dry with the heels of his hands. "I'm sorry. My brother's been gone for a year, so most of the time I feel nothing. But sometimes, this wave hits me, and I can't control it."

I shook my head gently. "I think it's beautiful. Or, I mean, it's beautiful that you loved him so much that you feel this way."

He gazed out over the cemetery. "I was thinking about how much he loved Johnny Cash and wanted to see Nashville. The only reason he never visited was because he thought it seemed too gay or something, and that suddenly struck me as profoundly sad. He was this hard, sort of angry dude, but he also had that in him, too."

I thought about all of the thoughts and emotions I suppressed, afraid they would scare people off. I understood the impulse.

"I'm sorry, I know that's kind of heavy, and you don't even know me—"

"No, I get it," I said, cutting him off. I had learned at an early age not to talk about my mom and dad—it could really clear a room. "Both of my parents are dead."

He coughed again, his face contorted with genuine concern.

"It's not as dramatic as it sounds. I never even met my dad. And I don't remember my mom. I was too young when she died. I couldn't even feel something at her grave earlier—I wanted to, but I just didn't," I confessed. "I'm envious."

His brow furrowed more deeply. "Hold on. Are you saying your mother is Belle Powers?"

I nodded hesitantly, not meaning to have revealed this so easily to a stranger.

"Jesus."

"Yeah."

He was quiet a beat. "So you don't remember her at all?"

I nodded. "But I want to. That's why I'm here." At the thought, a familiar feeling rose up, not a wave but maybe a ripple, that ached for the touch of another person.

As if he could feel it run through me, he reached out and put his hand over mine on the slats of the bench. I looked up at him, and his eyes glinted with that infinite mirth.

"What's your name?" I asked.

"Micah." He paused. "And yours?"

"Rhea."

He smiled for the first time, and the mirth spread from his eyes to each of his features, imbuing his face with a mischievous light. "The goddess herself."

That evening, I was invited to a country star's house for dinner.

On the way in the hired car, we passed a bronze statue of my mother posing with hands on hips like she owned the place, her wig glinting dull gold in the sunset. Down the road, we stopped at an intersection at the Country Music Hall of Fame, where her ten-foot grin flashed from a banner advertising a new exhibit.

Everywhere I looked in Nashville, I saw her, like she was a religious icon, and I had finally come to her holy city.

We arrived on the outskirts of town in a neighborhood of ornate iron gates and high foliage that obscured the properties beyond. The singer's house wasn't the gawdy mansion I expected, but rather a modest single-story colonial set back from the street in a dense thicket of trees. When I exited the car, it was like stepping into the woods.

The woman who answered the door was as tall as me, with an aging dark-haired, freckled beauty. She was dressed in all black and garnet lipstick like a beatnik, but she gave off a sense of Southern society and a magnetic warmth I'd never encountered before.

For a moment, she just studied me with an intense gaze, and I wasn't sure what to do. I was used to adults taking the lead. "Um, hi. I'm Rhea. You invited me for dinner?"

Her face spread into a grin and she laughed. "Well, of course. It's nice to meet you, Rhea. I'm Hess."

I had heard of Hess Walker, but I wasn't very familiar with her music. Only that one song, "Lady in Black," which my principal dedicated to his wife at every high school dance. It was the kind of song you heard at a gas station or a grocery store.

I put out my hand, but she took me by the shoulders instead and gave me a gentle hug. She smelled like wildflowers and hot stone, reminding me of a hiking trail back home, and I took another sniff, hoping she wouldn't notice.

When I pulled back, she studied me intensely once more, and I wondered if she was looking for *her*. But then she seemed to give up, and she showed me inside.

The house was elegant but cozy with a level of sophistication I'd never seen in real life. I had always known luxury as giant TVs and tarped Jet Skis in the driveway, but this woman had *taste*.

The furniture was expensive and eclectic in rich-hued textures like dark wood and olive velvet. She had real art on her walls that featured naked women and abstract designs. Glinting gold awards were scattered among other artifacts like an owl's white tail feather and a chunk of smoky quartz.

In the dining room, a redhead in a pink dress spotted me first and shrieked, wrapping her arms tightly around my shoulders. She smelled strongly of rose, and my stomach turned slightly. "Rhea! You've come back to us!!" she cried.

As soon as she released me, I was enveloped by a woman in a silver turtleneck I recognized as the R&B singer Tima Williams. She whispered in my ear, "Welcome home, baby."

Another woman with high cheekbones wearing a fringed suede jacket and worn cowboy boots held out her hand and calmly introduced herself as Martha, clearly trying to balance out the chaos.

"Are you sure you don't remember us?" the redhead, Phoebe, asked in a playful tone. "Anthony told us you didn't, but I just can't believe . . ."

I considered lying before deciding that would be the greater sin. "Honestly, I don't. I wish I did."

Tima put an arm around my shoulders. "We understand, baby. You were so little when your mama passed." She guided me into a seat, then everyone sat down at the table. "But we are happy to see you regardless. We were good friends of your mother's."

Hess disappeared into the kitchen, and I instantly wished she would come back. She had a grounding force, and this was a little overwhelming.

"So, Rhea, tell us all about you. I want to know every little thing we've missed," Phoebe demanded.

"Um."

"Are you a singer?"

"No."

"Do you play an instrument?"

"No."

Phoebe raised her eyebrows at the other girls. "What *are* you interested in?"

I hated questions like this. How was I supposed to sum up my entire being in a list of interests?

Tima saw me hesitate and jumped in. "Are you planning to go to college? My son is starting at Vanderbilt in the fall."

I smiled gratefully. At least that was easy to answer. "Yes, I'm going to

UCR," I said, and when I saw their confused looks, I clarified, "University of California at Riverside."

"Good for you," said Tima, though I could tell she'd never heard of it.

Phoebe gushed, "I *love* California. People are just happier there. Everyone on this coast is so tortured, blah blah blah. But California people, they're just lighter."

I had heard of this stereotype before, and I had to stop my eyes from rolling. I didn't consider any of the beleaguered, disillusioned adults I knew from back home as "happy" or "light."

She studied me. "Though *you* seem more like the tortured artist type. Like your mother and father."

My ears perked up, and I tried to ask a follow-up question, but she kept going.

"Have you *tried* singing?" she asked again.

Hess breezed in carrying a pie and cut her off. "Feebs, give it a rest. You sound like an old lady."

Tima laughed as Phoebe pretended to look chastened. "My God, you're right." She turned theatrically toward me. "Forgive me, dear. I can be a little much."

The rest of the dinner passed with the group of women sneaking in casual questions about me amid the merciless ragging they gave each other. I learned that Phoebe was a fashion designer who had designed my mother's wardrobe throughout her career. And Martha was a legendary session musician who'd played on the best country and rock albums of the '70s and '80s, including my mother's.

They had all met her living in a boardinghouse together when they were my age, and it wasn't hard to imagine them as young, bubbly girls. Even now, they seemed younger than most middle-aged women I knew, and I wondered if it was the effect they had on each other. I marveled at their gleeful intimacy, too intimidated to interject and ask any other questions.

The food itself also contributed to the general euphoria; the buttered lushness of the chicken pot pie was making me high.

After the blueberry cobbler and ice cream, Hess put down her napkin and announced, "It's time for a field trip," and the other women smirked knowingly and topped off their wineglasses.

At the front door, Hess handed me a flashlight but advised me not to turn it on yet. Then we skipped out into the night, their giddiness fizzing in the darkness. The air was heavy and warm against my skin in a way the cool, dry California nights never were—I was wrapped up and held against it.

We walked out to the main road and took a left, strolling casually in the middle of the street. Tima and Phoebe giggled arm in arm with their wineglasses in the front, then came Hess and me, with Martha loping in the back smoking a cigarette and looking up at the stars.

On the right, we passed an enormous white-columned house on a hill like a Greek temple. It was cast in shadow, as if it'd been abandoned by its followers. Hess saw me studying it and explained in a low voice, "My parents' house. Where I lived as a child."

"Wow. It's so . . . grand."

She smiled. "People used to say that Nashville was the Athens of the South, which is why many of the mansions around here are Greek Revival. My parents bought into it big-time."

"Do they still live there, or . . ."

"No, they moved to Florida decades ago. To be close to my sister and her family."

She said this with a tinge of wistfulness, though I wasn't sure for what. Maybe that was just how things sounded in Southern night air.

Hess continued, "What I remember about that house is silence—my parents didn't like music being played unless it was classical at a dinner party, and even then, my mother sometimes found it a bit overwhelming." She paused. "But I loved this area with all of the huge, ancient trees." She gestured around. "It's peaceful. Which is very different from silent for me. Peace is a kind of safety that lets you create without fear."

I gazed around at the hulking, shadowed oaks, and I tried to see it. Feel it. There was definitely something here, but I wasn't sure it was peace. In this place, everything felt more substantial, more dense with meaning.

"I know what you mean about the silence—it was like that in my house, too," I said.

"With your aunt and uncle?"

"Yeah, but they weren't against music, really—it was more like silence between us or something."

"What do you mean?"

"Like, we never talked, because I don't think they had a lot to say to me."

"Did they mistreat you?"

"No, not exactly." I considered mentioning my uncle's creepiness, but I didn't want to spoil the conversation with his stench. "They were just . . . indifferent, maybe? They didn't want me there, but I also didn't take up much space, so they just lived with it, I guess."

Hess was quiet for a moment as we continued to stroll. "That sounds hard, Rhea. I'm sorry it was like that for you."

Now I was embarrassed. "It wasn't that bad. I could have been in the system, or whatever. There was a kid at school who didn't have parents either, and I could tell his situation was pretty horrible. Honestly, I'm lucky. I don't know why I complain."

"But it shouldn't have been that way. If your mother was still alive—" She paused, chastened. "I'm sorry, forgive me."

I urged her on. "Please, don't stop. What were you going to say?"

She took a deep breath. "Only that, even if it wasn't so bad, you should have been loved." She looked away. "Your mother loved you so much."

My chest ached as it had earlier, this time more strongly than I'd ever felt it. I didn't know what to say, or what other questions I had. It was all I needed to know in that moment—that my mother had loved me.

Hess went to say something else, but then Phoebe squealed up ahead, "We're here!"

On the left stood a pink iron gate with BELLEWOOD written in gold metal cursive across the front.

"Is this . . . ?"

"Yes, this was your mother's house before she died. *Your* house." Hess smiled and stepped up to a keypad off to the side where she poked a few buttons. The gate swung open, and Phoebe skipped through, waving her flashlight over her head.

We followed on the unlit, winding drive as Hess explained how Lou had left provisions in her will to turn Bellewood into a museum whose proceeds would fund music education in rural Tennessee. The estate had partnered with the Country Music Hall of Fame to set up the exhibits, and now it was a popular side tour. Thousands visited every week.

"I wanted you to see it without all the crowds," she added.

We rounded a bend, and a house loomed into view, my eyes now accustomed to the dark. The front had the same Greek columns as Hess's parents' house, but these were painted hot pink, and two large pink wings extended from either side, making it look like the White House if it'd been designed for Barbie.

I saw a light blink near one of the bushes at the front, and I wondered if it was a faulty outdoor light. Then another one blinked a few feet away, and then another, and another, until the house glittered.

"Do you remember lightning bugs?" Hess asked me, and I shook my head in wonder. It was amazing what beauty a person could forget.

Hess disappeared for a bit, and then there was a heavy clang, and the house lit up all at once like a carnival ride, dispersing the twinkling bugs. The façade shimmered with tiny pink bulbs, and a Belle Powers song I didn't know poured from a fake rock speaker next to me.

Phoebe jumped up and down clapping, then led the charge up to the front door where Hess let us inside.

The entryway was a grand two-storied situation that led to a corded-off living room decorated entirely in different shades of pink. An enormous portrait of Belle Powers done in pink rhinestones instead of paint hung above the magenta fireplace.

I stood behind the plush exhibit rope and tried to remember something of this room, but it looked like no one had ever set foot here, much less played on its rug. The flamingo satin of the couch shone so slickly, I imagined you'd slide right off. And the smell only reminded me of church, with its crumbling carpet and burnt coffee.

The kitchen, which I expected to be homier, looked like it'd been dipped in liquid gold—gold counters, gold stove, gold fridge. There was a gold bowl of gold fruit sitting on the solid gold breakfast table in the corner. I couldn't imagine someone cooking, much less eating, in the kitchen without going blind.

I wandered into a more subdued room with nothing but a white grand piano and a desk stacked with notebooks, scribbled napkins, and a Krystal takeout menu with a few lines written in the spaces between the prices. I had been ignoring the accompanying placards to force my own memories, but now I read this one for the "Music Room."

It described Belle's voracious songwriting habit—at any moment, she might come up with a few lyrics or chords and have to write them down on whatever was available. One time she wrote a whole song in turquoise eyeliner on a hotel mirror and the maid left it for the next guest, afraid to scrub it off.

This was the room where she assembled the fragments into songs, and this space, at least, still buzzed with life. I wondered if she'd ever let me sit with her in here, or if this was a place she went to be alone to make her music. Even in this room, it was hard to imagine a child had ever lived in this house.

Upstairs, I found a series of themed guest bedrooms connected by a hallway lined with gold-framed pictures and small placards. The first showed a young Belle in a poofy vintage wedding dress and daisy-studded wig standing next to a middle-aged man in a tuxedo and lustrous tan.

I studied the date on the placard, 1967, and did the math. She was my age—*eighteen.*

The placard identified the man as her first husband, country star Clayton Redd. It said in '67, he was visiting a friend at a rival label's studio and heard Belle sing for the first time. He scooped her up from the competition, brought her out on tour, and, in essence, launched her career. Belle's first four albums were recorded with him, and then later, he produced her crossover albums that made her the big star she is remembered as today. While their romance didn't last, he would always be known as one of her most important collaborators.

Hess came up behind me and studied the picture over my shoulder. "She hated that dress. But Clayton insisted."

"How *old* was he?"

Hess pursed her lips. "I think he was mid-thirties . . . maybe thirty-four, thirty-five?"

"That's disgusting." She looked like a child bride sold off to this bronzed creep.

Hess laughed. "I know this sounds like a cop-out, but things were different back then." It seemed like she wanted to say more, but she stayed quiet.

"I didn't know she was married before my dad."

Hess smiled absently and nodded, but again, she didn't say more.

We moved on to Belle's master bedroom, which had a more restrained butterfly theme. Next to her bed, I saw the first photograph in the house that wasn't a splashy portrait or a posed photo with another celebrity.

I craned my neck to get a better look, but the rope partition kept me at the edge of the room. Hess scooted it aside and gestured forward. "Go ahead."

I crept gingerly over to the photo and picked up the frame. In it were two women about my age in matching dresses and holding guitars—one glossy, freckled brunette that was undoubtedly a young Hess. The other I didn't quite recognize—she was bone thin with frizzy copper hair like my own fanned around her head and a feral intensity in the face. I asked Hess who she was.

"That's Lou."

I stared back at the photo, embarrassed I hadn't placed her. But she looked so different from the images I'd seen, as to be an entirely separate person. Even the light inside her burned a different color.

"It's nothing to be ashamed of. When your mama took off her wig and makeup, no one recognized her. Even when she was real famous, we could go out to eat in the middle of Nashville and no one would have a clue who she was."

I stared even harder at the photo, trying to force some recognition beyond my own hair color, perhaps some connection to the warm chest I sometimes dreamt of. But nothing came.

Instead, I noticed what looked like dark branching lines showing through the chiffon neck of the dress.

"What are those?" I asked, pointing at them.

Hess squinted at the image and shook her head. "No idea. Must be a shadow from the camera." She took the frame from me and set it back on the table. "Let's see the next room."

Out in the hallway, the other women joined us as we approached the last door with a sign that said NO TRESPASSING in cheery pink cursive. Hess took a key from her pocket, opened it, and let me walk through first.

The child-sized four-poster bed looked like a castle with turrets built around each post. In the far-right corner, there was a wooden jungle gym with a slide leading down to a ball pit. On the other side, there was a tiny white baby grand, a miniature guitar, and a shelf lined with books and beautiful, pristine dolls.

On a small vanity arched with real glass bulbs, a few framed photos stood next to a set of silver hairbrushes. The first photo showed a younger, more effortless Phoebe at the beach with a girl of about two or three in a Tarzan-like bathing suit, flexing her tiny guns like a miniature body-builder.

A dark-purple mark slashed across her collarbone.

That little girl was me.

"You used to run around bellowing like a wild woman, so I made you a wild woman's bikini." Phoebe laughed from behind me.

I had never seen myself at such a young age; the few childhood pictures I had were from eight or later, and always showed me sitting at the periphery of my aunt's family, pale and sullen.

Phoebe opened the door next to the vanity, revealing a walk-in closet filled with frilly dresses and tiny patent-leather shoes and a wall affixed with hundreds of different-colored hair bows. She pulled a puff of pink tulle from a rack and held it up to me.

"You remember this? We designed this one together. We called it the cotton-candy dress."

I brushed my fingers against the tulle as if to test its veracity. I couldn't fathom such an enchanted childhood, much less one that had belonged to me.

I continued to browse the room and study the various pictures of me as a sunny, uninhibited child. Except for the one with Phoebe, all of them showed me alone.

"Why isn't Belle in any of these?" I asked. I was still too shy to call her "Lou" like they did.

Hess frowned. "I think she was always taking the pictures. And when she wasn't working, she didn't like to be photographed."

I could hear something false in the words, but perhaps it was my own disbelief. When I looked at the pictures, the yearning I felt to know my mother went even deeper, into that tender place where I ached to be close to her, to touch her, to be wrapped in her arms.

"What was she like?" I asked.

They all looked to Hess, and I knew then that she had been my mother's *best* friend.

"Well." She smiled. "She was very brave, and hardworking, and kind. And exceptionally talented, of course."

There was a beat of silence in the room.

"She could also be rough, and selfish, and secretive," Phoebe added good-naturedly. Hess frowned at her, and she said, "What? She should know that Lou wasn't perfect. That was part of who she was."

"She was *voracious*," Tima added. "That girl could eat four double cheeseburgers and four fries in one sitting. I have never seen such a little thing put it away." The women laughed, including Hess. "She was like that with a lot of things—the way she worked, and the way she loved."

"She knew music like it was her first language," Martha added from the corner. They all nodded, as if still in awe of their friend. "If you really want to know Lou, you should listen to her music. That's where you'll find her." Martha gestured dismissively at the room. "Not here."

Spirits were high as we made our way back to Hess's house and out to her screened-in porch. Martha and Hess picked up guitars, and Phoebe pulled me onto a couch with her so we could play the audience.

"Let's do some of the early stuff," Tima suggested.

"How early?" Hess asked.

"I'm talking *early early*. Rhea, did you know your mama and Hess used to be in a singing group together?"

"For a very brief time," Hess clarified.

"How about 'Let Me Out'?" Martha suggested.

Hess hesitated. "I don't think that's a good idea."

"Oh, come on, let's do it," Tima cajoled.

Hess exhaled. "All right."

In the moment before they began to play, I listened to the chirp of crickets out in the grass beyond the screens, and I remembered what Hess had said about peace. Here was a place you could explore whatever inspired you, and you didn't have to be afraid.

Then they began to strum, and as the music formed in my mind, I could feel its tightness, like someone squeezing at my throat. I wondered if I was the only one feeling it, but I could see Phoebe grimacing slightly next to me.

Tima sang in a rich, deep twang,

She sat in the room, watchin' the tree,
Waitin' for someone to set her free

The lyrics wound around me like smoke, choking off my air. That strange, claustrophobic feeling came over me, and the music faded to the background as I closed my eyes and focused on breathing.

In and out.

In and out.

The music stopped, and I heard a thud, then Hess was hunched over me asking, "Are you okay?" Her face was drained of color.

I nodded and tried to look normal. "Of course. I'm fine."

She handed me a glass of water, and I drank a few sips as if to appease her, though I couldn't deny the relief of the cold washing through my insides.

Phoebe sighed. "It's an interesting song, Hess, but it ain't the easiest to listen to." She and Tima chuckled, but Hess still studied me with concern. "It wasn't my idea."

"Please," I begged. "Don't stop playing."

After more back-and-forth, Hess finally conceded and picked up her guitar once again. They moved on to old country songs I'd never heard of, and I was grateful they didn't cajole me into singing. The sounds of their voices were like rare bird calls, beautiful and tinged with nature. How could I ever sing with people who could make music like that?

Instead, I lay down on the soft linen of the couch and closed my eyes, allowing the music to enter me without distraction.

I imagined I was a young child wrapped in gossamer and playing beneath a sun-dappled tree with a gleaming white dog. I watched Belle come toward me with her unadorned face—the one she showed only to those she trusted and loved.

She picked me up and held me to her warm chest, and the ache finally ceased.

5

lulabelle

1967

FIFTEEN YEARS LEFT

Those who pay attention know the perfect days are unplanned.

It was the first warm day of spring. Hess and I drove along a dirt road in the sunshine with my bare feet hanging out the window, tree branches tickling the bottoms as they moved to the beat of Dolly Parton's "Dumb Blonde" on the radio. I wanted to climb on the roof, put my arms out, and fly through the early afternoon.

I'd been at Mom's for a few months then, and for the first time in my sorry existence, life had slipped into a blissful rhythm.

Hess stopped the car at the edge of a small lake, and the radio went quiet. I'd gotten so used to being surrounded by people that I could hear the silence.

We were completely alone.

Hess pulled her dress off, revealing a red bikini, and ran through the grass toward the water. I undressed as I ran after her, and we both jumped in at the same time. The water was warm as a bathtub with cool spots that I liked to float over, imagining they were tunnels to some other place.

We'd come to hear the sound of our voices in water.

We swam to the center of the lake, where the water was so low from drought that Hess could still stand, but my tiny legs couldn't touch the bottom. I sang out a few bars of nonsense, and the dewy sound echoed between us, damp with its green. Hess matched the tone, and we cooed to one another like mermaids.

I noticed drops of water were pearled in Hess's eyelashes and at the corners of her lips. I tried not to stare at her too much because I didn't want to give her the creeps. But sometimes I couldn't help myself.

She stared back at me, unguarded. "You must be getting tired," she said.

I'd nearly forgotten my body, but now I could feel the burn in my limbs, and the beginning of that frantic need to find solid ground. "Yeah, a little."

"Why don't you hold on to me?"

I swam to her, and she reached out and brought my legs around her waist like a child, though I didn't feel like one. I kept my torso a few inches away to keep some distance between us, but she gently pulled my back toward her. I instinctively put my arms around her neck. Our faces were very close now, and I could smell the stone and petals of her natural scent, even in the lake water. I shivered against her warm body, and she held me tighter.

"Hey, Lou."

"Hey," I said, a bit unsteadily.

"I don't mean to pry . . ."

Even pressed together, she was still so damn polite. "Yes?"

"What is that on your chest?"

I looked down and saw the mud-colored branches fanning out from the top of my bathing suit, and my insides twitched. I'd forgotten about it entirely. Though I knew she'd seen it when I was sick, I'd been careful since moving into Mom's to keep myself covered.

I looked up at Hess's concerned face, and I wondered if I could really trust her. I knew I had to let myself be known, even in small ways. Otherwise, I'd truly disappear. I knew this, and yet, it was still hard for me to do it most of the time. Everyone I'd ever trusted had turned out to be a rat bastard.

But Hess was different.

I told her it was a birthmark. The trunk started at my belly button and followed up my chest, where its branches fanned out like a tree, with the tips grazing my collarbone. A mark like this was the sign of a trauma that happened to the mother during pregnancy. An experience so harrowing that it left a mark on the baby in her belly like a scar.

I told her when my mama was nine months pregnant, she was hit by a truck while crossing the road and landed in a black gum tree. She didn't survive, but somehow, cushioned by her body and the branches of that tree, I lived through it.

My daddy had left town months before, and he was never found, but his family took me in. Apparently my mother's people had wanted me, too, but they weren't exactly respected in the town. I didn't tell Hess that every woman in my mama's family, as far back as anyone could remember, had died at the age of 33 of some tragic accident. I knew she'd think I was crazy.

Instead, I told her I went to live in a small wooden house with my grandparents, aunt, uncle, and their three boys. My aunt had always wanted a girl, which was why they fought so hard for me. But soon after I came, she got pregnant again, this time with a girl, and I became dead weight.

I wasn't the kind of girl she wanted anyway—the kind who liked to stay at home and help with the cooking and gossip. I did what they asked, but I much preferred exploring the woods and writing songs by myself. When they found out I could sing, they started renting me out for things like people's parties and church stuff, and they treated me a little better. But I was more mule than daughter.

I'd been plotting my escape for years when fate stepped in and forced my hand. Of course, I couldn't tell her why I'd had to leave in the middle of the night in the dead of winter. That was a story I was taking to my grave.

Hess listened quietly the whole time I was speaking and never asked a question, or interrupted with her own story. When I was done, she held me a little harder against her, and I put my cheek to her chest. I didn't cry or anything, because this was just my life. But it felt good to rest my head against a body that cared for me; I could feel it like a force radiating from her skin.

I wanted to be somehow closer to her, inside her in a way, and I worried I might do something that would scare her off. I brought my head up and gently pushed away from her with a little splash to make a game of it. Something hard to read crossed her face, but then she splashed me in turn, and the moment passed.

As we floated on our backs, that old country tune "The Prisoner's Song" fluttered down and beat its wings in my head:

Oh, please meet me tonight in the moonlight
Please meet me tonight all alone

Hess came in on the next verse:

For I have a sad story to tell you

And then our voices came together in harmony, gliding across the water and wrapping us in its sound:

It's a story that's never been told

The tingle of the lake lingered in my skin as I flipped bologna sandwiches and restocked glasses that night at Darlene's Indigo Lounge. The place was a tiny, narrow honky-tonk around the corner from the Ryman, and just being close to the Opry gave it a bit of magic.

Hess sat at the end of the bar in her regular spot, reading a novel. She had this ability to block out all noise around her, creating a bell of serenity in the middle of the roughness. I refilled her Coca-Cola and tried to catch her eye, but she didn't look up.

"I'm So Lonesome I Could Cry" moaned from the jukebox for the eighth time in a row, and I watched as one of the regulars stared sorrowfully into his whiskey glass. It was a great song, but someone needed to put this guy out of his misery. The real music would be starting any moment, and I gazed longingly at the little stage. I'd asked Darlene a dozen times now if she'd let Hess and me play just one song up there, but she always said no without explanation.

I heard Darlene curse and slam the phone down in the back. She came out and asked Ronnie, the bartender, about his friend's band in a clipped voice. They sometimes filled in when someone flaked. The Opry had just let out, and people were starting to stream in, their voices rising above the wail of Hank Williams.

Ronnie told her the lead singer's wife had just had a baby, and he didn't think he would come. He started to name off alternatives, but I stepped between them and looked Darlene square in the eye.

"Let us play, Leenie. It'll take anyone else half an hour to get here. Look at all these people. You've got no other choice."

She eyed me. "I'd rather go up there and shake my fanny than let you do that. I told you—this place ain't your big break."

"Please. Just one song. If they hate us, you can shoo us off with the broom. I'll babysit your kids for free on Sunday. I'll goddamn do anything, just let us sing!"

She thought about it for a moment, taking in the growing herd pushing toward the bar. Live music acted as a gentle drug for this crowd, and she wouldn't be able to hold them off for much longer.

"Fine. One song. You got thirty seconds to be up on that stage. Don't get yourselves killed."

Hess had been listening, and without a word exchanged, she ran out of the bar. I unknotted my apron and plunged my fingertips into a glass of water sitting in the sink and tried to smooth my hair down. Ronnie poured me a shot of apple pie shine, and I threw it back. Hess returned with a guitar in each hand: her beautiful new Gibson and her old Kay I'd been using with its swirl of dark wood.

We fought our way through the roil of bodies with our guitars held above our heads like soldiers crossing a river with rifles. When we finally made it to the small platform, we elbowed a few out of the way, climbed up to the stage, and got into position.

Hess and I locked eyes, and I wondered if I looked as scared as I felt, as if I was about to face a firing squad. But Hess looked ready for battle, and it lit the warrior fire in me, too. With her by my side, I could do anything.

We strummed a few bars of the song's intro, and no one paid attention. Then I came in solo for the first verse I'd written all those weeks ago:

She sat in the room, watchin' the tree,
Waitin' for someone to set her free

People started to look up as my voice rang out through the place. My sound is high and rich at the same time, with a lilting roundness that comes from my accent. I know I'm not supposed to think things like this, like maybe it doesn't make me a real artist, but I love my voice. It isn't always perfect, and there've been times when I've strained to push the sound from my body. But I really think it's beautiful.

Hess came in low and steady underneath me for the chorus:

Let me out, Lord
Let me be free
Let me out, Lord
Who will I be?

Meanwhile that tight, coiled rhythm twisted around the room, and as more heads turned our way, I could feel the unrest building. The song was closing in, trapping them. One man called for us to cut it out, and then another joined in the heckle, and the tide built against us, even if I could tell some were intrigued by the sound.

In a pause in the lyrics, I whispered to Hess, and we gradually changed from her serpentine riff to "The Prisoner's Song" we'd sung earlier at the lake. We harmonized, taking the old tune and speeding it up for a bigger, more modern sound:

Now if I had wings like an angel
Over these prison walls I would fly
And I'd fly to the arms of my poor darlin'
And there I'd be willing to die

The atmosphere in the room changed immediately as we set the audience free, and pairs of dancers took turns in the space between the tables. The same men that had heckled us moments earlier now hollered up at the rafters and ordered more beers.

We started taking requests, as Hess and I knew a lot of songs between us. We'd been practicing together for weeks, and we had an unspoken language. It felt like we were sharing one brain, one heart, one set of hands. But there were two throats: the voice all my own floating up toward the ceiling and hers coming in to tether it to the ground.

After an hour or so, Darlene motioned for us to clear out for the next act, and we stumbled sweat-soaked and giggling into the women's bathroom. Hess went into a stall and pulled me in behind her, and we both leaned against opposite walls, still gasping from the elation. I had never felt so lifted before.

I stared freely at Hess's hair stuck to her glistening collarbone, her strong arms, the golden harvest of her body. I had that desperate, bone-aching feeling again of wanting to be closer to her, and I took a step forward. It was a tiny stall, so she only had to move a few inches more to bring us front to front, the outer tips of our bodies grazing against one another and filling me with red, electric pleasure. Hess moved even closer, pushing me back against the wall.

She nuzzled her nose against mine, and our mouths parted but didn't touch, held there in that space and time right before. It tasted like strawberries and their bitter green stems.

Then her mouth slid into mine, and the boundary between us fell away as it did when we played music, and there was only slick, smooth pleasure curving from side to side. I knew our hands were on each other, but I couldn't tell what we were touching, only that it felt good everywhere.

A rough knock rattled the door and startled us apart. A woman yelled at us to hurry up, and we scurried out with our eyes cast down.

I looked in the mirror at my mouth ringed in red and the wild tangle of my hair. Hess looked unblemished; if anything, her face shone a little brighter. She wet a corner of her dress with cold water and held it up to my skin, then raked her hands through my hair. I closed my eyes as her fingertips stroked my scalp, evoking the pleasure from before.

Then another woman came in, and Hess pulled her hands back. We each turned to the mirror and pretended to primp.

Once I was presentable, we returned to the main room, and I put my apron back on. Hess took her usual place at the bar, and she buried herself in her book once again. On the surface it was like nothing had happened.

But everything had changed.

As I made my rounds collecting glasses, the cowboys were more beautiful, the whiskey more jewel-like, the band's music sweeter to my ears. The bar blushed under its lights, and I made a game of waiting as long as I could to look in the far corner.

When I could no longer stand it, I allowed my eyes to wander where they wanted, and she was there, staring back at me.

My love.

6

lulabelle

1967

FIFTEEN YEARS LEFT

After the success of our performance, Darlene gave us a regular spot at the Indigo Lounge, and we started to hone our show into something less slapdash.

I'd heard someone ask when the country girl with the sweet voice was playing, and I didn't want that to be my only identity. I saw other acts pretending to be big, clowny hillbillies. Some called it pride, but I didn't see how jumping around, acting like a poor, ignorant idiot showed pride. To me, being a hillbilly was a refusal to let anyone tell me who I was.

And I wanted a new look.

But it was more than that, of course. Every time we went onstage, I worried someone would recognize me and turn me in. I didn't just need a stage costume—I needed a *disguise.*

Hess and I stood in our underwear in front of the floor-length mirror in Phoebe's room, watching each other in the glass as Phoebe ran a tape measure down the lengths of us. We'd seen each other in bathing suits plenty of times that spring, but there was something more intimate in the thin, pale nylons against our skin. My nipples were little pricks against my bra, and I hoped Phoebe would chalk it up to the breeze running through the room.

"So. Tell me what's in your head."

I took out a few pictures from magazines, of Hollywood starlets with their big, smooth platinum hair. Phoebe studied the photos, then dove into the artful garbage dump of her room and pulled out a periwinkle box. She took off the lid and reverently lifted a large blonde wig up by its roots and held it in front of me.

It glowed like a holy artifact.

When I nodded, she gave me a snipped foot of pantyhose, and I stuffed my unruly hair into it. She carefully placed the wig on my head and pulled it left and right. Then she turned me around to face the mirror.

The effect was arresting. I have such a tiny body, and the largesse of the hair and its polished metal color—well, it was imposing. Like a weapon fresh out of the military lab. It inspired awe, and maybe a little fear. It was exactly what I was looking for.

For the makeup, I asked for the full Pauline—a woman who used to sell herself around the logging camps near the holler. She painted her makeup so thick you couldn't see what was under it. Like a beautiful mask. That's what I wanted.

Phoebe had her own vision for the clothes. She could spin the most unexpected whimsy; she was the one responsible for Tima's enchanting silver suit. She'd watched her sing one night on the porch under a full moon, and a vision had come to her, of Tima dipped in moonlight.

For us, she'd taken inspiration from an afternoon we'd spent together in a wildflower meadow. She'd constructed a butterfly wing pattern out of strips of iridescent cloth in different colors, so that each dress looked like a psychedelic quilt, the colors shifting and coming alive as they transformed across the surface of the fabric.

I trailed my fingers over the skirt, and I couldn't believe it was made for me. It was the most beautiful thing I'd ever seen.

When we walked onstage that night, it felt like we were emerging as something new. I'd morphed inside my hillbilly chrysalis, and in that moment under the spotlight, I burst through it with two feet of blonde hair and a riot of color.

I stepped up to the mic and for the first time, introduced us as the Walker Sisters. It was my idea—it added an extra layer of protection to my identity, and if people thought we were sisters, they wouldn't wonder at our closeness.

We'd learned our lesson that first show—the audience wanted to hear songs they already knew, even if we changed them up a bit. Our specialty was taking familiar ballads and speeding them up so you could shake to them like the Monkees or the Beatles.

But that night our sound was different. Like it'd been dipped in nectar and rolled in butterfly shimmer. Since Hess and I had started fooling around, our voices had changed—I could hear it in the harmony when we sang. The touching and retreating, touching and retreating, the space between us charged with a palpable force.

The audience could feel it, too.

The heat.

It was late when I emerged in my cotton dress to close up for the night. A cool, composed man in a cream suit stood out among the red-faced cowboys and sweat-slick girls. While I emptied glasses and scrubbed the bar, he leaned against it and asked me where else we played and other probing questions. I thought he was hitting on me, and I answered with a polite distance.

Hess and I never talked openly about what we were doing or how we felt about each other, but there was an understanding that we would be true to one another. I didn't want anyone but her.

After I'd finished closing and was ready to strip off my apron and tell everyone to go home to their mamas, the man got down to business.

"Miss Lulabelle, my name is Randy Kane, and I work at ACM Records. I'd like to record you and your sister singing a few songs, maybe put together enough for an album. Y'all got something real special here."

I thought he was blowing rainbows up my skirt. "Bullshit."

He choked on his whiskey. "Excuse me, ma'am?"

"You're serious?"

"Yes, ma'am. This is a real offer. What do you say?"

I called Hess over, and he repeated everything to her. Hess, ever the cool operator, asked him how much he was going to pay us. That hadn't even crossed my mind. I'd have done it for free.

After a bit of negotiating, he gave us an address and a time for the next day. We waited until he'd left the bar before screeching up at the ceiling like cats. Hess took me by the waist and we started dancing around the room to our own tired voices singing Kitty Wells's "It Wasn't God Who Made Honky Tonk Angels." Darlene came out to see what the racket was, and I told her what had happened. She smiled, but she also looked a little worried, and she told us to be careful.

"If something's too good to be true, it probably is."

She sounded like the people back home, and while I appreciated her, I'd left the holler's negativity behind for a reason. I was lifting off the ground, and no one was gonna pull me back.

Late that night, Phoebe whipped us up a pair of simple creamy-green dresses. While she worked, Martha took us aside and, in a rare stretch of talking, coached us on how to conduct ourselves.

"First off, don't walk in and start giggling."

I was a little offended. "Martha, we ain't idiots. I know how to act right—" But she gave me a look, and I knew what she meant. Hess and I had fun with each other. There was a fair amount of giggling. It was a shame we couldn't just live in our joy, that we had to flatten ourselves to be taken seriously. But that was the reality.

"You're there for a job. You are an expert in singing, and they need to respect that. You got it?"

We both nodded. Sharing wisdom was an act of love for Martha.

In the hallway outside my bedroom, I passed Tima, who stuck her pinky out. I hooked mine in hers, and we met eyes as we kissed our fists. We didn't have to say the words.

Whatever it takes.

The next day, Hess and I showed up at the studio polished and serious faced in our dresses like mint ice cream. Randy led us down a hallway lined with rooms of singers performing into microphones, the sound muffled, each square like a scene from a silent movie. A red-nosed old man still belting from the heart, a dimpled boy singing from beneath a cowboy hat one size too large, a young woman shaking with nerves in her braids and gingham shirt.

We finally arrived at our room, where a small band of men sat looking bored. Hess and I explained we played our own guitars, but Randy assured us it was better to have *real* musicians for the recording. Our playing would do just fine at shows, but this had to be on a *different level.* I wasn't some big-time guitarist, but I thought Hess was pretty good. I felt the emotion of the music more when I could feel it vibrating through my hands, releasing the creature that stayed pent up inside me.

But I didn't say a word. I was too nervous that any objection would change his mind, and he'd ask us to leave.

Without any instruction, he told us to get on with it and start singing, and that's what we did. But soon he had to stop and show us how to sing for a recording, as if it was predictable that women wouldn't know such things. There was a lot of starting and stopping, adjusting and readjusting. When we did sing, it was hard to get to that place where I felt lifted. He treated us more like hotel maids than artists reaching toward the sublime.

Just as I was finally getting into the groove, I looked up, and there was famous country singer Clayton Redd standing in the booth, watching me sing. It was like seeing Jesus in the supermarket. I couldn't believe it was really him.

I glanced over at Hess, and her eyes widened in acknowledgment. I tried my very hardest for the rest of the track, wanting to impress him. When I finished the song, I searched for him in the booth to gauge his reaction, but he was gone.

After we'd been at it for an hour, Randy said Hess needed a bit of vocal coaching, and he sent her to a room down the hall. He told the band to take a break and get some lunch, and he and I stayed in the booth to work on the arrangements.

I thought, perhaps he did respect my instincts, even if I lacked experience and formal training. I was excited to learn from him and be a part of the process.

Once we were alone, he sat down on a couch against the wall and patted the cushion next to him. I sat on the other side, keeping my distance. He started to ask about where I grew up and what my family was like. I didn't talk about that with anyone, much less a strange man, and I steered the conversation back toward music. He kept turning it back to me and asking foolish questions about dresses and boys that I didn't give a damn about. While he talked, he crossed and uncrossed his legs and readjusted his jacket, so that with each movement he moved closer to me on the couch. Eventually, he was practically sitting in my lap.

He had that aging-man smell, the fumes of his rot releasing through the gray stubble on his chin. He might have looked fresh on the outside, but he was going bad on the inside.

When he put his hand on my leg, sweat broke along my hairline where the wig now sat like a weight, holding me down. I thought of the knife I kept in my corset, but I couldn't go there yet. Instead, I flicked through possible actions and their costs, attempting to find an option where we could keep recording music. I didn't want to be anyone's victim. So I searched inside myself for a way to like it. If I claimed the hand on my leg, I'd be in control.

He let his hand slide into the crease between my legs as if gravity had willed it. I went stiff as he slowly moved it up my thigh beneath my dress.

I tried to focus on owning that hand, convincing myself that *I* was the one moving it up my leg.

Then he leaned over and whispered with his rotten breath, "I want to see how juicy you are."

Without another thought, I drew my knife and held it up to his neck. He froze, and I told him in a low, quiet voice, "Take your hand outta my crotch." He obeyed slowly and placed it in his lap. I could see sweat beading at his temple, and he shook beneath the blade. Good. Now he knew what it felt like.

I removed the knife from his jugular, and he shot up from the couch, fleeing to the other side of the room. There was a dark stain on his pants where he'd pissed himself. When he saw me looking at it, his face flushed in angry shame, and he stormed out.

I sat there for a moment, pretending we still had a chance.

But I had made my choice.

I could feel the vague outline of regret, like a glimpse into a future where I might wish I had done what it took.

That was quickly pushed aside for clean, practical anger.

I stashed the knife in my bra, packed up our guitars, and left. There was no sign of Randy in the hallway. I went from room to room looking for Hess, and with each passing doorway empty of her, I became convinced she was in some secret corner of the building with another hairy hand between her legs. When I finally found her in the kitchen eating a sandwich alone, I couldn't help feeling angry.

I told her what happened without mentioning the knife, and since she was Hess, she ignored the accusation in my voice. She was solely focused on getting us the hell out of there.

We passed through the lobby at a near run and were almost to the front doors when I saw Clayton Redd sitting in one of the chairs. Hess pulled at my arm to keep us moving, but I couldn't help myself. I turned around and walked right up to him.

"Excuse me, Mr. Redd. I saw you in the studio earlier, and I wanted to introduce myself. I'm Lulabelle, and this is Hess. We're the Walker Sisters."

Clayton subtly smirked as he took us in.

Hess extended an elegant hand. "It's a pleasure to meet you, Mr. Redd."

Clayton gently took her hand and then released it. "The pleasure is all mine, young ladies. I hope you didn't mind me poking my head in. You hear a lot of the same stuff around here. But you all have something special. Miss Lulabelle, you have quite a voice on you."

I'd been cold and hard up to this point, but now I faltered. Clayton Redd liked *my* voice. I couldn't feel my arms.

"She keeps her voice so pretty by conserving it," Hess said to fill my silence, and the comedy of this helped pull me out of my trance.

"Thank you, Mr. Redd. That is real kind."

He smiled. "So when can I hear this album?"

The hand on my thigh seemed to belong to another life, where Clayton Redd didn't like my voice. "I'm afraid that's impossible. There's not gonna be any album."

Clayton studied me, and I noticed there was something different about him. An intensity behind the eyes, and a sort of aloofness that I couldn't put my finger on.

"I see." He asked the secretary for a piece of paper and a pen, and he scratched on it and handed it to me. "I'm about to head out on the county fair circuit, and our girl singer just dropped out. We like to have a female act in the lineup. Would you two be interested in coming on the road? The pay isn't good and the food's even worse, but you'll get some experience and exposure. What do you say?"

Hess and I were speechless. A few minutes ago our career had been over, and now a country legend was asking us on tour.

Clayton gracefully added, "I know you've had a long day. Think about it, and call that number when you're ready. They'll give you the details."

We were both strangely quiet in the car on the way home, as if holding our breaths. Once we shut the door behind us, safe in the womb of Mom's house, we started talking at the same time, burning through all that this could mean. Hess said this was how a lot of the big acts got started, working their way through the South and performing for the people who bought the records and drank at the honky-tonk shows.

This wasn't some grift to get in our pants. It was a real chance.

7

lulabelle

1967

FIFTEEN YEARS LEFT

Life on the road was dirty and strange. This was the county fair circuit smack dab in the sweaty crack of summer. We were all damp as frogs from sunup to sundown, smelling like the salt dust of the shelled peanuts we lived on.

And I quickly realized I was made for it. I had lived most of my life on the edge of existence like the other musicians.

Hess had a harder time acclimating. She was used to a certain standard of living, and she didn't say it out loud, but I knew she thought it was all a bit barbaric. The cheap hamburgers and passing the liquor bottle after the shows and taking naps in bus seats while we drove to the next town.

The one thing we both took to was the motel room we shared each night. We might have been surrounded by stained carpet and rusty sinks, but we didn't see it when we were together.

As much as I wanted more, before the tour, Hess and I had only kissed. We couldn't risk tiptoeing between our rooms after lights-out at Mom's. It was sweet torture to lie in bed touching myself, knowing that she was only a few feet away on the other side of the wall. Sometimes I'd put my hand up to it, and I swear I could feel it pulsing.

The first night on tour, we were given only one bed at the motel. It sat there, charged, in the middle of the room, and we both stared at it, paralyzed.

All of my yearnings had stored up like muscle memory in my body, so it was the force of those lonely fantasies that finally took her hand and led her over to the bed. Set free by my touch, Hess reached around and unzipped the back of my dress. She pulled the straps down and let it fall to my ankles. Then she gently brought my slip over my head and tossed it on the ground. I shivered.

Hess unhooked my bra, turning my breasts from cones to cakes. She got on her knees and put her face in them, and when her nose grazed my nipple, it plucked my insides. They were still humming when she gave it a furtive lick. We were feeling it out as we went, and maybe we were a little timid and clumsy, but it was better for that. Something so tender needs a light, fluttering touch, not force.

I ripped off my wig and flung it into the chair. She unclipped my pantyhose and pulled down my undergarments. I widened my legs, and she swept her fingers back and forth, gently again. There was something more to her touch, like I could feel the Hess of her buzzing against me. My knees went to jelly, and I nearly keeled over.

I clutched her shoulder to stay up, and I realized she still had all her clothes on. I pulled her up to standing and frantically stripped her, and the urgency created even more heat.

When she was naked, we lay down on the bed and pressed our bodies together. Finally, there was nothing between us. I could get as close as I wanted. I slid my fingers inside of her, desperate to give her something.

She had already given me so much.

But then she was touching me as well, and I stopped thinking my petty thoughts.

It was just us, back in the forest of our sound, rolling around on the moss.

As we touched each other, the buds of my tree sprouted into enormous triumphant blooms. They dripped nectar, coating their petals in fragrant honey.

When it became too much to bear, the flowers violently unfurled to their most exposed beauty. They stayed like this for a moment, raw and burning in the sunlight.

Then they curled at the edges and fell to the ground, spent but not dead. They would be absorbed back into the earth of me and come alive once again.

Afterward, we held each other on top of the bed and tried to catch our breaths. I felt soft-shelled and safe, like I never had as a child, and I wanted to tell her what I'd kept secret all these months. What lay at the hidden center of me, where my demon child heart beat.

"Hess?" I asked against her chest.

"Yes, my love?"

"My mother didn't just die in a tragic accident. Or, that's not the whole story."

"What do you mean?"

"Her mother also died in a tragic accident at the same age, 33. And her mother before that, and her mother before that. The women in my family are cursed."

Hess stopped playing with my hair and went silent. I continued, "When she was 33, my great-great-grandmother traded her soul to the devil for a beautiful singing voice. She didn't know she was cursing every woman in her bloodline thereafter with the gift to sing and the fate to die at 33, condemned to hell." Her cursed soul was handed down through the generations like a tattered wedding dress. I paused. "Which means when I turn 33, I'm going to die."

I had never dared tell anyone this outside the holler. I knew most would think I was out of my mind, or worse, stupid. They wouldn't understand that I grew up in a different place. After centuries living on this planet, people have thrown their own veil over the world. But in the holler, the veil is thin. We can see through it to nature and its truths.

I watched Hess carefully. She was calm and impassive, contemplating what I'd revealed.

"How does it feel? Knowing when you'll die?" she asked.

I thought on it. "Sometimes I can feel the seconds ticking by, and it makes me feel like I can't breathe. Every morning when I wake up, my first thought is: *Fifteen. Fifteen more years.*"

Hess nodded, urging me to go on.

"But it also makes me a little wilder, like I can take chances, 'cause I only got a bit of time left to do everything I want. It's now or never."

She took my hand and kissed it lightly. "It must be hard to live with, especially all by yourself."

I nodded and clenched my teeth, willing myself not to cry.

She *believed* me.

It was the best gift I'd ever received. She pushed me onto my back and lowered herself. She smiled. "We should make the most of our time, then." She kissed me, and I forgot about time. There was only her.

Hours later, I woke to cool air brushing against my bare skin, and I imagined someone barging in and seeing us like that. I tried to remember the noises we had made and how loud, and I wondered if the rooms on either side had heard. I'd been so possessed by the need to be alone with Hess that I hadn't paid attention to our neighboring room assignments. I sat up suddenly, seized by panic.

She sat up, too, and asked me what was wrong, and I told her. Then she smiled and lay back down on the bed, stretching her arms languidly above her head.

"Oh, darling, I'm sure no one heard. They're all passed out or having their own fun. No one cares about the sweet little Walker Sisters." She giggled and tried to pull me back down to her. I saw that this was one real difference between us. Hess had never lived in fear like I had.

I wasn't afraid of death; I knew when it would come for me.

But the world could make you wish you were dead if you weren't careful.

At each stop on the tour, we played the morning slot in the tent meant for women and children seeking shelter from the heat. I could see our audiences perking up at our music, so I knew we had some effect.

But without an original song, we'd just be the nameless girl singers with the nice voices who played the classics with a swing. It was no longer enough that we got to play, on a stage, for people. I wanted to play our own music.

One night I tossed and turned as a melody looped in my dreams, tormenting me with each note. When I woke, it was still there, teasing my mind. I hummed it up at the ceiling, rousing Hess from sleep. She hummed it back to me, and then as we rolled on our stockings and applied lipstick in the mirror, we hummed it together.

In the diner across the street, we talked about possible lyrics. We wanted this one to be funny. Flirtatious. There was such a lightness between us. We spoke mainly in private jokes that no one else could understand. We were in the blush of new love, and we didn't even have to hide it that much because we were young and sweet and apparently related.

One of our favorite jokes was mocking the way every venue host introduced us onstage, no matter the state:

"Now let's welcome to the stage a pair of *pretty little ladies* . . ."

"Get ready for some sweet music from these *pretty little ladies* . . ."

"My oh my, here are some *pretty little ladies* for you . . ."

We should have called ourselves the Pretty Little Ladies for all people cared who we were. It was doubly funny that I was such a rough-hewn hillbilly, hardly what many would call a "lady," and Hess was not what you would have called "little." She was proper, but she was taller and stronger than most of the men in our touring group.

And of course, our nighttime activities were hardly the actions of virginal, sugar-coated *pretty little ladies*.

I brought up the joke, and Hess said there was something there. We sat in the diner for an hour while our eggs went cold, making a list of all the traits of a pretty little lady, and then, all the realities of being a woman. We wanted to compare these in an upbeat, humorous story, where it felt like we were all laughing at ourselves by the end. That's how you pulled off something like that. If we were all laughing, no one was getting their drawers in a bunch.

When we met, you called me pretty little lady
You loved how I fit in your palm
At the church, they called me pretty little lady
In my sweet little white gown
In the kitch'n, you called me pretty little lady
As I sweated over open flame
In the delivery, you called me pretty little lady
As the big, bouncing baby came

That morning we were headed to the next town in the bus for the lesser artists—mostly a bunch of kids and old drunks still working the circuit. Usually I liked to look out the window and allow new music to enter me through the changing landscape. There was something about passing new scenery that rearranged my mind and created ideas.

But for this ride, we worked for the full two hours, coming up with the right words and matching them to the tune we'd hummed all day.

When we got to the motel that night, we picked up our guitars and started to play the song for real. Once we'd worked out all the kinks, we played it through without stopping.

Hess and I locked eyes over our strings still vibrating in the stale motel air.

We could feel it.

That feeling when an idea finally achieves sparkling, solid reality. When it officially joins the world.

When we first boarded the tour, we'd had to get our set list cleared by Clayton and his music director. It was just a bunch of classic country songs, so there'd been no issues. That was what they wanted from us—sweet, lady-pitched background music for people to eat corn dogs to in the shade. No one from the tour actually watched us past the first performance, so I figured it didn't really matter what we played. We could have tossed our guitars and whistled for all they cared.

So we were ready the next day when the announcer in Macon, Georgia, gave us the standard intro we'd hoped for:

"Now let's give a big Georgia welcome to these pretty little ladies . . ."

We came in with the first verse echoing his words, *We're just pretty little ladies*, and that made the audience laugh right off the bat. We gave him knowing glances, making it seem like he was in on it. We couldn't have him telling Clayton we made fun of him. Nothing's more fragile than the ego of a man with just a little bit of power.

As the song went on, the audience really got into it, and when they started clapping to the beat, I knew we had them.

We're just pretty little ladies
Like a flower bloomin' all year long
We're just pretty little ladies
It's a miracle we can sing this song

Hess and I laughed like madwomen right there onstage, we were so high and relieved they liked it.

The next day, there were a few more people in the tent, and we played it again, and at the next show, there were a few more. By the weekend, we had a real crowd. The announcer, who now felt a part of our act, delivered his line like a clown in a show. It was a little slapstick for my taste, but the audience loved it.

When we stepped off the stage at the end of the set, Clayton was waiting for us with his arms crossed.

"No one told me you were doing new material."

Hess jumped in to explain, but he put a hand up.

"It's a great song. Where'd you get it from?"

"It's ours, sir."

He studied us for a moment and clicked his tongue against his teeth. "I want you all to play before me now, in the evenings. Just that song."

I thought I might swallow my own heart.

8

lulabelle

1967

FIFTEEN YEARS LEFT

It was the Fourth of July, and we were in some backwater corner of Mississippi.

That night, Clayton had invited me onstage to sing a duet with him, and the crowd had loved it. He didn't curl his voice around mine like Hess did. He sang ahead, and the sound demanded I follow.

When the show had ended, the whole touring crew had herded from the grounds to a local park for a cookout with the rest of the town. The charcoal smoke hung heavy in the humid air, wrapping us in its primal smell.

Hess and I sat with the rest of the musicians in a circle of lawn chairs, eating hotdogs and jamming idly. Clayton approached and asked if he could speak with me privately, and we wandered off toward the pines lining the park on one side.

"Did you know I grew up in Amos?" he asked.

"No shit!" The words were out before I could look them over.

He smirked at me. "I thought you might know it. Where'd you say you were from?"

My blood went cold. I'd fed him the same "little holler" line I'd given everyone else, even Hess. Most people in Nashville didn't know or care about the tiny hamlets in the mountains, and no one *ever* asked me which one.

Was it possible he knew who I was? What I'd done?

He saw me hesitate and smiled reassuringly. "It's no matter. Your business is none of mine." He put more of his real accent into the last phrase, like he was slitting a finger and wiping his blood across the words. A pact.

"What I'm saying is I see myself in you. I think you could be a big star. And I want to help make that happen."

I eyed him, wondering if I could trust his word. He was like a chameleon, always shifting personas to blend in and get what he needed. We understood each other in that way, which was why I wasn't sure I could trust such a person. But did I have a choice?

"That's very kind of you. Could you introduce us to your producer, or someone at your label?"

He paused, considering his words. "I deeply admire Hess. I think she's a lovely girl and a gifted performer." He took a deep breath. "But she's not you. She doesn't have your voice, or your magic. I'm interested in helping you, and *only* you."

"But . . . you don't understand. She and I are a team. I'm only good because she's up there with me."

"What about our duet tonight? She wasn't there then, and you lit up the stage. I know it's hard to accept because she's special to you, but that's the reality of this business. Not everyone gets to be a star. And you have to make sacrifices if you want to make it. I know from experience."

This was what I'd been waiting for my whole life. I thought of the promise Tima and I had made to each other my first night with the girls—I had to take my chance, no matter the cost.

But Hess was everything to me. She was my music partner, my best friend, my love. The thought of hurting her made me sick.

Clayton must have read my silence as awed agreement because he kept talking.

"First thing we'll do is record an album together. I'll do a few songs, and you can record "Pretty Little Lady," and then we'll do some duets. The one we did tonight, and a few more we can get from these great songwriters I have back in Nashville."

With just one change to a song title, he had cut Hess out of the band.

As he continued to talk, I searched for her on the other side of the park and found her watching me. We met eyes, and she quickly turned away.

"We'll need to change your name. Lulabelle is a little long, and it has a common feel to it. I want something with more punch."

I looked up at him. "You want to change my name?"

"Not legally. Just for the public. You can still call yourself whatever you'd like in private. All the big stars do it. Look at Marilyn Monroe."

He sure knew how to appeal to me. "What about 'Lou'? That's what everyone calls me anyway."

"That's too boyish. It needs to be elegant, and a little sexy. What about . . . Belle?"

Clayton probably thought he'd come up with this idea, that he was telling me who I was, and I'd go along with it no matter what. The helpless little hick who ate up whatever they served her.

But that wasn't it.

I was no stranger to taking a piece of myself and giving it a new name. I'd already started to think of my stage persona as someone that could be taken on and off. It was the wig, and everything that was attached to it. Giving it a name felt natural. Logical, even. A way of separating them more cleanly. I was Lou with Hess, and at the boardinghouse with the girls, and at Darlene's when men needed their skulls knocked. But when I walked onto that stage, I became someone else.

Belle was sweet and polished, and country like a girl raised in a grand, decaying mansion. The name looked like a body to me, with curves that gave way to long, slender legs. It was musical, but it didn't ring so much as curl in the mouth like cream.

"Alrighty. I like it," I said, enchanted.

"We'll get started when we return to Nashville."

I nodded, my arms suddenly cold.

We rejoined the group, and Clayton picked up a guitar and started playing patriotic songs. Everyone sang along to them, spreading to neighboring grill-outs, so that it felt like hundreds of voices were singing together.

I noticed Hess wasn't singing with the rest of us. She sat next to me real quiet, staring off away from the group. She always took up so much space, was such a radiant, overwhelming presence in my life, that it was strange to see her like that. A little smaller, and turned in on herself. I didn't like it.

One of the fiddlers, who'd grown up in the town, whispered in my ear that some of the younger kids were sneaking up to the roof of the high school to watch the fireworks. I grabbed Hess's hand, and I could feel her spirit lift as we followed him away from the cookout across the street. We ran giddily through the darkening grass until we came to a ladder at the side of the brick building. The fiddler went first, and I climbed up after him, feeling a surge as I clung by my arms high up over the town.

At the top, I saw shadows milling about. The cherries of their cigarettes glowed on and off, and they passed bottle silhouettes in the dying light.

The fiddler told us it was about to start, and the shadows went quiet, and we were instructed to lie down on the loose rocks and look up. I reached out for Hess's hand, and it was there, waiting for me.

I heard a sound like an angry rooster call, and then something shot up into the sky. There was an explosion of sparks, and then they fell back to the earth, like it was raining green candlelight. I'd never seen anything like it. There was another burst in gold, and then another in purple and orange. I held my breath, waiting for the next one.

Hot, dark ash rained down on us, and most of the kids got up and ran for cover. But Hess and I stayed, holding hands and letting it coat us like volcano worshippers. It was like witnessing an act of God. I couldn't look away.

Afterward, we watched the smoke slowly drift and clear, revealing the stars above.

I told Hess what Clayton had said, and though I couldn't see her, I could feel her spirit sink again. I'd pushed my guilt away in the excitement of Clayton's plans for us, and now it rushed back in with greater strength. I told Hess I wouldn't do it without her.

At these words, she sat up and gave me a hard look. "Of course you're going to do it, Lou." Then she jumped to her feet and held out a hand to me, her face stern and hard to read. I took it, and we followed the ladder down to the sounds of the kids below.

The group of us broke into the school, and while the others shot baskets in the gym, Hess and I went to the girls' locker room to clean up. In the stark fluorescent light, we laughed at our soot-covered faces and clothes. We looked like chimney sweeps from *Mary Poppins.*

Hess's face went serious again. She pressed me up against the sink and kissed the clean patch on my neck. She put her hand up my gingham dress and found her way to my underwear. She moved it aside and rubbed small, gentle circles the way I liked, the light touches making my body reach for the sensation. She breathed against my ear,

"No matter what happens, I am yours."

"*Yes,*" I gasped.

"And you are mine."

"Yes."

I tried to put my hand up her dress, but she batted it away. She kneeled down and took each of my thighs in her strong palms and put her mouth between my legs. I leaned back and pressed my head against the glass of the mirror. I could feel its fragile grit against my skull; I imagined it shattering with the force.

And then, I was shattering, a shower of sparks raining down inside me.

9

rhea

1995

When I think of that summer in Nashville, I see Hess and me cruising down a sunflower-lined country road in her blue Mustang convertible, belting Shania Twain's "Man, I Feel Like a Woman."

She'd invited me to stay at her house instead of a hotel—she lived alone without a husband or children—and so her place became like a home to me.

Each morning was spent re-creating Belle's life—we got our hair done at her old salon, we bought pearls at her jeweler, we ate the tangy shreds of her favorite barbecue. I traded in my perfectly soiled Chucks for cowboy boots and squeezed into Belle's old clothes Hess kept in the attic. It was fun to pretend I was shedding my skin, finally becoming who I'd always been, rather than putting on a costume.

In the afternoons, when Hess was busy with meetings and appearances, I saw Micah.

He'd decided to stay in Nashville for a while, and we spent almost every day together getting to know the city and researching my mother. We went to museums filled with images of her face and her old things that didn't seem real under the lights. We went to the Grand Ole Opry and the cheesy honky-tonks along Broadway.

Mostly, we talked.

He told me about building a makeshift wrestling ring with his brother in their backyard and diving off the roof of their double-wide. He told me about the first time he saw classical music performed live at the Charleston Symphony; they played Ravel's "Pavane for a Dead Princess," and he'd felt emotions he didn't know existed, like a special, gilded melancholy that stayed with him for weeks after.

I told him about me and Shelli stealing her parents' liquor at thirteen, and me daring her to slap me across the face, just so I could see what it felt like. I told him about the summer I read *Dune* and found kinship with Paul and his haunting visions of the future.

In the beginning, it was more curiosity than attraction that pulled me toward Micah. Then as we spent more time together, and he became the person I wanted to talk to most, I could feel a kind of desire starting to creep in, stronger and more sickening than I'd ever felt it before.

I had liked sleeping with boys in high school—bringing them under my control, feeling their need moving against mine, briefly smothering the ache I felt to be touched. I only ever saw them as bodies, and I preferred when afterward they would disappear.

There was something different about Micah's honeyed accent, and I wanted to know what he thought about everything. When we weren't together, I obsessed over when I would see him next.

But he hadn't tried to kiss me, and I worried he only saw me as a friend.

For all of his wiliness and emotion, he could be incredibly disciplined. He was this mix of impulsivity and restraint, of primitive man and gentleman, and it left room for me to be the same. Both creature and girl.

That summer, Hess was the headliner for the Fourth of July show at the Tennessee State Fair. I'd never been backstage at a concert venue, and the frantic, sweat-soaked urgency of it was overwhelming. People breezed in and out of Hess's air-conditioned dressing room, paying their respects to the "grand dame," while I sat in the corner and listened to my Discman.

I'd started my music education with Belle's first album, *Clayton & Belle*. She recorded it with her first husband, Clayton Redd, and the cover featured the wedding photo I'd seen in Bellewood. Now when I looked at it, I saw the commanding look in her eyes and not the helpless child bride.

My favorite track was "Pretty Little Lady," which felt more like her than the rest of the songs that skewed a bit sappy. I could see her smirking as she wrote it, her eyes filled with mirth. I imagined us laughing over its irony, she and I the same age at the same time, no longer two trains passing in the night.

Hess had hired guitar and voice teachers so I could learn to make my own music, but the fingerings felt unnatural, and my voice was mediocre at best. I spent most of the lessons eyeing the clock, wishing I was lounging in the backyard with a sweet tea.

When Hess's dressing room got too crowded, I went to the wing and watched the show from the side in the sweltering air. I'd learned to sink into the wet heat like a bath and let my body become one with it.

One of the featured rising stars was performing—a twiggy brunette with tall, feathered hair and huge rhinestone earrings. There was a gravelly quality to her voice that made you lean in closer. As I swayed to her music, I felt someone come up next to me.

"Can you believe I found her singing at a little resort in the Ozarks?"

I recognized his twinkling, vintage movie-star eyes from the wedding photo. "You're Clayton Redd."

"Yes, ma'am. It's nice to see you."

I still couldn't get over the eeriness of meeting strangers who already knew me, like I was an amnesiac reentering my life after a lengthy coma. At least he didn't tell me how "grown-up" or how "beautiful like my mother" I was. I was 5'10" and broad with copper hair. I looked nothing like her.

The young singer finished her song, then took a bow to roaring applause. "There's something about her," I said. "I can't look away."

He smiled. "Reminds me of your mother."

I wondered if he still loved her, and what had really happened between them. He had an elegance I hadn't expected, and he didn't instantly repel me like other men his age. Seeing him now, it was a little easier to believe that Belle had once been in love with him.

"I've been listening to *Clayton & Belle*."

"Studying the classics, are we?"

"I keep wondering—did you fall in love *before* you wrote the album, or while you were recording it?"

He smiled again, though this time it seemed strained. "That is a hard question to answer, young lady." He paused. "What I can say is this: The first time I heard your mother sing, I fell in love with her voice."

I was seized with a sudden envy, as if this man didn't deserve to have these precious memories when I had none. I wished I remembered the first time I saw her, the first time I fell in love. Though I guess no child ever remembers that—the memory isn't necessary, because the love has always been there, like an organ pulsing in your body. To not have that love must be like a birth defect that deforms you for the rest of your life.

"What happened between you? Why did you break up?" I asked quietly. I wanted him to hurt like I did, and to remind him of his place in her story.

His eyes darkened. "Your mother valued freedom over everything else, and I didn't understand that until it was too late."

I tried to parse his words for meaning, but they seemed deliberately vague. "But then you worked together again, later."

Years after their divorce, when my mom started recording country pop and became really famous, Clayton was the producer on all of her albums, and this baffled me a little. Shelli's parents had been divorced since she was three, and they'd barely made eye contact at graduation.

"Yes, well, I'd learned my lesson. I was only ever meant to serve her greatness. Nothing more."

Why were people always giving me cryptic answers to my questions about her? "But how did it happen?" I pressed.

The twinkle returned to his eye. "After she signed her new record deal, she came out to LA for a bit. I was out there producing, expanding into rock and pop. When I heard she was in town, I begged her to have dinner with me. We got to talking about her vision for the new album—she said she wanted to be huge, like a Greek titan. A massive star. It would have sounded arrogant and delusional coming from anyone else, but she made it sound mythical, like she was a warrior from a great tale.

"I went home that night, and I played the demo she'd given me, what would become the *Mile High Woman* album. It sounded like God himself reaching down and thumping me in the chest. I knew I had to be a part of it, if it was the last thing I ever did. I called her up the next morning, and I asked her how it'd come to her, and you know what she said?" His eyes were shining. I shook my head.

"She said, 'It was the sound of my little girl coming into the world.'"

My face flushed, and the heat traveled down my neck and the backs of my arms.

With her set now over, the singer ran at us and jumped onto Clayton, hugging him tight. He grinned and held on to her like a grandfather, and I stepped away, still reeling.

Hess came up beside me in her black sequined suit. Her forehead was shiny with sweat, and it occurred to me that I'd never seen her like that; she always looked cool as a cucumber, no matter the temperature. "I see you met Clayton," she whispered.

"Yes."

"Is he what you expected?"

I shook my head dazedly. "No, not really." I looked over at him talking to the singer, his eyes crinkled at her excitement. "I assume all men his age are sort of . . ."

"Clueless?" she supplied.

I chuckled. "Yes. That."

"Well, you'd be right. But not Clayton. He's a different kind of cat." I watched her lock eyes with him across the way and give him a subtle nod that he returned. They clearly weren't close, but they seemed to share an understanding I wouldn't be able to penetrate, no matter what questions I asked.

Hess craned her neck around the barrier and peeked at the thousands of people in the crowd undulating like a sea in the shimmering heat.

"Do you ever get nervous?" I asked, and she smirked.

"I never did when your mother was with me. I thought I was one of those people born without stage fright until she was gone, and I had to go out there on my own. Even now, I still get a little sick right before." She took a long sip of water, and I saw a bead of sweat trickle down her temple.

Overhead, the announcer intoned, "And now, ladies and gentlemen, welcome to the stage: the grand dame of country, our hometown sweetheart, our lady in black, *Heeeeeess Walker*!"

She stuck out her tongue at me before plastering on a smile and walking out onstage.

The crowd screamed for her, and she waved back at them like a good-natured beauty queen.

As she launched into her set, I thought about what Clayton had said about my mother valuing freedom above all else. With each new fact I learned about her, I tried to color in her image a bit more. But it was hard to piece such disparate, sometimes abstract impressions of a person into a cohesive picture—the result was more Frankenstein's monster than mother.

It was easier to imagine her as different people, as I had as a child.

This new mother was a person who followed their own desires no matter the consequences. Who couldn't be tied down. I wondered what it was like for such a person to be a mother. Could they ever be happy? Or did it only trap them?

Out onstage, I heard Hess break off a verse and tilt her head away from the mic, gasping for breath. The back of her suit was drenched in sweat, and her hair was matted to her forehead. I waited for someone from the crew to rush on to help, but no one moved.

Without a thought, I ran out to her and put a hand on her arm to support her. I whispered, "Are you okay?" in her ear, and she nodded weakly.

"Are you sick? Should I call 911?"

She shook her head and whispered, "No. It's just a hot flash."

I only knew what menopause was from watching *Fried Green Tomatoes* with Shelli, but I understood enough. It had something to do with hormones, and it could make you feel hot and sort of crazy.

"I just need a moment." She picked up the water bottle by her feet and chugged.

I looked out on the crowd staring at us, some in confusion, others in concern. I heard a few boos echo through the mass, and I figured I should say something.

"Hi, everyone." The boom of my voice through the mic made me jump.

The people continued to stare, and the boos increased in volume.

"My name is Rhea . . ." I had to say something they would actually care about. "And Belle Powers was my mother."

At the mention of her name, the crowd broke into a roar. I glanced over at Hess, who was still red-faced and catching her breath. I needed to kill more time.

"Hess asked me to come out and help her sing one of Belle's songs. My favorite from early in her career, called 'Pretty Little Lady.'"

The crowd roared again.

"Will you get us started?" I asked them.

They screeched in response, and it was like communicating with an enormous sentient being who spoke only in guttural excitement.

I turned back toward the band, who began to play the song, and I thrust the microphone toward the crowd, praying they knew the words. They screamed:

When we met, you called me pretty little lady
You loved how I fit in your palm
At the church, they called me pretty little lady
In my sweet little white gown

I heard Hess chuckle next to me, and I whispered, "Are you all right now? Can you sing?"

She straightened. "Yes, I'm good. Let's do this."

She pulled the microphone back and began to sing with the crowd:

In the kitch'n, you called me pretty little lady
As I sweated over open flame
In the delivery, you called me pretty little lady
As the big bouncing baby came

Now that the emergency had passed, I stood there terrified, wondering what the hell I was doing in front of all these people. When it was time for the chorus, Hess pulled me into the mic, and I belted:

We're just pretty little ladies
Like a flower bloomin' all year long
We're just pretty little ladies
It's a miracle we can sing this song

Awash with adrenaline, I finished the song with Hess and the thousands of singers in the crowd. When it was over, they wailed like lunatics. Hess took my hand, and we stepped forward and bowed. I thought my heart might explode, and when she released me, I ran from the stage to the safety of the wing.

Once I was out of view, a crew member handed me a water bottle, and I tried to drink it while hunched over my knees.

"That was very brave," came a smooth voice above me. I looked up to see Clayton standing there, eyes twinkling.

"I don't know what I was thinking."

"It looked like you saved the day."

I smiled gratefully, still focused on catching my breath.

"I wonder if there's something here. An album, maybe. 'Greatest hits of Belle Powers as performed by her daughter.' Could be big if that crowd is any indication."

"But I'm not really a singer," I said, wondering if he might challenge me. Maybe I had a better voice than I thought, and I only needed the right person to spot it. Part of me still wondered if there was a remnant of Belle's talent lurking somewhere in me, just waiting for the right moment to reveal itself.

He furrowed his brow and pursed his lips. "Oh, that doesn't matter. We'd pair you with artists from that era for most of the songs. And nowadays you can take any voice and make it passable. Computers are remarkable things."

Deflated, I considered how to respond. It seemed like something I should be excited about, but the idea made me a bit queasy. Perhaps that was just the adrenaline leaving my body. I arranged my expression to one of enthusiasm. "I could sing some of my father's songs, too. A few of the big ones he wrote."

Clayton stiffened and looked away. "I mean no disrespect, but I have no interest in memorializing your father."

I bristled. Was this jealousy after so many years? It didn't seem like Clayton to hold on to such petty emotions.

"I'm sorry, I—"

"Please, it's no matter." He took a card out and placed it in my hand. "Give me a call, and we'll talk about the album. I can really see it." He looked me up and down and said, "You could even dress up like her for the cover."

As he walked away, I glanced at myself in the mirror used for touch-ups at the edge of the stage. I'd worn one of Belle's old dresses from the '70s in a lime polyester, and it strained across the middle and at my thighs. My hair, bleached to a red gold from the sun and teased up for more volume, had fallen since the morning. My eyeliner ran from the heat, and my hot-pink lipstick had faded, blurring the outline of my mouth.

I looked like a bad Halloween version of Belle—a night-worn, shameless imitation stumbling home late from a party.

I suddenly felt the tight itch of the polyester against my skin, like I was trapped in the dress. My chest constricted, and my stomach roiled. Instead of sinking into the heat, it smothered me now. I needed some air.

I left the stage area and walked through the searing neon fairground to meet Micah, as loud country pop pounded against my head and the smell of fried dough pressed against my nose like a thick blanket. I still felt like I couldn't take a full breath.

When I finally saw Micah at the Ferris wheel, he took one look at me and grimaced. "Are you okay?"

His beautiful face made my stomach turn even more. "I don't feel very good," I answered. "I think it's the heat." It didn't help that whenever he was close, I felt like I was going slightly insane. I couldn't stand another night of watching him out of the corner of my eye, wondering if he'd try to kiss me. "I'm sorry, I just need to get out of here."

I staggered toward the exit, but he said, "Wait," and caught my arm. We rarely touched, and an electricity passed between us.

I stopped and turned back to him.

"I know a place we can go."

We drove to a large row house a few doors down from Micah's hostel, and he led me through a gate to a swimming pool glowing oceanically in the dark. He began stripping off his clothes, and I couldn't help but stare at his lean, compact body.

"Whose pool is this?" I asked.

He smirked at me. "Not sure. But they haven't been home all summer. Someone might as well enjoy it." He backed up toward the edge in his boxers and let himself fall backward into the water.

I watched him paddle around for a while in the stifling heat, until I finally kicked off my boots, shimmied out of my dress, and jumped in.

God, it was so good. I could feel the sweat and makeup and hairspray rinsing away, and my summer muscles pounding furiously against the water. I surfaced, washed clean of that artifice, once again my unadorned, tortured self.

I swam toward the shallow end where Micah floated on his back, looking up at the stars. "Tell me a secret," I said. It was a game Shelli and I always played at the public pool.

He rolled over and stood in front of me with serious eyes and water dripping down his lips the color of cold plums. He was even more beautiful wet.

"My brother didn't die in an accident." While he hadn't said this explicitly, it had been implied. I raised an eyebrow, waiting. "He took his own life."

Micah was the one who found him in the woods behind their house. He'd shot himself in the head with their grandfather's pistol. He was only twenty years old.

"I don't like telling people," he explained. "It seems like too much to put on someone, and when you do, there's this feeling of being *tainted.* Most of my friends back home stopped talking to me after it happened." He paused. "But I feel like you're one of the only people who could actually understand."

I wanted to reach out and touch him, but I wasn't sure if that would be right. Instead, I nodded gently. "I used to feel that way, too, that I was tainted, because I thought my parents were these terrible people who had died because they didn't care about themselves, and that made me worthless as well." I paused, remembering the way people looked at me at school. "Now that I know the truth, you would think I'd feel better, and maybe I do a little, but the bad feeling is still there." I had been pretending for the last few weeks, and now here was the truth. "Maybe it's because I'm nothing like her—I feel so flawed in comparison."

He moved closer to me, but we still weren't touching. "But the image you have of her that's in these museums—it's not real, right? It's just a persona she created."

"I know. Which is why I've been trying to figure out who she really was, and I just can't seem to get it. I have little pieces, but it's not enough."

He nodded. "I think that's why I came here, too, because my brother always wanted to, and I thought it might reveal the part of him he kept hidden. But I still don't understand why . . ." He drifted off, unwilling to finish the thought.

"Did he leave a note?" I asked before I could take it back.

He shook his head. "He had a lot of issues—he could be really angry one day, and sort of lifeless the next. He'd get stuck on these bad thoughts, and he would stop sleeping. Instead of getting him help, my parents would tell him to stop being an asshole. They fought a lot in the last year—he was working for my dad's plumbing business, and he skipped a lot of jobs and it was creating this really bad situation in the house."

I related to some of this in my own way, but I stayed quiet.

"He started talking about how these people were out to get him, and he seemed really scared." He paused, his voice breaking. "But it was still shocking when it happened. I tried to imagine him doing it, and I just couldn't believe he'd actually pulled the trigger."

I nodded solemnly. "I can't imagine."

Silence fell over us for a moment, then he said, "It's your turn."

"What?"

"To tell a secret."

I had forgotten we were playing a game.

I wanted to tell him about the creature that lived inside of me, of the dread that I felt on birthdays, and sometimes on other days. But I couldn't now.

And maybe that was a good thing. I could still be anyone with him, the kind of person who claimed what she wanted without fear, like my mother had been.

"I *want* you," I said, and he paled in surprise. "I know you probably don't feel the same way, and that's okay. But I thought you should know."

His face turned serious. "What makes you think I don't want you?"

My heart was beating very fast, and I fought to control my voice. "It's been weeks and you haven't tried anything . . ."

He looked down, gliding his arms through the water. "Maybe I didn't want it to be . . . cheap."

My stomach curdled. "So you think kissing me would be cheap?" I asked.

He frowned. "No. What I mean is, I like when there is an order to things. My whole life I've watched people live carelessly, and I don't want to be like that."

We heard a pop in the distance, and then a shower of blue sparks rained down over the buildings to the east, turning the water and our faces a deep blue. Another pop came, and this time it was red, and then the next was gold. I watched Micah's awed expression change slightly with each shift in color.

He turned back to me. "I've never met anyone like you," he said seriously. "It's like discovering a member of my own species, when I thought they didn't exist. That I was the only one."

I took a shaky breath. "I feel that way, too."

He reached out and held his palm to mine, then laced our fingers together. Again, I felt that charge between us. He moved closer, wrapping his arms around my waist and pulling me toward his chest. Pressed against his body, it felt like my cells were regenerating, like more of myself was flowing into me.

"Do you feel that?" he asked.

I nodded, and before I could stop myself, I kissed him.

10

lulabelle

1967

FOURTEEN YEARS LEFT

If I was a creature of the road, I was also a creature of the studio session. I loved the manic late nights. The feverish collaboration. The worldless feel of it. We were only in that box, floating through space, separate from time and its demands.

Recording an album was me at my most primal. I didn't have to pretend to be anything other than someone who received music all day from the heavens.

We'd start recording around nine a.m. Clayton liked to get an early start, much to the chagrin of the players who were still drunk from the night before. As long as they played well, he didn't mind. They were the A team, a handful of musicians the labels used for all the high-profile sessions in Nashville.

I insisted Martha play on the record, and I saw their side-eye the first day. But that went away real quick when they heard her play. A lot of guitarists have a tang to their sound that can be too sour and bright. But Martha's playing is like honey; the guitar kind of melts away and all you can hear are the notes ringing in their sweetest form.

Clayton would hand out the music, and everyone would study it and put in their two cents. I'd never been taught how to read music, and Clayton had noticed early on. He said having a natural genius would only get me so far; I had to learn a few technical skills. Naturally, I balked at this, but eventually I came around.

When we were ready, I'd go in the corner by the door with a microphone. They'd turn the lights down and put on colored ones, in red or blue. The song would start, and the music would fill the room like a powerful perfume. It was so strong that it'd soak through my skin, marinating me like a chicken for hours. Around midday they wouldn't need me anymore, and I'd walk out into the world, the music still buzzing in my meat.

The studio was on Music Row, where record-label offices lined the street on either side. I couldn't go a few feet without being invited to a barbecue celebrating an album release. None of the big stars paid me any attention, but it was fun mingling with the backup singers and engineers and all the people that went into making a record. It was one big party, and it didn't matter which label you were with. We were all making music and having a good time.

Then I'd head to Darlene's to start my shift. I wasn't getting paid much for the sessions, and I still had to make rent at Mom's. Plus, I liked hanging around with the cowboys and listening to Darlene bitch about everyone. Hess still performed in our old slot, but Clayton forbade me from joining to rest my voice. It was hard not to jump onstage with her, but I loved watching her sing.

When I got off work at midnight, I'd head back to the studio with a brown paper bag of fried bologna sandwiches. They didn't need me, but I couldn't stay away. By that time, the room would be stuffy and warm from the steam rising off the musicians. They'd all be half drunk and excited to see me. Martha and Clayton were the only sober ones, keeping everyone on track and nailing the takes.

I'd stay until around two a.m., and then I'd get a ride home. First, I'd sneak into Hess's room and give her a kiss. Then I'd tiptoe to the kitchen, inhale the plate Mom left me, and sit on the back porch smoking a cigarette. I'd still be so high on music that I'd need a few hours to come down before my mind would quiet.

Sometimes I'd take long walks around the neighborhood, making larger and larger circles with Mom's house at the center. Time dissolved and blurred in the middle of the night, but it didn't feel any less valuable to me. It was still this precious time, wasted by so many, when I could experience more of what life had to offer.

By the time I was ready to sleep, it was time to get ready for the studio, and I'd launch back into it. For me, the album was recorded in one very long day.

~

After we finished the record, Clayton decided I needed fixing up.

We went to Harvey's and bought bigger wigs, designer makeup, fancy clothes. He tried to hire some fussy stylist, but I wouldn't let anyone but Phoebe dress me.

He took me to my first dentist. I had so many teeth that needed pulling they decided to start over and give me a whole new set made out of porcelain. Like a fancy toilet.

He took me to my first doctor with a medical degree. I was used to seeing the granny witch back in the holler, but I'd never been to an MD. He did a full examination from snout to tail, looking for all my creepy-crawlies. He gasped when he saw the birthmark on my chest. Said he'd never seen anything like it.

Turned out I was pretty healthy, considering I'd lived with total abandon my whole life. Afterward, Clayton asked to see my birthmark if I was comfortable, and I showed him the very top above my tits. He didn't seem seduced by it or anything, but he was intrigued. He said we'd keep it in mind for wardrobe, and that was that.

He brought me to see a lady in her nice house across town. She looked how I imagined Hess's mother: an elegant woman in pearls with a modest lilac dress and matching heels. She taught etiquette to the society girls in Nashville, and I wondered if she'd trained Hess. It made me laugh to think of her practicing her curtsy and pretending to eat soup with the right spoon.

For the first few hours, we went through speech drills, attempting to smooth my jagged speech into something sleek and curved, like Audrey Hepburn's transatlantic purr. But eventually she gave up. I could *pretend* to be whoever she wanted, and I could create endless new personas to suit my needs, but there was no version of me that wasn't from the country, or the South for that matter. She spent the next few hours teaching me all the basics of acting proper until Clayton seemed satisfied, and I went along with that part. I like to know what rules I'm breaking.

When the transformation was complete, he took me to a studio to have my picture taken. The photographer had all these ideas about me dressing up like a cowgirl straddling a hay bale and prancing around in a swimsuit with a beach ball, but I put a stop to that nonsense. I told him to just make me pretty, and I posed real nice for him, and that was all we needed. I refused to be someone's fool.

Then, it was time for the label to listen to the album. I called out of work and stayed by the phone all day at Mom's, waiting to hear from Clayton. Hess tried to distract me with board games and the new Loretta Lynn album, but nothing calmed my nerves. The opportunity still felt so precarious, so unreal, that I was afraid someone would come by and snatch it out of my hands. Or Clayton would wake up one morning and realize I was nothing special and dump me on the sidewalk with the rest of the trash.

Early in the evening, there was a knock on the door. It was Clayton. His face was calm and self-assured. Unreadable as ever. He asked if I'd like to go for a drive, and I said okay. I felt like a dead woman walking, like the mafia was about to pick me off.

When we got into his Cadillac, he asked me if I was hungry, and I said "always." I was a legend in the studio for the food I could put away.

We pulled into the Krystal's on Gallatin and waited for a waitress to skate to our window. The car was a quiet, dark space in the midst of the feral Saturday night crowd. Clayton didn't like to listen to the radio when he was working on a new album; he preferred to hold the songs in his mind without them getting infected by other sounds.

After a petite brunette took our order, Clayton went back to staring out the windshield. I couldn't take it anymore. "All right. Let me have it. They hated it, didn't they?"

He smiled. "They *loved* it. And they *loved* you. Your voice, and those pictures we had taken. They agree you're going to be a star."

There was this little jolt in my chest like I'd been struck by lightning. But I still sensed there was a catch. "Then why do I feel like you're gonna take me out?"

He folded his hands and held my gaze. "I have a proposition for you."

"That don't sound good."

He raised an eyebrow and continued. "I think we should get married."

I instantly thought of Hess and her goddess body. We struggled to find places we could be alone and really together, and we'd had less time to spend with one another with all the work on the album. Even so, it felt like she was the center of my little life.

I looked at Clayton, and I imagined his red face hovering above me, concentrating hard and pulsing to burst. I was suddenly aware of the small space of the car, and the fancy automatic locks on the doors. I pretended to adjust my dress, feeling for the knife in my bra. But I'd forgotten it in the excitement. Sweat broke along my hairline, and I scanned around the car, searching for anything I could make into a weapon.

"I appreciate the offer, but . . ."

He held up a hand. "I don't see you that way, either. I'm . . ." I looked over at him, forgetting the danger for a moment. I'd never seen Clayton at a loss for words. He was always so calm and collected, already waiting with the right thing to say. "I'm not interested in that kind of thing."

What did *that* mean?

"I don't enjoy being close to people . . . in a romantic fashion. I enjoy friendship, and professional and artistic collaboration. That's all I want from others."

I'd never heard of such a person, and I tried to wrap my head around it. Clayton was divorced and had a few kids that lived in Kentucky with their mom and her new husband. I'd always sensed something different about him, and I'd honestly thought it was that. I'd never met a divorced person before. It was still very taboo in the holler. People really thought it would send you to hell.

"Then why do you want to get married?"

"I think it would be good for the album. A little love story for the fans. Newlyweds singing to each other on their record players. We'd have the press cover the wedding so they could put it in papers and magazines."

It was an interesting idea. I saw the logic in it. But I was still skeptical. "What would I have to do?"

"You'd move into my house with me and my mother, but you'd have your own room. There's a whole wing just sitting under sheets with no one to fill it."

Another mother that wasn't mine. Another unknown, judgmental presence looming over me. I thought of Hess and Mom and the girls at the boardinghouse. It was a safe space I'd made for myself, and I didn't want to give it up. It was the first time I'd been in control of my own life. I'd never see Hess if I left.

"I don't know. I like living at Mom's. I don't wanna leave."

The brunette returned with our burgers in red plastic baskets and a slice of chocolate icebox pie on a plate for me. I tucked a napkin into my dress and started to eat immediately, stuffing the burger into my mouth and forgetting where I was.

Clayton eyed me and chuckled. "You'd be able to have visitors. I wouldn't want there to be a whole crowd all the time, but you'd be welcome to host Miss Walker whenever you'd like. She could even . . . sleep over."

I narrowed my eyes at him. "Well, that seems fair, since she's my sister and all . . ."

"Lou, I know she's not your sister. I know she's a very special friend, and you'd be free to be together, alone, without anyone around, if you lived with me. Do you understand what I'm saying?"

A piece of burger caught in my throat, and I sipped soda to dislodge it. I thought I might puke. I wanted to ask him how he'd found out, but I was afraid to even acknowledge it. I kept staring straight ahead, terrified of meeting his gaze.

He continued, "If we were married, no one would ask you questions about boyfriends or snoop around your love life. And believe me, once this album comes out, they'll be interested. They've been after me ever since my divorce."

I finally felt brave enough to look over at him. He didn't look disgusted or like he was trying to threaten me. He didn't seem bothered by it at all.

"What about your mama?"

He smiled to himself. "Ma is very old. She has a great team of nurses that take care of her twenty-four hours a day. You won't have to worry about her."

The judgmental mother of my imagination now morphed into my great-grandmother, a woman older than pond water who spent my early childhood on the porch looking out at the mountains through milky blue eyes.

"Our marriage wouldn't be traditional in many ways, but I hope it would be in this sense, that we could keep each other's secrets." He laid a hand on my arm, and it felt almost fatherly in its gentle warmth. When I looked into his eyes, they were open and empathetic, and I could feel that he accepted who I was, without saying it out loud or making a big deal of it.

My mouth filled with salt, and my eyes went cloudy. I swallowed back the tears and smiled at him. "Let me think about it."

After Clayton dropped me off, I crept into Hess's room and climbed under the covers with her. She was warm and heavy with sleep, and for a moment, I just nestled against her, feeling the length of her body against mine. She stirred and turned over, pulling me toward her.

I whispered in her ear about Clayton's proposal. Her eyes opened, and she sat up with a hand against her forehead. After a while she whispered, "Well? Are you going to say yes?"

I thought we'd have more of a discussion before it came to the question. I would tell her I couldn't do it, and she'd tell me that it was okay with her, and I'd protest a bit more, and she'd insist. She wasn't following the script.

"We could be together, alone, all the time, without anyone watching us."

"Except for Clayton and his mother."

"I don't think we have to worry about his mama. And Clayton is okay with it, that's what I'm saying. He doesn't care about us."

"Are you going to *sleep* with him?"

"What? No! Never." We both giggled at the thought. Then Hess went serious again.

"Do you love him?"

What did *I* know about love?

I never knew the love of my mama or daddy. I was treated like a worthless demon child by my aunt and uncle. I had a few cousins who were nice, but we were all fending for ourselves, trying to survive. I had to be selfish, and I couldn't let them see under my skin.

What Hess and I had didn't have a word. It contained too much and resembled nothing I'd ever seen between two people.

And as for Clayton, he was someone you got to know at a distance, and I didn't think you could ever love someone like that, which is how he wanted it. To not love them was to respect their wishes.

"No. I barely know the man. But I trust that he won't hurt me, or you. He'd only be doing this if he thought it was worth it."

Hess turned away from me and went over to the curtained window facing the backyard. She pulled aside the fabric and gazed down.

I waited breathlessly with my arms wrapped around my knees, watching her back muscles for some sort of sign. I wondered if I had just ruined this beautiful thing between us, this pure, filling love that I didn't deserve. I squeezed my knees tighter and imagined curling into a smaller and smaller shape until I disappeared.

Then she turned around, and there was a smile on her face. "Okay. I think you should say yes." She came over and took my hands in hers. "Imagine the dress Phoebe will make for you. It will be *divine*."

I could see the strain in her smile, and there was something brittle about her excitement. But I was so relieved that I decided to pretend it was real.

And soon, it was, as we sat on the bed, dreaming up everything we wanted for the wedding.

As if it was our own.

11

lulabelle

1967

FOURTEEN YEARS LEFT

The whole wedding was a performance.

Under Clayton's direction, Phoebe made a white dress with an enormous fluffy skirt and lace sleeves. Grand but traditional, it was a dress conceived for a broad audience and uglier than homemade sin.

At least Phoebe and I got to be creative with the hair—she sewed about fifty small silk daisies into my best wig. I looked like a fairy princess being married off to the human world.

When Clayton and I said our vows, Hess was only a few feet away, standing in a pink taffeta bridesmaid dress. I felt her presence burning behind me the entire time. Afterward, she stayed by my side, performing her maid of honor duties and keeping my champagne coupe filled.

I barely saw Clayton. When we weren't posing for pictures and greeting reporters, he was mingling with the partygoers. Nearly the entire guest list were his people. My group was small but mighty with Hess, Phoebe, Martha, Tima, Mom, and Darlene. All of these women who'd become like family to me in less than a year.

After it was over, Clayton and I got into his Cadillac and drove away from the church with tin cans bouncing from the bumper. The quiet wasn't a silence between us; we were both lost in our own thoughts.

We passed through an ornate metal gate and snaked up a long drive until a house like a palace revealed itself, shining on the hill. It was the grandest thing I'd ever seen.

He politely opened the front door for me, and I stood in the cavernous dark hall alone while he checked in on his mother. I was afraid to touch anything, and I worried I'd made a big mistake. Here was yet another space where I would have to creep around, an intruder in my own life, like I'd done as a child and when I'd first arrived at Mom's.

When he came back, he gave me the full tour. Living rooms, sitting rooms, dining rooms, all filled with pristine, unused furniture. More an idea of a house than a place for real living. In the kitchen he told me the cook would arrive in the morning and fix my breakfast. I could tell her my food preferences when we met. I'd spent my whole life eating what was given to me or what could be scavenged, and I wondered what I should say. There was so much I wanted to try.

We finally came upon a door he indicated as my "wing." Behind it was a modern but feminine sitting room with brand-new furniture arranged like a magazine photo. A set of glass doors led out to a terrace overlooking the pool in the backyard. He showed me a small spiral staircase looping down to the ground floor.

Leading off the sitting room was an enormous bedroom decorated in the same style. I had my own bathroom with a marble tub and a vanity with a gold stool. And then, there was the closet. It was its own little room filled with dresses, hats, shoes, purses, and God knows what else.

I was truly speechless. All I had in my suitcase were the few dresses Phoebe had made me and a ratty nightgown.

He watched me closely, searching for a reaction.

"Honest to God, I don't know what to say."

"That's a first." He smiled at me. I wanted to give him a hug, but I didn't know if that was okay without the cameras around. We were in such strange territory.

"Can I give you a hug? It's okay if you don't want me to. I ain't sure how to be a fake wife."

He laughed and motioned at me with his arms, and I wrapped myself around his warm chest. He was about a foot taller than me, and his shirt smelled like wood shavings. It was comforting, being with him. I felt safe.

"Thank you."

"It's my pleasure, Miss Belle."

I saw a phone on my bedside table, and I ran my finger along its smooth edge.

"That's your private line. With its own number. No one will be able to listen."

I knew who I wanted to call.

"I'll let you get settled in. Good night."

~

I was wigless and stripped down in the bath when I heard footsteps outside the bathroom. The door opened, and Hess tiptoed in as if we were back at Mom's and someone could catch us.

"Did you see that closet? Lord have mercy!" She grinned at me.

She looked as if she'd run here, still in her bridesmaid heels, like a Greek warrior delivering a message. She glowed.

I held my bubble-covered arms out to her. She quickly took her clothes off and got in at the other side of the tub, sloshing foamy water onto the floor. I turned around and lay back against her chest. We both looked out over the gleaming surfaces of the bathroom.

I knew she was used to nice things, but it was as if she could feel it for me, the awe of it. The soft, fluffy security of this new life. Mom's had been a wonderful place, but I'd never had any privacy, and I never forgot its precarious nature. If I didn't make rent, I didn't get to stay.

With Hess there, wrapped around my body, it felt more real. Everything always felt better and more real when she was there to witness it with me.

Her fingers slipped from my chest down my belly and stroked gently beneath the suds where I couldn't see them. A heat flared, warming the water to boiling, and she continued to stroke. That slick, erotic place was easy to find in the water, as if we were made to make love under the sea.

Afterward, we got out and put our hair up in plush towels and put on the two robes that hung in the bathroom. I was a little sick from all the champagne and the surprise of the room and the heady bathtub plunge. I was wrung out.

We climbed into the enormous bed with its thick floral blanket and mound of small, silly pillows matching the wallpaper. We tossed the pillows onto the floor and snuggled under the sheets with our hair still wet against the cotton.

Then Hess wrapped herself around me, and we slept curled and wet-headed, like two mermaids floating in the ocean on their wedding night.

12

lulabelle

1968

FOURTEEN YEARS LEFT

The first time I heard my voice on the radio, I was in Hess's Mustang in the middle of a snowstorm.

I'd convinced the girls to go night skating on the lake in Centennial Park, and we were all piled in the car wearing every item of clothing we owned. Snow streaked across the windshield as we slid on the icy asphalt, Hess white-knuckling the steering wheel and muttering that she couldn't believe I'd talked her into this.

I heard a familiar tune coming out of the speaker, and I turned up the knob to the sound of my own voice singing, *When we met, you called me pretty little lady.* Hess and I stared at each other, eyes bugged, as we skidded across the road into a ditch. We all screamed as the car came to a stop, then Phoebe leaned over the backseat, turned the song all the way up, and jumped out of the car. In the beam of the headlights, she danced by herself in the middle of the street. Then Tima got out, and Hess and I joined them, and then, finally, Martha.

Hess pulled me into her arms, and we waltzed madly across the asphalt to the beat of the song, nearly slipping a few times, our faces chapped with cold. The others danced around us, their whoops absorbed by the snowflakes falling thickly on our shoulders. Cars honked and swerved, but we didn't move from the street.

I had earned my place here in Nashville. That was *my voice* on the radio.

A few weeks later, our album hit #1 on the country charts, and I was invited to perform at the Grand Ole Opry with Clayton.

The inside smelled like a church with its old wooden frame, and the freshly washed bodies and fried chicken suppers laid across the laps of the audience. Phoebe, who was still in charge of my wardrobe, led me down a narrow hallway into the women's restroom where all the ladies got ready. It was cheek-stinging winter outside, but in that tiny room, it was hot as a bonfire. Packed wall to wall with women in slips and curlers, hairspray shot into the air from all angles, an assault of so many different perfumes that it numbed the nostrils.

Phoebe elbowed her way to a space in the corner, pulled out the dress she'd made, and helped me get into it. It was ivory with a high neck, inspired by Clayton's grandmother's wedding photo that hung in the hallway of his house. The Opry was all about tradition; you were supposed to pretend you were still a country girl singing for church on Sundays. The label had used our wedding photo as the album cover, so we were leaning into the wedding theme, and people loved it. At every performance, I came out in a different white dress with my daisy-studded wig. The perpetual bride.

There was no waiting room backstage, so we just hovered in the wing out of view, sweating it out until it was our turn. Hess kept dabbing around my hairline, sopping up the little beads of sweat. She didn't let go of my hand. When they finally called me and Clayton, she squeezed it hard and kissed me on the cheek. She whispered that she'd be right here, just a few feet away, watching me. I calmed, and then moved my hand to Clayton's and walked out to the cheers of the crowd.

I could hear my name out in the chaos of their sound, the roar forming into smooth pearls of "*Belle, Belle, Belle*." A row of teenage girls sat at the front wearing matching blonde wigs studded with daisies, and they held their arms up, reaching out to me as we headed to our mics.

Under the hot lights of the stage, I became Belle, smiling and waving at the crowd with all the good nature I had.

The band strummed the first few chords of our duet, and we launched into it, and as always, I became only the music.

And then, in a snap of my fingers, it was over.

Clayton bowed, then said my name and gestured toward me. I curtsied, and the crowd hollered louder, the sound deafening. We exited the stage, and the calamity continued, becoming a chant of my name once again.

"Belle! Belle! Belle!"

One of the producers came over and told me I'd better go out there for an encore or they'd tear the place apart.

I walked out alone onstage, feeling the empty space around me. I'd never performed solo before.

This time when I looked out, I saw that the Opry really was a church. The audience sat in wooden pews in a circle surrounding the stage, and I was at the center of it, like a preacher come to share the good word. They wanted me to tell them stories, so they could feel their own heartbreak. So they could take some solace home with them and feed on it for the week.

I remembered an old murder ballad from the holler. It was one of my favorites because it wasn't about a man killing a woman, which a lot of them were. It was about my great-great-grandmother, and a curse.

This was the story I wanted to tell.

I strummed my guitar and started to sing:

There was a woman in town who sang so sweet
Her beauty was beyond compare
But one day a bright specter she did meet
There aft she was no longer fair

There was only my voice and the twang of my guitar, and I could feel the richness of the sound in that room, the notes oiled to a high, smooth shine. It traveled out and stroked the ears of each person, like the building itself was an instrument, created for just this purpose.

I watched them close their eyes as the song took them over. The force of their feeling filled my spirit, my body lifting a few inches above the stage, hovering there beneath the stained glass and the beaming faces of the congregation.

Looking back, I realize I hadn't *made it* in that moment. No.

I had *risen*.

13

lulabelle

1972

TEN YEARS LEFT

The next few years were a blur.

We went on tour for the album, hitting all the Southern cities. Then it was time to make another one. The cycle repeated over and over. Album, tour. Album, tour. The only way to mark time was the changing of the seasons out the window.

Clayton curated every part of my life, and it was a beautiful one. I wanted for nothing.

He hired Hess as a fake assistant for me, and she left Mom's and moved into the house. A room was set up for her in my wing, but she never touched that bed. We lived perpetually a few feet from one another. At any moment of the day, I could reach out and feel her warm skin against my palm.

She stayed up with me when I couldn't stand to sleep, afraid of wasting precious moments. The music that came to me at night were strange, slanted tunes. Hess called them my night songs, and I had a whole drawer of them. I encouraged her to keep working on her music career, but she struggled to write songs on her own, and over time, that dream seemed to recede into the background for her.

We also stopped calling ourselves sisters, and no one asked questions. I no longer worried that someone would find me and lock me up.

Now that I was Clayton's wife, it was like everything I'd ever said and done had been wiped clean.

One morning during the recording of our fourth album, I awoke with the words *ten years* floating in my mind, as if they'd drifted in from somewhere else.

I realized it was my birthday. The *real* birthday that belonged to the demon child, that no one in this life knew about.

Ten years.

I have just ten years left.

I was usually good at pushing the thoughts away; I was so busy that it was easy to forget about everything else but the chaos of the moment.

But that morning, those two words refused to leave.

Hess stirred next to me, sensing my distress, and I told her I was fine when she asked. She was always watching me, looking for something she could make better. An uneasy feeling crept in, and I retreated downstairs to see if food would help.

Clayton was sitting at the breakfast table, fresh as a daisy in his starched suit, and he grimaced slightly when he saw my sorry state. Hair askew, bags under my eyes, still in the men's pajamas I liked to sleep in.

I sat down and the cook, Annie, served me a butter pecan diet shake in a fancy glass. I swear to God, that stuff tasted like sweet mud. I eyed Clayton's eggs and bacon across the table with murderous jealousy. He was trying to get ahead of my metabolism, convinced it'd never keep up with my eating habits now that I was *getting older.* Twenty-three, and already an old crone.

When I first moved in, Annie made me these incredible feasts that I scarfed down like a mad king. She loved it—cooks love to see people eat their food. Then Clayton put his foot down. I'm sure he knew Hess was sneaking Krystal burgers into the house at night, but I figured he'd stay quiet until my measurements changed. Then the real smackdown would come. My hillbilly scrawn was part of my look, and I couldn't risk losing it.

"We've talked about this," he said, gesturing at my disheveled appearance.

"But no one is here 'cept for you and Annie, and she don't mind." I looked over at Annie, who gave me the smallest wink.

"It's 'ex-cept' and 'doesn't mind.' And *I do* mind. As should you. If you're not going to respect yourself, how can you expect anyone else to?"

I huffed, feeling too edgy for one of his lectures.

"We do not get to choose how we come into this world, but we choose how we present ourselves. Anyone can become a person of status if they put in the effort. Honestly, show some class."

I had loved this idea of Clayton's, that I could be anyone I wanted no matter my upbringing, and whenever he was around, I usually made sure to have my hair done, my makeup tidy, my outfit spotless. Even when he wasn't there, I could hear him scolding me for looking like a dirty hillbilly with no sense.

But today it made me want to curl into a ball.

Upstairs, I took a scalding shower and inhaled the steam. That uneasy feeling strengthened, thrashing around like a wild cat in my lungs. I knew what it was. It was that feeling I'd had back home and in the shed, like I was trapped and couldn't escape, or maybe there was something trapped inside *me* that needed to get out.

In my closet, Clayton had laid out a powder-blue skirt suit, sensible pumps, and pearl earrings for me to wear to the studio that morning. I'd have liked to try a psychedelic minidress or a pair of jeans, but he was real particular about my look. The label didn't want anyone thinking we were engaging in free love. We were still good Christians singing about good values, never mind that Clayton didn't give a damn about those values. It was all about giving the people what they wanted.

Hess rolled pantyhose up each of my legs, caressing my calves as she did. I tried to pull her closer to me, but she said we couldn't. I'd get wrinkled and then we'd be late, and we knew how Clayton would react. It would ruin the whole day.

Outside, we got into the backseat of one of Clayton's Cadillacs with my hired driver sitting up front. I still had no idea how to drive; Clayton said when you were a star, you paid people for things like that. So I had Beau. Clayton gave him an itinerary every morning, and he took me and Hess wherever I was supposed to go.

A few hours later, I was in the booth singing a new song into the microphone. Clayton had co-written it with one of his regular songwriters, Dick Rhine. Another version of the same song they'd been reinventing over and over for each album, about my man doing me wrong and me hurting over it. This one was called "The Last Time."

You said you'd change
You said you'd stop
But now you gone and strayed
I know I've said it
But I really mean it
This is the last time

I injected my voice with a bluesy sadness like I had with all the others, and as the words drawled from my throat, I realized I felt nothing inside. It was a fake sadness, like a candy flavor. There was nothing aching in my chest like when I sang one of my own songs.

I'd never been in love with a man, much less so in love that I'd put up with that kind of shit. I didn't know that kind of desperation. With all the sadness I'd stored up over the years, it seemed strange that I'd have to fake it.

I got through the recording, but later I asked Clayton if I could show him a new song I'd written. Whenever I wasn't working, I was writing songs. Music still drifted down to me at all hours of the day. I knew they weren't all winners, but I could tell when one hit a chord. There was something addictive about the sound; I wanted to taste it in my mouth and swallow it down again and again.

I had this new one I'd worked on with Tima, one of my night songs, that was like steak against the teeth: thick, juicy, and silky in the middle.

I played the song for Clayton on my guitar and sang some rough lyrics about the hunger we all feel for a person who's left us, that aches in the bones. Hunger is the pain of something that's no longer there. The words worked perfectly with the rich melody, and it was a more complex sound than what they usually gave me. The heartbreak went deeper.

When I was done, I told him Tima and I wanted to do it as a duet. He'd seen Tima perform, and he knew how talented she was. We were lucky she was willing to record with me.

"You really got something there." He picked up a guitar and played the melody back. I started to play the rest of it with him, but he put his hand up. "No, not that. Just this." He played only a few bars of the melody, the real tender part at the center of it. "Dick just sent me some lyrics that might work. He closed his eyes and started to sing along with the melody:

God, send me a good woman
So I can be a good man
God, send me a good woman
So I can live your plan

We'd done this dance before. He'd take a piece of my song, the real tender kitten heart that would make it a hit, and then he'd change everything around it, including the words. They became these creatures I didn't recognize, with my little kitten hearts beating in their chests.

I could just see it. I'd open the album cover and find "written by Clayton Redd and Dick Rhine" underneath the song. The first time it happened, I asked Clayton about it, and he told me that was just the way they did it, because of contracts.

Not this time, buddy. I could feel the fire stoking in me. He was gonna harvest that little kitten heart over my cold, dead body.

"No."

He raised an eyebrow.

"That's not what the song is about. I like the one Tima and I wrote, and I want to sing it with her."

He paused. "Lou, I like what you wrote as well. I think it's clever and ambitious. But you can't honestly think we'd be able to do that song. That's not what our fans or the label expect from us."

I narrowed my eyes at him. I'd heard it all before.

"Besides. You know we can't have Tima on the record."

"Why the hell not?"

He gave me a look like he shouldn't have to say it, but I didn't give him the satisfaction. I jutted my chin, spurring him on.

"Don't play dumb with me. What would people think? And we couldn't tour with her—half the venues we play wouldn't let a Black woman onstage."

"I don't give a damn what they think. And if that's the truth, we shouldn't be playing those venues. You know I can't stand people who act like they're better than others. It makes no goddamn sense." He was such a coward. It made my blood boil.

"Come on, Lou, the label would have a fit."

"Isn't part of becoming successful that we can start doing what we want? You told me money is freedom. So if we got the money, why can't we have the freedom?"

He exhaled as if I was a petulant child. "Money gives you the freedom to not go hungry or have to work yourself to the bone for nothing. But to get that money, we have to do a job. We won't have money for long if we go around half-cocked, doing the job however we want."

I knew what he was doing. He was appealing to that fear in me, the one that worried at any moment it would all get snatched away, and I'd end up back in the holler, poor and forgotten, or worse.

It was true that he knew what people wanted to hear. He'd shown that in the way my star had risen steadily over the last few years. I had the fame I'd always dreamed of. People recognized me on the street now, and they all lined up to listen to me sing.

But the lyrics weren't my words. It felt like I was wearing Clayton's skin, singing with his throat, feeling with his heart when I was out there on that stage. None of it was my own.

I scowled at the floor, afraid of what I might say next. As angry as I could get, he was like a father to me, and I'd only defy him so much before I backed down. I still thought I'd be nothing without him.

He softened at my submission and put a gentle hand on my shoulder. "Next album. We'll figure something out. I promise."

He said this every time.

We finished recording that evening, and then Hess and I took off in her Mustang for a remote cabin in the mountains.

It was my first weekend off in months. I worked constantly, but when I got a few days off, Hess and I would always rent this one cabin and walk around naked and make love in the kitchen. It was far enough from the holler to be safe, but close enough that I could spend time among my trees, shielded from the rest of the world.

That morning, with Hess still asleep, I went out for a walk in the woods while the light was still coming up. I finally felt free, like my time was my own, and I could live in my true sound.

When the sun hit a certain point, the birds chanted all at once, raising their calls like a choir. My steps through the thick leaves added a rhythm, and the insect buzz added dimension. I became possessed by the music, breathless in the pure, early-morning chill.

But as the sun climbed higher and came into its power, I knew I'd have to go back. Hess would be worried something'd happened to me out here.

She didn't trust the woods like I did—to her, they only held mystery and monsters. She didn't know where the true dangers waited.

When I got back, she was in a yellow apron frying bacon in the kitchen. I leaned over and kissed her neck, careful not to disturb her concentration. She looked up at me, and I saw relief in her face. She wouldn't say anything, but she'd been holding her breath since she woke and saw me gone. Something in my chest tightened.

After breakfast, we sat in the living room and I practiced the new songs for the upcoming tour. It was the same mix of stuff I'd done for every album—two classic covers, one original about how much I loved my man, and another that warned my man that if he stepped too far out of line, there would be hell to pay, which in this case was "The Last Time."

There was something foolish about the defiance in the song, like a child rebelling against her father. What used to feel daring now felt cheap and silly. I thought back to my time in the woods and the breathless inspiration. The wild cat thrashed in my chest.

I stopped playing and thought about smashing the guitar against the hearth.

Hess gently took the instrument out of my hands and suggested we take a break and hike to a little meadow.

Nature was its usual balm as we walked through the trees. In the meadow, she laid out a blanket and lazily trailed her fingers over my blouse-covered nipples until I couldn't stand it any longer. We shed our clothes and made love in the stark sunshine. Our sensations were spotlit, made external by the light. Hess tasted like lemonade.

Afterward, we lay back in the soft plants and inhaled the mix of our citrus and the green of the wildflowers.

"What if we bought this place? Just for us?" Hess asked casually.

"With what money?"

Hess sat up on her forearms. "Lou, you have money in the bank. You could buy a little cabin in the woods."

Hess's family had cut her off a year prior. They'd been trying to set her up for years with eligible Nashville bachelors, and she finally told them she had no interest in getting married. She had this heap of money she was entitled to, but she'd only get it once she'd gotten hitched. Until then, it would just sit in a vault somewhere, collecting dust. She now relied on me and Clayton for whatever she needed.

"I don't even know how to get to it." The truth was Clayton controlled all of that; I had no idea how much I had in my own name. Anything I needed, he bought.

When I'd first started making royalties, he said he'd handle it for me, so I wouldn't go off and spend it like some of the people he knew who came from nothing. That way, when I needed it, it would be there.

"So you don't like the idea."

"No, that's not it."

"I'd like us to have a place where we can go and be a real couple. Not just Clayton's house, with him always around, making all the decisions. A place where we can do whatever we want."

"That does sound nice."

"And maybe we can adopt a few children. Clayton would legally be their father, but we'd raise them ourselves and he wouldn't have to do anything. I could live at the cabin with the children while you were touring, and when you were off, you could be with us."

I could tell this idea had been percolating inside of her for a while. She didn't come up with wild, impulsive plans like I did. She really wanted this.

She smiled and continued, "I have this vision, of you and me sitting on the porch in rocking chairs, listening to the kids playing in the house and watching the sun go down."

I gave her a half smile. "I didn't know you wanted a family so badly."

"I just think it would be fun to teach them what we know and have something to love and care for. After a while, you get bored of just taking care of your own needs."

Back then, I had no interest in taking care of children. I'd done it as a child myself. My aunt had so many kids that when a new one came along, the older ones were expected to feed them and wipe their butts and make sure they didn't cry too hard when my uncle was hungover. I knew how much time it took and how tired and hollowed you could feel while doing it. I only had ten years left, and I didn't want to spend it spooning slop into a baby's mouth.

I also wasn't keen on getting tied to one place and always feeling the pull back, as if my work was something taking me away from my real life. I wanted to live in the moment, to truly feel free. Or as free as you could be in this world.

I looked at Hess lying on her stomach, her naked butt gleaming in the sun. With each year, she'd become even more goddess-like, and at twenty-three, she could not have been more beautiful or self-possessed. I loved her more now than I ever had.

What I'm saying is: I'd have given her whatever she wanted if that was all that was at stake.

But she was imagining a future that couldn't be. She saw us growing old together on a porch in the woods with a pile of kids to love like we hadn't been loved. This would only ever be a fantasy. I'd be gone before it'd barely started, leaving her all alone after she'd spent her best years building a life around me. I couldn't do that to her.

"It's a lovely dream, but what about when I'm gone? Are you gonna raise them all by yourself?"

Her brow furrowed and she smiled slightly, as if I'd told a strange joke. "And where are you going, exactly?"

"Hess, I'll be dead in ten years."

The furrow deepened, and she sat up. "What are you talking about?"

My throat felt thick, and I sensed the first stirrings of anger. "You know perfectly well. I told you, I'm gonna die when I'm 33."

Her face smoothed, and I swear she almost laughed. "Oh, darling. Do you really believe in that curse?" She reached out and stroked my head like a child. "Baby, that's nothing but superstition."

My heart dropped. She didn't think it was real. Maybe she'd *never* thought it was real. All this time, I thought I was truly being seen, and she was just humoring me. The betrayal stung like a chestful of buckshot.

How could I explain it to her now? She hadn't grown up in the country, communing with the land and its spirits. She couldn't know the strangeness that lurked there.

"Just think about it, okay?" she said, lying back down in the grass.

I nodded, afraid of what I might say if I spoke. I listened to the screech of the insects in the grass, and I heard the words *ten years* whispering through their sound.

Ten years.

Ten years left.

I felt the wild cat clawing at my chest again, desperate to get out.

It was time to set it free.

And I had no idea how.

14

lulabelle

1972

TEN YEARS LEFT

That year, we were invited to the Country Music Association Awards at the Ryman. Clayton and I were nominated for a duet from our most recent album about two people who couldn't help loving one another.

The ceremony would be broadcast on television, so Phoebe and I spent weeks dreaming up my look. We'd long abandoned the child-bride style in favor of an evolving range of color and shape. The silhouettes were loosening from the stiff forms of the '50s and '60s. The fabric was beginning to flow. We settled on a long, diaphanous blue chiffon with a jeweled neck that covered my birthmark, and Clayton approved. It was the kind of sheer goddess toga that would have looked beautiful on Hess.

She wasn't invited to the actual ceremony, but she could come to the reception afterward at the Hermitage Hotel. On the surface, everything was the same, but I knew she could feel me pulling away. As much as I still loved her, I couldn't shake this feeling that something had broken between us. I had given her a glimpse of the demon child, the me beneath all of the lies and names, because she was the only person I really trusted. And she'd treated that inner part of me like ignorant trash that didn't know better.

Inside, the Ryman had been transformed into a sleek backdrop for the broadcast. I waited in my seat as they set up the enormous cameras and figured out the angles, the machinery buzzing something god awful. Clayton was busy roaming the rows and shaking hands with the other stars, while I was instructed to stay put and look pretty. I could feel that wild cat getting agitated. I needed to take a walk. Calm down. But then the orchestra started playing and everyone scurried back to their seats. It was time.

I waited patiently through the other categories and speeches like it was a wedding for someone I didn't know well. I'd been around a few years and I'd met folks along the way, but Clayton didn't introduce me much. I was usually sequestered somewhere with Hess when I wasn't performing. These people were still strangers to me.

When our category finally came around, I clenched my fists and focused hard on the voice of the announcer. He gave a dramatic pause, and then he was saying our names amid a roar of clapping, and Clayton was taking my hand and pulling me out of my seat. I'd told myself I didn't give a damn if I got some award.

But of course I did.

I floated above the boot-scuffed floor as Clayton led me to the stage by the hand. As we climbed the few steps, I prayed to God I wouldn't trip on my long, flowy gown. Then we were up behind the podium squinting into the bright lights. I couldn't see a damn thing.

Clayton stepped in front of me to speak into the microphone and kept hold of my hand, pulling me behind him like I was a child. His tall frame blocked the lights, so that all I could see then was the square of his dark-blue suit. I heard him thank the Country Music Association, and then he was tugging me off the stage. I tried to say a thank-you into the mic, but I was too far away for the sound to register.

It had been so quick, and now it was over. I sat in my seat as the other categories were called, buzzing and empty.

On the off chance we won, I'd rehearsed my speech in my head while I tried to sleep the night before. I debated whether I should thank Hess, or if people would get suspicious. Everyone knew we were best friends. A girl is allowed a best friend. So I decided I would thank all of the Mom Washburn girls together, with Hess in the honorary last spot, and that would be safe. Regardless of what happened between us, I owed my life to her. I also wanted to thank God and the golden place he'd created for music that sent me messages throughout the day. I knew people might think I was strange, but I didn't care. I was an artist.

None of it mattered now. I'd been blotted out by Clayton. I might as well have stayed in my seat; at least I'd have hung on to a little dignity. I bitterly mused whether he would have been nominated if it weren't for me. Everyone knew he was washed up. Our audience came to see me sing at our shows, to hear my voice and see what I was wearing. Phoebe had made me a fashion icon of sorts, though I only knew this from reading magazines. I was kept away from the rest of the world and the fans.

The mad cat thrashed around inside me, clawing to get out. I couldn't sit there burning up with resentment for the rest of my life.

Ten years.

I only had ten fucking years left.

There was no way I was using those to keep some man's career afloat, as much as I loved him in a complicated way. He'd taken such tender care of me, like the rich, sweet father I'd never had. And I truly believed he loved me as much as he could. But I also knew he'd built a comfy little prison for me with his care. He controlled every aspect of my life so I could never leave or move past him. He had me right where he wanted me.

At the after-party, I fumed. Clayton had no idea, because he was off schmoozing with our award in hand, receiving congratulations and clinking glasses. Hess and I were at a table in the far corner, and I barely spoke to her, focused instead on burning holes into the back of Clayton's hairpiece.

Hess put a hand on my arm. "Why don't we just leave? I can tell you're not having a good time, and we should get on the road anyway."

Hess and I were supposed to go to the cabin for a few days before the tour started. We'd planned to leave that night so we could wake up in the mountains the next morning.

But I didn't want to slink off, hiding myself away from the world. Wasting my precious time before I was forced to go back into the studio, to sing his words and spout his principles. Eat his food, wear his clothes, ride in his car, because neither he nor Hess would teach me how to drive.

I was in the mood for destruction.

"I don't want to leave tonight. I want to celebrate." I left Hess at the table and asked for a glass of vodka at the bar. The bartender hitched his eyebrows at the request, but I didn't take the bait. I shot it down like water, the sting of it matching my fury. I asked for another, and he poured.

"A lady after my own heart." The voice was creamy behind me, smelling of Tom Collins and gardenia. I turned around, and there was Alice Buckley in the flesh. She'd just lost best album of the year. She was another divorced country star like Clayton, and it gave her a haunted patina that I liked.

She signaled the bartender for two more, and he lined them up. Alice and I knocked glasses and downed them. I let out a guttural holler, and that was how I knew I was drunk. The hillbilly was coming out.

Alice slapped me on the back and laughed. "You are *not* what I expected. I thought you were this little lamb in a wedding dress following Clayton around." She dabbed her lipstick with a napkin and asked the bartender for another. "But you ain't that at all." She winked at me and slung it back.

I saw Hess and Clayton watching me from different sides of the room, and I started to sweat under the jeweled collar at my neck, suddenly aware that it was choking me. I tried to loosen it with my fingers, but it wouldn't give. "You think there's anything to get into around here? You know, something more than just jawing? I'm so antsy I might shed my skin."

Alice thought about it for a moment, and then she got this devilish look on her face. “I know just the thing.” She leaned over the bar and grabbed a bottle of champagne in each fist. The bartender didn’t try to stop her.

We pretended to hide the bottles behind our backs as we snaked around the edge of the party toward the doors, and then hightailed it down the hallway, giggling like banshees. We got in the elevator, and she asked the bewildered conductor to take us to the top floor.

As we ascended, the light dimmed, and the world tilted.

Next thing I knew I was on my knees on the hallway carpet as if I’d just tripped. Alice was hunched over laughing in front of me.

Then I was climbing a metal ladder up the side of the building with one hand, the bottle in the other. My heel slipped on a rung, and I kicked both shoes off into the void below like the world was my bedroom.

Then I was on my back on a hard, gritty surface looking up at the stars, reminding me of that Fourth of July years ago when Hess and I first fell in love.

I moved against a body. Thick, chemical-coated hair was in my mouth and eyes. There was only that feeling between my legs and the hair smothering all other perception.

And then there was a whole lot of nothing.

I came to in my soft, starchy bed. Consciousness was a heavy burden, and I longed to go back under and sleep forever. Or at least until I felt like a human being again. But when I turned over, I saw Hess hunched on the side of the bed, faced away from me. Her shoulders were shaking. I reached out for her, and she shrank away from my touch.

I closed my eyes with my arm still outstretched on the comforter, attempting to conjure some stronger self to rise to the moment. But I was destroyed.

I reopened them and watched Hess pace in front of the bed. I saw in the light slanting through the curtains that her face was bare and rubbed raw. Hess was the kind of woman who could swim all day in a creek, and she'd look better than most women could ever hope for. I'd woken up next to her hundreds of times, and she always looked fresh as a baby's bottom. I'd never seen her so unraveled. It scared me.

"Are you just going to lie there?" she asked icily. Her anger had only ever been the sweet, nourishing kind meant to help me find the right answer. I didn't recognize this voice.

"I'm not feeling very good." I half expected her to start tending to me, maybe get me some aspirin and a glass of cold water. But she just stood there, staring daggers into the wall. She'd yet to actually look at me.

"How could you? Just explain it to me. Because I don't understand how you could actually, physically do what you did. It is beyond my intelligence."

At the mention of the unnamed act, last night came back in chunks. The realization seeped in like bile. The regret was so immense I couldn't absorb it. It only sat there pooling, this sense that I had done something so awful that it couldn't be undone.

"Dear God. Hess, I'm so sorry." I thought I might spew if I said anything else. The sickness was overpowering. But I kept going. "It wasn't me. I mean . . . it was my body, but it wasn't me making it happen. It was like somebody else in my body calling the shots. Does that make sense?"

"I'm familiar with the concept of being drunk." She was quiet. "But Lou, you weren't drunk when you left me alone and went to the bar. I could tell you were on some kind of mission from hell. Which I might've understood if you'd talked to me. I could have come with you. We could have gotten drunk together."

"I needed to be alone for just one moment, so I could breathe. I've been feeling trapped lately. Like if I don't bust out, I'm gonna end up in pieces painting the walls."

She finally looked at me, and I flinched at the pain in her eyes. She sat down at the edge of the bed and smoothed the comforter. "You feel trapped with *me*?"

"It ain't just you. It's Clayton, too. Making all the decisions and running my life."

"But it is partly me, then." She brought her thumbnail to her mouth. "Is this about the kids? Lou, we don't have to have kids. It was just a daydream."

"No. It ain't about the kids. You know if you really wanted them, I'd do it for you." I'd already slit the skin open, so I just let the blood flow. "But you dream of a future for us, of us growing old together. And it just can't happen."

"Oh, Lou. I know we can't be together in front of people, but we can at our own house. You have Clayton to hide behind. We have the freedom to *be* whatever we want. You aren't trapped."

"I'm not talking about what other people think. I'm talking about *me.* I only got ten years left. What are you gonna do after I'm gone? It's not right for you to build a life around me." My mouth filled with salt. "I can't do that to you. And I . . . I can't be with someone who doesn't understand that." My vision went cloudy, and the tree on my chest felt like it might split in two.

She crawled across the bed and took both of my hands in hers. She focused hard on my eyes, making sure I was tuned in. "Listen to me. You are not cursed, Lulabelle Powers. That is just a silly story someone told you when you were a child. You are going to have a long, beautiful life. And we can have it together. All you have to do is say yes. And promise to never step out on me again. We can get through this. I know we can."

I pulled my hands back. "I've made up my mind. This can't go on any longer with us." I turned over so I wouldn't have to look at her face. "You should go."

"You can't do this. You don't want to do this."

I continued to stare at the wall in silence, refusing to answer any of her pleas.

I heard her slump to the floor, and then I listened to her weep for a while. I wanted to leap out of bed and wrap my arms around her and tell her I didn't mean it.

We had grown up together, from girlhood to whatever we were now, so that I wasn't quite sure where I ended and she began. Separating from her was crude and bloody. I imagined I was losing parts of myself in the severing. My body crooned with pain.

I knew I'd never love anyone like I loved her.

But there was a bitter relief in it, too. A part of me knew it was the right thing to do. She and I could both be free now.

After a while, I heard the door shut, and I could feel that she was gone.

I was truly alone now.

I could feel myself fading, losing color.

Then I disappeared, floating back into unconsciousness, grateful for its void.

I slept for eons. Civilizations collapsed and were reborn. The planet froze and thawed. The tree on my chest fell to the side and slowly returned to the land grain by grain, before reawakening once again.

On top of my hangover, I'd caught some nasty cold on that roof, and I stayed in bed for a week. Looking back, it might have just been heartbreak making me sick.

I kept waiting for Clayton to visit, to face his judgment, but he stayed away, looming on the horizon like a storm about to break. Then one morning when I woke, I saw him sitting in the corner watching me. His hair was freshly oiled, and he had on a clean, pressed suit.

I hadn't showered in centuries, and though I couldn't smell my own stink, I'm sure it was like a dead possum left under a house. My hair, which I kept short to fit under my wigs, was matted against my head like a dog's, and I knew my makeup was smeared down my face like an old whore.

It felt good to be so undone in his presence. Stripped down to my studs, I could really confront him.

I must have been smiling to myself because he said, "I'm curious to know what you find so amusing. From where I'm sitting, you don't have much to smile about."

"I was just thinking about how good it's gonna feel when this conversation is over."

He narrowed his eyes. "Do you have any idea what you've done? Employees from the hotel found you and Alice up there half naked and unconscious. They almost called the police." He took a deep breath. "Thankfully, I'm close with the manager, and he called me first. The staff were paid for their silence."

When I didn't respond, he looked me dead in the eye. "Hess moved out."

At the mention of her name, my chest jerked. I couldn't go there right now, not in front of him.

"I see she was unsparing. Good."

"My relationship with Hess is none of your business."

"You are my wife. Everything you do is my business."

I was ready to go for the throat. "I think I'd like to change that. The wife part. Clayton, I don't want to be married to you anymore."

A rare surprise crossed his face. He took a moment, carefully choosing his words. "Lou, I know I'm being severe, but it's only because I want you to understand the danger you put yourself in. If this got out, it wouldn't just end your career. It would ruin you. It could put you in jail." His face softened. "I don't want that to happen to you."

My anger receded. "This is about more than that night. I want to make my own music. Run my own life. I'm not a kid anymore, and I'm not your doll to dress up. I want to be my own person."

He took a deep breath. "I hear you, all right? You can have more input on the albums from now on. You can pick which songs you record for your solo tracks. I won't get in the way."

"When you say my songs don't fit on our albums, you're right. Because we don't fit together anymore. I want to explore new things. To experiment with a new sound. And that ain't you."

I could see him starting to panic. He was in negotiations for *The Clayton Redd Show* on TV, featuring me as the main entertainer. If anything proved how fucked things were, it was that. His name on the show, my ass playing my heart out. I knew it'd probably fall through if I didn't go along with it. But that was his problem, not mine.

He walked over and kneeled at the side of the bed. He took my hand and held it in his. "What's going to happen to you if I'm not around? People don't mess with Clayton Redd's wife. You know it's true."

I patted the top of his hand like he was a small child and I was his aging grandma, laid up sick in the bed. "You forget where I come from 'cause I'm so fancy now." Clayton smiled at this, taking in my sorry state. "I'm the meanest son of a bitch in this pretty city. They should be scared of *me*."

I wish I could say this story ends with a heartfelt goodbye. But this is a business, and there was money on the line.

I thought we could get a quick, easy divorce and not have to spend a lot on lawyers and whatnot. We were both from a place where people settled their fights amongst themselves without strangers getting in the middle.

When the divorce papers arrived at Martha's where I was staying, I forced myself to read every page, even though it was painful. I'm no illiterate, but that kind of language is made to confuse. To trick people into agreeing to whatever the other person wants.

And I was sure as hell confused. It said that Clayton would receive 50 percent of all my music earnings.

For the rest of my life.

Apparently I'd signed some agreement that guaranteed him part ownership of any music I ever made, even if he didn't work on it.

What right did he have to *my money*? To *my music*?

That was when I called Alice. We hadn't spoken since that night, and

I made it clear it wasn't a social call. I wanted to know what greasy son of a bitch helped her get a good divorce.

And thank God, she delivered.

Part of me thinks this was Clayton's way of trying to hold on to me. To keep me from leaving. There was a little tenderness to it.

But he also thought he owned me. That he *made* me, and that entitled him to some return on his investment. He wouldn't accept that I kept him afloat those years. His career would have died a slow, wheezing death, and instead, my pretty little ass came around and brought it back to life.

I'll spare you all the dry legal proceedings. What's important is that we ended up in a very different place from where we started. He still walked away with more than he'd earned. All the publishing rights, and most of the royalties. He'd set it up from the beginning so I got a tiny fraction of each record sale and nothing else.

But I had enough to strike out on my own and not have to depend on anyone. It's what I'd wanted all along, and I'd made it happen with just my voice.

I was my own person now, and all I had to do was figure out who that really was.

15

rhea

1995

In early August that summer, Micah and I went to Martha's for the first time. She lived across the river on the east side of Nashville, where long-haired tattooed locals walked amongst historic homes and the neon pulsed at a lower volume.

Inside Martha's modest bungalow, musicians of different ages sprawled across couches and hunched on the floor, smoking and drinking from jelly jars. Candles burned on every surface, illuminating shelves of records lining the walls as Judee Sill's "Down Where the Valleys Are Low" spun on the turntable.

Micah raised his eyebrows at me, clearly impressed, and I raised mine in response. I felt like we'd just entered the real Nashville, and everything up until this point had only been a performance.

Martha appeared and handed us each a jar of golden liquid. "Sparkling pear juice, if you dig. I keep a dry house." We each took a drink, and it tasted like something a fairy might sip. Martha elbowed me gently in the ribs. "I met your father at a party like this."

This was why I had called her. Since the Fourth, I'd ruminated on what Clayton had said about my father. I'd been so focused on Belle that I'd almost forgotten about him.

When I'd asked Hess, she'd bristled with disdain. She told me she never knew my dad, and when I asked why, she said something vague about a falling out with Belle. It'd taken a while, but lately I'd noticed that she often answered my questions about Belle with half answers.

I had the keen sense she was hiding things from me.

At the same time, I could feel her watching me. Tracking my movements. Sometimes she made passive-aggressive comments when I came home late.

When I'd introduced her to Micah, she'd been polite to the point of coldness, and the conversation had devolved into her grilling him on why he wasn't going to college. The past year had been tough for him with his brother's death, and his grades had slipped. He also didn't feel ready for college—he had no idea what he wanted to study, and shouldn't it be more deliberate than that? Especially when it was so expensive? I thought Hess would be impressed by his thoughtfulness, or at least sensitive to the fact that he clearly didn't come from money. But this only deepened her suspicion of him.

She and I had been so close at the beginning of the summer. But now that connection had stretched and strained, and I often couldn't wait to be out of the house, no longer under her watchful gaze.

As the weeks passed, I spent most of my time with Micah in a haze of early love. Even when we were just talking or eating or walking through the streets, being together felt historic, cosmic, *cataclysmic.*

Sometimes, though, when I hadn't seen him in a day or two and he hadn't called, I would imagine him dropping me, and the fear could be so intense I thought I was losing my mind. I still couldn't believe someone as special as him could love *me*—maybe want me, but not love me.

Martha continued, "Your father used to try out new songs at these house parties. Wasn't much of a singer, but nobody cared because his words were so beautiful."

I imagined the shaggy-haired Jesus-looking man I'd come to know from the scant pictures I'd found, sitting on the rug with a beat-up guitar and rasping out his latest poetry from a scribbled page.

"How did he meet my mom?"

"They also met at a party—I actually introduced them." She had an edge to her voice, like maybe she was a little bit ashamed of this fact.

I wanted her to tell me more, but then someone yelled her name from the kitchen, and she put up a finger. "Hold tight. I'll be back in a shake."

Micah and I drifted over to her records and thumbed carefully through them. There was everything you could imagine—Nina Simone, Joni Mitchell, Kate Bush, TLC.

Martha returned, and Micah said, "This is a sick collection—and so much that's not country."

"I love music," she answered simply. "Country is my first love, but there's too much out there to ignore. And they all borrow from each other. Your mama was the same way."

"Really?" I asked.

Martha nodded. "*Oh, yeah.* You'll never guess who she was into around the time she met your father."

"Who?"

"Black Sabbath."

"Holy shit."

"Yep."

Micah pulled an album from the shelf and showed it to us. "What's *this*?"

On the cover, a woman in a long black dress stood at a distance at the edge of a forest. She was far enough away that you couldn't make out her face, but you could feel her intense gaze searing into yours. Along the bottom in red cursive was written "The Cursed Woman" and then next to it, "Belle Powers."

I took it from him and studied it closely, as if it were an occult object. I'd listened to every album my mother had ever put out—all of them lined up on a special shelf in Hess's music room—and I'd never come across this one.

Martha's brow furrowed. "You've never seen this before?"

"No, definitely not."

"It's not in Hess's collection?"

"No."

Her mouth flattened. "Well, that is your mother's first solo album. And my favorite of hers, actually. I played on almost every track." She took the album from Micah and slid out the disc, then handed the sleeve back to me. "We're listening to this next."

Micah and I found a spot on the floor amid the sprawled musicians, and I studied the woman on the cover, searching for some stroke of Belle in her face. As I stared, the dots of color blurred and grayed, and I could feel myself being pulled into the image through the gaze of the woman, my body dissolving, my eyes the only thing left of me.

I felt a hand on mine, and I suddenly returned to the room, my scalp gone cold. Micah whispered that it was starting, and I turned the sleeve over for the track list, hiding the woman from view.

The first track, "Folk Song," began with simple, ominous guitar, and then she sang:

> **There was a woman in town who sang so sweet**
> **Her beauty was beyond compare**
> **But one day a bright specter she did meet**
> **There aft she was no longer fair**

I felt a cold finger drag down my spine, freezing my body in place.

> **She ranted and raved and ran over town**
> **Chased by somethin' not seen**
> **She ran so far that she came to a cliff**
> **And it chased her over to free'n**

The voice was my mother's at her most stripped down and magnetic, beckoning us around a fire so she could tell us a story.

When the last note died on the player, I felt my body relax, no longer frozen. I waited for the second track, my spine still tingling.

A fierce fiddle kicked up, and I checked the track list. "Duet with the Devil."

It told the story of a woman long ago who traded her soul for a beautiful singing voice, thereby cursing every woman in her bloodline to an early death.

And then the next track played, "Black Gum Tree," describing a pregnant woman hit by a car and thrown in a tree, saving her baby's life with her soft, powerful body. Not just an accident, but fate. One that couldn't be escaped.

The fourth, "Mountain Girl," began slower, with a sense of atmosphere between the fiddle and guitar plucks, like fog was rolling in. She sang about a little mountain girl, cursed from birth, who everyone called a demon child. But she didn't care because she had something they didn't have—when she walked among the trees, she heard music floating down from God above. It was the thing that transcended all of the pain, the thing that made her want to live.

Next played "Let Me Out," the song I'd heard that first night at Hess's, and I seized up immediately, feeling the same panic start to take over. I tried to shift focus to the conversation next to me, where a girl whispered to her friend, "Have you ever heard the rumors about her?"

"What do you mean?"

"Apparently she—"

Someone shooshed her, and the girl went silent. I turned to ask what she was going to say, but then the track ended, and I was distracted by the ascending movement of the music.

"The Cursed Woman."

Not what you would expect from a song with that name.

Belle sang in a round, hopeful voice about the girl finding release in finally accepting her fate. Then the song built to an almost ecstatic climax of joy, like she was having a religious awakening. She was rapturous, bathed in her own light, haunted but not chained.

She was the cursed woman. And she would live as such, chasing freedom and repelling fear.

The next track was called "Old Crone," where the cursed woman imagined the old age she would never experience—to some, it might have sounded like a blessing, but to her it was a loss. She saw herself growing old in New Orleans, her hair going coarse and gray like the Spanish moss hanging from the trees. No longer yoked to the demands of youth, free to walk unobserved through the world and delight herself however she saw fit.

Then I waited for the instrumental opening for the last track, "Lullaby for a Demon Child," but I heard only a delicate voice wafting through the air. It was close and quiet, as if she was speaking right in my ear:

Baby, don't be 'fraid
When I leave too soon
Baby, don't be 'fraid
I'll be your moon

Another voice repeated the verse, this one so rich and deep it made my belly ache, and then another voice sang the words, this one strong and clear like rushing water.

Then the trio was singing all together, and the harmony of their voices swaddled me and held me against its chest.

Baby, don't be 'fraid
When the white dog moan
Baby, don't be 'fraid
You'll nev'r be alone

I dug my nails into my fists to keep the tears from flowing. I knew without knowing, *I* was the child she was singing to.

Baby, don't be 'fraid
When you wake at night
Baby, don't be 'fraid
I'll be your light
Baby, don't be 'fraid
When it comes for you
Baby, don't be 'fraid
'Cause I'm there with you

The album ended, but the disc continued to spin on the turntable, emitting a fuzzy sound, and I strained to hear what it might be saying.

I felt a hand against my cheek, and I startled before seeing it was Micah. I told him I needed a minute, and I walked out the back to a small yard where a few smoked and murmured in the shadows. I took in the warm night as the adrenaline left my body, making me shake.

"Are you okay?" Martha asked from behind me, lighting a cigarette.

I took a deep breath and tried to compose myself. "Yeah, I'm fine. Just a little overwhelmed." I took another breath. "That album is . . ." I didn't even know how to describe it. "Why is it so different from her other stuff?"

Martha looked up at the sky. "She wrote it after she left Clayton and when she first met your father. It was the first album where she got to create her own sound. She said it was inspired by where she grew up in the mountains, and Eve and original sin—this idea of the cursed woman as created by the Bible." She blew out a stream of smoke. "But I think there was more to it than that."

"What do you mean?" I asked.

"She had demons, and I saw how they haunted her. I do think she felt like a cursed woman sometimes."

"Like something bad had happened to her?"

"I don't know for certain. She never talked about her past. But it was a sense I got—I've spent a lot of time around people like that."

"Did my dad hurt her? Was he a bad person?" This was the question that had been haunting me.

She exhaled. "I don't deal much in good and bad. He was like your mother—impulsive, creative, always in motion. I think that's why they got along so well. But he had his own demons."

"Like what?"

She paused. "He was so restless, and he wanted so many experiences that sometimes he hurt himself and others without meaning to—that was part of him being an addict." She paused. "There was also the trouble with his family—when he dropped out of college, his parents disowned him. And no matter how much you dislike your parents, that hurts in ways you might not be aware of."

I barely remembered my grandparents, but I knew the rigidity of my aunt and her "morals," deployed like weapons whenever it suited her. She'd always lacked a capacity for understanding other people, was proud of it even, and I never understood why someone would choose to live such a limited existence.

"Did my parents love each other?" I asked.

She looked over at me. "I think so."

"I wish I could have seen them together."

She smiled sadly. "Me too."

Back inside, I found Micah on the couch and curled up against his side. I told him everything Martha had said, and he stroked my arm as I tried to process this new information. Perhaps I had shared something with them after all, or maybe I was finally starting to see them as real people.

I suddenly felt Micah's body stiffen against my shoulder. "What's wrong?" I asked.

"I have to tell you something," he said, his voice serious.

My heart skipped. "What?"

"I'm leaving Nashville in a few days. I'm hiking the Appalachian Trail this year, and I don't want to miss the warm months up north."

My face heated, and I could feel my heart beating faster, but I told myself to stay calm. *Keep your voice level. Don't let him know how upset you are.* "I didn't know."

"I was actually headed to the trailhead in Maine when I stopped here. I didn't mean to stay this long, but I'm glad I did." He grabbed my hand and kissed my knuckles, but I could barely feel it.

"Right."

This was what I'd been worrying about all summer, that one day he was going to realize I was nothing special, that I was damaged, even, and he would leave me, and I would never see him again. There was a pathetic relief in it, like it was finally happening, and I could just be done with it now. I could stop pretending I was a person he could love.

He sat up and looked into my eyes. "Why don't you come with me?"

I pulled my hand from his. "What? No. I can't just leave."

"The trail goes through Tennessee—you could see the place your mom grew up and wrote about in her music." He tried to pull me back toward him, but I shrugged out of his grasp.

His mouth flattened, and he turned away from me. "The truth is, I don't want to live in the past anymore. I don't want to keep reliving the bad feelings. It's not good for me, and I don't think it's good for you, either."

He didn't understand. "I'm not ready."

He scowled. "Well, I don't have a choice. I'm out of money. I'll have just enough for the trail if I sell my brother's car in Maine. I'm not like you—someone didn't just show up at my house one day and give me millions of dollars."

I glared at the ground, my cheeks burning in shame.

He exhaled, and his voice softened. "I can't stay here any longer. I have to keep moving. But I want to be with you."

"And I'm supposed to just follow you?"

He sighed in frustration and stood up from the couch. "I'm not going to beg."

"Then don't." I could feel the meanness in it, like they weren't my words. He stared at me, and I'd never seen him so hurt, the mirth in his eyes extinguished.

As he moved toward the door, I called out to him, but he kept going, and then he was gone.

Around two a.m. that night, Hess and Martha found me in Hess's kitchen eating leftover fried chicken in the dark.

I'd left Martha's without telling her and walked all the way back through the city to Hess's house, imagining the woods from the album—this magical place where my mother had once heard music in the trees and where she'd discovered the thing that made her want to keep living.

"Where have you been?" Hess demanded sharply.

I glared at her, allowing all of the resentment of the last few weeks to rise to the surface. Even Lorraine and Carl had never tried to control me like this; for all of their indifference, at least in that house I'd had a bit of freedom.

"We were just worried," Martha said gently. "Tell us what happened."

So I told them about my fight with Micah. "The thing is," I explained, "I actually think he's right. I want to see the mountains where my mom grew up and be in those woods. Maybe I'll understand her better than I have being here, or maybe I'll find something of my own. I just felt like he was pressuring me."

"It's a nice idea," Hess said softly, as if I wasn't being serious.

"I mean it. I think it's what I need."

"But where is this coming from?" she asked.

"I've been thinking about 'Mountain Girl,' and—"

Hess turned to Martha. "You let her listen to that? You know how I feel—" She stopped, clearly unwilling to finish the sentence in front of me.

"Hess, you don't get to decide—" Martha shot back.

"Yes, I do—"

"Excuse me?" I interjected. "Can you please not talk about me as if I'm not here?"

Hess's face softened again. "I'm sorry, but—"

"What are you not telling me? I have a right to know."

"She's right—" started Martha, but Hess cut her off with a glare.

"I came here to learn more about my mom. The truth. Because I'm her *daughter*. But all you do is hide things and try to control me."

Hess frowned, attempting to keep her composure. "I am not trying to control you, honey. There are some things that you just wouldn't understand."

I was so tired of this, and in that moment, I knew it was time for me to leave. I might not have known my mother, but I was certain she wouldn't have squatted in the shell of someone else's life like I had the past few months. She would have gone out and found her own.

"I'm leaving, and I'm going with Micah," I declared, daring them to stop me.

"You barely know him," Hess answered.

"I barely know *you*, Hess."

She flinched. "What about college?"

"What *about* college?" I asked. So much had changed over the last few months that college and California felt like distant notions now. "My dad dropped out because he wanted to see the world and make art. College isn't the answer to everything."

Hess narrowed her eyes. "I wouldn't follow anything your father did—"

"That's not fair," Martha cut in, and I said, "You didn't even know him."

Hess took a deep breath and closed her eyes. "Never mind, that's not the point. What I'm trying to say is your mother wanted you to be educated. Part of why she left you all that money was to make sure you'd have the opportunities she never had."

Fury ignited in the back of my throat. "We don't know what she would have wanted because she's not here. She left me that money so I could exercise my *freedom*, and that's what I'm doing."

"I'm just trying to protect you," Hess added, more softly this time. "And to help guide you toward the right decisions."

"You're not my mother," I said with an edge in my voice. "That's not your job."

Hess grimaced, and I saw her eyes mist over. I instantly regretted my words. "Look, I'm sorry. I'm grateful for everything you've done for me. I just . . ."

Hess took a deep breath, and I watched her eyes dry and her face harden into that of a stranger. She turned the corners of her mouth up in a humorless smile. "No, I apologize. I didn't mean to cross a line. You are an adult, and you can make your own decisions."

My arms prickled, and I shivered in the AC.

I considered taking it all back, giving up on the hike with Micah, and continuing on as we had. But where would that take me? I couldn't pretend to be this cheap reproduction of my mother any longer.

I needed to find my own way.

The sun was just coming up when I arrived at Micah's hostel in an old, stately house near downtown. The heavy-lidded desk clerk told me it was too early for visitors, but then I heard someone coming down the stairs, and there he was, his eyes bloodshot and his beautiful hair askew.

"I thought I heard your voice," he said, standing a few feet away. "I haven't slept all night."

"Me neither."

I walked into his arms, and we held each other for a long moment, allowing our cells to regenerate.

"I'm sorry I didn't tell you earlier," he said into my shoulder. "And I shouldn't have tried to force you—"

"I want to go with you," I said, pulling back to look at him. "I just—I wanted it to be my decision."

He tucked a piece of hair behind my ear. "Are you sure?"

I nodded. "I think you're right, that this could be good for me," I said, smiling. "I want to stop living in the past and move on—with you."

He smiled back, his eyes sparkling with mirth once again.

We walked to a twenty-four-hour diner down the block, and over eggs and pie, he laid out the plan for the next six months—our great adventure into the wilderness, the sacred, untouched place where, just maybe, we could find a way forward after everything, and everyone, we'd lost.

Afterward, we curled up in his twin hostel bed in the morning light, and he fell asleep in the crook of my arm.

I stared up at the cobwebbed ceiling of the bunk room, and I tried to hold on to the bliss I'd felt for the last few hours.

But I could already feel it receding, replaced by the cold, tight fear that I was tempting the universe. Surely no one was allowed to feel this good and get away with it.

As hard as I tried to shake it off, I knew, somewhere deep inside me, that something terrible was lurking on the horizon.

And there was no escaping it.

16

lulabelle

1973

NINE YEARS LEFT

After the divorce, I took my sack of money and bought a little white house with a red door. It gleamed with being mine.

It looked like a tidy hobo lived inside. There was one brocade couch with a cigarette burn that Martha and I found trolling the rich neighborhoods in her truck. A few plates and glasses and forks and a frying pan. A mattress on the floor in the bedroom.

I had to make my money stretch now. The label had dropped me during the legal battle with Clayton. So had all the managers and lawyers and men in suits who surrounded Clayton like a wool cocoon. There were no offers coming in. My new phone was silent. Life had been a constant stream of activity for years, and it had fed me.

Now, life stood still.

For the first time, I slept. I slept most of the day. And in the evening, Phoebe or Martha would wake me and make me eat a bit. Draw me a bath. Tima was out on tour, making her way through the summer festival circuit. She called me late at night when she knew I'd be up and told me road stories to make me laugh.

The girls knew not to talk about Hess. All I'd heard was she'd moved back in with her parents, but that was it. At some point the girls had realized she and I were more than friends, but we never discussed it—one day they just knew, and it wasn't a problem.

I wanted to ask if they'd seen her, and how she was doing. I wanted to know what she'd had for breakfast that morning. If she was wearing her hair the same way. If a touch behind the ear still made her shiver.

But I couldn't keep opening the wound. So we pretended like she'd never existed.

I tried to work on music. I had this whole wooden trunk of songs. But when I played them, the words went bitter in my mouth. They all reminded me of her.

There were no new songs in my head, either. It was like Hess had taken my music with her, just as she'd restored it when we first met. I was back to that sad, sorry girl locked in the shed, no longer able to receive the music floating down from the heavens. It was worse than death. The tree on my chest withered to a husk.

One night Phoebe brought over a box of paints and brushes to *stimulate my creativity*. We laid down old sheets on the floor and put on Tammy Wynette. But that just made me cry. So Phoebe switched it out for Donny Osmond, but that just made me annoyed.

Undeterred, she pulled out a record she'd borrowed from Martha. The band was called Black Sabbath, and a witch in a long black dress stood watching me from the cover.

Something seized up in me like I'd been caught. Like the devil had finally found me and now fixed me with his one yellow eye. I told her I couldn't listen to the devil's music, and she laughed and put it on anyway.

Rain poured down around us, and a church bell tolled in the distance. The guitar lurched through the scene like a funeral procession, slow and ominous. A man wailed as an evil figure approached, bringing his own destruction.

The song wasn't afraid to acknowledge we were all doomed. In fact, it reveled in it.

I felt my own damned fate looming in the corner of the room, and for the first time in my life, I wondered what it would be like to give myself over to it. To stop pretending, or trying to hide from it. To open up my arms and let the devil in.

Phoebe offered me a canvas, but I waved it away. Instead, I dipped my hands in a pot of syrupy red paint. The guitar riffs picked up speed, and I smeared it on the living room wall in thick slashes. Phoebe squealed and dipped her own hands, and we stroked along with the music.

We were women possessed. It felt good.

~

When I woke the next evening with red under my nails, I was still empty of new music. My night of devil worship hadn't worked.

Martha came by with a bag of Krystal burgers. After I'd eaten, she led me into the bathroom and told me to get cleaned up. We were going out.

We drove to the outskirts of town. In the middle of a dark, quiet neighborhood, one house was lit up and crawling with people. The men had long hair and beards that hung scraggled over their leather vests, and the women wore no makeup and walked barefoot in the grass.

As Martha and I made our way through the throng into the house, I touched my wig self-consciously. I hadn't worn it since I went into hibernation. Sometimes it felt like armor, and other times, a weapon. It *always* gave me confidence. But now I could feel its weight on my neck, the scratch of it against my scalp, the slick cheapness of its strands.

We snaked our way through the house and then out the back to the yard. There was a small fire surrounded by old lawn chairs and a few long-haired boys strumming lazily on guitars.

We sat in empty chairs, and one of the men looked me over.

"Hey, ain't you that girl who sings with Clayton Redd?"

"Not anymore. My name is Belle. Belle Powers." I extended my hand for him to shake, but he just went back to strumming.

Another boy added, "My mama's got all his albums. She likes to play them at Christmas. Makes me wanna blow my brains out." He made his hand into a pistol and shot himself in the head. They all guffawed.

I still had a lot of anger for Clayton. But some of his music had been *my music*. Or at least, I'd been singing it. And the way these boys were dismissing him, as if they knew what it took to get where he'd gotten. It just pissed me off.

"So what are *your* names?" I asked.

They mumbled their names around the circle, and I crossed my arms.

"Huh. Never heard of you."

I stalked off from the fire to the other side of the yard where a pair of old metal swings sat rusting. I sat down and started pumping my legs. It was like being back in school. Me, all alone on the swings, smarting from someone calling me a demon child. I went higher and higher, getting closer to the stars with each climb.

A man walked over and started swinging next to me. It was dark in this corner of the yard, and I could only see the gleam of his blue eyes and the pearl of his smile as we soared higher together. At the highest point, we both paused and let ourselves fall back to the earth.

I slowed, and then stopped, and he did the same. We were both a little out of breath, and a giggle escaped from my lips. It was the first time I'd laughed since Hess left, and the release felt foreign in my chest. I looked down, dragging my shoes through the dust.

"I hope I'm not intruding."

His voice was crisp and clear, with an unfamiliar accent that was like cold milk and peanuts in my ears. Different from the people I'd grown up with and met in Nashville. Even Hess, for all of her schooling and proper speaking, still had a bit of sweetgrass in her voice.

"Not at all." I tried to see what he looked like, but he was still just a glint of eye and teeth in the night.

He reached over and offered his hand. "Tate Larsen."

I took it, and my hand slid against the thin calluses on his palm. Not like the thick pads of men who've worked for years; these were new—rough over smooth.

"Belle. Belle Powers."

"I know who you are."

"Yeah, what, 'Clayton Redd's girl singer'?"

He smirked. "I saw you sing at Darlene's when I first got to Nashville in '67. And when I saw you were playing the Opry the next year, I spent my rent money on a ticket."

I laughed. "I bet you regretted that."

He smiled. "I'd do it again in a heartbeat. You have a magical voice, Ms. Powers."

The way his words reverberated through me made me a little angry. I didn't need another man telling me I had a great voice. I knew I did. I didn't need his approval. None of it.

"I should probably get going. It's late." I stood up out of my swing.

"If that's what you need to do."

"I just . . . I don't need you blowing rainbows up my skirt, okay?"

He smirked. "I promise not to compliment your voice again. Scout's honor."

I sat back down. "Well, I don't know about that . . ." I returned the smirk. It was nice to talk to someone who knew nothing about my real life. "Where you from? I know it ain't here."

He relaxed back into his swing. "Minnesota. What about you?"

"The mountains."

"An authentic country girl. Rare these days."

"And I still got all my teeth, can you believe it?" I bared my fake teeth in an unsettling grin, and he laughed.

I heard Martha calling my name, and I saw that most of the party had congregated around the fire in a big jagged circle. Tate and I stood up and joined everyone, separating to sit with our respective friends.

A man in his thirties with a guitar slung across his middle introduced himself as Don and welcomed everyone to his home. Half the circle were clutching guitars or basses, and there were handheld percussion instruments scattered throughout. I even saw someone with spoons.

Don played the first chords of an old Bob Wills tune, and a couple guitars joined in. Another man with a russet beard started to sing, and his sound was coarse against the sweet melody, like stubble rubbing against my face.

I saw Tate across the circle, lit up now by the flames. He was beautiful in the way teen boys were beautiful, with a tenderness beneath a serious, rough exterior. His hair was thick and shaggy to his chin, and his beard was more neat than some of the others.

I leaned over and whispered to Martha, "Do you know that guy? The one with the old Gibson?"

She searched for him in a sea of men clutching Gibsons. "Oh, Tate. Yeah. Fine voice. Good player. *Amazing* songwriter." I loved that this is what Martha thought of first—his qualities as a musician. "He's written a few songs for big artists."

"Is he married or . . ."

"No, he's single." She looked concerned. "I don't know, Lou. He's kind of a heartbreaker."

I thought, *Yes.*

Across the circle, I heard a familiar tune start up. Tate was strumming the first bars of the old murder ballad I played that time at the Opry.

He was staring right at me, daring me to sing. I accepted the challenge.

There was a woman in town who sang so sweet
Her beauty was beyond compare
But one day a bright specter she did meet
There aft she was no longer fair

I could feel the rough edge of something new in my voice catching as the song slid out of my throat. The pain of the last few months had added depth to my sound.

But the words themselves, they had come before I ever met Hess, and it felt good to sing something without a trace of her.

There was an honesty in singing about my curse this way, in front of all these people. A morbid acceptance. I remembered how lifted I felt when I performed it at the Opry.

She ranted and raved and ran over town
Chased by somethin' not seen
She ran so far that she came to a cliff
And it chased her over to free'n

Later, when we walked en masse back to our cars in the early-morning light, there came a clear, crisp voice behind my ear, "Come back to my place."

"No."

"Then come tomorrow."

"It *is* tomorrow."

"Come later, then. Whenever you want. It's the one with the pirate flag on Blossom Road. I'll be there."

When I looked behind me, he was gone.

17

lulabelle

1973

NINE YEARS LEFT

Tate lived on the far edge of town where the trees breathed. I found my way there the next afternoon, and we sat behind his house, watching them inhale and exhale.

We were waiting for the right moment to enter the woods. I wasn't sure when that would be; something inside me would align, and then it'd be time. But right then, the world was still shifting. We were in this in-between space, this fuzzy black-and-white space, where the world around us hadn't decided what it wanted to be.

I had never done LSD before, so I couldn't be sure if this was normal. But it didn't feel dangerous.

Tate dragged a finger across the top of my hand lying flat in the grass. I could feel the weight and quality of his mind in that touch, fizzing against my skin like powder mixed with vinegar. I looked into his eyes, and he suddenly blazed into full, radiant peaches and blues against the black and white.

The scene around us burst into color as well, and the trees stood before us, beckoning with their swelling purple trunks. He and I stood up. We clasped hands. And we walked toward the wall of nature like a portal.

In the woods, I took off my shoes and flung my wig onto a branch. I became a child again.

We walked slowly between the trees, touching every surface, savoring every sensation. If I looked at anything for too long, it would start to expand and unfurl. Moss sprouted small blooms and tree bark swirled into intricate patterns. My gaze had the power to unlock new life.

We found a little pond with a few fish wiggling under the surface. Tate told me about ice fishing in Minnesota where he'd grown up. They'd make a little house on the ice, cut a hole in it, and lower their line. His parents were conservative churchgoing people, but when they were out on the ice or crouching in a deer stand, his dad would let him have a bit of whiskey in his hot chocolate. The normal rules didn't apply in these special places.

He asked me about my childhood, and I told him that I'd once slept for a week in an abandoned deer stand. It was summer, and in the absence of school, I needed an escape from my aunt's family. I stole a blanket from the house and used dried weeds to soften the wood boards. I lived off wild blackberries and a sack of jerky I'd swiped from the cellar. When I finally returned seven days later, my aunt asked where I'd been all day. She needed help with the wash.

Tate asked me quietly what happened to my parents. I started to tell him the canned version of my story, the one I'd dreamed up in that truck on the way to Nashville and had given for years in interviews.

My parents were taken home to Heaven in a car accident, and I was raised by my loving aunt and uncle, accepted as one of their own in a beautiful mountain holler, where we loved God and lived a humble, peaceful life.

To tell you the truth, I was sick of that story.

I had kept my secrets so long from others, afraid of what would happen if I exposed them, and yet, the thing I'd feared had already happened. The person I loved most hadn't believed me, had treated me like a dumb hillbilly, and I was still standing, wasn't I? I didn't want to hide anymore. Maybe now, I could live some version of the truth.

I asked Tate to sit in the leaves with me, and I told him that my father had left, and my mother had died at 33 from a family curse. I unbuttoned my shirt and bared myself to him, showing him my tree in all its glory. The tree that killed my mother.

The air danced over my naked skin, and my breasts pebbled. I watched his face, searching for a glimmer of doubt in his eye. But he only stared thoughtfully, and after a long silence, he asked me what it was like to know I would die in nine years.

It was the same question Hess had asked me, and I wondered what that meant. Perhaps he really believed me. Perhaps not. It didn't matter anymore, did it? This was my truth, whether he believed it or not.

I told him what I'd told Hess, that it weighed heavily on me, but it also inspired me to take risks. I didn't live as if my days were infinite; I squeezed the blood out of life and painted my cheeks with it.

But that wasn't the whole story, was it?

I'd been told all my life that I was a demon child, that I was going to hell. And so when I was little, I had often imagined where I was headed: a place of pain without escape, a place where the only sound was a terrible noise. It haunted me at all hours of the day—in my sleep, at my desk at school, in the pew at church.

That was the demon child's greatest secret—she was very, very afraid. And it wasn't just the idea of hell—it was that she was supposed to spend the rest of eternity there. And whenever she tried to imagine that cursed eternity, a terrible, suffocating feeling would overtake her, and she'd want to die—not twenty-five years from now, but right then and there, struck by lightning while her granddaddy gave his sermon from the pulpit. It would get so bad, she'd tell her aunt she needed to use the bathroom, and instead of going to the outhouse, the demon child would head into the trees, running through them until she was deep enough to hear the music drifting down in the shafts of sun.

Music is what had saved her—it allowed her to escape such thoughts, to live in a place where hell and eternal pain didn't exist. If not for music, she might have gone insane.

The woods suddenly grayed and darkened around us. I stood up, trying to clear the new mood, but it only deepened. When I put my hand on a tree to steady myself, I felt something wrong emanating from its bark. Dread seeped in like a cold liquid.

Tate looked at me with fear. He could feel it, too. "We need to change locations. Let's go to my house."

We fled the way we came, desperate to outrun whatever had descended over the woods. When I looked back, a thick fog obscured our trail, and the outline of a figure stood in the cloud, watching me. I ran faster.

When we finally returned to the field, I saw Tate's house shining on the hill. This would be our sanctuary.

Inside, the living room was a velvet-lined, wood-ribbed whale, and we settled into its cushioned belly with weary relief. The walls inhaled . . . and exhaled.

Tate put on Blind Willie Johnson's "Dark Was the Night, Cold Was the Ground." I lay back in a pile of pillows and let the blues soak me through.

I became the demon child again, lying awake after bedtime, sandwiched between two of my cousins with a thin blanket spread over us. I could smell the older boys in the next bed over.

I lay there and touched the skin on my neck, searching for comfort. I didn't have a special blanket or a stuffed animal I could stroke and soothe myself with. I only had my own body, so I rubbed my soft neck skin between my fingers and sucked on my tongue.

I reached for a memory that I saved for the real bad times, afraid overuse would wear it too thin:

It was dark, and I was warm and wet.

And then, out of the blackness, there was a sound. It vibrated against my body.

Then it entered me, filling up my head and chest like a yellowroot unfurling in spring. It felt so good. Better than anything I'd ever experienced.

It was my mother, singing to me while I was still inside her belly. My first music.

I started to hum the tune, and Tate turned off the record player. I sang what I remembered:

Baby, don't be 'fraid
When I leave too soon
Baby, don't be 'fraid
I'll be your moon
Baby, don't be 'fraid
When the white dog moan
Baby, don't be 'fraid
You'll nev'r be alone
Baby, don't be 'fraid
When you wake at night
Baby, don't be 'fraid
I'll be your light
Baby, don't be 'fraid
When it comes for you
Baby, don't be 'fraid
'Cause I'm there with you

Tate leaned over and brushed his thumb across my wet cheek. I almost never cried, especially in front of people. It was much easier to keep it inside and heat it to steam, let it escape as anger.

"What was that? I don't think I've ever heard anything so sad and beautiful."

"My mama used to sing it . . . it must be some folk song." But as I said this, I wondered if that was true. The lyrics were so specific, so clearly made for a cursed woman speaking to her child, knowing she will soon leave them, and that one day, they, too, will suffer. The song conferred a haunting comfort, a tenderness meant for a demon child. Perhaps it was written by my mother, or my grandmother, or my great-grandmother.

The tears continued to flow, and I let them drip warmly down the sides of my face into the rug.

"I'm so scared, Tate. I don't want to die."

There was a beat of silence, and then he said, "I used to be scared of death. I would think about it all the time, and it almost made me want to die, just so I didn't have to worry about it anymore." He looked away. "But then, in school, I read something that helped me move beyond it."

He got up on his knees and unbuttoned his own shirt this time, revealing a pale, hairy chest covered in thin ridges. I sat up to get closer, and I saw that they were words carved into his skin and healed into white scars. I traced them lightly with my finger. All together, they said, *Amor Fati*.

"What does it mean?" I asked.

"It is a saying of the Stoics. It means to love one's fate. It reminds me to welcome all of life's experiences, good and bad. Even death."

"But how can you love your fate if you know you're headed to hell?"

He let go of his shirt and let the fabric hang down over his chest. "How do you know you're going to hell?"

I got on my knees so we were eye to eye. "So you don't believe me, huh?"

"What I'm saying," he explained, "is even if this curse is in your family, and you're certain you're going to die at 33, how do you know you're going to hell afterward?"

I thought back to the first time I ever heard about the curse.

It was my fifth birthday, and a neighbor who doted on me brought me a cake and got everyone to sing. I'd never gotten so much attention, and I'm sure I was beaming with it.

After she left, my uncle got into his secret stash and tied one on. He could barely stand as he roamed the house, looking for something to torture.

Us kids knew to make ourselves scarce, but it was oddly cold that night. My shoes were worn to holes at the bottom, and I imagined my feet turning to ice if I escaped to the woods. When I tried to join the others in the various hiding spots around the house—the cellar, the space under their parents' bed, my aunt's bureau—they wouldn't let me nestle in with them. They said there wasn't room.

So I stood in the middle of the kitchen with my small five-year-old body and dared him to do his worst. If I couldn't hide, I sure as hell wouldn't cower.

When I didn't scamper, he got angry. He lunged at me slow and sloppy, and I dodged him easily. He tried again, and I dodged him again. He peered at me with bloodshot eyes and said, "You think you're real special, don't ya? That lady only felt sorry for you, 'cause she knows where you're headed."

I looked at him curiously, and he said, "Everybody knows that the women in your mama's family are *cursed*. They all die at 33 of some gruesome accident—just like your mama." He leaned in closer, and his voice went low, like he was telling a ghost story. "And it's all because one of your kin from way back made a deal with the *devil*. Traded her soul so she could sing like an angel." He grabbed my wrist with his meaty hand. "Your mama and your grandmama and all those other ladies are in hell right now, burning alive. And one day . . ." He paused, bringing his mouth right up to my ear. "You're gonna join them."

I knew my uncle liked to torture things just for fun, and I shouldn't pay him any mind. But deep in my gut, I knew he was right. I was the demon child, and I was damned to hell, just as my mother had been. I saw the place I imagined in church, the place where the only music was a terrible sound. I saw my mother there, the house dress from the only picture I had of her set aflame.

"The devil owns my soul. Where else would I go?" I said to Tate.

"I don't know. I just have a hard time believing you are destined for hell. When you sing, it's like I can see God's light pouring out of you."

It was true that since I was a girl, I had also felt the Lord with me. The devil might have given me my voice, but it was God who sent me music.

I didn't know how to fit these two ideas into who I was or what I was destined for; perhaps as a damned girl, a demon child, God took the greatest pity on me. Maybe he even had a big, grand plan for me, and one day all of the ecstasy and sorrow would come together in one striking image, and I'd see what He'd intended.

Perhaps all I needed was to let go, as Tate had. Love my fate. Welcome the good with the bad and watch it unfold.

It was dark when Tate dropped me off at home. We were two travelers at the end of a long journey; there was nothing left to say. We nodded at each other, and then I walked inside.

I'd come back down to earth from the LSD, but things were still a little cockeyed. I lay down on the couch and tried to sleep, but the brocade pattern kept pestering me. The world wouldn't let me turn off.

I must have drifted off at some point because I woke to a hammering on my door. It was early evening in spring, and the smell of wet daffodils wafted through the screen window. When I looked at the brocade, it stayed mercifully still.

Another knock came at the door.

I opened it, and there was Tate. It felt natural that he should be there, like the next chord in the song of my life. We both reached out and brought our palms together, testing reality. I felt none of the drug now, but our connection was still there, a luscious vibration where our skin met. I wanted to feel more of it, and so I snaked my arms inside of his jean jacket and pushed my hands beneath his shirt to his warm, bare back. He did the same, and we stood there, clutching one another under our clothes.

I looked up at the dark-blue sky over his shoulder, and I heard something in the distance. At first it was just a little tinkle in my brain, and then it got louder and more complex, and my body shivered as it crackled through me like an electrical current.

It was a new song. A special one. About a cursed woman, searching for a bit of light.

18

lulabelle

1973

NINE YEARS LEFT

I can only describe it as a fever. The constraints of day and night, of breakfast, lunch, and dinner, did not apply to us. We ate when our thoughts turned to vapor, and we slept when we could no longer think at all.

When we needed a break, we lit a joint and fucked on the couch or the floor. I thought it'd be hard to sleep with someone after Hess, but it was different with Tate. It wasn't charged with so much love and devotion; we each did it to serve ourselves.

But what we mainly did was write songs.

Me, in my bedroom on the mattress, and Tate in the living room on the couch. Every so often, one of us would come into the other's space, and they'd share what they'd written, and the other would give feedback, and then we'd separate once again.

I was burning up with this idea that had sprouted during the acid trip and now grew inside me like kudzu. I wanted to make a concept album about a figure I was calling "the cursed woman," starting with the song my mama sang to me in the womb, titled "Lullaby for a Demon Child" and that old murder ballad from the holler. There'd also be several original songs, like the one Hess and I had written years ago when we first met.

Tate had gone to college in the northeast before he became a songwriter, and he'd studied the great literature. He taught me how to elevate my writing without sucking the life out of it. One of the songs he helped with, the hardest one for me to write and what would become the title track, was about accepting one's fate, even reveling in it.

I imagined Hess listening to each song and the notes she might have given. I did everything I could to keep from thinking about her.

But I was also committed to telling the goddamn truth this time. That was the way to make real art, to expose the truth at the core of you.

I was finally bringing my night songs into the light.

~

One morning I woke and Tate was gone. There was no note. No answer at his house. Martha didn't know where he'd gone, but she told me this was what he did. He would disappear for weeks and show back up with stories of poker games with cross-country truckers and riding rodeo bulls and selling a new song to a rock star in San Francisco.

It was a good kind of pain to feel abandoned by Tate, wondering if he was with someone else out there. If he'd ever come back. I reminded myself that this was what I wanted: someone who didn't need me. I was the Cursed Woman, fated to walk the earth alone.

Without anyone watching, I stayed up for days at a time working on the songs. I painted the lyrics on the walls in thick black letters. I only went out at night, when everyone else was asleep, and I could walk unobserved for miles in the cold, clear air, dreaming up my next song.

Three weeks later, Tate showed up at my doorstep with a small cooler in hand. He acted as if he'd just gone out for groceries, the way he casually stepped inside without a hug and strode to the kitchen. He took out a bundle wrapped in paper and unfurled it with his back to me. Then he turned around and presented a dark-red knot of meat on a plate, his face reverent.

"My goddess, I've brought you the heart of a deer as an offering. May I cook it for you?"

I nodded in surprise, and he pulled out a long, sharp knife from the cooler and cut thin, bloody slices from the heart. They went into the frying pan with butter, and the smell of it was dark and loamy, like hot, fertile soil.

When he was done, he fed me a piece from a fork. The meat was blood rich and lean. I could taste the leaves and berries the creature ate, its power and wildness. He fed me another, and another. The juices ran down my chin.

When I'd consumed the entire heart, he put down the plate and carried me into the bedroom. The meat had only made me more hungry for him, the desire painful and moaning. I tore off his shirt, and he took off his pants, and then he pulled off my dress, finding me naked underneath. He buried his face between my legs and licked me like an animal. I bucked at the tender force.

Afterward, he lit a joint and we lay there in the dark. He told me about deer hunting in Minnesota, not as an explanation for his absence but as a good story. I didn't ask for any details, or whether he'd gone elsewhere in his time away.

He noticed the words in black on the walls, and he turned on the lamp to read them. Any other person would have thought I'd lost my mind. In all fairness, it looked like a satanist was squatting in my house. But he only stood up to get a better look and remarked, "You figured out the tree metaphor. It really works now. Feels consistent all the way through."

I'd struggled with this song. I'd kept the images real loose when I first wrote it, and Tate had encouraged me to tighten it up, make sure I wasn't mixing my metaphors like many did in songwriting. It was called "Black Gum Tree," and it was about my mother's death.

I was serious—this time I would tell the *goddamn truth*.

When the album was ready to record, no label wanted to make it.

I hadn't recorded or performed in a year, and my face was already fading from the collective mind. They said I didn't have value without Clayton, and even Clayton himself wasn't so valuable anymore. His latest solo album had done mediocre at best.

What they didn't say was that my new look might not have value, either. I'd stopped wearing wigs and slapping on the makeup, and Phoebe had made me these long, flowy black dresses after listening to the demo. I was no longer the child bride.

I was the Cursed Woman.

Then there was the music. I knew it wasn't the clean, easy sound they were used to. But I'd seen so many musicians break out and expand over the last few years. I thought, surely there was space for it. And yet, I could feel their fear. I was a hardened, haunted woman they couldn't control. A real outlaw.

Martha told me the house where I'd met Tate was also the home of a small label and recording studio, different from the big labels on Music Row. The owner, Don, had a vision for a country music that wasn't afraid to get its hands dirty. There were no suits milling around, calling the shots. Just a few guys plucking strings and trying to make something special.

I was skeptical of something so slapdash after I'd spent years recording in Nashville's best studios with Clayton. I didn't want to move backward, or look like I couldn't make it without him.

But, of course, that was only the fear talking.

In the daylight, the unassuming yellow ranch looked like any other modest family home. You'd never suspect people were making music in its rooms. The studio itself was just a soundproofed basement with instruments and microphones scattered about. That first day, Martha and I set up while Don's regular guys got situated. They all had the same long hair and beards, and it was hard to tell them apart.

The first song we recorded was "Lullaby for a Demon Child." The sound felt off for some reason, and instead of stuffing my concerns like I'd done with Clayton, I told Don it wasn't right. So he asked me what we should change, and we did another take, and I realized there were voices missing. I could hear their absence. The song needed to be three female voices harmonizing together.

I was lucky Tima was in town because she spent most of her time touring. I went over to her house that night and played her the song and described how I heard it in my head. We sang it through a few times, and we could both feel it. We really had something.

We got in Tima's car and went over to Mom's uninvited. She had a whole new crop of girls living in her house, but we still felt like her *real* girls come home. It was late, and she was already in her curlers and robe. We sat on the back porch like old times, and we sang it for her. It took a bit of cajoling, but eventually she agreed to sing with us on the record.

The next day at the studio, we all gathered around the mic. I'd decided I only wanted voices on the track. So all the boys and Martha were hanging out in the makeshift booth with Don. He had his doubts about recording a country song with no instruments, but bless his heart, he was willing to walk into the fire with me.

I asked him to turn out all the lights, and the studio plunged into darkness.

I sang the first line, and then Tima came in with her voice, and then Mom. Then we all sang together, and repeated the round. Goose bumps prickled up my arms and a shiver ran through my shoulders.

Baby, don't be 'fraid
When I leave too soon
Baby, don't be 'fraid
I'll be your moon

The studio faded away, replaced by a dark, log-lined room lit only by the moon, and us three women rocking babies in our arms. The sound was round and berry-tart with that vein of mournful truth running through.

We consoled our babies for the suffering they would have in this life and perhaps the next.

When it was over, the sound lingered in the air like smoke from a candle. The booth was quiet, and some of them boys looked like they'd seen a ghost.

Don said, "Well, goddamn, Lou. I mean . . . *goddamn.*"

19

rhea

1995

We started the southbound trail in mid-August in windblown, craggy Maine. I'd never been that far north before, and it had a crisp, head-clearing quality perfect for the beginning of our great trek.

On day one, we scrambled up a rocky mountain with full packs weighing heavily on our shoulders and black flies swarming our sweat-coated faces. With each trudge, I thought, *I have made a terrible mistake*, but I was too afraid to say it out loud. I didn't want Micah to think I was soft.

By day three, I had decided to quit. We hadn't even made it off the first mountain yet. My feet were like raw meat from my new hiking boots, and my soul ached for a hot shower. I had imagined Micah and I having these endless, roving conversations while we walked during the day and wild, passionate tent sex at night, but we'd barely spoken or touched since we started the trail. Reality was starting to seep in, and I didn't like it.

That evening, lightheaded from exhaustion and despair, I studied Micah across the small fire he had built, and for a moment, in a flicker of light, with his head tilted at just the right angle, I saw him once again as a stranger. I was all alone in the wilderness with this man, and we barely knew each other. A tight flush crept along the back of my neck, and I shivered in the cool night.

Our eyes met, and he started to shake with silent laughter. At first I thought this was some sort of psychotic episode coming on, finally revealing him as the killer I had missed, and I should run away now while I still could.

But the laughter was also infectious, and I started to laugh, too, the tension releasing from my shoulders against my better judgment.

"This sucks," he said, when he caught his breath.

"Oh, thank god," I rasped.

"I'm sorry, you just looked so miserable. I couldn't help it." He exhaled slowly into a low whistle. "I feel bad, because this was my idea. I'm supposed to make sure you have a good time."

I kept laughing and shook my head. "No, no, it's not on you. I'm the one who thought I could do this."

He smiled more soberly. "You can. I know you can. We just have to get through this first part. From what I've read, it only gets easier." He looked me in the eye. "Will you hang in there just a little longer? I think it'll be worth it."

Leaving the trail had been a seductive thought; its promise was the only thing that had kept me going that day. But the Micah I recognized had returned, and I knew I wanted to be with him. To be the kind of person who stayed, the kind of person he saw when he looked at me.

Fifteen weeks later, our trek led us back to Tennessee.

I was still taken by the wet green of the place; I could feel it in my lungs and on my skin. Its fresh, earthy smell mixed with my own foul scent, which I'd grown accustomed to over the miles of sweating and nature. At its most pungent, it reminded me of the rare flowers our next-door neighbors in California grew—a sweetness so nauseating it made my mouth water. Like roadkill, Carl used to say.

Micah and I had walked through ten states together, talking about everything that mattered and everything that didn't matter, unburdening the thoughts and opinions we'd been holding in for years, and forming new ones. I could articulate what was inside me in a way I hadn't been able to before, and I never thought back on our conversations and regretted my words.

We'd crafted our own little world; being with him felt like a home that we carried on our backs wherever we went. A place where I felt like the best version of myself.

On that first day in Tennessee, Micah hiked ahead like he sometimes did, so I was left alone on the trail. I took off my headphones and walked quietly through the forest, imagining my mother as a child wandering among these same trees, barefoot and dirty-kneed, listening to the music emanating from them. I stretched my own ears toward them now, straining to hear it for myself.

There was the twinkling of birds, the screech of insects, the skitter of a breeze moving through branches. I stopped, silencing the crunch of my footsteps, and held my breath.

There was a low, unmistakable tone echoing from the trees, pulsing to the rhythm of my own heartbeat thumping in my head.

Is that what she'd heard? Had she made music out of such a thing?

The pulse followed me as I finished that day's mileage, keeping me company with its beat.

When I came upon Micah waiting at our meeting place, the pulse abruptly stopped, and for a moment I felt lonely, almost bereft. Then Micah pulled me in for a sweaty hug, and I rejoined our little world, content once again.

Near the shelter where we'd sleep that night, an older woman in white braids and a long, flowing white dress stood by the open trunk of her car, offering trail magic to the hikers. We were used to hiking provisions of Gushers, protein bars, and bags of chips, but her spread was uniquely lavish: bowls of glistening fruit, a pot of honeycomb, tiny glass bottles of moonshine. I watched her sharp eyes linger on my birthmark poking out from my tank top, and I ignored it. Most strangers couldn't help but stare.

Micah asked her for "safety supplies" with a knowing voice. She nodded and retrieved an ornate wooden box from the backseat of her car. With her body angled away from passersby, she opened the lid, revealing a pile of dried, curling mushrooms resting on plum velvet.

Micah raised an eyebrow at me as if to say, "Do we dare?" and I nodded furtively. We had discussed doing mushrooms before the trek was over, and while I'd been a bit skeptical, this seemed like the type of thing you shouldn't pass up. When a forest witch gives you magic mushrooms, you take them.

We thanked her and moved on to the shelter, which was a one-room cabin filled with musty bunks. Once settled, Micah cut the mushrooms up and laid them on bread slathered in peanut butter. I chewed quickly through their ethereal, spongy texture and swallowed with a sense of gravitas; there was no turning back now.

It had been a short day, and the sun was still setting, so we lay on our backs in the grass outside. Fellow hikers arriving for the night waved to us but didn't disturb; they could sense it—we were on our own trip now.

The coming up was gradual, mirroring the dying of the light. I ascended as the sun descended, meeting the night sky as if it was pressed right up to my cheek.

The stars shimmered with greater intelligence—they weren't just flat pinpricks of light, were they? They were vast heavenly bodies, larger than I could fathom, or they had once been, and now I could only see their shimmer.

That was all I would ever get, wasn't it? The last bit of shine of something long gone, a bit of shimmer in my periphery, reminding me of what could have been. I felt the old dread open up like a black hole inside me, sucking in all other thoughts with its thick gravity.

"Do you think that woman was a witch?" I asked Micah, attempting to pull myself out.

"Maybe," he said in a dreamy voice.

"Do you think there are supernatural phenomena that really exist out there? Like stuff that can't be explained?"

"Of course," he said, moving his hand back and forth over the sky, creating ripples in the black that separated into the colors it'd absorbed—purple, green, blue, gold.

"Do you think it's possible, to like, sense something bad is going to happen? To have real premonitions?"

He kept moving his hand and said, "Yeah, I think so." He hesitated, then continued, "The night before my brother died, I dreamt about my family going to a gathering dressed all in black. And when I looked at my brother, I couldn't see his face, like it was blurred."

I could feel my heart beating slowly, and I wondered if my body was getting enough blood or if it was slowly shutting down. Everything around me seemed to be moving in slow motion, like the world itself was slowing. "That must have been freaky," I said absently, drawing out the syllables. But Micah didn't seem to notice.

"I just pretended it didn't happen—I've actually never told anyone before." His voice thickened, and I looked over and saw tears running down the sides of his face into the grass. I knew I should comfort him, but I couldn't take on his sadness right then. It was all too much.

I said, "Sometimes I just feel this intense dread, like I know something terrible is about to happen, maybe not right now or even soon, but sometime in the future. Or all of a sudden I'll just have this strong impulse to do something terrible, like I'll imagine the most vile, unspeakable thing I could do in a situation, and the thoughts don't feel like mine—it's like they come from somewhere else, or another place inside me, and I can't control them or get rid of them." I took a deep breath, suddenly aware of the act of breathing. "Does that ever happen to you?" I wheezed.

"No," he said with fear in his voice. "Does that really happen to you?"

"Um, yeah, I mean, not all the time—"

Micah suddenly sat up, his eyes darting around. “Something feels wrong,” he whispered.

“I’m sorry, I didn’t—”

“Please. Don’t talk about it anymore. It’s putting me in a bad place. I can’t . . . I don’t want to go there. I want to think about good things. This is supposed to be fun.” He sounded scared, but also a little angry, like he was scolding me for not knowing how to have a good trip. “We need to go inside,” he declared. “It’s getting cold.”

In the cabin, someone had made a fire in the hearth, and most were already asleep in their bunks. I lay down in my bottom bed, and Micah lay in the top. He said our trips had diverged, and it was best for us to ride them out alone.

I stretched out on top of my sleeping bag, and I felt a choking loneliness crawl up my throat, reminding me of nights spent alone in my aunt and uncle’s house as a child. They liked to send me up to bed and have movie nights with Dinah in the den beneath my room. I would listen to their shouts and laughter from below, and my chest would burn with the desire to be touched.

I felt a wetness on my cheeks, and I realized I was crying, something I never did in front of others. I searched around the room to see if anyone else was watching.

But as I scanned, I noticed the bunk beds were slowly dissolving one by one, so that eventually they were gone, replaced by shapeless furniture and pictures hanging on the walls.

I was alone in the room now, crouched in a child’s squat.

A woman suddenly approached and kneeled in front of me, grabbing my arms. She had muted blue eyes framed by a cloud of hair the color of an old penny.

Lulabelle.

Her secret, unadorned self. She leaned closer, and I saw her eyes were bloodshot and her lips were cracked.

She said, "Rhea. Angel. I need you to listen to me." She squeezed harder, and I winced in pain. "What I'm about to tell you is the honest to God truth. People will tell you it isn't, but don't listen to them, you hear me?"

She paused, waiting for an answer, and my head nodded of its own will. I tried desperately to stand up and speak to her, but my body and mouth wouldn't move. I only crouched there, paralyzed.

I saw her mouth move again, and I heard noise coming out of it, but this time I couldn't make out what she was saying. I strained to piece together words from the strange tones, but it was impossible.

A pounding came from the door, and she jerked her head toward it. She let go of me, crept over to one of the curtained windows and peeked through the slit.

She gasped and stepped back quickly, bringing a hand to her chest. The pounding came again, shaking the wood in its hinges.

She ran over to me and pulled me up from the couch into her arms.

Again, that strange tone came from her mouth as she spoke to me with fear in her eyes.

Then, the room was getting darker, and her face was going out of focus, and I squinted, attempting to make her out as best I could, but I could feel her slipping away . . .

Then, there was only darkness, complete and smothering. I tried to move, but my body was still paralyzed. When I opened my mouth to scream, no sound came out. The trapped feeling I'd experienced since I was a child filled my being, thick and fresh as if for the first time—

Then there was a flash of light, blinding me for a moment.

When my vision cleared, I was standing in the middle of the woods. I touched my face, and I realized I could move again. I scanned around and saw no sign of the shelter's outdoor light. I had no headlamp, and so the trees formed thick, impenetrable walls around me, studded with the pearly eyeballs of creatures prowling in the shadows. I thought of the woman who'd gotten lost on the trail, found dead months later just a few miles from civilization.

Out of the darkness, a brilliant white animal emerged, and I froze, afraid it might be a coyote or mountain lion. It amiably padded over and rubbed its head against my side, and I saw that it was only a large shaggy dog. Dogs were off-limits in this part of the trail, and I wondered if someone had snuck him in and then lost him or if he'd run away from a nearby house. I patted his head, and a deep calm settled over me.

He took a few steps ahead and then looked back, as if beckoning me to come along.

I followed him in the darkness, and I finally began to breathe normally, my heart no longer thumping in my veins. I had the sense that nothing could hurt me when this dog was around.

After a while, we came upon a clearing bright with opal moonlight and with a large, twisting tree at its center. The dog disappeared behind the tree, and a pale man stepped from behind it wearing a crisp white suit. I should have been frightened, but I wasn't. It seemed entirely natural that he would be there. Perhaps he was the dog's owner.

I walked closer to the man and the tree, feeling a sudden desire to touch its dark, lustrous trunk. Perhaps I could curl up inside its hollow and wait for Micah to find me.

But when I put my hand out, the man grabbed my wrist. I couldn't see his face through the glare of the moon. I inhaled sharply, and he pulled me toward him, his breath sweet and hot on my cheek.

Fifteen years, he whispered.

And that's the last thing I remember.

I woke the next morning in my bunk to the faint embers of a fire and Micah curled in the bed above me, dead to the world. I had no idea how I'd gotten back, or if I'd ever left.

I walked out of the shelter to a viewpoint overlooking the mountains, and I let the chill wash away the rot in my head.

I didn't know what to think of the vision of my mother. It had been glorious to see her in the flesh, moving and talking in three dimensions, to finally witness a moment only I had with her.

But was it real? It reminded me of the recurring nightmare I'd had as a kid, and when stitched together with the encounter with the man in white, it seemed more dream than memory. What had he meant by "fifteen years"? In fifteen years, I would be 33. The same age as my mother when she died.

But what did that mean?

I had tried for so long to remember her love and what we'd had together, and now that I might finally have a piece of it, rather than comfort, it only bewildered me.

I craved memories and visions that were real, that I could rely on and bring to life. I wanted solidity, stability, my feet on the ground. That was what I needed.

I heard footsteps behind me, and then I felt Micah's warm body against my back. He wrapped a blanket around both of us and held me in silence as we looked out over the mountains wreathed in fog.

"I'm sorry I freaked out last night," he said into my neck.

"No, it's my fault—the mushrooms took me to a really weird place. I didn't even mean most of what I said."

"Me too." He pulled me in tighter. "I don't want to do that again—get lost in another world. I like being in this one, with you, without make-believe problems."

"I want that, too," I said, hesitating. "I actually have an idea, but I don't want you to think I'm crazy."

"I won't. Tell me."

I whispered, "Let's get married."

Three weeks later at the end of the trail in Georgia, Micah and I were married at the top of Springer Mountain by a fellow hiker known as

"Friar Tuck." We were sweat salted and dirt streaked, and we wore the same clothes we'd used for the last six months, now forever scented with the baked, weedy smell of our insides. When we kissed in the thin air of the summit, I swooned with a happiness that not even dread could penetrate.

Afterward, at our little reception of Ruffles potato chips and cheap red wine, all I wanted was to call Hess. But I was afraid of what she would say. I knew it would seem quick, but Micah and I had revealed every piece of ourselves over the hundreds of hours of walking. We knew exactly who the other person was in a way that usually took years to accomplish, so that our marriage felt like a natural progression—not rushed, but right.

A few days later, I broke down and called her anyway. I hoped she'd surprise me. With no family to tell, she was the next best thing.

When I said hello, she exhaled dramatically, her voice unsteady. "Oh, Rhea, I'm so glad you called. I've thought about you every day, wondering if you're okay. Not that you wouldn't be," she added carefully. "I'm so sorry for how I behaved, honey. Will you please forgive me?"

I was giddy with relief, and I told her, "Of course. I'm sorry I was such a brat. But listen, I have some news." I took a deep breath. "Micah and I got married."

Hess was silent on the other end, and I kept talking. "It was this beautiful ceremony on top of a mountain in Georgia, and another hiker officiated, and it was just . . . magical. I've never been so happy in my life."

"Well, that's, um, that's lovely, dear," she said quietly.

"You don't sound very excited," I said.

"What do you want me to say? You're only eighteen, and you barely know him."

"That's not true. I know him better than anyone I've ever met."

"I'm sure it feels that way now, but what about in a few months? Does he know about your money? Did you at least get him to sign a prenup?"

I didn't know what a prenup was, but it sounded offensive. "No, I didn't." Why had I called her? I had felt so good in spite of myself, and now she was making me feel like shit. "I was hoping you would be happy for me because I can't tell my mom. But I guess that was too much to ask."

She paused for a moment. "Honey, I'm sorry, but your mom would've agreed with me—"

"But she got married at my exact age," I spat back.

"Because she didn't have a choice," Hess retorted coldly. We were both silent for a beat, and I wondered fleetingly what she meant. "But you do," Hess added more gently.

"Exactly. And this is what I've chosen."

"Rhea, please—"

"If you can't support me or the person I love, then I don't think there's a point in us keeping in touch."

"Wait, I'm—"

But I hung up before she could say anything else.

For the next few weeks, Micah and I stayed in Georgia and plotted what we would do with our lives. He had seen a glassblowing demonstration in North Carolina during a day in town, and he wanted to apprentice at a hot shop. I was interested in going to college now, though what I would major in still eluded me. With my mother's money, I could take my time.

After applying around the country, Micah was offered an apprenticeship in Arizona. There were plenty of colleges there, and after our trek through the wilderness, I was intrigued by living a simple, brutal existence in the desert. It was a series of decisions that we made together, and I saw that this was what marriage would be.

I imagined an alternate reality in which I'd never met Micah, and I'd completed the journey solo and now planned my life alone, according to only my desires. The reality of marriage, that it was a decision that cut off all futures where I might be alone again, started to sink in. I had been lonely for as long as I could remember, but I'd never been on my own. I wondered if I was making a mistake, and if I should be chasing my freedom as my mother once had.

But I really loved him. And when he looked at me, he saw the best version of me—someone worth loving. Maybe through the force of his belief and my desire, I could actually become that person.

In that way, I would be free.

20

lulabelle

1974

EIGHT YEARS LEFT

When *The Cursed Woman* came out, good Lord, you couldn't imagine the noise it made.

You'd've thought I'd posed for *Playboy* the way people carried on. It was just *too much* for a lot of country fans. Maybe it made them feel something they didn't know what to do with. But instead of digging deeper into their own selves, they called me a devil worshipper. A witch. This made me laugh. I'd known a real witch in the holler. She was an old woman who lived in the woods and healed people all day. She was like your grandma if she lived a little more free.

But there were those who loved the album. People outside the country world, like folk music fans and young people. I wondered if Hess had bought it, and what she thought about each song. I'd never recorded anything without her, and it was strange not having her there, as if it wasn't quite real.

Don helped set me up with a manager, an old veteran who'd gotten tired of the system and started working on the fringes. Only taking clients he really believed in. He organized a tour across the country for me, and Martha and I put a touring band together, with Tate tagging along for the experience. I'd only ever toured in the South and a bit in the Midwest. The conventional wisdom was those were the only places people listened to country music. Of course, that was horseshit. People listen to it anywhere there's sorrow, and a yearning to hear a story that we all live. A story we all tell ourselves.

~

New York was not what I expected. It was dirty, and everyone seemed poor and desperate. Even some of the famous people Tate wrote songs for were hollow. Strung out. It was the first stop on the tour, and I was fresh. Maybe a little too bright-eyed for those folk, but I could tell they kind of dug it.

One night Tate, Martha, and I went to an apartment in SoHo called "The Loft" and paid $2.50 to get in. It was dark, and Aretha Franklin was playing. I'd never seen so many people of different races in one place, grooving together.

Tate pulled me into the bathroom and tipped out a little powder from a tiny glass vial. He raked it into a single line with his license and showed me how to suck it up my nose without blowing it away. It was bitter in the back of my throat, and it wrapped me in a fuzzy shine. We giggled and made out in the stall.

When we finally made it to the dance floor, I could feel it. That elusive collective rhythm. We grooved together like limbs on the same body: foreheads glittering with sweat, cheekbones sharp and glowing, curves haunting with their swing. I'd lose Tate for a song or two, caught up in my own movement. But then I'd catch a glimpse of him, of his beauty in the darkness, and I would feel love in its heady, all-consuming warmth.

I forgot I was ever going to die.

Performing my music became its own kind of drug. Tima and Mom couldn't tour with us because they had their own lives, so I recruited local singers at each stop to perform "Lullaby." At the first show in New York, both singers didn't show up. I thought, *shit*. Then I looked out in the crowd and saw all these women, and I thought, *hell yeah*. We saved it for the last song, and I invited anyone up who knew the words and wanted to harmonize with me.

Then I asked them to turn off the lights.

The boot scuffing and drink clinking ceased, and it was silent in the club as all those voices came together, pooling into a deep well, telling their babies the truth.

I thought I might cry.

Our next stop was New Orleans, which always reminds me of back home in a way. The veil over the natural world is thin there, and I have loved it since Clayton and I visited on our first tour. They understand curses, the power of the land, the different planes of existence. I could feel it at my show that night; we were all mourning our own curses, but also reveling in them. Taking a drink, and toasting to them. I was serious in "Old Crone"—in another life, I would have happily settled down there. Let myself go dry and gray like the Spanish moss hanging from the trees.

And then, there was *Austin*.

Austin was like traveling to the future. They were years ahead of Nashville. There were actual country fans there who understood my album.

When I played at the Armadillo World Headquarters, I got to feel seen by my own people. We were all dirty outlaws screaming into the void, looking for some comfort in the strange.

Just before Christmas, Tate and I came off the road and played it straight in Nashville for a week as a half joke. Neither of us wanted the easy life of cocktails in the den, five p.m. dinners, a kiss before bed.

What we didn't admit was that we both needed it.

At some point on tour, the music had gone quiet in my head, and I needed to dry out and vibe on that sober high for a bit. Martha had been hinting that I should slow down, and I knew she was right. When you're messed up for long stretches of time, sobriety becomes its own drug. A world that is still and washed clean. Intriguing for its solidity and simple images.

One morning Tate and I woke to find a rare snow had fallen. A layer of pure, cold sparkle covered everything. No sound but the cardinals in the trees and our panting. Drugs would have ruined it, painted pink and paisley over its crystal simplicity.

We spent hours sliding down the hill on metal sheet pans and wrestling in the snow. When I couldn't feel my fingers, Tate warmed them in his mouth.

On Christmas day, he blindfolded me with a silk scarf and pulled me out to the driveway. When he yanked off the scarf, I saw a black Ford Gran Torino sitting there shiny and sinister on the concrete.

"Tate, you damn fool, you know I don't drive."

He smiled at me. "I think we can fix that."

He spent the rest of the day teaching me in an empty supermarket parking lot. Once I got the hang of it, I took the car out on the snow-slushed road. There was hardly anyone out; everyone was home for Christmas. When the sun went down, I drove us around neighborhoods all over Nashville ogling the lights on the houses. I imagined what the families were doing inside, but I didn't envy them. Freedom vibrated beneath my hands. I could go anywhere at any time, and no one could stop me.

That evening, we went to dinner at Mom's house with Martha, Phoebe, and Tima. It was our yearly tradition, and I tried not to stare at the empty chair at the end of the table.

Christmas was a sad time for me as a kid; my aunt and uncle would always "forget" to get me a present, and I learned to sit quietly while my cousins opened their packages around the tree.

I remember waking my first Christmas morning with Hess and finding a pile of beautifully wrapped presents under a tree she'd set up in the corner of my suite at Clayton's. Each one was something she'd picked out just for me, and I finally understood why people liked Christmas so much. It wasn't about getting a pile of junk; it was about feeling that someone truly saw you.

Even with Tate by my side and all of my friends around the table that night, even with all of the blessings I'd been given, it didn't feel like Christmas without Hess there.

New Year's came and went, and my head was still empty. There was no new music.

When I finally confessed this to Tate one night under the covers, he said I just needed to get back out there. Get some new experiences. That's what always unblocked him.

I'd been invited to play a small tour in England. Neither of us had ever left the country, and Tate convinced me this was exactly what I needed to find my music again. And this time, I needed to watch. Observe. Look for that next little spark.

I was surprised to find England wasn't so different from where I'd grown up. The Brits had a real sense of humor that was dry and self-deprecating. Life was pretty simple and gray there, but they got a laugh out of it.

Martha and I played small clubs out in the countryside, and then afterward Tate and I got pissed on pints with the locals. There wasn't much to do but drink.

Tate knew a band who'd rented a house nearby, and he, Martha, and I went to visit them. No one answered the door when we rang the bell, so after a while we just walked in.

It was this big manor house, and it was covered in trash and cigarette butts and splintered furniture. It looked like a nuclear bomb had gone off, so when we stumbled upon a bedroom with men strewn about it, I thought they'd truly gone and died.

Tate shook the shoulder of one with messy black hair, and he stirred a bit and finally opened his eyes. He shrieked at the sight of Tate, and at the noise, the others rose from the floor like zombies.

That afternoon a group of old women came in and cleaned away the filth. An Indian feast appeared, and we ate it with our fingers and drank red wine out of crystal goblets around a massive molding table.

They told us charming stories about Tate and their escapades, leaving out key details. They treated Martha like a fellow musician, but they were giving me the pretty-little-wife treatment. It was like watching animals pretend to be humans. It was really quite funny. They hadn't even asked my name.

Tate eventually got around to telling them who I was, and only then did they finally see me. One of them prowled over to a stack of records in the corner and pulled *The Cursed Woman* from the top.

I was on the cover, but you couldn't see my face very well. I was more of a haunting figure looming there, watching *you* as opposed to being watched.

"I thought you'd be, like, a witch."

"How you know I ain't?"

He studied me. "Too . . . pretty." He brought a finger to his lips. "Although . . . there is something *feral* about you. I can see it in the way you watch everything. Me, the food, Tate. Like a big wild cat." He curled his fingers into claws and lashed out at the air.

I laughed, and we understood each other then. There was no more of the gentleman routine.

Shortly before midnight, hordes of people descended upon the mansion. Young and old, glamorous and plain. I doubt they knew very many of them, but it didn't seem to matter. As long as you were *cool.*

Martha warned me to be careful. She'd heard bad things about these guys. I pretended to heed her warning and left her in a corner talking music theory with a long-haired professor, eager to escape her watchful eye.

In the upstairs balcony, one of the boys gave me a piece of tin foil with a black bead in the center and put a straw between my lips. He lit the bottom of it with a lighter while I inhaled from the straw and chased the bead around, watching it create a tar-black design with its trail.

For a few seconds there was nothing.

And then there was pleasure. Everywhere, all at once. Searing, surging pleasure pushed to its limit, red and orange, like something held up too close to the sun.

I looked up at the sky above me with its endless black pricked with puncture wounds of light. I used to feel like a little wound, like God poked a hole in the skin of reality and made me. Now I felt infinite as the sky, and for a moment, it truly felt like I was more than just the curse. That I could grow and widen until its evil was only a prick of light in *my* expanse.

No longer strong enough to bring me down.

The rest of the tour was like a dream, the logic of it just beyond my understanding. There I was, singing onstage, doing lines in between songs off the amps. We'd go out after and thrash around to frenzied rock in tiny clubs until daybreak. Or if we were feeling mellow, we would light a dirty cigarette in the hotel bed and float out to sea. One night, we woke to our room engulfed in flames, and we had to jump out our second-story window into the dumpster below.

At some point, Martha confronted me. She was worried. She wanted me to slow down for real this time, get clean. I thought she didn't have a demon in her like I did, that she couldn't understand.

I told her if she wanted to leave, she should leave.

So she did.

Tate and I traveled to Paris next, which filled my head with noise. A rich, billowing static. Sometimes a rhythm under it like stones dropped in deep water. But always, the static. I wanted to capture the sound and make music from it.

Tate had a friend of a friend with a studio in the city, and we spent a few heady days laying down tracks. We talked about how we were evolving: our sound, our lifestyle, our expectations. What had we been seeking all this time?

We couldn't remember.

21

lulabelle

1975

EIGHT YEARS LEFT

That summer, I was asked to play a Fourth of July show down in Austin. It was a *scene.*

Thousands of long-haired young people descended on the ranch, kicking up dust with their secondhand boots and handmade sandals. Folks were sitting on blankets and lighting up and dancing to the music with their shirts off.

I was hanging out behind the stage with Tate and the other musicians when Tima showed up in her silver jumpsuit. I hadn't seen her since Christmas, and when she hugged me, I went a little limp in her arms. She pulled away and turned my face up to hers, scanning my eyes.

"Are you okay, little lady?"

"Of course, mama." I backed away from her and spun in a circle, showing her how good a time I was having. We'd been passing the tequila bottle since that morning, and I was real loose.

She laughed and twirled me around, and it was like old times again. We went over to the BBQ pit where they were serving up ribs and fixin's for the musicians. I was so geared up for the show that I was almost breathless, and the idea of chewing and swallowing anything made me sick.

Tima saw me decline a plate and arched an eyebrow. "I have never seen Lulabelle Powers turn down food in my life. Must be the heat." She was trying to make light of it, but I saw her watching me again.

I wondered if she'd been talking to Martha and Phoebe. I hadn't spoken to Martha since she'd quit the band, so God knows what she'd told them. When I saw Phoebe last, she'd looked at me real close, and I didn't like it.

Tima and I shook off the awkward moment and caught up. She was touring as a solo country artist and doing well, but it was an uphill battle. Most venues were still segregated in all ways but legal, and neither Black nor White promoters wanted to call her music "country." They were still trying to tell her who she was, and I could see she was fraying at the edges. She was engaged to a lawyer back in Nashville, and while he hadn't pressured her to come home, she was thinking about taking a break.

I thought back to when we were eighteen, and we'd sworn to never let anything get in the way of our music. I knew she was up against things I'd never have to face, but I still felt like she was betraying those girls on that balcony, in a way. I, for one, couldn't imagine going home and being a little wife.

It was ignorant and unfair of me, of course—but that just shows how far gone I really was.

I went on in the early evening in the soft desert air. The crowd was blasted off the last act, and lots of tequila and grass. Violence was starting to brew at the front near the stage, where people clamored for the best spots with unsteady, childish anger. Local toughs in long beards and leather tried to keep the peace, but the crowd could not be tamed. This was why they'd come: to escape their parents, who didn't understand them, and their bosses, who wanted to rule their lives.

The fighting escalated, and the festival manager warned me it might be dangerous to go out there. There'd recently been deaths at a few shows.

But I knew today wasn't my day to die. And if anyone could soothe a crowd of beasts, it was me.

Tima and I walked onstage together to sing "Lullaby," Tima shining in silver, me in my long black dress like Death herself. We huddled around the microphone, and our voices drifted unaccompanied over the endless crowd receding into the horizon.

I watched the angry people at the front look up, curious. The red drained from their faces, and they abandoned their fights. The crowd quieted to a low, atmospheric hum, and they all swayed from side to side in a rippling current, rocking their babies and themselves. I saw one rough in the front row get shiny-eyed, and I imagined he was thinking of his mama when she was happy and young, and so was he.

I'd never reached so many people before. The tree on my chest shook a bit from the weight of it.

When the show was over, we hitched a ride in a truck bed to the after-party. As we sailed over the scrubland, we spotted fireworks exploding over the horizon, and I remembered the time I'd watched them with Hess on the roof. Even with all the booze and drugs and the high from singing, nothing ever felt quite as magical as it had with her.

By the time we arrived at the house, I was ready to do some damage. I'd been sipping tequila all day to avoid sobering up, but now it was time to really descend. Someone poured a mound of blow on the coffee table, and Tate and I did lines in between swigs.

At one point Tima pulled me into a bedroom and locked the door. She was a bit hazy in the dim light, and I had to sit on the bed to steady myself. She took me by the shoulders and asked me to look her in the eyes.

"Lou, I'm going to be honest with you. I'm worried."

"About what?"

"Martha told me you were in trouble. But damn, girl. I wasn't expecting this."

"Wow, that's real nice of you."

"You know what I mean. What's going on? Is Tate treating you right?"

I couldn't believe I was getting this from her. We were artists. We were supposed to allow each other the space to experiment and live outside the lines. Instead, my friends had been talking shit about me like some dirt child they had to take care of. I stood up to go. "I am completely fine. Tate is a great friend, unlike you or the rest of the girls. Y'all can stuff that shit where it don't shine."

I didn't see Tima after that. She probably went back to the hotel.

At some point, we all got naked and jumped into a makeshift pool in the backyard. I wrapped my legs around Tate and we floated around, making conversation with clusters of people. We were all hurling mad gibberish at each other and having a great time. My memory of the evening dissolves there in the water, fading to black.

~

I dreamt I was in a grassy field bordered by trees. Soldiers in tattered uniforms fought with rifles and muskets in the sunshine. It was my job to tend to the wounded and distribute supplies where needed.

One man was laid off to the side wailing and clutching his leg. It looked like it'd been shredded by a bear. I needed to stop the bleeding, so I tied a tourniquet and wrapped the wound with dirty cloth torn from my apron. It was the only thing I had.

Another man called for ammunition, and I ran to him, pulling metal balls from a bag tied around my waist.

Then all of the soldiers disappeared from the field, except for one man by a large, twisting tree at the edge of the clearing.

I went to him, skimming quickly over the grass as if I were flying. He was faceless, indistinct. I laid him down on his back like he was wounded, and I pulled down his white trousers. I hiked up my skirt and straddled him on the ground, guiding him inside of me. I rocked back and forth in the grass.

A sound trickled into my mind like it once had, and I thought, *Is this the music? Has it finally returned?* But as it grew and developed in the dark space of my brain, it became a deformed, chilling piece. It was pure, uncut despair, with nothing to balance it out. No flicker of hope. No love or beauty to pull you back from the edge.

I looked down at the man between my legs, and I realized I knew him. He was the man in the white suit, the one from my vision behind the shed all those years ago. I could see the outline of his features now, but they seemed to shift with each movement, from round and womanly, to broad and craggy.

I ran from the man, stumbling to my knees in the field. The large white dog appeared, glowing in the dying light, and he padded over and sniffed my ear with his wet nose. Desperate for comfort, I sat up and put my arms around his neck, and he patiently stood there, letting me hold him.

I put my cheek to the dog's and smelled salt and rust. At the very edge of his black gums, the fur was stained dark red. He opened his jaw, and the iron smell wafted strong and thick.

The volume in my head turned up, the terrible music screeching through my mind, and I was lost to blackness once again.

Then I remember waking before the sun had risen, naked and still messed up but aware of a tense soberness at my core. The space between my legs burned.

My eyes acclimated to the dark, and something caught my attention across the room. It was the vulpine angle of Tate's nose. He was naked and lying on a futon, asleep. There were heaps of nude bodies strewn around us.

I tried to remember what had happened, and who I'd been with, and while no images came to mind, a feeling lingered, of my body no longer under my control.

Beneath the chorus of breathing in the room, I thought I could hear a voice echoing from a forgotten corner of my mind:

Eight years.

Eight years.

Eight years.

At the first hint of light over the dusty, jagged peaks, I searched for my dress among the mounds of clothing. I found it balled at the bottom of one pile, but I couldn't find my underwear or my shoes. I crept quietly outside in bare feet to the desert-cooled air. The gravel cut into the bottoms, and it was a simple, easy pain.

My black Gran Torino waited for me in the driveway like the devil's chariot. I got in and blazed out for the open road, the only car on the two-lane highway surrounded by miles of dust and cacti. It was too open, too exposed. I thought I might lift into the air and drift like dandelion fluff to an even more desolate place.

I longed for home, where the trees held me in from the sides. I put my foot to the gas, willing myself there.

22

lulabelle

1975

EIGHT YEARS LEFT

I showed up at Mom's around dinnertime. I stood on the porch for a while without knocking, watching through the lit-up window as young women gathered around the old dining room table. They laughed and gossiped as they passed dishes of chicken and green beans, and I remembered all the dinners I'd had with Mom and the girls. My first real family, the way I thought of it. That warm-belly feeling of food on the table and people you loved around it.

One of the girls must have spotted me peeking through the window because Mom came out looking to scare off a prowler. I didn't know how far gone I was until I saw her face. There was genuine fear in her eyes. I had barely slept or eaten in days, and I near collapsed in her arms.

She put me in one of the empty rooms, and I woke to softness and steaming broth just as I had years ago when I'd escaped the shed. Time folded in on itself as I made my way downstairs and found a wrapped plate on the table. I didn't feel much like eating, but I pushed the chicken around and nibbled the potatoes to make Mom feel good.

I passed a large mirror in the hall and caught the first sober glimpse of myself in a while. I was bone thin, and my skin was dull and gray. I was blurred at the edges, fading. The lonely ghost once again.

I found them out on the back porch talking in low voices over candles. Tima was curled up in her usual chair, Phoebe sat on the ground with her feet bare, and Martha and Mom were on the couch. I tried not to think about who was missing. I was too raw to unearth her right now; every thought and movement felt like it was brushing against an open scrape.

They all got up and wrapped around me in a big cluster. I seized up inside, waiting for it to be over. I didn't want to be touched.

They set me up on the couch and swaddled me in a thick blanket. Mom gave me some hot tea, and I sipped on it. What I wanted was something stronger, to blunt all that I was feeling. I thought about what I had stashed in the glove compartment of my car, or various coat pockets and drawers in my house. I could make an excuse about needing to be alone. It would be easy.

I tried to stand up, and Martha pulled me back down. She whispered that I wasn't going anywhere. I was gonna stay right there and drink my goddamn tea.

I thought about telling them what had happened in Austin. But when I tried to put it into words, it didn't make sense. I'd gotten naked among strangers, and maybe something'd happened, or maybe it hadn't. Maybe I had cheated on Tate. I couldn't be certain of any of it, but either way I felt used up, dirty. A worthless demon child.

I spent the next few days in a tense fog of paranoia and formless rage. I ate plate after plate of Mom's meatloaf and potatoes, heat radiating from my skin, and then puked it up in oily streams. Afterward, instead of feeling relief, this black hole opened up in the empty space.

There were times I could hear a dog panting in the corner of the room, or I'd see a flash of white moving just out of view. Some moments, I felt I was already in hell.

All I really wanted was a drink, or a bump, or a little bead of heroin. I'd have taken anything set in front of me if it promised a world in which my every nerve wasn't exposed to blistering reality, or where every regret didn't come streaming back to torment me.

More than anything, even more than the drugs, I yearned for Hess. The grounding comfort of her presence, and the way she always knew what to do. I had never felt warmer and more whole than when she was there, caring for me. Loving me.

I knew why I'd driven her away, but part of me wondered if it'd all been selfish whim. This petty need to experiment and be free when all I really wanted was someone to love and be loved by. I had always done my best work when she was with me; I was only truly solid in her presence.

But that part of my life was over, and I couldn't go back.

Mom came in after a few days and told me Tate was there to see me. I couldn't talk to him the way I was. Part of me blamed him for what had happened, that he hadn't protected me. Another part felt guilty and ashamed, like I'd betrayed him, and myself.

So I told her to tell him to leave me alone.

But he came back one night, late. He knelt in the front yard and yelled up at my window. I saw Mom trying to get him to leave, but he wouldn't go until I came down. I was starting to feel better, and I couldn't let Mom deal with him for me. She'd already done so much.

I went downstairs in my borrowed housecoat and slippers. I must have looked like a little old lady, because Tate smirked at me in this glazed way. He was on his knees in the grass, and his dark-blue shirt was soaked through with sweat. He looked pitiful in a way I'd never seen him; we'd never been separated by altered states like this.

"Lou. You are my goddess of the night. Of the forest. Of the forest at night." His eyes swiveled in their sockets. "I am your disciple. I dedicate my life to the worship of you."

He unbuttoned his shirt and opened it to reveal his chest. Blood trickled down from long, thin slashes across his pecs, forming the letters L-O-U.

Mom gasped and brought her hand to her mouth, taking a step back toward the house. I wasn't sure what to do for a moment. He looked so pathetic kneeling there. Not like someone who was dangerous or deserved punishment, but someone in pain who desperately needed help.

I crawled to him in the grass, and I put my arms around him. Then I pulled him up to his feet and supported his swaying body as we went inside. Mom kept her distance as I dressed his wounds and gave him some water.

I packed up my scant possessions and led him half conscious to my car. Mom offered to let him stay, but we both knew it wasn't right. Her house was a sanctuary for young women. They couldn't be worried about some handsome junkie moaning from the next room.

We went back to my house, and I put him to bed. While he slept, I had to find something to do with my hands and my brain. The house hadn't been cleaned in months, so I started clearing away trash, wiping down every surface, hand-washing the floorboards. I went to the grocery store as soon as it opened and bought enough food for an army. I covered the kitchen with trays of muffins. Tate took bites, and then threw them up into a trash can next to the bed. I held back his beautiful, tangled hair. Mostly I let him ride the wave alone. There was no saving him from it.

The studio in Paris had sent a demo pressing of the tracks Tate and I'd recorded. I finally opened the package, took out the record, and set it on the player.

The sound was dissonant, hard on the ears, lacking any melody. It made my skin crawl. It was like receiving a letter from a self far gone, and I imagined her still in Europe smoking junk in a bathroom while the building burned down around her, awaiting my response.

I didn't have the heart to tell her it was pure dog shit. This wasn't music. This was the sound of a hammer flattening a mind into a thin disc.

I put logs and old newspaper in the fireplace and lit it with a match. I watched the flames catch and grow, and when it was big and hot, I tossed the record in. It melted slowly, the black goo hissing as it covered the wood, banishing that terrible sound back to wherever it came from.

Tate stepped out of the bedroom for the first time and sat next to me in a pile of blankets.

Neither of us had anything to say.

Instead, we watched the fire together, and we lost ourselves in its shifting, primal power.

23

lulabelle

1975

SEVEN YEARS LEFT

For the first few weeks, we floated around the house, avoiding each other. I worried if we got too close, I would feel his need and he would feel mine, and the power of it would pull us both under.

The only thing that kept me going was the hope that the music would return once my body was clean and ready to receive it again. I woke up every morning and craned my ear toward the heavens, listening for the golden sound.

But it never came.

Tate got himself some religion to get through it. A preacher drove the devil from his body and introduced him to the healing power of Jesus's love. I was happy for him, but I didn't have the stomach for church after the way I'd been treated as a child. I was truly afraid that God had forsaken me for my sins—why else would he take my music away? And I didn't think going to church every Sunday would fix it.

I needed to heal my soul.

So I threw myself into the study of music. I had to relearn it from the beginning now that I no longer had a direct line to its source. I took lessons in piano to understand composition, and in drums to understand the beat. I read books about music history and theory.

I listened to the symphonies of Beethoven and Mahler, Renaissance church choirs, and the rock operas of Queen. Ethiopian jazz, tango, and Tibetan chants. This was grand, lifting music that captured and transcended existence, that connected with the divine. I'd always relied so heavily on the sounds in my own head, that I hadn't truly explored the music that lived outside of it. As my world opened up, I became obsessed with creating a large, all-encompassing sound.

After I sobered up, I also apologized to my friends for the way I'd treated them. It was easier with Phoebe and Tima because we hadn't toured together.

But Martha had seen the worst.

Sometimes I would get a flash of one of our arguments from her last days on tour, and my own words would turn my stomach. I couldn't believe some of the things I'd said to push her away. I'd disrespected her and put her career in jeopardy. I'd taken her hard-won trust, and I'd thrown it in the trash. Even after she forgave me, there was still a distance between us.

I tried to reach her through music, which had always brought us together, but when I went to a bar or a venue, all I wanted was a drink. The music scene in Nashville was not a dry environment.

Undeterred, Tate organized these sober music nights at my house. It was amazing how much the sound in Nashville had changed; now everyone wanted to be an outlaw. I watched this skinny young thing play in our living room one night, and I could tell she was shaking a bit. It reminded me of when I was starting out, and I'd wanted it so badly. I'd been filled with this light of music that I'd squandered. But I tried not to wallow in self-pity. Instead, I talked to the girl afterward and offered advice. I made new friends.

Drugs have a way of turning you in on yourself, of flattening your emotions and your interactions with other people. You become gray and solitary, despite the colors that surge inside when it hits. An illusion of vibrance.

Now, I was finding new colors. I was returning to people.

But if I'm being honest—and that's what I want to do, be honest here—some days the music and people just weren't enough.

I only had seven years left. Did I really want to live my last years denying myself pleasure? Or relief? I understood it for Tate, who could live for fifty more years if he wanted. But for me, I was starting to question the point of it. Sobriety and goodness hadn't returned my music or God's light to my life.

One night I walked in toe-numbing cold to our usual diner. I sat in the booth eating pie and ice cream and staring hard at the table's glitter-flecked linoleum. The pie was flavorless, and I was empty. Not even Linda Ronstadt's "Long Long Time" playing on the jukebox could provoke a feeling. It was music, goddammit, the one thing that had always fed me. And I felt *nothing*.

I wondered if I'd ever feel good again, or if this was as good as sober got.

I thought about the plans I'd been making. The tricky part would be hiding it from my people. I imagined a double life, where I could have everything I wanted, and no one would get hurt.

I felt the table tilt, and I looked up to see Martha sitting across from me with a stony expression. I glanced around the diner to see if anyone else had noticed her; I thought I was hallucinating.

"Tate called. He woke up and you were gone." She lit a cigarette. "Thought I might find you here."

I was afraid to open my mouth. I didn't know what would come tumbling out.

"I know that look." She paused, exhaled. "When I stopped drinking, the hardest part was the time after I got sober and put my life back together, maybe weeks or months later, when I thought I'd get back to where I was before. But all I felt was nothing."

She looked up at me to see if it was registering. "That right there"—she tapped a finger on the table—"that nothing was the greatest danger."

I didn't know she'd had a problem. I'd thought the not drinking was part of her stoic musician persona.

"I'll tell you what we're gonna do." She signaled to the waitress for a cup of coffee. "I'm gonna make a phone call, during which you are gonna stay in that seat and not move." She eyed me like *don't fuck with me, girl.* "Then we're gonna sit here and drink our coffee until the sun comes up."

Later, as we drove away from town, purple light spread across the horizon. I was right on the edge, living moment to moment. One more minute gone. Then another. Just make it to that stop sign. Just make it to that tree. Just make it to wherever Martha was taking us.

We pulled up on a small airstrip in a field miles away from civilization. There were a few baby planes lined up next to a large barn. A man in his forties or so greeted us in the morning chill, and he pulled Martha in for a long hug before he turned to me.

"Good morning, Ms. Powers, I'm Rick." He was handsome in a quiet, weather-beaten way. "I hear you need a little help."

I should have been angrier than a hornet—a stranger? Now? But I was grateful for the distraction, and there was something comforting about how much life had worn this man in.

He led me over to a tiny two-seater plane and opened the door. I looked back at Martha, who leaned against her truck, watching us from a distance. She urged me on with her silence.

I climbed in. It smelled like oil and old wool, and I was surprised by the simplicity of the interface. Rick gave me a headset and fiddled with the controls while he explained each action. The engine started, and the propellers whirred. He steered us toward the small runway, the vibration shaking my teeth.

Then he floored it, and we shot down the asphalt, gaining speed, until we lifted up, my stomach twisting, gravity clinging to my body.

As we rose through the air, rising above the sun, the heavy pull evaporated.

I floated, weightless.

When we hit sky, he showed me how to steer the plane, and he let me take over the controls.

I should have been scared, but I wasn't. I knew when I would die.

The country looked small beneath us as I carved our path toward the horizon. It was safe up there, like nothing could touch you—not the devil, or man, or any of their laws. It was a new kind of nature—one with true open spaces.

A flock of birds came up next to us, and as we flew together, something like a song filled my head—not exactly music, but a feeling so high and colored that it felt like a melody. I spotted a cloud up ahead, outlined in flaring pink gold, and it looked like Heaven must be behind it.

After a while, Rick took over and returned us to the land of the living and the dead. The weight returned, but it was lighter and easier to bear.

Neither of us felt the need to speak as Martha drove us back toward town.

I had felt something up there, and I wanted more of it. Maybe that was the addict talking, but I didn't care.

I wanted to fly.

24

lulabelle

1976

SIX YEARS LEFT

I remember waking that morning to the smell of salt and iron. Tate sat at the edge of the bed with a plate of bacon still hot from the skillet, smiling serenely. His hair was wet from the shower and curling at the ends like a little boy's.

I was usually in a plane by sunup, getting my hours in for the day. But Rick was busy, and I'd somehow slept the whole night. I felt bruised from lying down for so long, and my mouth watered for the food.

As I ate, we talked about the big trip we were taking south, through Mexico and all those little countries on into South America. Tate wanted to help out at some churches down there, and I wanted to hear Latin music straight from the source. I needed to feel the twist of the instruments, the sound bouncing off the walls of the places they'd been forged, the smells and the heat settling around the strings as the descendants of their makers played. We weren't rolling in dough because we'd been shit at looking after our money, but we had enough to bum around and travel.

After breakfast, I drove to the travel agency to finalize the details, and Tate headed downtown to volunteer. He and a few of the church folk went out and found junkies to talk them into getting clean. It was funny to imagine those uptight church people trying to talk to someone who'd had such a hard life. But I thought Tate was probably pretty good at it; at least he understood the need.

I went over to Martha's in the afternoon. She was my only unmarried friend by then—even Tima had married her lawyer beau. I was happy for them, but I longed for the days when we looked out only for each other. I knew they'd always have my back, and I also knew it would never be the same again.

Martha and I worked on a few ideas with me singing and her on piano. It still felt a little strange to make music in such an effortful way, instead of just listening to the music that drifted into my head. But I'd learned so much about music, and there was still so much to discover. I was trying to make peace with the fact that it wasn't coming back. I'd found other ways to be with God, and that would have to be enough.

We worked until her keys fuzzed and grayed, and we realized we'd forgotten to turn on the lights as the sun fell. That was my cue to head home.

Every evening Tate and I made dinner together, and then we put on a new record, or he read out loud to me from one of his college books. He'd introduced me to writers like Mary Shelley, Flannery O'Connor, and Sylvia Plath. "My freaks," he liked to call them. They were my people.

I drove home in my Gran Torino with the windows down. We were right on the edge of fall, and the maples were just starting to turn. Wood smoke curled in on the breeze, and I had this good, clean feeling that maybe I was finally figuring out how to live this brief life.

When I got in, the table was already laid with a feast. Emmylou Harris's "Boulder to Birmingham" was playing on the record player with its mournful beauty. It was bluer than we'd been leaning since we got sober.

I found him in the bedroom with his bicep tied off with a belt and a needle still in his arm. He must have injected seconds prior, because his lashes were fluttering like he was launching up and away. As if the whole world was passing behind his eyes.

I pulled the needle out and ripped off the belt. I held him in my lap and said his name. He opened his eyes, and they were glazed like donuts. He smiled dreamily and reached up to touch my jaw as if testing its solidity.

"I waited for you. I was going to show you, and then we were going to decide. To be or not to be. To be or not to be . . ."

I told him I was sorry. I told him this was just one slipup. He would ride this one out, and I'd flush the rest of it, and we'd just pick up where we left off. As I said this, I eyed the half-full baggie that sat forlornly on the nightstand.

His hand released my jaw and fell limply against the bed. His eyes rolled to the back of his head, and his throat made this horrific gurgling sound.

"No, no, no," I pleaded, trying to prop him up, as if erect posture would bring him back to consciousness, but he was like a scarecrow in my arms. I turned him on his side so he wouldn't choke on his vomit, but nothing came out. I held my finger under his nose and felt his chest, but there was no movement. He wasn't breathing.

I put my mouth around his and tried to give him my air. I'd give him everything I had—my lungs, my heart, my brain. Anything he needed to start living again.

But he only turned cold and blue in my arms, the warmth fading from him like the end of summer out on the road.

As I called for an ambulance, I felt this stark loneliness sweep into the room, and I looked down and saw that he was gone.

Since the night I met him, we'd been on this journey together. Even when he was off on his solo adventures, we were still linked, traveling like two connected particles through the universe.

But now I was utterly alone.

A lone traveler.

Hurtling through time and space toward my inevitable death with nothing but emptiness before me.

25

rhea

2002

When we first arrived in Phoenix, it felt like we'd crash-landed on an alien planet, with the red Mars soil and rock formations, the agave with their spiked tentacles, the shops selling crystals glinting with energy.

And it was this strange backdrop, this separation from everything we'd known before, that had allowed us to build a new life together over the past six years.

That afternoon, Micah and I sat at our kitchen island while I showed him the teaser my partner had cut for our latest documentary. Micah paused it on a clip of a woman walking rows of heirloom corn, her dexterous fingers smoothing back the silks and running over the purple kernels.

"I like this, but I think we need a better sense of the setting—this is agriculture in the middle of the desert. Life in a place thought to be lifeless," he said, tucking a piece of hair behind my ear.

I let the rest of the video play through, nodding. "You're totally right. I'll let Mike know."

After a few years exploring in college, I'd finally declared history as my major. Not because of an inherent love for the subject, but for the courses that blew everything I thought I knew about a topic apart, that challenged me to scrape beneath the surface and find the truth. I was addicted to that kind of obliteration.

It was in my final year that I met Mike, a film major, and we put together our first documentary as a joint thesis project. After graduation, instead of taking a low-paying job, hoping one day someone would let me do what I actually loved, I started a production company with my mother's money and began doing what I wanted right away, no permission required. Mike and I had made a handful of documentaries on subjects that interested us, getting better each time, and this latest was set to be something special—a profile on a chef in Arizona who was using local indigenous ingredients to return us to a lost way of life.

Micah was showing me his latest blown-glass piece—from a series of creatures inspired by the desert vegetation—when my phone rang. It was Hess.

Without saying hello, as if all she could muster were three words, she whispered, "Martha is gone."

Martha had recently been diagnosed with lung cancer. It took her quick, and in some ways it seemed like a kindness. Once her ability to play music went, life wasn't worth living for her.

The funeral was a big Nashville affair—not the type you might see for a star, but everyone in the industry was there. I saw Hess from afar fielding visitors and playing the good hostess as usual. Micah and I gave her quick hugs, and though her words were warm, she avoided meeting my eye. I tried to ask how she was doing, but then she was pulled aside by another mourner, and I moved along.

I had seen Hess many times over the last six years. She had apologized to me and Micah, and she was always especially nice to him, as if perpetually making up for the past. She called frequently and sent us Christmas gifts, and on the surface, we kept in touch.

But she and I had never gotten back to where we were that summer. I had forgiven her, of course; I could see now that her intentions had been good. And yet, there was still this wall between us, and I didn't know how to bring it down. She was the closest I'd ever come to having something resembling family besides Micah—and I couldn't help feeling I'd ruined it.

During the service, as people recounted stories of Martha guiding their careers as young musicians, I remembered how Martha had made me feel like a person worthy of respect over the years, especially when it felt like no one else did, and at the thought, my eyes welled. I realized *this* was true mourning, like I'd never been able to feel for my parents. Holding the singular beauty of someone in your mind and realizing you would never witness it again.

The reception was held at Tima's house, where Micah and I mostly kept to ourselves in the corner, eating the Southern foods that only tasted this way in Nashville. We lingered after everyone left, and Tima asked me to take a plate to Hess upstairs where she'd gone to freshen up.

I didn't find her in any of the second-floor rooms, and so I searched the rest of the house, the paper plate going limp in my hand. I finally found her in the garage, curled up in the backseat of Martha's black Gran Torino with her face pressed into the leather.

I opened the door and got in next to her, but she didn't stir.

"I'm so sorry," I whispered to the thick, hot air of the garage, and I wasn't just talking about Martha.

She turned over and faced me, and I saw most of her makeup had rubbed off, leaving her face gray and drawn. "Oh, honey. Don't be."

God, I felt so ashamed. "I'm sorry, this isn't about me. This is about Martha."

She smiled tearily. "I think Martha would have loved for us to have a real talk." She heaved herself up and leaned back against the seat.

"I know it's been years, but I feel like there's still this distance between us. And I don't know what to do about it. I know it's my fault."

"No, honey, it's not." She ran a hand through her hair. "I wanted to respect your boundaries like you asked, but I think I went a little overboard." She patted my leg. "I've been thinking about how Martha wanted me to be honest with you that summer, and I didn't listen to her."

I gestured for her to go on.

She folded her hands in her lap. "I didn't talk to you about your father back then because I didn't want to color your perception of him, or make you think badly of Lou. Part of me blames him for a lot of things I shouldn't." She paused for a long moment, then continued, "Tate got Lou into drugs when they first met—she was on them when she wrote *The Cursed Woman* and throughout the time she spent with him, until the end when they both got clean. And I blamed him for bringing that kind of suffering into her life—still do, in a way, if I'm honest. It's hard to let go of."

The beautiful dope-fiend version of my mother I'd crafted as a child reappeared in my mind like the memory of an old enemy. "So there was some truth to what my aunt told me after all."

Hess's eyes hardened, and I tensed against the soft leather seat. "Every word that woman ever told you about your mother was a *lie*. Do you understand me?"

I nodded, afraid to say anything more, and Hess softened. "I'm sorry, honey. I just . . . I don't want you to get the wrong idea about her."

"Is that why you and mom had the falling out? Over the drugs?"

"No, it happened before that. But we didn't become friends again until she was sober."

Something else popped into my mind then—the image of my mother with bloodshot eyes and chapped lips from my mushroom vision. I had never asked Hess about it, partly because it seemed too strange to articulate, but now it was cast in a new light.

"Did my mom have a cabin when I was little? I think I might have a memory of us going to a cabin and her being scared and wanting to tell me something important."

Hess's face paled for a moment, then righted. "That was probably my cabin. She used to bring you to visit quite a bit, though I'm not sure of the time you're talking about. What do you remember?"

I told her, and she nodded absently, looking off into the distance.

"Could she have been on drugs then?" I asked. There had clearly been something off about her in the memory.

Hess's brow furrowed. "No, she stayed clean once she had you." For a moment it seemed she wanted to say more, but then she stopped. I waited, but she remained quiet, and I was lost to my own thoughts. I remember thinking, *At least there was a cabin*. Perhaps it wasn't just a fever dream, but a fragment of something larger, filtered through a child's perception.

"Micah seems like a wonderful person," Hess said to fill the silence.

"He's the best person I know," I said, and Hess smiled.

"Thank the Lord for *that*."

There was another beat of silence, and I noticed Martha's signature aviators still clipped to the visor up front. "This car is so cool."

"Martha left it to you in her will."

I looked over at Hess, shocked, and she smiled again and caressed the door. "It used to be your mother's. Your father actually gave it to her for Christmas one year. He taught her how to drive."

I studied the interior with new interest, as if there might be clues hiding in the black leather. I imagined my parents riding in it together, golden with '70s glamour, my mother's bare feet propped on the dash.

Hess and I really talked then, about my marriage to Micah and how I'd stopped worrying about him leaving me.

Hess told me about a new album she'd been writing, inspired by her experience with menopause, though of course, she couldn't say it outright. She had to use metaphors so that only the women who understood would get it.

We heard a guitar kick up inside the house, and the voices of Phoebe and Tima calling for us. At the sound, I saw Hess's face suddenly wilt, and tears finally make their appearance. "I don't want to sing without Martha," she rasped, and I took her hand in mine and let her ride the wave.

When she calmed, we walked inside to Tima's son playing guitar while Tima sang and Phoebe danced around the living room with Micah and her granddaughter.

I left Hess there to join in, and I went to the kitchen to help clean up, preferring to be out of the fray. Tima's daughter, her husband, and their two children were already there, and I watched as they washed and dried dishes together among the retro wood panels.

The children were young—maybe eight and nine—and as they helped their parents wipe the plates, the family seemed to move in concert. They made strange inside jokes with one another as if they were speaking their own language, and when they laughed, the sounds of their joy blended in harmony.

It was such a specific world they'd created—a small glowing bubble of a world that fit them completely. There was something familiar about it that I couldn't place.

I wondered what it would have been like if my mom were still alive, and I had grown up in her world. It was hard to imagine her as a mother—she had spent so much of her life chasing her dream and making music that I couldn't see her tied down, sequestered to a warm bubble. And perhaps it wasn't something she had wanted, and she had made the best of it.

But when I looked over at Micah dancing with Phoebe's tiny granddaughter in the living room, I *knew* I wanted to share the world we'd created, built on love and respect and joy and truth, with children of our own.

And in the next moment, a voice inside me whispered, *What do you know about being a mother?*

But as we traveled back to Arizona, the desire only grew stronger.

For days after we returned, I hid from myself and focused on work.

Then at some point, as I stared into the blue light of my computer screen, I realized I had been my own mother all these years. And I wouldn't be raising a child by myself. I had Micah.

But I was nervous about what he would say. We'd never talked about children—it was one of the only things we'd failed to discuss that year we fell in love. We were so young back then that the possibility had seemed remote. And the specter of his brother loomed there, telling me to be quiet.

I wondered if Micah had decided never to put himself in the position of his parents and risk the kind of loss that had destroyed him and his family.

Then one night while we ate dinner, I was suddenly seized by the need to tell him. I couldn't hold it in any longer.

"I want to have a baby."

Micah stopped shoveling lentil soup into his mouth and set his spoon down. I couldn't see his face at first, but when he finally lifted it toward me, his eyes were shining like the glass sculptures that took up every surface of our home.

"I want one, too."

"Really? Why didn't you say anything?"

"I didn't want to *force* it on you. I'm not the one who has to carry it. I thought I'd sound like a dick if I said, 'Rhea, let's put a baby in there!'"

I laughed. The relief was intoxicating.

I got up and sat in his lap. I put my forehead to his, and I felt that restoring energy, our cells regenerating.

Then he fucked me with hearty purpose, right there on the cold clay of the kitchen floor.

26

rhea

2003

It was a game at first. To see how many times we could have sex in one twenty-four-hour period. We fucked in the bathroom at the hot shop, and in the backseat of Micah's green Volvo, and in the prickly bushes of a weekend hike.

I listened to my mother's *Mile High Woman* album on loop, remembering Clayton's words: *She said it was the sound of you coming into the world.* The music was grand and bursting with life, the album cover featuring a giant Belle in a flowing white dress reclining in a green valley like a sexy Paul Bunyan. I imagined growing my baby, and hearing my own choir as the tiny life entered the world. My own little act of creation.

When after a few months I still wasn't pregnant, we did a bit of research. We started tracking my cycle and making it count.

Months passed, still nothing. So we went to the doctor. I remember there was this oil painting hanging behind his desk, of a cream-colored coyote howling at the moon while a Native American man looked on from a distance surrounded by saguaros. I'd never seen so many desert art clichés in one piece.

The doctor's face was grim as he delivered the results of the tests. "We found scarring in your fallopian tubes, Rhea." He paused. "Have you ever been diagnosed with chlamydia?"

What? Micah let go of my hand. "No."

The doctor nodded knowingly. "There's a chance you might have contracted it in the past without knowing it. When left untreated, it can cause scarring and infertility in women."

I could feel Micah looking at me, but I didn't return his gaze. "Does that mean I can't have children at all?" I asked.

"No. There's an operation we can perform that might help. I also recommend changing your diet and ceasing any alcohol, smoking, or drug use. You want to create a clean environment for the embryo."

I shifted in my seat, my vagina itching like I hadn't washed in days.

We scheduled the procedure, and then we drove home without speaking.

At home, I immediately jumped in the shower and turned it to scalding. I wanted to bend over and let it stream into me, sanitizing my insides.

In college, I had taken an evolutionary biology class that explained to me that the creature inside me wasn't necessarily a creature at all, but a series of survival instincts left over from my primitive ancestors that I couldn't always control, especially before my brain had fully developed. I had seen the double bind we were all in—the gap between our instincts and what society demanded of us. For a while now, I had stopped thinking of myself as the little tortured thing. I felt more in control and less shame.

But I had made the decisions that led me here. I had thought there was liberation in being so reckless with my body, as if it was worth nothing. No matter where the impulse came from, creature or no, it had happened, and now I was paying the price. Regret curdled in my stomach.

At dinner, Micah was the first to break the silence. "I want you to know that I don't blame you."

" . . . Okay."

"Whatever you did before we were together is your business."

I narrowed my eyes at him. "What if *you're* the one who gave me chlamydia?"

"That's unlikely."

"Why?"

"Because I didn't have that many partners before you."

"Neither did I," I said, and it was true. But I couldn't stop picturing the boys I'd slept with in high school, their doughy faces pathetic with surprise beneath me.

"I'm sorry," he said. "I know how that sounded. I was trying too hard to say the right thing."

Of course I knew I was to blame. I had let myself become infected, and now I had a scarred body. "No, this is my punishment," I said in a small voice. "This is what I deserve."

"Hey," he said harshly. "Don't say things like that. Get those thoughts out of your head. You're never going to get pregnant thinking that way."

"But I can't just stop—"

"Don't. Don't say it. You'll have the operation, and then you'll get pregnant. I know it will happen for us. It's just a matter of when."

I nodded, attempting to clear the thoughts, but the regret and shame continued to accumulate as we ate, and I imagined it polluting my body even more.

I felt the overwhelming desire to purge, to flush all of the poison out. I wanted to be clean.

Over the next few months, I changed to a vegan diet and stopped drinking. I swore off all sugar, fat, and preservatives. I only bought produce at farmer's markets, and made elaborate, colorful meals lurid with vitamins.

I surrounded our bed with white chunks of purifying selenite. I got acupuncture once a week. I drove to the outskirts of the city where a friend placed her hands on my womb and removed an energy blockage that I imagined as a thick, gray clot at the center of my belly.

I tried to move through the world in a way that would atone for my sins. I was kinder and more empathetic to everyone I met.

I took in deep cleansing breaths.

When it was time for the procedure, I felt clean and pure, the space inside me as sterile as the operating room where they put me under.

The surgery was successful.

But three months later, there was still no baby.

We tried everything my mother's money could buy—new fertility treatments with sharp-angled acronyms like ART, IVF, FSH. Trips to Spain and Thailand to sample their local fertility offerings. But they simply didn't work.

I remember grieving in a strange void where only I floated, mourning something that had never existed. It was like the grief I had for my parents—amorphous and unjustified, missing someone I did not know nor could picture in my mind with any emotional specificity. It was grief without an object—only a terrible wrongness reaching to every corner of my body.

Micah and I discussed adoption, and while I objectively loved the concept, I could feel myself resisting the notion. It wasn't that I didn't think I could love such a child. There was a surplus of love stored up in my body, ready to be directed at any sweet, vulnerable thing.

But some nights, when Micah was asleep and my thoughts were allowed to ferment undisturbed, I wondered if my infertility was something even more elemental, more *fated* than anything I'd done in this life. Perhaps I was not meant to have children. A girl with a creature inside of her who had no memory of her mother's love and could not control the terrible thoughts that entered her mind. Who sometimes sensed a nameless, shapeless doom on the horizon, waiting for her.

Perhaps such a person was not meant to be a mother.

So I did what people have been doing for centuries to cope with pain—I buried myself in work. If I was unable to create life, at least I could create something else. With my mother's money, I co-financed a documentary investigating a popular company's corrupt business practices, and for the next few months, I lost myself in the greed of strangers.

I drifted to another part of the world I'd built with Micah, far enough away that he couldn't touch me, but close enough that he knew I was still there.

I was working on something important, so he couldn't directly fault it. Instead, he matched my commitment, devoting himself even more obsessively to his own work, spending early mornings and late nights in the hot shop, coming home streaked with ash. We were two dedicated people, working side by side on things we loved, and wasn't there something inherently romantic about that? Even if we'd stopped being romantic with one another? I didn't care if it was delusional; I wanted delusion. It was comfortable. I clung to it.

In February, Hess flew to Arizona to escape the winter, and I put on a happy face. She wanted to go hiking, so we drove two hours north to a trailhead in a valley of red rock formations jutting up from the earth. I had heard of this place from friends who talked of it being an "energy vortex," but Micah and I had never taken the trip.

This was life sucked of moisture, reduced to its vibrant, chalky essence.

And yet for all of its dryness, there was something soft about the air, like an element other than water moved through it, caressing my skin as Hess and I scrambled up the rocky incline.

At the top of the hike, we sat on a large flat rock and looked out over the valley between the two pillars of the cathedral formation. We were the only ones there, and the silence had the same softness as the air, like silk against my eardrums.

I tried to feel for the energy that supposedly buzzed straight from the earth's core up into this rock. Maybe that was the strange softness—the energy releasing and becoming like tiny, smooth particles in the air.

"What's going on, Rhea?"

I tensed, suddenly feeling cornered. It was just me and her up here, with miles of scorching, bone-dry desert spreading out in every direction.

"What do you mean? Everything's good," I said casually, careful not to sound too defensive. Hess knew I'd had an operation to boost my fertility, but I'd downplayed the situation, and she didn't know how long we'd been trying.

She put her hand on mine. "I know you, honey. You can tell me."

I felt a crack form, and something warm and salty leaked into my chest. I was so careful about what I said to Micah for fear that I'd express a toxic thought. Even around friends, when they could stand listening to me talk about fertility, I didn't dare tell them how I was really feeling. Giving air to the thoughts and feelings, I believed, would make them even more poisonous.

But it had been so long since I'd let it all out, and I felt safe with Hess, like maybe it wouldn't count if I told just her. It'd be like talking to myself.

I told her I had tried to make my body into a pure, beautiful place. Somewhere untainted where someone else might want to live.

But it hadn't worked.

And I didn't think it was just bad luck.

The universe knew something I didn't, that there was something inherently wrong with me, and I wasn't supposed to have a baby.

She studied me suspiciously. "What would make you think that? That the universe doesn't want you to have a baby?"

"How else am I supposed to interpret things? It's clearly not in the cards for me."

"That's it?" she asked, and I was a little confused.

"Um . . . yes? What else?"

She looked like she might say more, but then she stopped, and I swear I could see relief pass over her face before she settled into a motherly concern. "Never mind." She paused. "I'm just sorry you've been going through that, honey."

"Thanks." I didn't know what else to say.

"I lost a child once." The words seemed to echo around us, rebounding against the rock. "And I was never the same after. Everyone has their own experience, so I won't pretend I know what you are feeling, because I don't." She looked away and wiped a tear. "But for a long time, I also felt like I hadn't deserved to be a mother. Like there was something deeply wrong with me, and maybe God was punishing me." She looked out over the horizon. "It took me a lot of time, and therapy, to realize that wasn't true." She turned toward me. "So I promise you, it doesn't mean there is something wrong with you, or you're not 'meant' to be a mother."

"Thank you," I said, still shocked by her confession. "I can't believe you went through that."

She shook her head and smiled self-consciously. "It was a long time ago. Eventually, life grew around the loss into something totally unexpected, and I tried to embrace it."

Since the night I met Hess, I had sensed a sort of loneliness in her, and it'd only added depth to her warmth; she was one of those people who cared for others close up, meeting their pain with hers, and not at a distance. I had always thought it came from her never having met the right person, and she'd decided to build a different kind of life instead of wallowing, and I'd respected her for it. But perhaps I'd been wrong—maybe her loneliness was a type of grief.

I waited to see if she would share more, but she just looked out over the parched horizon, lost in her own mind. Maybe one day she would tell me the whole story.

"Did my mom have a hard time getting pregnant?" I asked.

She broke from her reverie and shook her head. "No, she didn't. I think it happened pretty easily, actually."

I couldn't help feeling jealous; of course Belle had been effortlessly fertile. "Did she ever want more kids?"

Hess thought for a moment. "There was some talk, but I think you were enough for her."

Perhaps there was comfort in that—my mother had been grateful for what she had. She didn't waste time yearning for what was not.

As we made our way down with the sun at our backs, chasing our shadows across the rocks, I thought of what she'd said—*life grew around the loss.*

Off the highway, Hess pulled over at a burger place styled like an old Western saloon. I studied the laminated menu, searching for any item made of plants. When the waiter came by, Hess ordered two double cheeseburgers, a basket of fries, and two beers. I ordered a salad and a water for myself, and Hess raised an eyebrow but conceded.

When our food came, the pile of mixed greens was soggy with balsamic. I looked over at Hess's plate. It had been months since I'd let myself have anything resembling a cheeseburger with its dirty fats and preservatives. It looked so good it glistened.

"You don't have to keep punishing yourself."

"There's nothing wrong with taking care of my body."

"Of course not. I do the same. But we all need little pleasures." She smiled slightly, picked up her knife and fork, and cut a piece of the burger. She put the small bite on the edge of my salad bowl, the red fat-sequined juices running into the mound of wet leaves. I stared at it, canines itching. Then I took the piece between my fingers and stuffed it in my mouth.

It was golden soft and fatty against my teeth. Salty and cheesy and tangy against my tongue. When it was gone, my mouth vibrated for more.

She pushed her beer toward me, and I took a furtive sip. It was cold and herbal sliding down my throat. I took another sip, the liquid flowing through my veins, and my body sighed.

She cut another piece, this one larger, and I stuffed that in as well. She cut bite after bite until the burger was finished, and I was forced to stop.

I leaned back in the chair, belly protruding and eyelids heavy. I yearned to lie down.

She flagged down the waiter and asked them to wrap up another cheeseburger. "Let's go," she said, and I followed her out into the purple light.

I had not been living these past months—only retreating, hiding, starving all other parts of my being except for the one that loved to dig against the surface and uncover some other truth to bury myself in.

Hess's words repeated once again in my head:

Life grew around the loss.

Back at the house, we found Micah eating a burrito alone at the kitchen table, and Hess said a quick hello and headed to her room.

"How was the hike?" he asked.

"Fine," I answered blandly. We were so careful with one another now. "We can't keep living like this," I said before I could chicken out.

"Like what?" he asked, turning to face me. I could tell he knew what I meant, but he wanted me to say it.

"Like this." I gestured at the distance between our bodies.

"I know," he said, meeting my eyes. "I was trying to give you space. I thought that's what you wanted."

"I did, but—" I took a deep breath. "It's been hard for me to talk to you because I feel like you don't want to hear what I have to say."

"Of course I want to hear—"

"Even if it seems toxic and fatalistic to you?"

He exhaled. "I'm not saying you can't have those kind of thoughts, just that it's not good to dwell on them. What is the point?"

"Sometimes I can't help it. Sometimes I think there is something wrong with me, and as much as I don't want to and would like to be a different person, I can't not think it. That's just how my mind works."

He nodded slowly, contemplating.

"And I feel so bad about it, and I keep it bottled up because you don't want to hear it, and it's easier to just not say anything than make up something inane to say instead."

He kept nodding. "Okay. I'm sorry. I wasn't trying to—I just." He sighed. "I think about my brother and how he used to wallow in all these terrible, negative thoughts, and he would get in this really bad place, and eventually, you know, he just couldn't take it, and it scares me to think—"

"I'm not your brother," I cut in before he could take it there.

"I know."

"I can have negative thoughts, and everything will still be okay."

"I believe you." He folded his hands on the table and looked up at me. "All right. I'm ready to listen now."

"Are you sure?"

"Yes. Please. I want to know." His eyes sparkled with genuine interest, and I remembered why I'd first fallen in love with him.

So I told him what I'd been holding back the past few months—my fear that something was inherently wrong with me, or that I was being punished, or that the universe knew something I didn't, that I wasn't meant to have a child.

I didn't tell him everything in my head because some of it was only for me.

But he listened this time and didn't cut me off. I told him I wanted to find our way back to each other, to the closeness we had when we'd carried our home on our backs.

If our family together was only me and him, then I was okay with that. It was so much more than I had ever had before I met him, when I was just an angry, lonely teenager. I would no longer organize my life around this void at the center of it, and I would stop punishing myself for whatever sins, real or imagined, that may have led me here.

I wanted to live again.

27

lulabelle

1976

SIX YEARS LEFT

For the next few weeks, it felt like the grief was transforming my body. Every morning I woke to waves of sickness, brought on by the memory of what had happened to Tate. I could barely eat, and when I did, I couldn't keep it down. I was exhausted, and I spent days on end in bed. Various bowls and casserole dishes surrounded the mattress from people who had come by to take care of me, and when I couldn't bear to leave the room, I peed in these and left them on the floor.

I'm not sure how long this went on. But one morning I woke up and felt better.

In fact, I felt wonderful. I walked stiffly into the bathroom and looked in the mirror. I'd lost weight from my convalescence, but somehow my boobs had grown. My complexion was milky and mixed with light. Mourning had endowed me with a tragic beauty. I was radiant with grief.

But above all, I was *hungry*. No, not hungry. *Ravenous*.

I called Phoebe, who was in town, and she came right over with a sack of cheeseburgers. She took one look at me and her face dropped. "Dear God."

"I know, right? I'm *gorgeous*. Look at this shit!" I twirled around in front of her.

"No, Lou." She put a hand on my shoulder and lowered me to the couch. "I don't know how to say this." She looked like she had before Tate's funeral, when she tried to get me out of bed.

"What? Did something happen? Is everyone okay?" If someone else had died, I'd take my beautiful ass to some cliff and jump right off.

"No, everyone is fine. It's nothing like that." She took a deep breath. "But darlin', I think you're pregnant."

Everything stopped for a moment.

I'd been careful. So fucking careful. I was on the new pill they offered, and it'd felt like armor against such threats. I'd imagined my body made of steel. *Impregnable.*

Then, I felt a flicker of something. Not like I was special, exactly, but like I'd been touched by a bit of magic. There was a kernel inside me that contained infinite lives. The last fragment of my relationship with Tate, this little memento of our journey together. I imagined his soft golden hair glinting on the head of a small child.

At the image of this tiny, innocent figure, a thick dread began to seep coldly down my throat and over my ribs. It covered every other thought and feeling in its muck.

What if it was a girl?

I had told myself years ago that I would never inflict my curse on another human being, especially my own child. How could I deliberately put her through such pain, of first my loss, and then her own doomed existence?

It was one of the reasons I'd ended things with Hess.

God, *Hess.*

The person I never let myself think of, and the one I thought of every day anyway.

I imagined her sitting there with me, perched on the arm of the couch as Phoebe delivered the news. She would have been so happy. It was what she'd dreamed of: a little family of our own.

Every time I'd contemplated going back to her over the years, I'd told myself it was the wrong thing to do. But the truth was, I was ashamed.

I had taken her tender loving care for granted, fashioned it into a trap. And look at where I'd ended up without it. I would never regret my time with Tate because of what it led me to, but it was undeniable that the years had been hard on me. There I was: no music in my head, a baby in my belly, my body and mind barely hanging on.

And so what if Hess didn't believe in the curse? Who would want to believe their love was going to die so soon? She didn't let things like mortality get in the way of her enjoying life and caring for other people the way I did.

I had wanted to protect her, of course. But who was I to make that decision for her? Who knew when she or anyone else would die? Look at Tate.

I was such a goddamn fool.

She was my Great Love, and she was *alive*, but at any moment, she could be taken from this world just like him. How had I spent four years without her? How could I live one more moment on this earth without being in her presence?

I had six years left.

And I wanted to spend them loving someone and being loved by them. I wanted to give Hess what she'd always wanted, the love and family she deserved.

And just maybe, if I was lucky, I could give it to her now.

~

Phoebe took me to the doctor, and they confirmed her suspicions. I was knocked up.

She knew how I felt about children, so she didn't treat it like this great miracle as the nurses had at the doctor's office. She solemnly watched the road as she drove me home, and I stared out the window, trying to organize my thoughts.

An image came to me of my aunt laid out on a bed when I was about six years old. The granny witch dangled a gold band from a string over her pregnant belly, and the entire family watched, our breaths held. The ring finally moved, making a circle over the bump, and my uncle grunted in the corner.

Another goddamn girl.

Back at home, I went to my bedroom and Phoebe followed, saying, "Lou, we need to make a plan—" But I held a hand up, cutting her off. I lay down on the bed, then I unclasped the simple silver chain around my neck and took off the wedding ring Phoebe had loaned me for the doctor's office. I strung the gold band on the chain and reclasped it, letting it hang down like a hypnotizing instrument.

I took a deep breath and held it above my belly.

"What are you doing?" Phoebe asked, bewildered.

"Please. Just watch. I want to try something."

She didn't say another word, and we both stared intently at the necklace.

Slowly, the thread of metal started to move, the gold glinting as it swung back and forth over my middle in a straight line.

I exhaled, and Phoebe instinctively did the same, not knowing what had just happened.

I was having a boy.

And he would not be cursed.

I knew I wasn't meant to be a mother. I was too wild and strange, and I would be gone before he really remembered me.

But Hess certainly was.

He belonged to her. I knew this in my bones.

When I died, I wouldn't be leaving him or Hess behind, alone. I'd be leaving them with each other. This child would not grow up motherless as I had, but with the best mother I could imagine, the woman who had saved me time and again.

"What just happened?" Phoebe asked, dumbfounded.

"Have you heard from Hess lately?" I responded, ignoring her question.

"What?" Her name hadn't been spoken between us in four years. "Why?"

"I just need to know. Tell me what she's been up to."

"Lord, you have lost your mind," she began, but I pleaded, "Please."

She sat down on the bed and exhaled. "She moved back home after y'all parted ways. Got sucked back into her parents' fancy world, going to all the society parties and whatever else rich people do. Shove tennis rackets up each other's butts, who knows."

I laughed for the first time in weeks.

"I don't hear from her too often. I think I remind her of you, and it hurts too much." She bit her lip, and I knew something was coming.

"Come on. Give it to me straight. I can handle it."

"About a month ago, I got an invitation in the mail. For her wedding. She's getting married to this guy whose family owns all the gas stations in the state. Never met him before."

I was speechless. I couldn't believe she'd fallen for someone else. And a *man* at that. While I'd always been attracted to both sides, Hess had told me men did nothing for her.

"Does she love him?"

"Lou, I don't know. She's getting married to him, so that has to mean something, right? Should we be talking about this right now? There are bigger things to worry about." She put her hand on mine and lowered her voice. "I know someone who can help you. It's safe. Not like what you hear sometimes. He's a real doctor."

"Can you ask her for me?"

"Lou, come on. She's marrying the guy tomorrow. I'm not doing that to her."

Phoebe's heart was in the right place. But I needed to know for myself. I wasn't going to give her up not knowing.

I told myself I'd just ask her, and if she was happy, I'd let her go. I really would.

I'd never been to Hess's house before. Her family didn't exactly approve of "hillbilly music" and all the shady types that played it, and I'd never been real eager to meet them either. I can't stand people who think they're better than anyone else.

But good lord, their house was magnificent. It rose up like a Greek temple on this big piece of land surrounded by trees. I parked my car down the road and walked through the woods so I wouldn't be spotted by the people moving in and out of the house. Phoebe's invitation said the wedding would be at the First Baptist Church followed by a reception in the ballroom at the Walker Estate.

I stood there in the trees like a little dirt child, studying the house and wondering how exactly I was going to get in to see her.

At the side facing me, I spotted a large oak tree with a thick, gnarled limb reaching out toward a balcony on the third floor. I remembered Hess's story of the oak she climbed down to sneak out for shows in high school.

Bingo.

I ran across the open lawn, praying no one would see me. I usually didn't run unless I was being chased, but I was fast when I did. I reached the side of the house mercifully undetected and flattened myself against it to catch my breath.

I'd decided to wear heels because I wanted to look good for Hess, but now I was forced to kick them off into the grass. I wrapped my arms around the trunk of the tree and used my bare feet to inch my way up until I could grab hold of the lowest branch. I climbed from branch to branch, flexing the old muscles. Soon I was on the final limb arcing out over the terrace, and I quietly jumped down onto the tiled floor.

The doors were curtained, but I could see a light was on inside. I put my ear up to the glass. I'd imagined a room of female relatives that I'd have to contend with. But it was strangely quiet.

I tested the knob and found it unlocked, so I slowly pushed it in and stepped inside. The room was a riot of pink and white lace, a little princess bedroom that I'd have mocked back in the day. In one corner, a white vanity was strewn with makeup and hot rollers. Dresses and suits were heaped on the bed.

But the room was empty.

My heart dropped—she'd already left for the church. I was too late.

And then, she was walking out of the closet, already in her wedding dress but with the curlers still in her hair.

My entire body stilled, and a glorious feeling rang through me. It was like music, but without the sound.

She froze at the sight of me. I saw relief pass through her, but then there was something else. A shadow like anger. She set her mouth in a straight line, went over to her vanity, and started unraveling the curlers.

"Who let you in here?"

She said it like I was some cat burglar. I knew I deserved it, but it still hurt like hell.

"Nobody. I climbed up the tree." I pointed toward the open doorway of the terrace.

She looked down at my feet, bare once again, like the first time I came to her years ago. A little smile poked through, and she exhaled loudly, "Oh, Lou." There she was. The Hess I knew. But then her face hardened, and she was gone once again. "What in the world are you doing here?"

"I just need to ask you a question."

She arched an eyebrow. "You need to ask me a question."

"Yes. Just one question. And then I'll go. I swear."

She paused for a moment. "Okay. Fine. What is it?"

Here it was. The moment of truth. "Do you love him?"

Her face contorted. "*Do I love him?* That's your question?" She waited as if I might respond. "How dare you come here and ask me that. *On my wedding day.* You're exactly the same, aren't you? Still only thinking of yourself." She turned back toward the mirror and yanked violently on a curler.

"Please, just tell me if you love him. If you do, I'll go away. I promise."

"What does it matter, Lou? It's none of your business. You made sure it was none of your business. That was *your* decision."

"I know. I'm sorry. I'm so sorry I hurt you. It hurt me, too. You don't know how hard it was."

This made her even more mad. "*I don't know?* I don't know how hard it was? Have you lost your mind?" She shot hairspray at the curls, slashing the can through the air and filling it with toxic fumes.

I was getting frustrated. She was taking it all wrong. This was not how it was supposed to go. "Hess, goddammit, do you love him? Do you love the rat bastard? Just answer the goddamn question!"

"NO!! OKAY? I DON'T LOVE HIM," she screeched. I'd never heard her raise her voice like that.

Her shoulders drooped, and she looked back at the mirror, gently combing out an unruly curl. "Of course I don't love him. But this is my life now," she said quietly, tears collecting at the corners of her eyes. "I think you should go."

I went over to her and got on my knees, but I didn't touch her. I sensed that would be a mistake. "This doesn't have to be your life." She turned her head and looked into my eyes as I continued. "I made a mistake. I never should have asked you to go. I love you, Hess. You are my great love, and I want to be together. For the rest of our lives."

She turned away, her voice now thick with tears. "You have no idea how much I've wanted to hear you say that. I used to think you'd show up one day and realize your mistake. But you never came, and I moved on from that fantasy. I can't risk feeling like that again. It was too painful."

"I understand. I really do. But it will be different this time. We won't be just you and me, hiding in my bedroom at Clayton's. I want to be a family. A real family. Like you wanted."

"What do you mean? How can we be a real family?"

"I'm pregnant."

Hess whipped back toward me. "What?"

"I'm going to have a baby, and I want it to be yours. I mean, it is yours. Already. He's your baby."

Her eyes were shining, but it wasn't just sorrow now. "He?"

"It's a little boy, and you're his mama. I just know it."

Her expression hardened. "Now, wait a minute. How did you get pregnant? Who is the father?"

My breath hitched. I wasn't prepared to talk about Tate. I'd forgotten he was a part of this at all. "The father is a man named Tate Larsen. We were sort of together for the last few years."

Hess narrowed her eyes. "I've heard. Won't he be upset if you take his baby away from him?" Her voice had returned to its icy tone.

"You don't have to worry about him."

Her face reddened. "So you're still treating people like dirt, huh? No thank you, I don't want any part in this. You need to leave now."

"Stop. Just listen. You don't have to worry about him because he's dead. Overdosed. A few weeks ago."

Hess paled. "Good Jesus. I didn't know." We sat there in silence for a few beats. She had avoided making eye contact since I'd arrived, but now she really looked at me, her gaze reaching deep inside to my little demon child heart.

She got on her knees with her wedding dress pooling around her, and she pulled me into her arms. I laid my head on her chest, and the glorious feeling rang through me once again.

"He was a complicated man, but I loved him. Not like I love you, but like a real friend who truly knew me." I paused, imagining if Tate had been able to meet Hess. "I think he'd be happy for his baby to have a mama like you." Hess's chest contracted against my cheek, and I held her tighter.

When I finally pulled back, she deflated a bit and looked in the mirror. Even with mascara running down her cheeks, she was still a goddess. "Good lord, Lou. I'm supposed to get married in an hour. Daddy had two hundred lobsters flown in from Maine."

"Fuck 'em."

She laughed. "That's not very nice. You know, the rat bastard isn't such a rat bastard. He's a perfectly fine person."

"I'm sure he's not a total devil if you decided to spend eternity with him." I tried to get real serious. "But this is bigger than other people, and bigger than lobsters. This is us, Hess. This is everything."

A knock came from the door, and then an older woman's elegant voice trilled, "Hestia, darling? It's time to go to the church. Are you ready?" The door started to open, but Hess flew across the room and slammed it shut. She turned the lock.

"What on earth? What's going on?"

"It's nothing, Mother! I need a couple more minutes to myself. I'll be down in just a few!"

"Young lady, you open this door right now. What has gotten into you?"

Hess locked eyes with me and whispered, "What are we going to do?"

"Is someone in there with you? Let me in this instant!" the mother crowed.

"We can leave the way I came." I flashed a wily grin at Hess and gestured toward the terrace.

"But you're pregnant!"

"I was pregnant when I came up just a minute ago. And besides, it ain't much of a baby yet. He'll be fine."

A deeper voice came from behind the door. "Hestia Walker. Open this door at once. It's time to go to the church."

"Just a minute!"

Hess and I ran out to the terrace. I jumped on to the branch and eased from limb to limb, going a bit more slowly this time, knowing it would make Hess less nervous. When I got to the bottom, I watched as she wobbled in heels on the top limb with her wedding dress bunched around her legs. As she moved toward the trunk, the tulle snagged on a branch and tore in half. She cursed and tied the rest into a knot between her legs, kicked off the heels, and swung the rest of the way down like an ape.

As she touched down below the tree, someone yelled from the driveway that they'd spotted Hess. We took off in our bare feet across the lawn and made it to the woods with a few of the staff chasing us.

But they were no match for a country girl and Hess's long goddess legs. We moved swiftly through the trees, floating on a joy that I could barely contain. When we reached my car, Hess got in on the driver's side out of habit, but I pushed her over and took the wheel. I floored it, quickly putting distance between us and the property, and she shrieked as she tore off the rest of the tulle and threw it out the window.

Moments later, I skidded into my driveway, and we ran from the car to the house. Before the door had even closed behind us, I jumped into Hess's arms and wrapped my legs around her. She pushed me against the wall and we kissed ferociously, painfully, trying to get too close too fast, jamming years of desire into the space of a moment.

Hess pulled her head from mine, and we caught our breaths. I put my mouth gently on hers, savoring it this time, the feeling of her washing over me with each small movement.

I guided her toward the bedroom at the back of the house with my legs still wrapped around her waist. She laid me down on the bed, and I was eighteen again, finding real love for the first time in motel rooms sweltering with summer heat. I flipped over on top of her, and I was twenty-one again, filled with the confidence of someone who thinks love will never leave them. I bent down and kissed her, and I was twenty-seven, scarred by heartbreak and ever closer to death, someone who vowed never to leave this woman as long as I walked the earth.

28

rhea

2009

When I turned thirty-two, Hess threw me a birthday party in Nashville.

Lanterns hung from the hulking trees in her backyard and fairy lights twinkled from the bushes like fireflies. I could see the real thing blinking in the darkness beyond the light and roar of the party, and I had that feeling again, that this was a place of more magic and meaning than others, Hess's place of peace. I saw her at the far end of the yard talking to one of Martha's old protégés, and we briefly met eyes.

Micah joined me at the deck railing and gently pulled my hair back to place a soft kiss on my neck. Feist's "I Feel It All" came on the outdoor speakers, and it was like Martha was there for a moment, selecting the perfect song. We touched our heads together, and I let myself disappear for a moment.

"How are you holding up?" he whispered in my ear.

Every year we'd been married, he'd dutifully abstained from celebrating my birthday—he would let me lie in bed all day and watch TV alone as I waited for the dread to recede, delivering my favorite foods on trays like offerings and excusing himself quietly from the room.

But this year something felt different, and I'd finally caved to Hess and the girls' desire to celebrate. The dread was still there, but I could treat it as an unwelcome house guest who would be leaving in the morning.

"I'm doing all right."

Phoebe sashayed through the crowd toward us, balancing a plate of mini cheeseburgers and three cups of punch. "Food and drink for the birthday queen," she said, bowing. I took a cup from her and stuffed one of the burgers into my mouth. "Your mama's favorite," she purred.

Tima came up behind us and knocked her cup against mine. "Happy birthday, baby. The thirties are the best decade." She paused. "That is, until you hit the forties." She winked.

"What about the fifties?"

She flicked a wrist in the air. "Divine."

After I scarfed a few more of the dollhouse cheeseburgers, Phoebe whirled toward the crowd. "C'mon, y'all. It's time for presents."

She led me over to a chair tied with balloons in the shape of a "3" and "2" and everyone clustered around me like I was a bratty five-year-old. Hess watched from across the circle with amusement playing over her face; she knew how much I hated to be the center of attention.

After opening a few gifts, Micah came toward me with a box. I could tell by the cautious way he walked that there was glass inside.

I carefully took it from him and balanced it on my lap, holding my breath. Even now, after years of being surrounded by his glass creations and opening countless fragile gifts, I was still afraid I would shatter it.

I opened the lid and pushed aside the tissue paper to reveal a dark-purple shape attached to a length of fishing line. I pulled it out, suspending it in the air so that everyone could see. The glass sparkled mysteriously in the light, the color deep and impenetrable.

It took me a moment, but when it came together in my mind, my stomach turned.

It was a tree branch extended horizontally through the air, like the birthmark on my chest.

My stomach churned more violently, and I winced, nearly dropping the sculpture. Micah lurched forward and took it from my hand, and I doubled over. Hess quickly led me to the trash can where I vomited pink chunks in front of the party guests.

Inside the house, I lay down in the bedroom. Micah was sent to the store for Gatorade and medicine while Phoebe played doctor, with Hess and Tima looking on.

"What are your symptoms?"

"Vomiting, obviously. A bit of a headache. I've been sick in general lately, but I think it's all the travel I've been doing." *And the birthday dread*, I didn't say. I'd been traveling recently for a documentary series that was getting some publicity.

Phoebe was uncharacteristically quiet, and I glanced over to find her looking very concerned. "What?"

"I'm not sure I should say it."

"Oh my god, what is it? What's wrong with me?"

"No, it's not that, I just . . ."

"Jesus Christ, Feebs, just spit it out."

She sighed. "I think you might be pregnant."

My heart stopped, and my skin went cold. Years ago, I might have felt a high, manic hope at these words, but I had since inoculated myself against that feeling. Instead, I went straight to tense, pragmatic anxiety.

Micah and I no longer had the dutiful monthly sex in anticipation of ovulation. We had sex when we wanted to, and I'm sure many of those times had been during that window, but nothing had come of it for years.

Now, *this*.

Had I even had my period last month? I didn't think so. And the month before that? It had been so light, I hadn't had to use a tampon, but I hadn't paid much attention. With all of the travel, I'd lost track of my body in time.

I did some quick math, still adept at such equations. *Twelve weeks.* One of the magic numbers of pregnancy when the chance of miscarriage plummets.

I could be twelve weeks if this was real.

Hess helped me up and led me into the bathroom. From deep in the recesses of the cabinet, she pulled a pregnancy test. We all stared at her, and she gave us an incredulous look. "What?"

"What are *you* doing with a pregnancy test?" Phoebe asked for all of us.

She sneered like we were being ridiculous. "My assistant was trying to get pregnant a few years ago and kept some boxes here." She examined it. "Hasn't expired yet."

Hess handed it to me, and I carefully slid the test out of its wrapper and squatted over the toilet while they averted their eyes. A few trickles came down, and I caught them on the tip without getting my fingertips wet. I was a pro.

I replaced the plastic cap, laid the stick face up on the counter, and set the timer on my phone like Micah always did. He insisted we adhere to the instructions every time.

Hess and I sat on the edge of the tub, out of view of the test, and Phoebe and Tima leaned against the wall.

"How are you feeling?" Hess asked.

"I don't know." I eyed the timer on my phone. Three minutes and thirty seconds left.

We were quiet for a moment, then Hess said, "Did you know I was there when you were born?"

"Really?"

Hess smiled. "Yes, ma'am. Of course, your father had already passed, and I didn't want Lou to be alone. The nurse actually tried to kick me out of the delivery room, but I said something quite unladylike, and she let me stay."

"What did you say?"

Hess only smirked in response. "Lou had to have an emergency

C-section, so she was knocked out when you were born. Your first cry was this powerful, earth-shattering shriek, as if you were *life* itself. I was the first one who held you, and I remember looking down at your face, so angry and determined. When you opened your eyes, I saw you, already in there, ready to take on the world."

I tried to imagine myself as a tiny being entering this life for the first time, full of fury.

My phone blared, signaling the time was up. We all stared at the test from across the room, unmoving.

"What's going on?" Micah asked from behind us. He was holding a canvas bag and studying us curiously.

"Phoebe thinks I could be pregnant." I met his eyes. "I could be twelve weeks."

"Holy shit," he whispered.

"I took a test."

"What did it say?"

"We haven't looked yet." I nodded toward the test balanced on the rim of the sink.

He walked furtively over and peered into the little window. His back was turned to me, so I couldn't see his face.

"Well?"

He turned around, and his eyes were wet. I lunged across the bathroom and snatched the stick. In the window, there were two lines. *Two miraculous lines.*

Phoebe grabbed it from my hand and shrieked, but I still couldn't feel anything. My body wouldn't let me be disappointed one more time; this must be some sort of trick.

"I'm going to be a dad . . ." Micah said dreamily, and I grabbed his wrist.

"No. Stop." As if Hess read my mind, she pulled the rest of the boxes from beneath the sink and handed them to me. I unpackaged every test so that they formed a fan in my hand and squatted over the toilet. "Just wait a second." I searched for some secret reserve of pee deep inside my body and squeezed it out onto the sticks.

This time, the minutes passed quickly. When Micah's phone went off, he and Phoebe eagerly checked them.

He came over to me with the tears collecting in the rims of his eyes, and put his arms around me. "They're all positive." He squeezed me hard. "You did it. We're having a baby."

Something gave way inside me, and all of the feeling I'd been suppressing for the last few years rushed forward in a dizzying flood. I wept into his shoulder, and I felt Hess and the girls come around my back and wrap their arms, so that I was encircled on both sides. I should have hated it, but for some reason it didn't feel suffocating.

My body was a place of love. And someone, or for now, *something*, had decided to stay.

29

lulabelle

1977

SIX YEARS LEFT

I was listening to Linda Martell's "Color Him Father" on the record player when my contractions started. That first pain rolled through, and I thought, *Here we go.*

I didn't say anything to Hess at first. She'd never seen a baby get born, so I knew she'd be flying off the handle and rushing us out the door. But I'd seen plenty of births, and it took hours. I wanted to spend as little time at the hospital as possible.

I'd wanted to give birth at the house, but Hess had insisted on a hospital, and she'd eventually worn me down. She'd heard horror stories from friends about complications that only a doctor could fix. Even though I'd left the holler behind, I'd imagined myself giving birth at home with the old granny witch catching it. I'd watched her put her hands on my aunt and sense the geological shifts happening inside, responding in kind. She treated women with animal tenderness. I couldn't imagine anything better than that.

I switched the player to an album by a band called the Runaways that Martha had given me. The guitar chopped rhythmically through the air, and the pain pulsed with it. The women screamed from the speaker, and my body screamed with them. I rode the waves from song to song, willing myself to hold on.

When the contractions got so quick and intense that I was having a hard time breathing, I hollered for Hess. She took one look at me and knew what I'd done, but she hid her anger as she helped me into the Gran Torino.

I made it to the hospital intact. The nurses did not share our sense of urgency. I wanted to scream as they casually found my chart, put me in a wheelchair, and rolled me into the delivery room. It was cold and smelled like a factory floor. I felt like I was about to be plucked and stripped.

A nurse came into the room and checked me out, then left without a word. No one would tell us anything. I'd decided to have him without drugs because of my past, but the nurse kept pushing them on me anyway. *Are you sure? Do you understand the pain in store?* As if I was a child who couldn't make decisions for herself. I knew pain. I knew it better than she could comprehend.

Sometime later, as the pain took over, I thought back to her words and wondered if I'd let my own pride get the better of me.

It was truly remarkable.

The waves of pain crested higher and higher, while the relief in between got shorter. The nurse kept telling me to breathe, but how the hell was I supposed to breathe through something like that? I kept getting out of bed, looking for some way to escape the pain. But the nurse kept forcing me back down, making me lie still like a child at nap time. Hess was there for every moment, humming some new melody in my ear, and I clung to it like a raft.

When it was time to push, I felt something leave me, and I looked woozily over at my hand hanging there alone with the gold wedding band digging into my bloated finger. It was Hess's idea to tell people I'd been married to Tate; that way the doctors and nurses would treat me well, and the new baby wouldn't be shunned for being a bastard.

My head swiveled to the other side of the room, where they were trying to force Hess out the door. A panic rose at the thought of not having her there. I just knew I'd fade away and the baby would fade with me if she left. I tried to cry out in objection, but the pain strangled the sound from my throat. It came out as an animal grunt.

Hess said something to the nurse I couldn't make out, and the nurse's face drained of color. She backed away from Hess and came back over to me with her rubber gloves, ready to assist the doctor.

Hess returned to her spot by my head and gripped my hand. She said I could squeeze as hard as I needed to.

At the other end of me, a harsh voice told me to stop pushing. I could feel it. Something was wrong. His hands were probing inside me and creating sharp, pinching pains where before the pain had been more global, like tectonic plates moving.

Then they were wheeling me down the hallway, and Hess refused once again to leave me. No one told us what was going on. In the operating room, I was strapped down like a mental patient and administered drugs without anyone asking me. As I tried to struggle against it, I fell back into a familiar oblivion.

I'd have thought it would be a relief to finally return to that place.

But the nothingness felt wrong. I couldn't see or hear very well, like a glaze had been applied to my perception, and my thoughts came slow and syrupy. When I tried to move my body, it was no longer under my control.

A panic seized me, but I was locked in, unable to articulate this to even Hess. Not even able to squeeze her hand.

I sank into the panic, and at some point I was lost to a deeper nothing.

Next thing I remember was hearing a little melody in my head, and for a moment, I thought music had returned to me. I lay there, trying to soak it in. There was something familiar about it that I couldn't place yet.

I opened my eyes, and I saw a fuzzy Hess pacing in front of the bed with a bundle cradled in her arms. That new melody hummed from her throat.

She saw that I was awake, and she smiled at me. Everything was softer about her, like God had rounded her edges and mixed light with her colors. The bundle gurgled, and I saw that it was the baby. Small and red and swaddled in white cotton.

Hess swayed toward the side of the bed, and I could see the baby better now, covered in fine, dark hair and sleeping peacefully in the nest of his mother's arms.

"Meet our daughter, Rhea. Named for the Greek goddess." She smiled shyly. "Only if you like it, of course, but it feels so perfect—"

"You mean our son."

"No, darling, she's a girl."

"No. I had a boy."

"Lou—"

"It's a mistake. It has to be. They gave you the wrong baby." My face was cold, and I couldn't get enough air.

Hess frowned softly. "I saw them pull her out of you with my own eyes." She folded back the blanket to reveal a dark-purple birthmark reaching across the baby's collarbone like the devil's gnarled finger. "She's hard to miss."

My stomach churned, and my mouth filled with saliva. I leaned over and vomited onto the linoleum.

Hess jumped back and clutched the baby to her chest. "Oh, honey, let me get you a nurse."

I lay back on the bed. Cold sweat beaded on my cheeks.

How had I let this happen?

Shame oozed into my hollow stomach, and I thought I might be sick again.

Another demon child. Another soul brought into this world, cursed from the start.

Hess, still holding the baby, returned with a nurse, and she cleaned me up and gave me fluids. She said it was perfectly normal, but I doubted most mothers got sick at the sight of their own babies.

When the nurse left, Hess tried to put the baby in my arms. "She's hungry, darling. She needs to be fed."

But I couldn't look at either of them. I turned over and pretended to fall asleep, and Hess gave up.

Later, I woke to a room blue with dusk. Hess was gone, but the baby was there, sleeping in a bassinet next to my bed.

She stirred and wriggled. Then she opened her black eyes and stared hard into mine. An understanding passed between us like electricity, crackling through my insides and filling me with charged love.

She was such fragile magic. It felt wrong that she should be outside me now, where she was vulnerable to the elements. The cold, abrasive air. The stinging smell of the hospital. The intrusion of its noises. It had been so much easier to protect her when she was inside of me.

I thought of my own mother, never given the opportunity to hold her baby. She wasn't there to protect me once I was out.

I reached into the bassinet, and I took the baby into my arms, resting her head on my chest. Her mouth opened like a baby bird, searching for my tit, and I pulled it out and helped her latch on to the nipple. She sucked, and this wave of feeling rose and washed over me.

I was here. I could protect her.

I imagined my body hardening and expanding, growing beyond the confines of the room, reaching up into the air until it towered above the hospital and the city beyond. I would hold her in my giant hand, shielding her from the evils of the world.

A grand, heroic music entered my vision, surrounding my towering body and ringing out over the mountains in the distance like God's choir. I realized it was the sound I'd been searching for since I got clean.

I would become so large and imposing, so unstoppable, that the devil couldn't slide me down his gullet, no matter the curse. I would be five thousand feet tall, one mile high, my wig puncturing the sky.

I would defy time and space, and Rhea would be safe.

30

rhea

2009

At first my body just roiled, like the ocean was churning in my gut. I didn't know if it was anxiety, or the swirling, sucking motion of life being made.

Then, I became a fertile, supernatural creature. My pubic hair grew into a long luxurious beard, and my nails grew into strong white talons. At night, I prowled around the neighborhood with my newly powerful nose, smelling desert jasmine, fresh mulch, meat charring on the grill.

When I saw the shadow on the ultrasound, batting at something unseen, it was difficult to grasp it was happening inside me. When I thought about it too hard, I would sometimes seize up, imagining how claustrophobic it must be inside the tight, dark space of my body, and I would have to push the image away.

The doctor moved the wand around, and there was a flash of silver I couldn't identify. She pointed and said, *Look, right there. The little penis.*

It was a boy.

When he started to kick, he felt like a dolphin flicking his fins against my insides. He demanded food at all hours of the day, and I was happy to oblige him, cramming in stacks of banana pancakes and well-cooked cheeseburgers and heaps of vegetables whenever I could. I was proud of how strong he seemed, my big, vital baby. Perhaps my creature would make a good boy—the raw energy of it creating a powerful specimen in my abdomen.

But that wouldn't be all he was—he was also half Micah, and so he would be sweet and contemplative. Micah made a playlist of soft indie music for him—dubbed amniotic rock—and we listened to it in the car, imagining him floating in his little ocean with his arms waving in wonder, surrounded by the gossamer sounds of Fleet Foxes and Band of Horses.

I also played Belle's music for him, running through her entire catalogue, from the Clayton albums to *The Cursed Woman* to *Mile High Woman* and her other pop albums. If he would never meet her, at least he would know her voice, and how she'd seen the world through her many transformations.

When I called Hess with updates, she was so happy that it was almost like getting to tell my own mother and feeling the warmth of bringing a new member of the family into the world. The pride of having fulfilled some sort of ancient duty, as archaic as it sounded.

I didn't want to just pick a name out of a book. I wanted to somehow discover it in nature—a name with a greater meaning that would root him to the world. We thought of naming him after Micah's brother Kenny, or perhaps Tate, after my father, but I worried it would be a bad omen to name a child after men who had died so young.

Everywhere Micah and I went, there were now the three of us, the little world I'd dreamed of just coming into being. We talked about how we would do things differently than how we were raised—we would not shame him for his emotions. We would encourage his talents. We would, above all, make him feel loved in a way that we were never loved.

We knew this was a futile exercise—there was only so much you could control, of course, we knew that—but what was the harm in fantasizing? Sometimes it felt like the baby was creating me, rather than me creating him—I was calmer, happier, less prone to anxiety and dread. As unnatural as it was for me, I was able to lean into the joy without reservation.

When I was twenty weeks, I dreamt I was back on that rocky cliff in California with Shelli, except this time there was a crowd of people there both alive and dead—Hess, Martha, Micah and his brother, Dinah—and we were all passing the Mad Dog bottle and having a wonderful time.

When I walked to the tip of the ledge to jump, they cheered me on.

This time the quarry water was warm, and I sank instantly into that sliver of night beneath the surface. I floated serenely until my foot kicked against whatever that slick, solid thing had been. I tried to swim to the surface, but this time it caught my ankle, and it started to pull me down.

I looked beneath me and saw the man in white from my mushroom vision, his skin glowing in the murk, his long, thin fingers wrapped around my ankle like jellyfish tendrils. I could see the outlines of his face rippling in his own light, fine-boned and feminine at one angle, then almost brutish in another. For a moment, we stared at each other, unmoving.

Then from up above, breaking through the surface, I heard a scream. It was happening again, I needed to save her, but the man in white began to pull me down once more, tugging me down deeper into the darkness below.

I woke with a start in bed, still feeling the water on my skin. I ripped the covers off, and blood soaked through my underwear, pluming around me in a large, lurid blot.

Micah rushed me to the hospital in silence as I panted in the passenger seat. I was grateful for the unrelenting pain; I clung to it. I wanted more, and more.

At the hospital, the doctor said I'd lost too much blood, and they needed to get me into surgery right away. Through the haze of the pain, it seemed we'd skipped a few steps and I asked, "Is he gone?"

The doctor and Micah exchanged charged looks, as if this had already been discussed. Micah tried to answer, but then his face twisted up and he couldn't get the words out. He turned away, and the doctor took my hand instead. "I'm so sorry. The fetus didn't make it."

In the operating room, as the nurse counted back from one hundred, I didn't feel myself falling into blackness as I'd expected; I could still see her and the flurry of activity around me, but now I couldn't move or speak, as if I was trapped in my own body. My old claustrophobic panic rose up quicker and hotter than I'd ever felt it before, flooding my insides, making my very being scream with pain.

The beige walls and the masked people fell away, replaced by the wood panels of a cabin room. It was the same cabin from my mushroom vision.

My mother suddenly approached and crouched in front of me as she had before, eyes bloodshot and lips cracked, grabbing my arms. I could feel how rough her grip was, my wrists pulsing between her fingers.

Again she said, "Rhea. Angel. I need you to listen to me." She squeezed harder, and I winced in pain. "What I'm about to tell you is the honest to God truth. People will tell you it isn't, but don't listen to them, you hear me?"

Again, my head nodded of its own will.

"All right." She closed her eyes and inhaled deeply. "Many years ago, when your great-great-great-grandmother was 33, she made a deal with the devil. She traded her soul for a beautiful singin' voice. But he played a trick on her. He didn't tell her that for the rest of time, her female descendants would inherit this deal, this curse, and die from a tragic accident at 33."

She searched my face, making sure I understood. "My mother died on her 33rd birthday, hit by a truck while crossin' the street. When my grandmother turned 33 she fell from a bridge and drowned in the river. Do you see what I'm sayin'? It ain't just a story. It's real, angel."

I felt my head nod.

She took a deep breath. "My birthday is real close—"

"But your birthday was in May," my little voice chirped.

She waved me away. "I'm talkin' about my real birthday, darlin'. Now, listen. I don't got much time left. But we are gonna stop this thing, okay? Me and you."

I could feel myself shaking now, a warm sob rising up in my chest without resistance in a way I'd never felt before. "I'm scared, Belly . . ."

Her mouth screwed up, and she squeezed her eyes together. "Oh, angel, I know, I'm scared, too." Her eyes watered, and her grip loosened on my arms. "I'm so sorry. I never wanted this to happen. But I'm gonna make it right—"

A pounding came from the door, and she jerked her head toward it. She let go of me, crept over to one of the curtained windows and peeked through the slit between the fabric and the frame.

She gasped and stepped back quickly, bringing a hand to her chest. The pounding came again, shaking the wood in its hinges.

She ran over to me and pulled me up from the couch into her arms. "There's been a change of plans, angel. I don't think I can take you with me. It's too dangerous. So, just listen to me now. When you get older, and things start goin' bad, remember this: You are not crazy. You are cursed. And remember what I'm about to tell you, okay?" Her face was stern and focused now. "A few months before—"

The pounding came again, this time even harder and more brutal against the wood. She cried out in frustration.

"Okay, okay, never mind." Her eyes darted around the room. "We're gonna play a game," she said, as she carried me over to a large wooden trunk in the corner. "There's a monster comin', and I need you to hide from him." She opened the old-fashioned padlock with shaking hands and frantically pulled out the afghans, leaving a hollow space. She picked me up and placed me inside. I instinctively crouched down, and she tried to smile, but I could see the fear pulling at her features.

"Stay very, very quiet, and the monster won't find you. All right?"

I heard my child's voice say, "But what about you, Belly? Where are you going to hide?"

She almost smiled at this. "I'm gonna fight the monster, angel. Now, remember . . ." She put a finger up to her lips and closed the trunk lid over me. It was dark and cramped inside, but there was comfort in it. I felt safe and contained.

Outside the trunk, I heard the door open, and then footsteps so heavy they rattled the roots of my teeth. I could hear her voice, like she was pleading for something, but I couldn't make out the words through the thick wood.

Footsteps, movement, her voice, too much to isolate and discern what was happening. Then, the door shut once again. Silence.

Endless, stretching silence.

I thrusted up on the lid to open it, but it didn't budge. I heard the padlock jangling against the outside.

My breathing quickened and my body warmed as I tried to force the lid open with my small hands. I thrashed around, going dizzy, not getting enough air. I screamed for my mother, hoping she or someone would hear me, but there was no answer.

Then the lid was opening, flooding the chamber with blinding light and cold, raw air.

I was in a hospital room, and Micah stood over me, his face drawn in concern. He seemed to have aged five years in the last five minutes. He tried to smile when we met eyes, but I could see how forced it was. He started to tell me the operation was successful, but I wasn't listening.

All I could hear was the monster's hooves against the floorboards, my own shallow breaths reverberating against the tight space. And my mother's voice like sweet, smoky music, whispering,

Remember this.

I held my breath.

You are cursed.

31

rhea

2009

SIX MONTHS LEFT

I don't recall coming home from the hospital, or slipping into bed, but these things must have happened, because I remember lying on the mattress, weightless, and the feeling of floating out to sea.

I was certain that what I'd seen at the hospital was not a dream, but a real memory from my childhood.

I searched for my old Discman in the bedside drawer, dusty from lack of use. I put on the headphones and pressed play.

My mother sang "Folk Song" in her hypnotic voice,

There was a woman in town who sang so sweet
Her beauty was beyond compare
But one day a bright specter she did meet
There aft she was no longer fair
She ranted and raved and ran over town
Chased by somethin' not seen
She ran so far that she came to a cliff
And it chased her over to free'n

The low tone of prophecy vibrated beneath the words now, still echoing in the earpieces after the track had gone quiet.

The Cursed Woman was not just a concept album—it was also a confession. A story passed down through my mother's family, only just now reaching me.

The next tracks played—"Duet with the Devil," "Black Gum Tree," "Mountain Girl," "Let Me Out"—and instead of imagining my mother conjuring these stories, I saw the real people behind them.

My ancestor meeting a devil at a crossroads and exchanging her soul for a beautiful singing voice, the same cursed soul that she would pass down from girl to girl like a tattered wedding dress.

My grandmother getting hit by a truck and landing in a tree on her 33rd birthday.

My mother growing up alone and unloved in the mountains with her aunt and uncle, reviled for her curse, her only consolation the music that damned her in the first place. Her deep desire to escape her little town, and to live freely out in the world and become a star.

A few images kept recurring in the songs: a white dog, a bright specter or a man in white, and a big, hulking tree.

I remembered my mushroom vision: the white dog leading me to the tree in the moonlight, and the man in the white suit leaned against the trunk, waiting for me.

The man pulling me deeper into the quarry, my body drenched in blood.

Then the high, joyful chords of the title track rang through the mesh, and this time I did not feel lifted.

It told the story of a woman damned from birth who, try as she might, could not escape her fate.

It was better if she did not try to hold on to things, to have people who needed her, because everything she touched crumbled in her fist.

I thought, What if it wasn't random? What if this curse had done this to my baby? Perhaps it was the creature that had haunted me all this time. Perhaps it had taken this beautiful, sweet thing inside me and poisoned it.

My musing was interrupted by the voices of the final track, "Lullaby for a Demon Child."

My mother sang that even though she was leaving too soon, that when I got scared, she would still guide me. She would be my moon, my light.

It felt like she was reaching out through the music and touching her fingertips to mine, our twin shadows finally meeting.

For so long, I had wanted to feel connected to her, to feel there was some piece of her magic inside me, just waiting to be unearthed.

And this was it, wasn't it?

This was the little shard of her lodged in my gut. Not a beautiful voice or a creative genius.

A curse.

~

Days might have passed, but I wasn't sure. One morning, it was like I finally blinked back into consciousness. There was a spoiled, creamy taste in my mouth like expired milk.

When I looked in the bathroom mirror, I saw a stranger.

My belly sagged. My hair was long and matted, and new moles had formed on my flesh. I looked like I'd been floating on the bottom of the ocean.

I robotically scrubbed away the grime and put on clean clothes that hid my middle. Then I went downstairs to find Micah making dinner in the kitchen. He'd grown a scraggly beard like he had on the trail, but there was something more unhinged in the jutting of the hairs.

When he saw me standing at the kitchen island, his face softened and he came around and clutched me delicately. "How are you feeling?" he asked with fear in his eyes.

I could see he'd been suffering these past few days, and I understood that he needed me to be good for him. I could give him that. "Much better now."

"Good." He released me and went back to the stove. "I need to ask you about something you said a few days ago—about a curse? Your mother told you that you were cursed? I figured it was just a dream or a side effect of the medication, but you seemed very agitated about it."

I wanted to tell him—he was the person I told everything.

"Yeah, I think I might have uncovered a memory where my mother told me about a family curse that makes every woman in the bloodline die at 33."

He looked up from the stove and studied me for a long moment. "Are you sure you don't want to see someone?" He said it as if we'd discussed it before, and I wondered what else had happened over the last few days that I didn't remember.

He continued, "Because it might be worth it. You know, I've seen this kind of thing before, when someone goes dormant and starts believing in delusions, and it might not seem like a big deal now, but one day it might be too much and . . ."

My heart sank. He thought his brother and I were the same, that the curse was just a postpartum nightmare, something to be medicated and reasoned away. The last few days had been rough, but now that I was up and no longer on the pain meds, my mind was clear. This wasn't a delusion. It was something to be investigated. But Micah clearly couldn't be a part of that.

"Yes, I'm sure. I'm better now. I just needed some time." I knew this was the right thing to say—the perfect words to soothe him. "And I didn't mean that I thought the curse was real—just that I might have uncovered a strange memory from my childhood. Who knows what my mom meant, or if I'm remembering right. Maybe it was just a crazy dream from the anesthesia."

I watched Micah's shoulders relax. "Thank god. I was worried." He gestured at an old-fashioned dessert tin on the counter with bright flowers printed on the metal. "Hess left those—chocolate chip cookies without the chocolate chips." My favorite.

I had no memory of Hess's visit—had I spoken to her, or had Micah sent her away?

He served us dinner at the table, and I tried to remember how one behaves during a meal with her husband. I must have done a passable job, because he kissed my knuckles and told me he was happy I was feeling better.

I gazed in the mirror hanging on the wall behind him and saw the stranger staring back at me.

I watched her mouth curve into a smile.

32

rhea

2009

SIX MONTHS LEFT

If you search for a record of Lulabelle Powers in the state of Tennessee, you will find no trace of a person with that name before her arrival in Nashville in 1967. No birth records. No medical records. No school records. Widen the parameters, and you will find two Lulabelle Powers—a nurse who served in the West Virginia branch of the Union army during the Civil War, and a housewife who died in the 1930s in Atlanta.

Twenty-eight unauthorized biographies have been written about my mother's life. Four full-length documentaries are available to watch. Thousands of hours and pages of interviews and articles.

And not one named the town she'd grown up in. Only "a little mountain holler" or "near Pigeon Forge" or endless variations of the same evasive answer.

If I was going to find out more about the curse, I needed to know where it came from.

But how could I do that if I didn't even know my mother's real name?

Judging from my search results, and from her comment about her "real birthday," I suspected that she'd changed her identity when she first came to Nashville.

So I combed through the records of every town in the mountains, some of them unnamed or unincorporated, as if they existed in a dimension separate from the rest of the world. I searched birth records for a baby girl with a deceased mother, or with a birth date of July 25, the date of Belle's death, but I found none. I searched adoption records for a girl taken in by an aunt and uncle, but there were few adoption records to begin with—there were honestly very few records at all, considering how many people must have lived and died in that region over the decades. It was clear that recordkeeping, at least back then, had not been a common practice.

If I couldn't find it online, I would need to consult the only people she had bared herself to—the people who must know her secrets.

A week later, I booked a trip to Nashville under the guise of Christmas shopping to see Hess and the girls. On the way to the airport, I felt a little funny driving over the flat, dusty roads, as if I wasn't quite connected to the ground. At the bar near the gate, I ordered sweet potato fries and a beer, attempting to center myself. I had always found planes comforting—I liked giving myself over to the journey, cozy in my small compartment, watching the saddest movies I could find and letting the sorrow flow freely.

But as I got in line to board, my heart beat faster and my cheeks flushed. When I tried to take a step forward, I couldn't feel my feet against the carpet. Somehow, I made it to my seat in first class, and for a moment, I was swept along in the tide of activity as the attendant helped stow my bag and asked if I would like a drink. I ordered a tequila on the rocks with lime and hoped that would be enough to calm my nerves.

But as I sat there waiting for it, studying the interior of the cabin, I imagined the flight attendant shutting and sealing the door, us lifting into the air. I saw the cabin suddenly plummeting, luggage flying, oxygen masks hanging like loose eyeballs above the seats as the passengers screamed. Me sitting there in a state of panic, irrevocably trapped. Us crashing into the parched terrain and dying in a blaze against the red rock.

Blood pulsed in my face, and I struggled to breathe, convinced they weren't pumping enough oxygen into the cabin. As the final passengers stepped on to the plane, I stood up, grabbed my bag, and asked to leave.

On the drive back home, my hands shook against the steering wheel. I took an overpass arcing above four layers of highway, and I felt myself leave my body and float up toward the ceiling, no longer in control of the wheel or the pedals, like one of those nightmares where you're riding in the backseat, and you realize no one is driving the car. I imagined careening into the van in front of me, shooting through the glass of my windshield, landing splayed on the asphalt.

I took the first exit, pulled over on the side of the road, and called Micah, pretending that the car had broken down. He picked me up, and we had it towed to the shop nearby. When he asked me why I hadn't gotten on the plane, I told him I wasn't feeling well.

I pretended to be sick in bed for the next week and called the girls instead.

"What was my mother's real name?" I asked Hess after we'd indulged in the usual small talk.

"What do you mean? You know Lulabelle was her real name."

"No, I mean like her *real* name. The one she was born with."

Hess was quiet for a moment. "Honey, as far as I know, your mother was born Lulabelle Powers." She paused. "Why do you ask?"

I could hear the suspicion in her voice, and I remembered the cover story I'd crafted. "I'm researching Belle's life. A little side project. There's hardly anything real about her out there," I explained lightheartedly. "And I realized I know almost nothing about her family, and I've had a hard time tracking anything down in the public records. I thought she might have gone by a different name at one point."

Hess exhaled. "Oh, okay. That sounds interesting. But like I said, I'm pretty sure she was born Lulabelle Powers. Maybe they didn't keep consistent records back then. It was a long time ago."

"What was the name of the town where she grew up?"

"I don't think it was a separate town—I think it was part of Pigeon Forge or whatever county that is. I'm sure you'll find something if you search in that area."

I couldn't tell if she was lying or she truly didn't know.

"I'm also having some trouble with *The Cursed Woman* piece of her story. She didn't give many interviews about that album, so I don't have a lot to go on in terms of her inspiration. I know you aren't the biggest fan of that one, but did she ever talk to you about it, or . . . ?"

Hess was quiet again. "Rhea, you know I wasn't around for that, so I can't help you there."

"I know, but I thought maybe later she told you—"

"No. She didn't." There was a rare edge to her voice, and I decided it wasn't worth pushing harder.

"Okay, that's fine, thanks for answering my questions."

There was a beat of silence. "Honey, do you need me to come there? That bug you have sounds nasty." I had told her I was too sick to fly. "I could be on a plane in a few hours."

"Aren't you recording right now?"

"Yes, but I could take a break. I know you've been struggling."

"You really don't need to come. It's just a virus, I promise. And it's been good to lose myself in this project. Helps me not fixate on . . . *it*. Let's talk again soon. We can figure out plans for Christmas."

She hesitated, then said, "Well, all right. Bye, dear."

"Bye."

My calls with Phoebe and Tima produced the same results, as if they'd decided to say the same exact thing. I wished Martha were still around—she had sensed my mother was hiding something in *The Cursed Woman* album; she would have told me everything she knew.

My next call was to the office of Mr. Blau. A few months ago, I had gotten a call from him informing me he was retiring. While I'd rarely seen him in person over the years, he'd been a constant in my life—mailing me financial statements, calling with requests for the estate, guiding me on major decisions like the purchase of our house and cars. What I imagined a father might do, without the pesky emotional baggage.

When I called his office, I was hoping they could look at his Belle Powers files for any trace of a real name, birth certificate, or place of birth, but the attorney found nothing. When I asked for Mr. Blau's home phone number, I was informed he was suffering from Alzheimer's, and his family preferred he not talk or visit with anyone who might confuse him. I had no idea he'd been sick, but it seemed like him, to elegantly make his exit before anyone could see him fall apart.

My final call was to Clayton Redd, whom I hadn't spoken to since our meeting at the state fair over a decade ago. Hess gave me his number, but when I tried it, he didn't answer. I left a voicemail and waited. A week passed and still no word from him. So I called again, left another voicemail. Sent a few texts. No response. I wanted to ask Hess to call him for me, but I was never sure where they stood with one another. They didn't seem exactly friendly.

In lieu of any other avenue of information, I went searching in the deeper annals of the internet. I always avoided this route in my research unless absolutely necessary, and even then, I only saw it as a source of garbage some people were gullible or deranged enough to believe.

But this time, I went looking for answers.

My mother had been known for two seemingly contradictory things—her emotional vulnerability, and her intense secrecy. Fans felt like they really knew her, and at the same time, very little was known. It was why so many rumors swirled online—why did she never show her chest? What was hiding under her wig? Where did her songs really come from? How did she really die? The internet was filled with speculation.

But what interested me the most were the subreddits and YouTube videos dedicated to the cult of *The Cursed Woman*.

These particular fans believed Belle Powers was haunted by a real curse, and the album held clues as to how she would eventually die.

On the cover of the album, my mother held her right arm out to the side, pointing west, indicating the direction of the place where she would meet her end—the West Coast, Santa Barbara, California.

The light on the cover was just at the end of golden hour, but when you flipped it over, the background was of a forest at night, indicating the time of her death.

When "Let Me Out" was played backward, fans swore it sounded like she was saying *I will crash into the sea* beneath the serpentine rhythm at the beginning of the song.

I studied all of these clues for myself, including using software to play the entire album backward. I could see how someone looking for a message might hear something in the sounds beneath the guitar, but to me it sounded like recording fuzz. All of it, honestly, seemed like too much of a stretch. I couldn't help feeling like these fans were just getting off on being spooked, rather than searching for the real truth.

And above all, this idea kept eating at me—if she knew exactly how and when she was going to die, why hadn't she stopped it somehow? In the cabin memory, she had seemed determined to stop the curse, no matter what it took.

But they weren't all dead ends—on one subreddit, buried deep in a link to an album of photos, I found a rare image that'd been taken at a *Cursed Woman* show in Austin. It showed Belle in a black dress, her hair natural and wavy, thick black shadow smudged around her eyes. The top of her dress had come undone, and I saw something on her chest. At first glance, it appeared to be a shadow or a smudge, but there was more than one, spaced out over her skin. I remembered what I'd seen years ago in that photo of her at Bellewood, the dark lines beneath the chiffon. It reminded me a bit of my own birthmark, and I wondered if we'd both been marked, and what it meant.

I posted about it on the page, and while some seemed to dig it, most voted me down as a poser. I apparently didn't know what I was talking about.

It wasn't until a few weeks later that I received the message. A user named maryshelley25—the name my mother famously used to check in to hotels on the sly—had DMed me a link to a lo-fi website dedicated to the conspiracy of Belle Powers's death.

This page was different from the others—it focused on the real circumstances around her death, not secret messages in album art.

My mother's plane crashed into the ocean off the coast of Santa Barbara, California, around 10:30 p.m. on July 25, 1982. Micah and I had spent an afternoon in the main branch of the Nashville Public Library that first summer looking at the news clippings of the crash, but I had forgotten the details.

I clicked on a link labeled "black box evidence" and it took me to an official report filed by the National Transportation Safety Board. It stated in a thick typewritten font that the plane had not malfunctioned prior to impact. There had been no strange weather event or interference from any other aircraft. I came to the final line of the report, and my blood went cold.

It was as if the plane suddenly fell from the sky.

For Christmas, Hess came to Arizona. We usually spent it in Nashville at her house with the other girls' families, but I made an excuse about not feeling like traveling. I was still using the miscarriage as a cover with Hess and Micah, and I wondered how long it would last.

I had stopped leaving the house very much, except for the occasional walk to the grocery store when I was feeling solid. Driving was out of the question now, as was any situation where I felt I couldn't easily leave. Sometimes, even when I was just walking around, I would start to feel light headed, and then I couldn't feel my feet against the pavement, and I would imagine myself walking out into traffic and ending up tangled beneath someone's car. Or falling over the side of an overpass onto the hard cement below. Other times, it felt like I was simply fading from existence, my body evaporating cell by cell into the desert air until I was only soft vapor.

I kept Micah in the dark about all of this, and instead made up an excuse about a sensitive project requiring an NDA. I knew I couldn't tell him about the curse; his reaction when I first brought it up was evidence enough. He would think it was crazy, and would try to stop my research, and I couldn't risk him derailing my efforts now. I had to keep going. I only had six months left until I turned 33.

But I agreed to go to a therapist at his request, and I told her about the new panic that was like the old claustrophobic panic but much, much worse. I told her that sometimes it wasn't enough to be able to escape wherever I was—sometimes my body itself felt like it was closing in on me. Even more than an airplane, it was the only space I truly couldn't escape.

I thought of telling her about the visions of my death, but that was dangerously close to the curse, which I would certainly not be mentioning. I worried that if someone had these types of visions, did the therapist assume they wished for death? Was it some sort of subconscious suicidal tendency in their eyes? I was afraid of being misinterpreted and misdiagnosed. I didn't want to die; in fact, I was doing everything I could to try to stop it.

So I mostly kept my mouth shut, and I didn't expect her to be able to help, but it did feel good to unburden myself in small ways to someone else.

To cope with the panic, she trained me to imagine a safe place. And when this didn't work, to imagine Micah's comforting presence in these new panic-inducing situations.

But while Micah had once been a source of comfort and stability, now it was more complicated. When he was around, I pretended everything was fine, clenching my teeth the entire time. It took so much energy that

I would be exhausted afterward and have to make an excuse to escape and rest.

On Christmas Eve, Hess prepared the full Southern feast that I usually looked forward to every year. I moved the food around and took a few bites to make her happy, but something about the glossy richness of the food, like a staged photo from an old-fashioned cookbook, made me want to gag. It was a quieter meal without the flurry of grandchildren and a wine-drunk Phoebe making everyone laugh, but it wasn't stiff. I participated well enough, and I got Micah on a glassblowing tangent that lasted a good twenty minutes, eating up most of the time.

Late that night, after they had both gone to bed, I snuck downstairs with the hope of spending some time in the basement where I did my research. But I found Hess sitting on the couch in the dark, the only illumination the warm light of the Christmas tree.

"Honey, come sit with me for a minute," she said, unsurprised.

I obeyed and snuggled under a blanket next to her.

"You know, your mother hardly ever slept. She said she didn't like to waste the time."

I didn't know where this was going. "I usually sleep fine, I just couldn't tonight. Maybe it was all the wine." I smiled playfully at her, but she didn't return it.

"I'm going to tell you something I should have told you a long time ago." Hess took a deep breath and placed her hands in her lap.

"Okay." I was on edge now, but I also couldn't wait to hear what she would say.

"When your mother and I first met, she told me that the women in her family were cursed to die at 33. I didn't think she really believed it then. Your mother was always making up stories for her songs, so I thought it was just something from her imagination. I didn't realize it was real for her until years later."

The wording "real for her" wasn't lost on me. "Okay," I said again, pretending to be bewildered.

Hess looked up at the ceiling and then back at me. "During her last tour in 1982, a few months before her death, she withdrew into herself, stopped sleeping or eating, started recording these secret songs. One night she collapsed onstage, and we had to cancel the rest of the tour. She told me it was the curse, and of course I told her it wasn't real. I wasn't around when she was experimenting with drugs, but Martha was and . . . she said it seemed like she was using again."

Secret songs? I hadn't come across anything about secret unreleased songs.

"About a week before she died, I went out to run errands for your mother, and when I came back, you were both gone. When I tracked you down at my cabin a day later, it was empty. Then I heard your little voice coming from the trunk in the living room. It was locked, and the key was missing. I had to drive to my nearest neighbor to get bolt cutters to slice through the metal padlock. When we lifted you out, you were so pale. You could barely stay awake. At the hospital they said you were severely dehydrated and in shock. You were too scared to speak for fear that a monster would hear you. It took you a while to tell us what had happened, and even then, it was hard to know what was real." She took a deep breath. "I thought someone had come and kidnapped Lou. Stolen her car. So I filed a missing person's report with the police."

I saw the room lined in wood, my mother's terrified face, the dark space of the trunk.

"She showed up at the cabin a week later looking terrible and acting strange. She wouldn't tell me where she'd been. I was furious with her but I also wanted to get her help. She refused. We decided it was best if she left you with me while she went out to California to shoot her movie." She knitted her brow. "She was trying to do what was right."

She turned away and quieted. "Two days later, I got the call from the police in Santa Barbara about the crash." She paused. "I will always regret not being there for her when she needed me."

I took this in. The memory from the cabin was *real*, and my mother really had believed in the curse. I wasn't insane.

It also meant that Hess had lied to me years ago. "So all this time, you knew what had happened in the cabin—when I asked you about it after Martha's funeral, you acted like you had no idea, but you knew."

Hess grimaced. "I know. I'm sorry. You had such a small fragment that I thought it was better not to dredge it up. What good could come from you reliving such a terrible time?"

"But you don't get to make that decision for me. We've talked about this."

"I was trying to protect you—"

"Well, it backfired. A few weeks ago, I remembered what happened at the cabin when she took me there. She warned me about the curse."

Hess's face went stricken. "What do you remember?"

I recounted it for her, and as Hess listened, her face remained grave. "That must have been terrifying."

"It might have been less terrifying if you'd been honest with me."

Hess closed her eyes, and I knew she was trying not to cry.

"Were you telling the truth when you said you didn't know her real name?" I asked accusingly.

"Yes, I promise."

"What about where she came from?"

"Yes, I promise I was telling the truth. She made it clear she never wanted to go back there, and I didn't push her."

Was there anyone who had really known her?

"What are you trying to find?" Hess asked quietly.

"I already told you—I'm working on a documentary about Belle." I avoided meeting Hess's eye.

Hess was quiet for a moment, then she said, "I don't think Lou would want anyone knowing about this."

"I know that. I would never put this in the piece. But I need the full story in order to figure out which parts to tell."

Hess nodded, still studying me closely.

"So do you think she was on drugs when the plane went down? Is that why she crashed? You lied about that, too." It was a convenient explanation for what had happened—so much easier for people to believe than an old curse.

Hess's brow furrowed. "It's the most logical conclusion."

I nodded, pretending to absorb this information.

"When she left you in that trunk, she wasn't herself—she loved you so deeply, honey. I never want you to think otherwise."

I nodded again, and I let Hess put her arms around me. As much as I hated the lying, I knew she meant well. I had already forgiven Belle—I knew she had done it to protect me, though I still wasn't sure of the details. And it was nice to think of the good in her, especially after spending so much time focusing on the damned part.

But as Hess walked me upstairs to bed, I did not think about Belle's love for me. I thought of Hess's story, and my mother's week-long disappearance before she died, with two questions repeating in my mind:

Where did she go?

And more importantly—

What did she find?

33

lulabelle

1982

SIX MONTHS LEFT

Home is a fickle thing for a demon child; it's always changing.

A few months ago, we returned to Nashville for a show at the Opry. I'd been touring for most of the year, and I was looking forward to coming home to my city.

I remember driving through downtown with the window down, passing the Ryman. I'd been back many times, and it was the closest thing I had to a church.

But it'd been a few years since the final show there, when the Opry moved to the new complex out by the highway, and as I got closer, I saw the old theater looked abandoned. It was cracked and sagging with age, like a great uncle left to rot in a nursing home.

A deep wrong settled over me as we turned left onto Broadway, and I searched for something else to ground me.

The street had changed over the last few years, with many of the old honky-tonks replaced by adult bookstores and nightclubs where music wasn't the main draw. As I passed open doorways, I saw people with their heads down on bars and laid up in the booths like corpses. The air smelled like dirty crotch and sewer sludge, and the light seemed to dim, the color filtering through a different lens.

Something had happened to Nashville. It was going bad at the root.

At the show that night, I shook off the dread and went out onstage like I always did—I can perform half dead with one eye closed if I have to. It was the Opry, after all. Even in the flashy new theater, it still felt like my church.

Usually when I play, my mind turns off, and whatever song I'm singing flows through me. But that night, right in the middle of my set, I heard a new song slowly crawl into my mind with a spider's delicate steps. At first it was faint.

Then the music grew louder, the melody underneath it dissonant and unsettling. Then lyrics emerged, rising to the surface of the sound.

They told the story of a woman, and the many ways she might die.

Electricity streams through the microphone pressed to her lips, melting their red onto the metal and filling her insides with sparks.

A stage light drops from the ceiling, crushing her head in a single blow.

The song said these deaths weren't chance. No "tragic accidents." They had happened because *he* willed it so.

I stared out at the audience in terror. If I opened my mouth, I knew I would sing this new song. I could feel it threatening to come up and out like bile.

I noticed a streak of pure white amid the muted tones of the audience, slowly snaking its way from the back of the theater toward the stage. It crawled on its hands and knees.

As it got closer, I saw that it was not a person, but a white dog. That white dog with the bloodstained jaws from my dream. Or was it a dog? It was a dog, and not a dog.

I couldn't breathe. I couldn't get enough air. My hands and feet evaporated, then my arms, my legs, my head, and finally, my chest, with the tree at its center, pulsing with that terrible music.

Next thing I remember was waking up in a hospital bed. Hess and a man in a white coat hovered over me. The doctor said I'd likely collapsed from exhaustion and dehydration, but they were still running tests.

I was so relieved when he finally went away, and it was just Hess and me. I was so scared of what was coming. I needed her now.

I'd been trying to stay in motion the last few years, growing to mythic size and constantly traveling from place to place, so that he wouldn't be able to catch me.

But I was never going to get away.

And I didn't want to face it alone. I needed someone to understand what was really happening before it took over.

I said to Hess, "I have to tell you something."

Hess scooted closer and took my hand. "What is it?"

"My birthday is coming up. I'm gonna be 33."

She smiled and exhaled. "I know how old you are, Lou. Do you want to plan something special? Maybe a trip so you can relax? Anywhere you want to go."

"No. Listen to me."

"I *am* listening. It doesn't have to be a trip. Whatever you want."

"That's not what I'm talking about. I'm turning *33*." I took a deep breath, steeling myself. "And I'm scared about the curse. I'm scared something is going to happen. I've got this terrible feeling—"

Hess patted my hand, cutting me off. "Oh, Lou. I didn't know you still believed in all that. I know it must be hard after what happened with your mother. But you are not going to die. I promise you. Nothing bad is going to happen."

"But I can *hear* it—"

She cut me off again.

"It's just the exhaustion. The doctor said it himself. What you need is a break. I'll talk to the tour manager about suspending your dates until you get better. I know you think you can just stay up for days on end and work yourself to the bone, but even you need rest, my love. It'll all be okay. I promise." She kissed my knuckles and then laid them back down.

My heart sank.

I don't know why I thought she'd believe me this time. Maybe because it wasn't just a scary story anymore—it was real, and it was happening to me.

But I knew then that she wouldn't be able to help me. This was beyond her, and it always would be.

We'd built this new reality together, this little life. But I could feel them starting to separate. Her in one world, me in another, the boundary like the edge of a storm: on one side, sunshine, on the other, billowing clouds and lightning thrashing through the air. The low rumble of thunder telling stories of how I might die.

After the doc officially diagnosed me with exhaustion, they canceled the last stops on the tour. It really burned my britches for people to think that I couldn't perform because I was *too tired.*

But I'm afraid to tell anyone else what is really happening. They might lock me up somewhere, and then I really wouldn't be able to escape. I can't trust anyone. Not anymore.

Lou has become a costume like Belle. When I have to, I put on a Lou who can sit in the living room with her family and not feel the presence of something dangerous in her periphery, waiting.

But with the tour canceled and me on doctor's orders to relax, things are often still and quiet, and there is nothing to block out the voice. I spend most of my time in bed pretending to rest while I grit my teeth against the songs that continue to fill my head every night:

Someone leaves the stove on, and the house slowly fills with gas as we suffocate in our sleep.

An errant ember jumps from the fireplace and sets the floorboards on fire, spreading from fabric to wood until the entire house is engulfed in flames and we die in our beds, reduced to piles of ash. I imagine them finding my wigs, somehow still intact and blazing platinum in the dark rubble—the only sign that Belle Powers ever walked the earth.

I have died a thousand times. My body feels each one, the damage piling up so that I feel more like a corpse and less like a person each day.

My night songs have always been a bit sideways. That's what makes them night songs. It's why I love 'em.

But these are something different. It feels like my mind has been tuned to a different station, like someone new has taken over the broadcast from that golden place.

I've never in my life wanted music to stop entering my mind. I've gone to great lengths to try to get it back when I've lost it.

But now, I wish it would stop. Because I know it's *him*.

I always imagined he'd show up for me one day, and that'd be the end. One tragic accident I didn't see coming, and whoosh, I'd be gone.

But it won't be that easy.

Papa loved to preach about the devil in church, even more than he liked to talk about God. I remember him leering from the pulpit, warning us that the devil could take many forms. A serpent. A man. A lover.

Sometimes he was only a voice, whispering in your ear.

And other times, he could enter you. Take over your body and mind.

I can feel him now like a swarm of bugs, burrowing into my skin and gradually eating me from the inside out.

I won't be *taken* by the curse. I will *become* it.

But I refuse to just sit here like some idjit standing on the train tracks, waiting for the train to hit them.

I have to do everything I can to stop it, no matter the cost. If not for me then for you, angel.

You and I will go back to the source, and I will lift this curse come hell or high water.

Rhea, that is my promise to you.

34

rhea

2010

EIGHT DAYS LEFT

For the next few months, I lost myself in research.

I studied every interview Belle had ever given, every televised performance, every word she'd ever said, for clues. I combed every album line by line, but especially, of course, *The Cursed Woman*. There was one line in particular from "Mountain Girl" that I kept coming back to:

In the hidden cave where we worship the Lord,
The preacher points and thunders,
Cast out her demon with your sword,
Cast it out, tear her asunder

Could this mean a church in an actual cave? That couldn't have been common. And yet, all of my searches only returned results from places like Hungary or Bulgaria. Perhaps the cave was only a metaphor.

But sometimes it felt like she was speaking directly to me in these songs, and this was one of those moments—there was something important here, I could feel it.

I looked into the secret songs Hess had mentioned, and I found no reference to them anywhere, not even in the most obscure of the conspiracy feeds. When I brought them up again to Hess, she said she'd never heard them and didn't know where they were, but that Clayton would know. I tried him yet again, and again, he didn't return my call.

I also delved deeper into the circumstances of the plane crash, and I kept coming back to this notion: Why did she get in that plane? Had she been forced somehow? Or was it her escape plan? Did she think she'd be safer in the air? I still had so many questions and so few answers.

Most nights I only slept for a few hours on the couch in the basement. Micah was set to have an exhibition at the Corning Museum of Glass in the summer—the highest honor for a glassblower—and he barely left his studio either. All I had to do to seem normal was make an appearance here and there, put together a simple meal, pretend to have slept in the guest room to "avoid disturbing him," all while reassuring him that I was fine by myself and happy to support him however he needed.

This was the life we'd agreed to—if we could not have children, we could be people who sometimes lost themselves in their work.

But in the pit of my stomach, I knew I was running out of time. I knew it, and I also didn't know it, as time had begun to slip away from me. Sometimes weeks would pass, and I couldn't recall their events.

And then one morning, I went on a rare walk outside. I thought being out in nature would give me the answers, that I'd been ignoring this essential fact by squatting in the basement.

But everywhere I walked, I saw bright, blinding figures in my periphery, disappearing every time I turned to see them. My head ached, as if I'd been staring into the sun.

When I came home, Micah's car was in the driveway. A strange sight in the daylight. When I walked inside the house, he wasn't in the kitchen or the bedroom. And then I realized where he must be.

I dashed down the stairs to the basement and found him standing in front of one wall covered in printed pages of song lyrics, each so meticulously noted in my cramped black writing that you could barely read the lyrics themselves.

He turned and looked at me with this expression that I didn't recognize and couldn't read, as if I'd replaced my knowledge of him.

He moved unspeaking to another wall, the one that I knew would be most damning. I had drawn a four-foot-tall image of the tree from my mushroom vision, the one I assumed my grandmother had died in on the side of the road. I had also drawn the man in the white suit and the white dog, though these were smaller and accompanied by printed sketches I'd found online, of similar men in white suits and white dogs other people had seen and believed to be the devil.

"What *is* this?" he asked.

I swallowed hard. Maybe this time he would believe me. Maybe all I needed was to trust him. "Remember when I told you about the memory I recovered about the family curse? Well, I've been doing a lot of research, and I think it might be real. I know it sounds insane, but if you'll just let me show you—"

His face drained, and I stopped talking. "Oh, Rhea," he whispered.

My stomach dropped, and I was afraid to speak again for fear of incriminating myself further. No matter what I said, I knew he wouldn't believe me now.

"How long have you been working on this?" he asked, but I stayed quiet. He continued to walk around, glancing over my map of the mountains with the tiny towns labeled, documents from the crash, the picture of my mother from Austin with the shadows on her chest blown up to try to make out any detail.

He went upstairs without another word, and I stayed in the basement, shaking, unsure of what to do. I could hear him on the phone, but the sound was too muffled to make out the words. I'm not sure how long he was up there, but eventually he came back down, his face now set in an unflinching expression.

"I found you an in-patient facility. It's very nice. Highest rated in the state. We'll check in tomorrow morning."

Here was the man I had loved since I was a child, the man I had built a world with, who had loved me in spite of everything. And he wanted to lock me up. Trap me in a place where I couldn't escape, with people who wouldn't believe me. It was a greater nightmare than the curse itself.

"I know it's not what you want, but I can't handle this by myself. You need real help." His voice cracked. "I can't let what happened to my brother happen to you. I can't do it, Rhea. I love you too much."

I could see it in his eyes—I had become what he'd always feared. Another damaged person who would leave him. He no longer saw that person I'd wanted to be for him, the person I'd told myself I was for years. That was all over now.

"I'm sorry. I'm so sorry. I promise I'll be better," I pleaded.

"No. Not this time. You have to go."

I imagined being lashed to a hospital bed, completely powerless to stop the curse. I only had eight days before my 33rd birthday. I couldn't waste another minute researching online and pretending it wasn't coming. It was time to act now—before it was too late.

"If you won't go willingly, I will have you committed. I don't want to do that." His voice faltered a bit, but he pulled himself together. "But I will. I can't let this happen again. I won't survive it."

It was then that I shut down completely. This was about my survival. Nothing else. I would pretend to go along with Micah's plan, and I would escape before he had a chance to trap me. I couldn't think about him or anyone else. I had precious little time left.

I stepped toward him and looked him in the eye. "Okay, I'll go."

He exhaled. "Thank you." He closed the gap between us and wrapped his arms around me. "You are still you. You are still the same person I fell in love with. I can see it. It's going to be okay."

If only that could have been true, I would have given up anything. Instead, I squeezed him hard, knowing it might be the last time.

That night, I listened breathlessly outside of his room. When I heard his snoring even out to a rhythmic sawing, I quietly picked up the bag I'd pretended to pack for the treatment center, tiptoed down the stairs, and slipped soundlessly out the front door.

I walked for an hour to a Walmart in the next neighborhood and used their half-broken pay phone to call a taxi from a number I'd scrawled on a piece of paper. I'd left my dead phone at the bottom of a box of cereal Micah hated, and I doubted if anyone would ever find it.

While I waited for the taxi, I went inside and browsed the hair aisle, searching for a wig. When I found only hairpieces, I went up and down the aisles until I spotted a small costume section near the sewing supplies. There was one long, voluminous blonde wig and another of the same in brunette. I selected the blonde, picked up a prepaid phone, paid for both with cash, then locked myself in the bathroom.

I put on the wig and stared at myself in the mirror, the blonde strands glowing under the fluorescents like they were radioactive. I'd selected this shade because it was the furthest from my dark copper as I could get, but now I saw the strangeness of the choice.

Even when I tried to disappear, it somehow came back to *her.*

Outside, I got into the taxi idling by the entrance and gave him the address to the Amtrak station in Maricopa. I looked in the rearview mirror, searching the driver's eyes to see if he could be trusted.

But in the dark interior, the glass showed only the outline of a blonde woman sitting in the backseat, haloed in desert neon.

35

rhea

2010

FOUR DAYS LEFT

For the last sixty hours, I've sat on this train streaking east.

For most of it, I was the only one awake in the quiet car; the passengers even slept silently here, their mouths closed and their bodies still as corpses. I haven't slept so much as sat in a trance for the last three days, reliving the past.

I noticed a soft, fuzzy sound like whispering coming from somewhere nearby, and I imagined a renegade passenger hunched in their seat, murmuring to themselves just so they could hear their own voice.

I put on my special noise-canceling headphones and selected "Let Me Out" from *The Cursed Woman* album on my iPod. The opening riff twisted like a snake over the houses passing through the window.

She sat in the room, watchin' the tree,
Waitin' for someone to set her free

I had made the same mistake. I had waited for people to free me, but I had since learned that no one could set you free. You had to do it yourself.

By any means necessary.

Let me out, Lord
Let me be free
Let me out, Lord
Who will I be?

The last line lingered in my mind, and I realized I had missed something in the song. This decision to set yourself free made you a new person, perhaps even a stranger.

I reached for my phone, and I saw the date glowing from the screen.

6.09.2010

Four days until I turned 33.

I wasn't entirely free. Not yet.

But I would be.

My head suddenly went light, and I saw my hands were shaking around the phone. It was time for food. In the dining car, I ordered a cheeseburger, and I watched the attendant microwave it inside a plastic wrapper. When he handed it to me, a cancerous steam filled the bag. I ate the chips instead.

Back at my seat, I saw the sun coming up over the green fields whizzing by. I opened the small vent of the window and inhaled.

Tennessee.

The land of my birth, and the place I'd fallen in love. I smelled the earthy sweetness in the air, and a sense of organic belonging sprouted inside me, like a native plant recognizing its soil.

Here I would find answers.

A few hours later, we arrived in Nashville.

I walked eight blocks in the warm evening to the closest public library and found an open computer. I searched my name and the word "missing." The first entry was a local news article about a man with my last name murdering a woman with my first name.

I imagined myself splitting into two, one part of me stabbing the other with a kitchen knife.

There were no relevant results. The news wasn't out yet.

I found a taxi outside the library, and we streaked west past the city, where the hills rolled and the houses became small farms.

After about an hour, we pulled up to a nondescript cattle gate surrounded by green. I lowered the window and pressed the button on a communication box.

"How can I help you?" came a garbled voice.

"My name is Rhea Larsen. I'd like to speak to Mr. Redd."

There was silence on the other end, and then: "I'm sorry, that won't be possible."

"Please, I've come a long way, if you could just ask him—"

"Ma'am, this is private property. If you don't leave, I'll have to call the police."

I could feel the driver studying me in the rearview, calculating how he might dislodge this crazy woman from his car. I had made him my unwitting accomplice.

"Look, I'm Belle Powers's daughter. And I really need to speak to him. It's very important. A matter of life and death."

Silence again. Then: "All right. Come on through."

We meandered down a long drive before coming upon a house at the end that was modern and sparkling against the farmland surrounding it.

Clayton met me in the front entry in cream seersucker, and when he smiled, his forehead remained taut and shining. He looked older than when I last saw him, but he was remarkably well preserved for a man in his early eighties.

"Well, if it isn't Rhea Larsen," he said.

I smiled back uncertainly. "Thank you for letting me in. I'm sorry for dropping by like this, but you haven't returned any of my calls, and I didn't know what else to do."

His brow furrowed. "I'm the one who should apologize. I had no idea you were trying to get in touch with me. I don't really handle my own phone anymore—I rely on my assistant for that. She should have given me your messages."

I watched him take me in head to toe, and I rushed to say, "I'm sorry for being such a mess—I spent the night on the train."

He cocked an eyebrow, then waved it away. "Are you all right? You said it was a serious matter?"

"Oh, yes, I'm fine. I just need to speak with you about something."

He nodded. "I was just about to have my lunch. You can join me."

On the back patio, a table was set with barbecued chicken and vegetables grilled whole.

"So how can I help you, dear?"

"I was hoping you could answer some questions about my mother."

He nodded. "I assumed that's why you came." He put his fork down and folded his hands. "What do you want to know?"

"What was her real name?"

The twinkle in his eye dimmed, and his brow furrowed again. "Well, it was Lulabelle Powers, of course. That's widely known." He caught my gaze across the table.

"I mean her *real* name. The one on her birth certificate."

His expression deepened, and the lines on his face finally emerged. "I'm not sure what you're talking about."

"Lulabelle Powers was a fake name." I watched him closely. "Did you really not know that?"

He bristled. "I was not aware."

"You were *married* to her."

I watched his body still and his face flatten to something unreadable. "Pardon me, miss, but I'm not going to be interrogated."

"Okay, I'm sorry—"

"It might be best if you leave."

"Please," I begged softly. "I'm sorry."

We sat in silence for a moment, and I felt like a child awaiting punishment. Finally, he said, "I was not aware, but . . . I'm not surprised. She had her secrets, and I had mine." It seemed like he wanted to say more, but he left it at that.

"Do you know where she grew up?" I asked gently. "The name of the town?"

"No, not the name. I think it was close to Amos, where I'm from, but there are lots of little communities in the mountains. Some so small they don't show up on maps."

Here was something. "Do you know anything about a town with a cave church in that area?"

"A cave church?"

"Like a church where they held services in a cave? I don't know if they held all their services in the cave, or just special ones."

He looked out over the land and squinted with one eye. "No, I don't think so."

I wondered if he was telling the truth, or if he was still keeping her secrets after all these years.

"Did she record any songs before she died? Anything that was never released, that she might have left unfinished or kept private for some reason?"

He shifted his gaze back to me. "Why do you ask?"

"Hess mentioned something about secret songs, and I thought you might know, being her producer."

He paused, running his lips over his knuckles. "Are you sure you want to go down this road?"

"Yes."

He was silent for a moment, giving away nothing. "All right. I have something to show you."

We made our way to the east wing where the walls were lined with gold and platinum records in frames. At the end of the hall, there was a studio with a professional soundboard and a vocal booth with instruments scattered about. He went to a safe the size of a refrigerator in the corner, pressed in a code, and the thick door popped open. I could see from across the room that it contained rows of glossy tapes with tiny, illegible labels on the sides.

He pulled one from its slot, closed the safe, and sat at the soundboard. He stared down at the tape in his hand as if it were a haunted relic.

"A few months before she died, Lou and I started recording this project she called *Night Songs* that she didn't want anyone to know about. Not even Martha or Hess. Usually, Martha was part of the composing, and Hess weighed in on the songs as they were coming together. But this time they weren't allowed in the studio. Only me and Lou."

He looked up at the microphone dangling behind the glass in front of us. "She would show up at my place in the evening, and she'd want to record all night. Lou could be impulsive and didn't sleep very much, so that part didn't seem too strange. But the *music*—that had a different feel."

He pulled the tape from its case and popped it into a machine to the right of the soundboard. "Lou made me promise never to show this tape to anyone, and I've kept my word all these years. It was the least I could do for her. But I don't think she'd mind if I played it for you."

He pressed a button, and the machine whirred.

We waited in silence for a few beats, and then sound oozed from the speakers, like an animal moaning in pain. I thought it must be a guitar, but I'd never heard someone play like that.

Then Belle's voice came in as a grating whisper, the sound like ice crunching against my molars:

I roll down my beloved Broadway
Seedy clubs where music used to play
Shadows in the corner booth
Nashville is rottin' at the tooth
My head is tuned to a different channel
From Almighty God to the crafty Devil
Songs about a woman dying

And when I hear them, I can't help crying,
Save me, Lord, save my child
Save us from the cursed wild

The song went on, describing the many ways she might die:

Onstage, being electrocuted through her microphone; a stage light crushing her skull; asphyxiating on a gas leak; a disastrous house fire leaving only her wigs behind.

And throughout the song, she kept begging.

Save me, Lord, save my child
Save us from the cursed wild

They reminded me of the visions I had, too, of the various ways I saw myself dying.

The song degraded, so that the lyrics were unintelligible, and the music sounded like the watery notes of a broken record, dissolving into nothing but the tap, tap, tapping of no disc.

Beneath the tapping, in a voice so close it felt she was right behind my ear, I heard,

Remember this.

Remember what I am about to tell you.

. . .

You are cursed.

My vision went black for a few moments, and then cleared to reveal Clayton hovering over me with silver stubble sparkling from his chin. "Rhea, are you all right?"

I nodded, afraid my voice would sound too frail if I spoke.

He shook his head. "Please forgive me for showing you that song."

I took a deep breath, and felt my body start to return. "No, I'm glad you did." I took another deep breath. "What are the other songs like?"

He eyed me, then said, "Every song is the same—the only thing that changes are the different ways the woman dies." He glanced at me again and continued, "She said the songs were coming to her at night, like her head had gotten stuck on the wrong channel. She said she couldn't write any other kind of music, and it was driving her nuts. She thought recording would banish them. That's how it usually worked when she had a song in her head."

"Did it work?"

"I don't know. I didn't ask. I . . . I thought I was respecting her privacy." He looked away, ashamed. "I wasn't around when she was using drugs. But it reminded me of people I'd known in the past. I can't say for sure, but I wondered . . ." He drifted off, uncertain of whether he should continue.

That same theory again. I wondered if he and Hess had spoken or merely arrived at the same conclusion separately.

"Did she tell you anything about a curse?"

He frowned. "A *curse*? What do you mean?"

"Like a family curse."

His frown deepened. "No."

"What about the *Cursed Woman* album?"

He gave me a perplexed look. "I didn't work on that one."

"She never spoke about the inspiration behind it?"

"No, we didn't talk about her old work. Not even the albums we'd made together in the past. She was always focused on what was next."

"Okay." I paused. "Can I listen to the rest of the tape?" I asked furtively.

He eyed me. "I don't think that's a good idea."

"Please. I need to hear it."

He clicked his tongue and exhaled. "All right."

The next few tracks were just like the first one—unsettling, spine-tingling music set to lyrics that imagined different ways she might die. I gritted my teeth against the visions, attempting to stay focused on the words themselves and what I could learn from them.

Around the fourth or fifth track, instead of music or singing coming through the speakers, I heard only my mother's voice, telling a story:

I was surprised to find England wasn't so different from where I'd grown up. The Brits had a real sense of humor that was dry and self-deprecating. Life was pretty simple and gray there, but they got a laugh out of it.

Martha and I played small clubs out in the countryside, and then afterward Tate and I got pissed on pints with the locals. There wasn't much to do but drink.

Tate knew a band who'd rented a house nearby, and he, Martha, and I went to visit them . . .

"What is this?" I asked him.

"Oh, right. I forgot about that one. She asked me to cut that out and send it to her on a separate tape, but I never got around to it. She said she was recording stories for you so you could have them when you got older."

Holy shit.

I continued to listen as my mother told me a story about doing heroin with my father for the first time at an English manor rented out by a rock band. It sounded more elegant than tawdry, a young person experimenting with ecstasy. I could see why she had done it, and also how it might have taken over her life. It didn't seem as simple as Hess had made it—my father had been part of the introduction, but my mother had tried it on her own, of her own free will. Was it fair to blame him?

"Are there more stories on here?" I asked.

He shook his head. "No, that's the only one. I think it came to her while she was in the booth, and she wanted to get it down before she forgot."

My heart sank. "Do you know where the other recordings are?"

He shook his head again. "No, I don't."

If only I could find those tapes.

His eyes watered, and I saw that he was exhausted. "If you need to rest, please go ahead. But would it be okay if I stayed here and kept listening?"

He looked like he might say no, but then he seemed to give into the fatigue. "Sure. Let me know if you need anything."

He got up, and I continued to play the tape.

I went from track to track in feverish concentration, and when the album ended, I started it over again. There had to be clues in these songs. Perhaps even clues she'd left for me on purpose, knowing that one day I would need them.

It was during my fifth or sixth time listening to the heroin story that a quiet voice came from behind me.

"Rhea."

I jumped, adrenaline shooting through my veins. I switched off the track.

The voice said "Rhea" again, and this time I recognized it. I turned and found Hess standing in the doorway, her face pale but calm. My first instinct was to be relieved, and my next was terror.

Micah must have called her. She's going to drag me back to Arizona. They're going to lock me up.

My eyes scanned the room quickly, noting that there were no windows in the studio. The only way out was through the door behind Hess, which she had closed. If I could just get around her, I could leave, run through the house, and be outside before she could stop me.

"Rhea, are you okay?"

I turned my gaze back to her. "Did Micah call you?"

She didn't hesitate. "Yes. He said you ran away and asked if I knew where you were."

"What did you tell him?"

"I told him I didn't know, which was the truth until about an hour ago, when Clayton called me."

"Why would Clayton call you?"

"He was worried after you just showed up here unannounced."

"Does Micah know I'm here?"

"No."

"Are you going to tell him?"

"Not if you don't want me to."

How can I trust her? What can she possibly say that I can believe?

My eyes flicked to the door again, visualizing stepping around her and pulling down on the handle. It would be easier if she moved farther into the room.

I went over to a cluster of couches and took the seat closest to the door. Hess instinctively followed, sitting a polite distance away, clearing the way for my escape. I pretended to relax back into the cushions.

"How is *Night Songs*?" Hess asked, catching me off guard. "Part of me always wondered what it sounded like, and the other part didn't want to know."

Clayton must have told her. I wanted to feel violated, but I liked that she didn't pretend not to know.

"Honestly, it's pretty disturbing."

She nodded soberly. "Is it like *The Cursed Woman*?"

"No. That album tells a story, and it is so . . . emotionally complex." I paused. "When I listen to these songs, all I feel is her fear."

Hess put the back of her hand up to her mouth and turned away for a moment. I sat there with her, the unease of the recordings still lingering in the air.

"I think I know why you're here," Hess said, turning back. "You're looking for answers about who your mother really was and what really happened to her."

I stared at her, unwilling to confirm or deny this.

"I want those answers, too," she said. "I've had the same questions for almost thirty years."

I studied her face, considering if this was a trap. *Is she trying to lure me into a false sense of security?* I imagined men outside the studio, waiting to grab me and force me into a van so they could take me to whatever local facility Micah had picked out.

Despite the things she had kept from me over the years, there was still a part of me that trusted her implicitly.

But I'd learned that even, or perhaps especially, the people you loved and trusted the most could betray you.

"Let me help," she pleaded.

"How do I know you won't just tell Micah where I am?"

She thought for a moment, then pulled out her phone and, sidling closer to me, showed me her conversation with Micah. His last text was from an hour ago, and it said: `Still no word?`

I imagined him hunched over his phone, eyes bloodshot, and I pushed the image away.

Hess typed `Sorry, no word yet.` into the text box and hit send.

It didn't prove anything—she could still contact him. But I needed her help—I had less than four days left. And as long as I kept my guard up, I could still escape at any time.

"All right." I paused. "I still haven't found the name of the town."

She nodded. "So what's our next move?"

"I think we should go to the records office in Pigeon Forge and see if there's anything in the physical files there. It's all I have to go on."

"That sounds like a good plan. It's too late to go out there tonight, so why don't you come back to my place? Tima and Phoebe are there, and maybe you can pick their brains more. We can leave first thing in the morning."

She could trap me there. I will wake up, and there will be people waiting to take me away.

"Rhea, all I want to do is help. I promise."

What choice did I have? I had to see where this would go. I had the strong sense that she might hold the key to this mystery.

36

rhea

2010

THREE DAYS LEFT

Hess drove us out of the countryside, and I stared out the window, avoiding conversation. She turned on the radio, and Elvis Presley's ecstatic, mournful rendition of "Unchained Melody" filled the car.

We hit town and rode past Broadway in its roil of families on vacation and bachelorette parties ducking in and out of honky-tonks in plastic cowboy hats, the street littered with bottles. Musicians in Old West costumes played in every window, the sound blaring from the doorways. I remembered the lyrics of the first track on *Night Songs*:

I roll down my beloved Broadway
Seedy clubs where music used to play

I saw a man in a spandex bodysuit singing half-heartedly in the street for the wasted tourists, some of them barely able to stay on their feet.

Shadows in the corner booth
Nashville is rottin' at the tooth

I wondered if Nashville had ever felt real, or if it had always felt like a parody of itself. When Belle arrived in the sixties with a dream, had it felt real then? And now, every night, did they pantomime *that* time in the past, that one *real* time?

I could feel Belle's story and mine converging, becoming two tracks running side by side. Hurtling toward the same cliff.

At Hess's house, she eyed me in the front hall. "Your room's ready for you. Why don't you freshen up? There are towels in the closet."

I went to protest, but then I saw her face. I *needed* to take a shower.

After I washed, I found clean clothes laid out on the bed. It was a relief to go without the wig for a while. I crept to the kitchen for water and heard people talking on the back porch.

I froze, wondering if they were there to take me away.

Then I recognized the voices, and I relaxed slightly. I needed so desperately to be alone. I felt like my body was slowly evaporating from exhaustion. But I forced myself to open the door and step outside.

The screened porch was awash in candlelight where Hess, Tima, and Phoebe sat around a low table laden with glazed ham and sides. Tima beckoned me to a spot next to her, saying, "Hey, lady," and Phoebe cried out, "Rhea! You're here!"

Tima fixed a plate of everything and put it in front of me with a smile. I took a small bite of a biscuit and murmured with enjoyment as they watched.

Tima smiled wider. "Y'all remember how much Lou could put away? Good lord." This was something she'd said before, but it felt forced this time. The other women smiled in agreement, as if they were putting on a play.

"I don't know *where* she put it, though. Skinnier than sin no matter what she did." Tima clucked her tongue.

I studied my own wrists, now thin and translucent as they never were before, even when I was vegan. I had always thought being skinny would feel powerful, but I felt weak and fragile. My smaller body was always curving in on itself, trying to get warm.

Phoebe poured wine for herself and Tima, and sparkling water for Hess. "Wine, darlin'?" She held the bottle up to me.

"No, thank you."

Phoebe poured me the sparkling, then held up her glass. "To Mom, to Lou, and to Martha."

We echoed her and clinked our glasses.

Hess set down her glass after a small sip. "Ladies, we're here tonight because Rhea needs our help. Is there anything we can remember about where Lou grew up? Anything she told us over the years?"

"I've been thinking on it," Phoebe started, "and I remember her granddaddy was a preacher. So there must have been a church in her town."

Tima raised an eyebrow. "You throw a rock in this state, you're gonna hit a church. I don't think that exactly narrows it down."

Phoebe scoffed. "I thought this was a brainstorm."

I jumped in, "I'm actually glad you brought that up. Have any of you ever heard of a cave church in Tennessee?"

They all contemplated this, then shook their heads.

Tima looked at the other girls, then, fingertips grazing her lips, she said, "I have something that might help, but I hesitate to say it because I don't know for certain, but . . ." She paused, then continued, "when your mama first came to Nashville, it seemed like she was running away from something. Like the law."

Hess narrowed her eyes. "What are you talking about? That's ridiculous."

"Is it? You found her squattin' in a damn shed."

Hess glared, unwilling to concede.

Phoebe chimed in, "I wondered the same thing." Hess turned the glare on her, and she shrugged. "When she came to me wanting a new look for the stage, she kept saying she didn't want anyone to recognize her, like she was trying to hide her real identity or something." She exhaled. "And now we find out Lulabelle Powers wasn't her real name? You have to admit it's suspicious."

I had suspected this myself, given the name change and how carefully she had guarded the secret. I had searched arrest warrants for someone who might have matched her description, but none of them had stood out either way. A few drugstore robberies, some prostitution hits, and a handful of arrests for nonviolent protests. They'd contained no pictures and very few identifying details.

"I think you might be onto something," I said, and described the research I'd already done. "Did she say anything specific that might have given you a clue?"

"She said it was trouble back home that made her run away, and that she could never go back," Tima offered in a low, dry voice, as if it hurt to break her friend's confidence after all this time.

"She told you that?" Hess asked, almost as an accusation.

Tima nodded. "The first night I met her."

I could use it to narrow my parameters, but I wasn't optimistic. I'd noticed there weren't many domestic disputes reported in these towns, and I assumed people kept such matters to themselves.

I leaned back against the couch, a wave of exhaustion rolling over me. *Another day gone.*

"Why don't we play a little music? Maybe that'll shake something loose," Hess suggested. She picked up her guitar and started to tune it as she discussed song choice with Tima.

I stared out into the dark beyond the candlelight of the porch, waiting for my eyes to adjust. As the shapes of the backyard emerged, I saw a streak of white dash across the blackness, disappearing into a thicket of trees. I waited, unbreathing, to see if it would reappear.

But the darkness remained still.

Another wave rolled over me, and I couldn't pretend any longer. I needed to be alone. I stood up abruptly. "I'm sorry, I have to go to bed."

Phoebe went to protest, but Hess cut her off. "Of course. We'll see you in the morning."

In the guest room, I allowed myself to unravel, huddling under the covers and clenching my teeth as I watched the shadows in the corners and listened for strange noises.

I felt the deep vibrations of a guitar coming through the walls from the porch, followed by a rich vocal melody like butter melting in my eardrums. I let the warmth of the music wrap around me, and I was grateful that I could take its comfort on my own terms, without being watched.

I imagined it was like being in the womb—protected in my chrysalis, while life went on around me at a safe distance.

I could feel myself drifting off, and I suddenly clung to consciousness, afraid of what might happen if I fell asleep. I needed to stay awake. Alert. Ready to leave at a moment's notice.

But the force of the music was too strong, and I found my body curling up of its own will like a wild creature in a hollow, and then I was floating away on the sensation, no longer strong enough to fight it.

And for the first time in many nights, I slept.

37

rhea

2010

THREE DAYS LEFT

My burner phone blared from the side table, stirring me from a weighted slumber. I checked that the number wasn't Micah's and answered.

"Hello?" I said in a hoarse voice in case it might be the police.

"Rhea? Is that you?" came Clayton's elegant rasp.

"Yes, sorry," I said normally, pretending to clear my throat.

"I'm sorry for calling so early, but I had to phone you right away. I . . . I remembered the cave church you mentioned. A long time ago, when I was a boy, I heard talk of it around Amos."

My heart pounded, and I sat up in bed. "Tell me everything."

"I remember it was in this little town a ways away that people used to talk about—a real weird place where a lot of strange things happened. A friend of my mama's came around gossiping about a church that was holding services in a cave like they were vampires."

I held my breath. "Do you remember the name?"

"Yes. It was Craw Valley."

That afternoon, Hess and I headed east in Belle's Gran Torino. I kept the car at her house to use whenever I was in Nashville.

As we wound deeper into the mountains, it felt like a slow ascent into the unimaginable, haunted place of my origin, where all of my visions had come from. The place I'd been seeking for months. I didn't know if the buzzing in my blood was elation or terror. I could no longer tell them apart.

Craw Valley.

Just a little town nestled in the backwoods and newly popular with tourists for its quaintness and autumn foliage. We still didn't have Belle's real name, but in such a small place, I figured it wouldn't be hard to root out.

At a distance, the main drag of Craw Valley looked like it hadn't changed since the day my mother left. There was an old-fashioned burger joint, a general store with a giant pencil for a sign, and a vintage movie house. Sprinkled amongst these were fast food places and abandoned storefronts, and as we got closer, I saw the true age of the place—it seemed to be slowly crumbling, returning to the nature that surrounded it.

We came upon a brick building with silver letters spelling CRAW VALLEY SHERIFF'S DEPARTMENT and parked in its small lot. Inside the tiny office, it smelled of burnt toast and dark urine. A young man in a uniform came out of the back and smiled when he saw us.

"Welcome!"

Hess returned the smile and introduced us. He shook both of our hands enthusiastically.

"Well, look at that. A real-life country star in Craw Valley. I can't believe it." He mimed wiping sweat from his brow.

Jesus.

"Is there someone we could talk to who would've been around in the sixties? I'm assuming that isn't you." Hess winked, and he put a meaty hand behind his head.

"You'd be right about that. But the sheriff could help you. He was a deputy 'round that time. He's in the back."

A few minutes later, an old wiry man in a tan uniform that hung from his frame shuffled into the room. "Johnson tells me y'all wanna talk about the old days."

"Yes, sir."

"My memory ain't what it used to be, but I'll do my darndest. What d'you wanna know?"

Hess pulled out a picture of Belle from when they first met. "Do you remember this woman? She would have been about eighteen in 1967."

He grunted. "Well, of course. The Arwood girl. Ernestine, I believe. Lived with her daddy's sister and husband over yonder."

My heart jerked. *Finally.*

Ernestine Arwood.

The name conjured the hardy mountain girl I'd sometimes imagined Belle to be, and I knew this was right. "What do you remember about her?" I asked.

"She had a voice like an angel. But she was troubled. Wasn't really her fault on account of her blood."

"What do you mean?"

"Her mama's blood was bad. All the women in that family died real young, real tragic-like. Made 'em act crazy sometimes."

"Oh, really?" Hess asked, coaxing him along.

"Yes'm, I remember when she run off after almost killing her uncle. I tried to get 'im to make a statement, but he refused, so I left it alone. The family never recovered. They all either died or left—not one of 'em is still in the Valley."

We were speechless for a moment. "So none of her relatives are around?" I asked in a quiet voice.

"Some of her mama's people are still here. Hasil, and his son, um, Enoch."

"Could you tell us where they live?" I asked, perhaps too eagerly.

He eyed me. "What you want with 'em?"

My mind whirred, calculating what would be safe to reveal. It felt like we'd entered that separate dimension I'd imagined, cut off from the rest of the world. I decided to take a chance. "Ernestine was my family."

He eyed me. "I can believe it." He clucked his tongue against his teeth. "All right. I'll give you directions."

We drove out to where he pointed us, burrowing deeper into the mountains. There were no businesses in this part, just a two-lane road running through the forest with houses nestled here and there on either side. We passed one property where a deer hung by its neck from an invisible string in the yard, as if it were suspended mid-escape. Its belly was split open, and the camo-clad man attending to it stopped his work and watched our car, unblinking, until we rolled along.

"*Ernestine*," I said in disbelief.

"I know," Hess said, looking at me. "No wonder she changed it."

Down the road, we saw the milky blue of the door the sheriff had described peeking through the trees, and we parked in front. It was a little scary approaching a house in this area; I had the feeling that I could be shot at any moment, and no one would care.

The moment we stepped onto the porch, the door swung open. Another old man, this one even older than the sheriff, stood in the doorway.

"What y'all want?" he barked. A middle-aged man with a similar face came around the side of him and put a hand on his shoulder.

"Dad, don't be rude." He turned to us. "I'm sorry, y'all, he's gone salty in his old age." The old man grunted in response. "How can I help y'all?"

Hess went to speak, but I put my hand on her arm.

"My name is Rhea Miller. My mother was Ernestine Arwood. I think we might be family."

"My God," said the old man, his jaw going slack.

His son smiled wide. "Well, I'll be damned. Why don't y'all come inside?"

We followed them into the modest house and made our introductions. The old man was my mother's uncle Hasil, and the other man was his son, Enoch. There was a bit of fussing around with iced tea and a plate of cookies, and the whole time I was biting my tongue, waiting for the moment I could start asking questions.

When we'd finally settled, I launched in. "What can you tell me about the curse?"

Hasil's face went pale, and Enoch coughed.

"Your mama never told you?" Hasil asked.

"I think she did when I was little. But I didn't get to ask her any questions."

He nodded, unsurprised. "So she passed?"

"Yes. When she was 33. Plane crash."

Hasil shook his head. "That's a damn shame. Sorry to hear it."

"She actually came to see us," Enoch added.

"When?"

"About a week before she turned 33."

Hess and I shared a look. *This* was where Belle had disappeared to after she left me at the cabin.

"So her birthday was July twenty-fifth?" I asked.

"Yes'm," Hasil replied, looking a little confused. "Same as Aileen. I'll never forget that day."

"Aileen was his sister," Enoch clarified. "Ernestine's mother. *Your* grandmother."

"Do you remember what time Ernestine was born?"

Hasil nodded. "Around 10:30 or so at night. I remember lookin' at my watch when they come to tell me."

It is true. She had, in fact, died on her birthday, just as she turned 33. "How long was she here? What did she say?"

"We only saw her for a few hours. She asked about the curse, the same as you. She wanted to know how to stop it," Enoch said.

My blood cooled, and I felt our two timelines converging once again, becoming one track. "And what did you tell her?"

"Ain't no stoppin' it," Hasil declared. "I took Aileen to the granny witch myself. She tried to get the demon out of her, but it didn't work."

"The granny witch is a local healer," Enoch translated once again.

Hasil kept speaking as if he hadn't heard him. "After her birthday dinner, Aileen was crossin' the street, and boom, a truck come out of nowhere and launched her into a tree. When I pulled her down, I could still hear a heartbeat. I ran her to the hospital, and the doctor said it was the baby's heart I was hearin'. Aileen was already gone."

"Black Gum Tree" played in my head, telling of the tragic death of the cursed woman's mother. It wasn't just a story—it was *real.*

"I wanted to raise Ernestine as my own, but the wife wouldn't let me . . ." The old man trailed off, and his gaze went unfocused.

"Dad?" Enoch prompted.

"Hey, um, E, fetch me that box under the bed."

Enoch heaved himself up and retrieved an old-fashioned blue hatbox from a back room. Hasil opened it and pulled out a small yellow blanket and held it out to me. I took it and studied the embroidery in one corner. It spelled out "Lulabelle" in pink thread with simple blue flowers stitched around the letters.

"What is this?"

He smiled. "Aileen made it for her baby when she was pregnant. Wanted to name her Lulabelle."

"Did Ernestine know?"

His smile faded. "I told the Arwoods when they took 'er, but they didn't listen. I didn't see 'er much 'cause the Arwoods weren't real keen on me, but at church one time, I told her 'bout the name." He pulled out a small photograph and gazed at it before handing it to me.

The image's black and white had faded to gray and yellow tones, but I could make out a young girl with a feral expression posing in a dress a few sizes too big. Those same dark branching lines peeked out of the low neckline.

"What are those?" I asked, pointing at them.

Hasil squinted at the photo. "She had a birthmark that went clear from her belly button to her neck that looked just like a tree. I saw it when they pulled her out at the hospital. Craziest thing I'd ever seen." He shook his head. "It was part of why my wife wouldn't take her in."

Her mark was a tree, and mine was a branch.

I handed him the blanket and the photo, and he put them back in the box and gave me the whole thing. "You should have this." His eyes paled and watered, but I couldn't tell if it was emotion or just old age.

"What happened with the uncle who raised her? The sheriff mentioned an incident," I asked.

He scowled. "I don't rightly know 'cause I only heard the rumors, but they said her aunt found him near dead on the kitchen floor and Ernestine gone. I saw 'im in church a few weeks after, and he looked like a daggum monster."

He sucked his teeth, and I interjected, "In the cave church?"

He cocked an eyebrow. "As a matter of fact, yes. We held services in a cave back then; thought it brought us closer to the land. A little wacky, but it made worship feel more ancient-like. They stopped doing it years ago." He cast his eyes around as if he'd lost his train of thought.

"You were saying about her uncle . . ."

"Oh, yes, he told people he'd been thrown from his horse, but we all knew the truth. I thought about tryin' to find 'er, but I figured she left for a reason, and she was better for it." The old man's face sagged. "I should have looked out for her. I promised Aileen I would. But I was a coward . . ." He trailed off, and his head drooped to the side.

Enoch turned to his father. "Dad, why don't you take a nap? I'll entertain these ladies."

The old man nodded distantly and shuffled into a back room without another word.

We sat in silence for a beat, just looking at each other. Then I said, "Enoch, is there anything else you can tell us?"

Enoch put a finger up, then made a show of cocking his ear toward his father's room. Soon, we heard a low snoring coming from inside, and he leaned back in his chair. "I do, actually." He lowered his voice. "When Ernestine showed up in '82, she didn't look good. Real thin, and like she hadn't slept in a week. Dad told her the same thing he told you. They tried to stop the curse; it didn't work. But later, when he was out of the room, I told her that wasn't the whole story." He took a deep breath.

"Growing up, Dad didn't tell me about the curse, but I heard about it from other kids. It's sorta like a ghost story in town—everyone knows it. Dad never said anything, but he must have been relieved he didn't have any daughters. Just me and my two brothers.

"Years ago, Dad got real drunk on Christmas Eve. He went out to the porch to sober up, and I sat with him. He started talking about his mother—his only memory of her was one Christmas Eve when it started snowing. He and Aileen went out with her into the backyard and tried to catch snowflakes with their tongues. He started crying a little bit, and I didn't say anything. I don't think I'd ever seen him cry.

"Then he started talking about the day Aileen died. He kept saying he found her hanging from the tree, and I asked him what he meant. He said she was hanging from a rope. I was confused because I knew she'd been hit by a truck. He said no, she hung herself in the tree and he found her. He could barely say the words. He said he climbed up and cut her down. She was still warm, and he could feel a heartbeat when he checked her, so he ran with her over his shoulder to his car and took her to the hospital, and they cut Ernestine out, like he usually tells the story.

"I didn't know what to say to him. I couldn't believe he'd kept this secret all those years. I asked him why he lied and told everyone the truck story, and he said people out here don't like it when someone takes their own life, especially back then. It woulda been real bad for our family, and for Ernestine growing up. Her daddy's sister might not have taken her in.

"Then at Aileen's funeral, an old friend of his mother's told him his mother hadn't fallen from that bridge. She'd jumped.

"You have to understand that back in the day, people thought mental illness was a sign of devil possession, or something supernatural. Not sure how'd you diagnose it, exactly, but my guess is that the family curse is a mental illness of some kind, passed down through the genes."

But what about Belle's birthmark in the shape of the tree? The branch on my chest? Each woman dying exactly on their 33rd birthday? The dog? And the man in white?

It was all too strange to be explained so easily. Ever since I was a child, before I even knew how to give it language, I had carried a creature inside me, and I had sensed a terrible fate looming on the horizon. As much as I wanted there to be an easy solution, I *knew* there wasn't.

I could see how it might have looked like a suicide from the outside. But he didn't know how evil could crawl inside you, fill your head with poison, make you do things you never imagined doing.

This thing didn't play by their rules; it was governed by an older, more elusive force.

When I didn't respond, Hess jumped in. "Thank you for sharing that with us. We really appreciate it."

"Is the granny witch still around?" I asked.

"No, she passed." He paused, deliberating, then he sighed. "But her granddaughter is. She still sees people, if that's what you're after."

I asked him where she lived, and after another long hesitation, he showed us on the map.

The witch's property sat deep in the woods, and I could tell Hess was a bit nervous as we pulled up to the cabin.

The place was surrounded by wildflowers, and I could hear a low buzzing like someone humming in my ear. A few women were draped across couches on the front porch, smoking cigarettes, one of them with a black eye. She hollered into the house for someone named Belva, and a woman in her fifties with dark hair came out in her apron.

"How can I help you?" she asked.

Hess pulled the photo of Belle from her purse and held it up. "Do you remember this woman? She would have come here about thirty years ago, in July of 1982."

The witch studied the photo and nodded her head. "Yes, ma'am, I remember her. My grandma was still around, and she talked to her. She'd tried to heal her mother, Aileen, and she told her the story."

"Do you remember it?" Rhea asked.

She closed her eyes for a moment. "Yes." She gestured for them to sit down, and the other women disappeared inside the house. When she was settled, she took a deep breath and began. "Hasil brought Aileen to my grandma when Aileen was about six months pregnant. She wasn't sleeping or eating. She told my grandma it was the family curse that was tormenting her. Of course, she knew what she was talking about. She'd heard from her own granny about it. Aileen was just shy of her 33rd birthday, and it wouldn't be long before it took her.

"Hasil asked my grandma if she could get rid of the curse. She'd done it before for others in the community: mostly little hexes people placed on each other when they'd had words and a few bigger curses put on by angry spirits. Those were tougher, but she'd always been able to pull it out of them.

"So she said yes. She lit the candles. She anointed Aileen with her most powerful stump water. She passed her hands from head to foot. When she made the final motion of the work, the candles snuffed out. In the darkness, she saw the outline of a figure looming above Aileen's body. Its voice slithered through her skull and said, *Old woman, this ain't your place. Do not try this again.*

"She told me she was paralyzed for a while, staring out into the room, looking for that outline. But it was gone. When she could finally move, she relit the candles and woke Aileen up. Aileen was angry, and she told her she'd only made it worse.

"Grandma wanted to help her so badly, try to take away her pain. But it was bigger than her. She told Hasil the birth would probably get rid of it to give him peace of mind, and they left. She never saw Aileen again."

I nodded, taking it all in. "What about you?" I asked the witch. "Do you think you could get rid of the curse?"

"Your mama asked the same thing. I wish I could help, but I wouldn't dare."

My blood went cold. "How'd you know she was my mother?"

The witch's eyes crinkled in a sad smile. "I could taste *it* the moment you set foot on the property. Like rotten eggs in my mouth." She paused, as if she wanted to say something else, then thought better of it. "How much time you got left?"

"Three days."

"Lord have mercy," she whispered. "You know, she asked about you. Asked if I could take the curse from a child before it had gotten its grip on them. But I told her it'd been inside you since the moment you were born."

"Can you please just try? Please."

"I told you no, and I meant it."

"What about . . . what if I made a new deal with the devil? Could that work?"

The witch studied her. "Your mama tried that, too." *Same track.* "Even if you did, the devil knows how to twist your words to get what he wants. You could end up in worse shape than you are now." She gave me another long look. "You keep that in mind."

"How would I talk to him?" I asked, ignoring her warning.

The witch sucked her teeth. "You go to a crossroads at midnight and think about what you want to tell him."

"That's it?"

"That's it. People like to add all these bells and whistles, but the devil don't make it hard. He's always looking for new friends."

38

rhea

2010

TWO DAYS LEFT

A few hours later, we drove out to the place the witch had told us about, where the road intersected with another in a cross. She said no one took this route anymore, since they built the highway to the east.

I stared out the window at the dense forest, and I imagined some*where*, some *time*, Belle was among these very trees, waiting for the devil to come and strike a new deal.

I imagined each of us putting a palm up to the time barrier between us, unable to touch but comforted knowing the other was there, gripped by the same fear.

We pulled to a stop on the shoulder beneath the dense canopy. The clock on the dash said 11:00. One hour until midnight. We sat with the windows rolled up and the air dying in the car.

"What are you going to do if he comes?" Hess asked.

I'd been wondering the same thing. First, I would plead for mercy. But if that didn't work, what did I have to give? What could I trade for my life? I had not inherited the ability to sing—only the curse attached to it. Perhaps that was something to discuss. If I had not been given the talent, then why should I suffer the punishment? That was the essence of the deal, and he had not held up his end of the bargain.

"I'm still working it out," I answered.

Hess turned her head and gazed out the window. "Being here is so . . ." She trailed off. "I feel like I understand Lou better now, experiencing it. I used to get kind of annoyed when she teased me for being a rich city girl, as if she was so different—sometimes it felt like she oversold her bit about being a 'hillbilly.'" I turned toward her, and she put up her hands. "Her word, not mine." She looked back out the window. "But we really did come from completely different worlds."

I knew what she meant—it had been one thing to immerse myself in the research of these mountains and the curse, but it was an entirely different experience to be here, at the source. Even my time hiking the AT hadn't prepared me for it. I thought back to Clayton's memory of Craw Valley as a strange town that many in the area avoided. There was certainly something about the place that made my mind tingle—not exactly in a bad way, but not in a good way, either.

"I keep thinking about what Enoch said," Hess continued, "about Lou's mother and her grandmother taking their own lives." She stopped, weighing whether she wanted to continue. "I always wondered if maybe Lou had done that, too."

I looked over at Hess, surprised by her honesty. "You don't think she was high when the plane went down?"

She furrowed her brow and kept looking out the window. "Well, it could have been both. There's a fine line there. But the truth is, I thought a lot of things when she first died. I wondered if it was drugs, or if she did it on purpose, or if it was truly an accident. In my wildest moments, I wondered if someone had tampered with her plane and it had been some sort of elaborate murder." Her eyes unfocused, lost to another time. "But eventually, I had to admit to myself that I didn't know. And the not knowing . . . that was more painful than any explanation could have been." She pressed her lips together. "So I guess that's my real answer. I still have no idea."

There was something comforting in her honesty. Even if Hess could never understand what I was going through, I could meet her in this space of unknowing.

Her phone suddenly vibrated in the cupholder. "It's Tima. She's probably just checking on us." She accepted the call, and I opened the door and stepped out.

Insects buzzed in the sweltering evening, and electricity hummed in the air, though I couldn't see any power lines among the treetops. I wandered around the dark undergrowth, feeling vibrations coming up from the ground as well. Where it felt the strongest, I lay down in the grass.

I stared up at the starlit sky through a gap in the trees, and I felt my body shrink under its expanse. I held my hands up and saw that they were a few sizes smaller than normal, the fingers glowing childlike in the dark.

I glanced over at the black car gleaming like new in the moonlight. Where Hess once sat, the window was now empty.

The thick foliage gradually receded from the road, taming itself, reversing its encroachment.

I fished in my pocket for my phone, but I found I was now wearing a dress, and my only way of telling time was a thin gold wristwatch I had never seen before.

Something was happening. Something new. My body wasn't evaporating this time, so much as changing, the sensations familiar but with a tinge of weirdness, like being in a stranger's body. I knew what it was to be in a body, but not in *this* body . . .

The tiny clock face read one minute to midnight.

Soon, it would be time.

She imagined her great-great-grandmother lying in the same dirt and looking up at the sky, wishing with all her being for beauty that she didn't have to pay for, for something no one could take away from her. Oh, to make music with her own body. She couldn't imagine anything more divine.

Could she blame her for making such a deal?

She watched the minute hand move in a circle around the mother-of-pearl face, and she demanded he talk to her.

She wanted to make a new deal. He owed her at least that. After all these years. After all the deaths, and all the lonely children left without anyone to love them.

Still, he did not answer. After tormenting her for months, his voice in her ear singing those terrible songs and showing up at the cabin to threaten her child, only now, when she really needed him, he refused to speak.

Midnight came, and then went.

She screamed for him, but she received no answer. Only the sound of buzzards beating their wings in the treetops and the caw of crows gliding over the empty road.

This was only a game to him.

She stood up and walked into the woods toward Papa's old church. He'd died a decade prior, along with her grandmother, her aunt, and her bastard uncle. The rest were still here somewhere, tucked away in the hills. She wondered if they'd recognize her, but she was kidding herself; she knew they would. Now, more than ever, she could feel herself returning to what she once was—a lonely demon child roaming the woods, listening to songs no one else could hear.

As she walked among the trees in the dark, she thought of the night she left Craw Valley for good. Her uncle had come home drunk from the logging camp, stripped down to his stained white underwear, and cornered her in the kitchen with his large pale body glowing beneath the full moon.

She'd tried to dodge him like she usually did, but that night he was quick, and he grabbed her by the shoulders and thrust her over the counter. She heard him fumbling with his buckle, and she reached for the knife in the butcher block and plunged it into his side. He reeled back and fell to the ground, and she sat on his chest. She pulled the knife from his fleshy belly, and blood sprayed her face and clothes. She held the knife above him, the blade sparkling in the moonlight, and watched the black holes in his eyes expand. Then she cut a slash in each cheek, so that even when she was gone, she'd never be forgotten.

Up ahead in the trees, a faint light appeared, and she saw it was the cave, lit up at the mouth, music pulsing from within. She walked toward it, daring herself to keep going. Then she entered, and a wall of life engulfed her. The cavernous hollow was filled with people and flickering candles. The air was humid with damp and sweat. A woman clanged away on the warped piano as if possessed, and the choir shrieked.

The preacher, a young man with unforgiving blue eyes in a white robe, was calling for all those in the grip of the devil to come forth. One by one, people from the crowd wandered up to the pulpit as if in a daze, and she wandered up with them.

She stood before the preacher, and he brought his hand up and passed it over her face.

He told her he could sense him. The devil. He was in her, all right.

It felt so good to be validated. To be in the presence of a believer.

The preacher told her to kneel in front of him, and she obeyed. She bowed her head, and he shouted for the sinners to think of all that they had done, the rot inside of them that the devil feasted on.

Every Sunday when she was a little girl, they forced her to go to the front and have the devil cast out from her body. She never felt a thing.

This time, though, she felt something. She thought of everyone she'd hurt: Hess, Rhea, Tima, Phoebe, Martha, Clayton, Tate, even her own mama. Everyone she'd ever loved, she'd lied to and betrayed. What had she done with her life other than follow her silly dream of becoming a star? She was so ashamed.

Maybe she deserved it. The curse.

But maybe there was a path to redemption.

Maybe this man could cast her evil out.

She felt hands placed all over her body, and then the preacher started to bark again, this time addressing the devil directly.

He said, "Out, demon! Out, devil! By the power of the Almighty and the Everlasting Love of his Son, I order you to leave this woman. This church. This holler. Slither back to the wet hole you come out of!"

She felt something wriggling in her belly, moving up through her chest, and then up her throat, nearly choking her. She watched a snake slowly exit through her mouth, its silken scales rubbing against her lips.

Afraid to move, she watched its corn-colored body slide across the dirt floor to the preacher in front of her, moving up his shoe and disappearing beneath his white pant leg.

She tried to warn him, but no sound came from her mouth. When she looked into his blue eyes, she no longer saw his indifferent cruelty.

There was wily evil staring back at her. It was him.

She shouted, "Let's make a deal, you son of a bitch."

He smiled. "What does thou have to offer?"

"I'll give you whatever you want—my voice, my money, my fame."

"But I do not desire those things."

"What about my life? I'll give you my life, if you will spare my daughter's."

He laughed and shook his head. Then he leaned down and whispered into her ear, "Darling, I already have your life."

She shook violently, the sound slithering through her veins like a cold snake. A crowd formed around her, and she tried to untangle herself, but their palms held her down. They thought she was resisting purification. They wouldn't let her turn away from the blinding light of the Lord.

She thrust upward, attempting to escape, but they just held her down harder, the panic rising—

Suddenly, the weight of the hands disappeared, except for one gentle pair, rubbing my back and whispering into my ear, *Rhea. It's okay. I'm here.*

I looked up and saw Hess's beautiful, comforting face. The cave was empty now, and morning light streamed through the entrance.

I breathed heavily, my heart thumping in my chest, and I took a moment to try to ground myself, using the icy stone beneath me to cool my blood and slow my heartbeat. Hess quietly watched me but didn't intervene.

When I was calm, she led me out of the forest to the car parked on the side of the road. She pulled the leaves and twigs from my hair, wrapped me in a blanket from the trunk, then fed me water and a granola bar. As I chewed, we sat there in silence with the car doors closed to the outside.

"Rhea?"

I didn't have the energy to respond.

"Are you okay?"

Hess's concern was heavy, weighing me down even deeper into the seat. "I'm fine," I answered weakly.

"You scared me half to death. I thought you'd gotten lost in the woods, that you might have fallen or worse—I spent all night driving up and down these roads looking for you . . ."

"I'm sorry," I said, avoiding her eye. I never asked her to come with me; I didn't have the energy to manage her feelings right now.

"Thank God I went back to Hasil's. We thought you might be at the cave church, and Enoch gave me directions." She paused, then whispered, "What happened in there?"

Hess would never believe that my mother and I had become one for a moment, that we'd entered one time, one life. "At the crossroads, it didn't work. He didn't answer me. I thought if I found the church, maybe he would answer me there." I hoped that was enough. "But I was wrong."

I could feel her staring at me, trying to meet my eye, but I kept looking forward. She exhaled. "All right. Do you want to go to the hospital? They should probably look you over if you've been outside all night."

"No. I'm fine."

She looked out the window. "Let's at least find a hotel where you can rest, then."

I didn't have time to lay in bed pretending to sleep, so I could prove I was normal to Hess. That ship had sailed. "No. I said I'm fine. What I need is to find out where Belle went after she left the church. We still have three days unaccounted for."

Hess opened her mouth, then closed it. "Fine." She paused, then continued, "When I went back to Hasil's, Enoch told me something he'd forgotten—during Lou's last visit, she went to that church, too. Rumor had it something scared her real bad during the service, and she ran off. Someone saw her get picked up by the police out on the highway."

It lined up with what I'd seen. "Okay, let's start there."

We returned to the police station and asked the sheriff if Ernestine Arwood had ever been arrested. He disappeared for a while and eventually came back with an old brown accordion file filled with papers. He opened it on the desk in front of us and scanned through the pages until he stopped on one. He read to himself for a bit, his mouth moving slightly, and then he said,

"Looks like on July 20, 1982, Ernestine Arwood was picked up walking along the highway a few miles from Craw Valley. She was dirty and disoriented and making 'crazy claims.' They took her to the hospital where she was committed to the psychiatric ward." He flipped through a few more pages, then stopped again. "A report came in three days later that she'd left without proper discharge. We kept an eye out for her, but she was never spotted again."

I imagined waking up in a room alone. Finding my wrists and ankles encased in thick cuffs and chained to the bedposts. The organ-melting dread when I realized I couldn't move.

I had read horror stories online of people committed against their will by family members, and hospitals still using restraints even now, leaving patients for hours on end to wet themselves. Forcing them to take medications that kept them near comatose. I couldn't imagine how bad it was back then, in a rural place like this. It must have been torture for her.

"Rhea?" I felt a hand on my arm and looked up to see Hess's concerned expression once again.

"Yes?"

"I was trying to get your attention—"

"Sorry, I zoned out." I tried to smile, but Hess didn't return it. "What were you saying?"

"I asked if you wanted to go to the hospital."

What?

"To see if there's anyone that remembers her, or if they have any records of Lou's time there."

It's a trick. She's trying to trap me.

"You can't just get us the records?" I asked the sheriff.

He shook his head. "No, hon, you'd have to do that. But it don't matter either way—that hospital shut down in the mid-eighties. It's a Walmart now. I doubt you'll be able to find anything."

I deflated, relief and despair mixing like cold and heat in my gut.

As we made our way across the parking lot, no longer in view of the sheriff, I felt the façade I'd been holding up begin to melt into the asphalt, my body evaporating again, my feet no longer connecting to the pavement. "Can we go somewhere private?" I asked Hess. "I need to regroup."

"Yes, of course. We can go to a hotel."

I imagined walking into the lobby, speaking to the front desk clerk, the other guests watching me. I shook my head. "No, I need to be away from people."

Hess paused, deliberating. "My cabin is not too far from here. About an hour."

"*The* cabin?" I asked.

Hess nodded.

I had always thought of the room in the cabin as a place that only existed in my mind, like a tiny dark compartment in my brain. "Why didn't you say something earlier?"

"I don't know. I guess I wasn't thinking."

I could taste the lie. "Okay, thanks, that sounds better."

Hess looked away, as if she regretted bringing it up. "I have to warn you, though . . . I haven't been back in decades. It's probably a wreck." She paused. "I could just drive us back to Nashville now. We could be there by nightfall."

"No, it's okay. I want to see the cabin." I tried to catch her eye, but Hess wouldn't look at me. *What's at this cabin?* "Look, I can go alone. Why don't you go home? I'm sure you're tired, and you've already done so much to help me."

Hess seemed to snap out of whatever had held her, and she finally met my eye. "No, no. I'm fine. Of course I'll go with you."

39

rhea

2010

TWO DAYS LEFT

Out on the back roads, we turned onto a one-lane gravel drive that twisted through forest slowly reclaiming its territory, forcing us to get out every few minutes and move a fallen branch or clear away brush.

I kept looking for a strange hook in a tree or a distinctive boulder, some trigger of recognition, but the trees were only trees. The rocks only rocks.

The cabin appeared, looking old and vaguely creepy, like the ones they used in horror films. A few of the slats on the porch railing were missing, and a tree had fallen into the roof on one side. I searched again for some gooey feeling of nostalgia, but there was nothing.

Hess studied the place through the window, wincing. "I'm sorry it's such a disaster. It's just been sitting here." She seemed hesitant to leave the car, but once I was out, she followed.

The wooden boards of the porch were surprisingly sturdy under my feet. Hess pulled a tarnished gold key from her ring, and I wondered why she'd carried it around all these years. She turned it in the lock and pushed the door open slowly.

A pile of mail sat at the entrance, and thick sediment covered everything in the small living room. My steps made footprints in the dust as I toed aside the mountain of paper and moved farther in.

There was a table against the wall holding a collection of framed photos obscured by grime, and I used my jacket sleeve to wipe the glass of one. It showed a barefaced Belle leaning against Hess with trees behind them. Hess's arms were wrapped around Belle's waist, and her face was wedged into the crook of her neck. It was an intimate, possessive position, like that of lovers.

I picked up the next frame and wiped. Hess held a baby against her freckled chest, her face serene and shining with the light of new motherhood. In another, Hess and a young girl walked hand in hand through an orange grove. The girl sat in Hess's lap on a tour bus. The girl flipped pancakes in the cabin kitchen, helping Hess make breakfast.

I looked up from the frames and studied the cabin with a new filter, and flashes came to me, of squatting on the floor of the living room with a Barbie in my fist as a guitar trilled in the background. The smell of pancakes browning and a rush of water, and this warmth that was muscular in its strength and solidity.

I looked back at Hess, who was standing a few feet away and watching me with shining eyes.

I moved down the hall leading off the main room and opened the doors as I passed. Closet, bathroom, and finally, bedroom. There was a large bed in the middle, and I remembered taking a running start and leaping onto it.

Mom and Belly's room.

Mom.

My head went light, and I floated from the room back into the hall. At the very end, there was one more door. I opened it, and there it was.

A tiny bed sat in the corner with a blue gingham comforter. A pair of small brown boots were lined up next to the dresser. A tiny wooden piano was pushed against the wall. The room smelled old and dusty, like an antique store, not like the pine and static cling that I remembered. More than the fantasy room at Bellewood, this was where a child had lived.

I sat down on the bed and fingered the blanket, trying to regain my bearings.

Hess came in and sat down next to me. There was that muscular warmth again, but now it was here, radiating from this woman.

"You were my mother."

Hess nodded.

The unsettling, many-faced image of my mother that I had long held split into two distinct people in my mind. Two mothers.

"But, how . . . ?"

Hess exhaled, her body shaking slightly. "Your mom and I got together when we were eighteen—she was the first and only girl I ever fell in love with. I'd had crushes before, but I'd never wanted someone until I met her."

She smiled through her tears. "Clayton knew about us—they only got married for the album sales. And so he could control her, of course, but we didn't know that at the time. We were very young." Her smile turned dour. "Lou left both of us at the same time, when she was twenty-three. Broke my heart. I honestly don't remember those years without her very well—I gave up control of my life to my parents and just watched from afar as it unfolded. And then after your father died"—she eyed me sympathetically—"Lou crawled through my window an hour before my wedding and told me she loved me, and that she was pregnant and she wanted to start a family. I was still so mad at her. I wanted to say no. I told myself I would say no, and I wouldn't back down. But I couldn't. She was the love of my life." She shrugged, as if she hadn't had a choice.

"When you were born, we bought this cabin, and I raised you as mine." She gazed at the walls of the room. "This was our special place—me, you, and Lou. We could be a real family here. Not like in Nashville where we had to be so careful. We told people I was your nanny, or I was a relative. But here, we could be ourselves."

I picked up another framed photo from a cluster on the nightstand, of me on Hess's shoulders in the forest. We both looked up at the sunshine filtering through the canopy.

"If we were a family, why are there never any photos of Belle and me, even here?"

Hess's brow furrowed, studying the photograph. "She was careful to keep her distance. Not because she didn't love you. Lord, she loved you." She paused, selecting her words. "I think she was worried she'd hurt you. She thought if I was your mother and she didn't get too close, she wouldn't infect you. And when she did pass away, you wouldn't be as upset. When I look back on it now, I think that was her plan. For us to be a family after she was gone."

My stomach dropped. "Then why weren't we? Why did I live with my dad's family after she died?"

Hess scowled. "When you were born, Lou got in touch with them through one of Tate's friends. She'd never met them—she was too upset to go to the funeral. But they had little interest in Tate's life after he dropped out of college, and that included any baby. They wanted to pretend he'd disappeared one day and wound up in Heaven somehow."

"Then how did I end up with them?" I asked again.

"Lou wrote her will so that I would receive custody of you and her entire estate until the day in which it could be passed on to you. I was planning to buy a new house in Nashville for us to live full-time before you started kindergarten. We couldn't live in Bellewood, obviously. We almost never spent any time there—it was meant to be more of a showpiece. We'd keep the cabin, but being out here didn't allow you to go to a good school. I was going to give you the best childhood I could.

"Then the lawyer told me Tate's parents and sister had contacted him. They had secured their own lawyer to sue for full custody. I was shocked. They'd wanted nothing to do with you until then." She shook her head. "First, I tried to talk to them. But they refused to even meet with me. So I fought it hard. They didn't understand that I was your *mother*. There was no way I was going to let some strangers take you away from me. There was a lot of back-and-forth. It got very ugly. I might not have been 'blood family' as they liked to put it, but I had the legal will on my side. My lawyers were optimistic their case wouldn't hold up.

"As you know, a few weeks after the crash, we had a big funeral for Lou with an empty casket in Nashville. Tate's parents and sister were there, and they asked to speak with me in a back room of the church. With their lawyer sitting next to them, your grandmother told me they'd hired a private investigator. He'd discovered that Lou and I had been lovers, the *sin* we'd been committing. I remember she said it like she was spitting. She said if I didn't give you up, they'd leak it to the press. At first I thought fine, bitch, leak it to the press. See if I care. But then she kept talking. *Everyone will know what you are. Everyone will know what Rhea comes from.* I imagined the fallout. Lou's legacy ruined. And you were about to go to school. Everywhere we went, we'd be ostracized. It was possible Child Protective Services would try to take you away. The beautiful, normal life I'd imagined for you was no longer possible, except, maybe, if I let you go with these people. For all of their vinegar, they seemed to genuinely want you. And they were your family. They weren't, in all honesty, strangers. Even as I reasoned with myself, a part of me screamed that I'd never give you up.

"But, as is my nature, my rational self won out. I was afraid. It was such a different time. If it was now, we might have had a chance. But back then . . . I don't know. Maybe we could have moved overseas to a place where people didn't know us. I still have a lot of shame, that I let you go. It's the greatest regret of my life." A tear snaked down her cheek and she wiped it away.

"I asked your grandparents if I could come visit, and they said yes, when you were settled. They wanted to take you right then, and I said I needed to pack your things, but they insisted they'd buy you new stuff. They gave us a few minutes to say goodbye, alone. I remember you standing there in the back room of the church, and I said to myself, *Hess, don't you dare break down.*

"I told you that you were going on a trip, but I wasn't coming. You started to get upset, asking why, and I said you needed to spend time with your grandparents. You'd never had grandparents, but I knew you understood the concept, so that seemed to calm you down a bit. We hadn't spent more than a night apart your whole life. I think you assumed you'd see me soon. You didn't know to question something so fundamental, like the presence of the sun, or the sky.

"I told you I loved you, but I didn't make it a big, dramatic moment. I didn't want to scare you. There was a bit of crying, but you tried to be a good girl and you went with them anyway. I remember waving goodbye as they drove away and watching your little arm wave back until they turned the corner at the end of the street."

I searched my memory for some fragments of this moment. Maybe a flash of skin or a burst of sun as we rounded the corner and headed toward the highway. But there was nothing solid. I didn't remember the sadness until later, at my grandparents' house, playing alone in my father's old room with his Lincoln Logs. Gripped by a profound feeling of loss that I'd never shaken.

"I didn't waste any time. I had their address from all of the legal documents, so I took a plane up to Minnesota and went around with a Realtor. Once I'd found a place, I got in touch with your grandparents and let them know I'd found a house nearby, and I would be available to help with childcare whenever they needed. They told me not to come anywhere near them, or you. God, my stomach dropped. I should have known, considering the kind of people they were. But I wasn't going to give up. I went by the house and your school, always looking for a way to see you. But your teacher had been warned, and I never got more than a few glimpses. I started staking out your recess, but the teacher called the police, and they made me leave. Eventually your grandparents filed a restraining order. I had no legal rights; I'd given those up. There was nothing I could do. I've never been so angry in my life. I prayed the whole family would die so I could take back custody. When God didn't answer my prayers, I went back to Nashville, and I wrote 'Lady in Black.'"

I had heard the song many times, and I tried to conjure the lyrics:

I go from room to room
Watchin' him live his life
With joy and kids and love
And me not by his side
I once cooked in the kitchen
I once laughed on that spot
But now I've been forgotten
Without a second thought
It's like I never existed
I'm erased, invisible, gone
I'll haunt this house forever
I'm the Lady in Black

"'Lady in Black' is about Belle?"

"Not just about her. For years, I had this family—you and Lou. It wasn't perfect, but we were happy. I even thought we might try to have another baby." Hess wiped another tear. "Then Lou dies. And in all of the press and at the funeral, I'm not mentioned once. Only Clayton and Tate, the two loves of her life. I wasn't famous then. No one treated me like her widow, except for the girls, but we had to be careful with so many people and reporters around. And then your grandparents took you and shut me out, and it was like I'd been erased from my own life. Like I was never a wife or a mother. I was a ghost, grieving in the shadows, invisible to the world."

I thought of how it'd been the last few months, knowing that no one believed me. Feeling utterly alone and silenced. It was an awful, desolate feeling.

Hess wiped her cheeks with the backs of her hands. "So anyway, I channeled all of that heartbreak into an album, and my career took off. It was a strange feeling, losing everything and at the same time, unlocking the creative life I'd always wanted but never thought I'd have. It took me a while to fully embrace it—for years I'd suppressed my talent or used it to help your mother's career. I finally got to be the singer I'd dreamed of being, with my own voice and something to say with it." She paused, finding my eyes. "But every morning, when I wake up, my first thought is of you."

I stared into space, trying to take all of this in.

More lies. More secrets. I looked down at my hands, and I didn't recognize them. The fingers were thick and wrinkled, and the left ring finger curved to one side like the bones had grown the wrong way. My body had become an alien, unpredictable thing. It constantly betrayed me.

And it was hiding things. Memories of being held by a wonderful mother, hoarded away to somewhere I couldn't reach, left to think I was an unloved little thing. A demon child, like my mother.

I peered into Hess's wet eyes, and beyond her sadness, all I could think was that she'd been lying this whole time. Keeping this from me while pretending to be my mother's best friend, my devoted auntie. How could I possibly trust her now?

You can't.

What else was she keeping from me?

Who knows.

I got up and left the room, and I could hear Hess hovering behind me. "Are you all right? Are you okay?"

"Yes," I whispered. "I just need to be alone."

In the bathroom, I locked the door and sat on the lid of the toilet. My breaths were coming short and shallow, and I wondered if the air was thinner at this elevation. Maybe I wasn't getting the oxygen I needed. Maybe I was slowly suffocating.

I stood up and looked into the mirror, the light going fuzzy with dusk and blurring the edges of my hair. I'd forgotten all about the wig. I pulled on one of the pasta-colored strands, and it tugged on my scalp like it was fused to my skull.

I saw Belle, almost thirty years ago, staring into the same glass and contemplating what she should do.

I had accomplished so much over the last few days—I had solved the mystery of Belle's true name and birthplace. I had verified the curse and investigated its depths. I had discovered where she'd disappeared to that week and most of what she'd learned. I had even found my mother.

But none of it was going to save me.

Death was coming, and there was no telling what kind of pain I would be forced to endure at the end.

I felt like I was sinking through the floor. There was no hope left in me. Only the heavy desire of wanting to escape this body, this feeling.

What if I can choose?

What if I can decide when? And where. And how.

I imagined sneaking out of the cabin that night when Hess was asleep, going out to the woods, and doing what needed to be done.

Visions of my death had haunted me for months, but now the very thought of it made my shoulders lower a few notches. My breathing slowed. For the first time in a very long time, I felt the luscious pleasure of control. Sometime soon, at a time of my choosing, all of the pain and fear and unknowing would be over, and I would finally be free.

I unlocked the bathroom door and went out into the hall, which was now lit by a serene blue light. Hess was on her knees hunched over the mountain of mail, most of it dried and soiled to ancient parchment, nervously sorting.

I kneeled next to her and picked up a husky credit card offer for a company long defunct. I tossed it on to the brightly colored junk pile.

Now that I had a plan, I could be sweet and obliging. I could feel the simple pleasure of sorting, unbothered by the seconds dissolving. I could be like a normal girl.

Toward the middle of the mound, I spotted something larger and unearthed a small box. On the top was the cabin's address with no return listed. A Santa Barbara post office insignia was stamped in the right corner.

"What's this?" I asked Hess, and she paled.

"Oh my Lord."

"What?"

She held her hand out, stroking the letters on the cardboard. "That's Lou's handwriting."

"You're sure?" I asked, my heart beating fast.

"Yes, I'm positive."

I quickly pried open the flaps to reveal two rows of glossy cassette tapes stacked like square jewels inside the box. On top lay a small folded piece of paper. I opened it and read,

Hess, my love.

I have one last favor to ask. I know it's not fair, and I'm sure you hate me right now, but please, if you ever loved me, honor this last wish.

Do not listen to these tapes or share them with anyone else under any circumstances, unless one day, when Rhea is older, she comes to you looking for answers about the curse. Then, please, give these to her. My greatest hope is that she'll never need them. But if she does, I won't be there to guide her. Hopefully these can.

All my love,

Lou

Tears streamed down Hess's face next to me, and she was shaking. "I can't believe it. After all this time," she whispered. She took the paper from me and scanned the words again.

I ran my finger over the rows. Here were the tapes Clayton had described. The story of her life. There were so many of them, perhaps hundreds of hours of audio, and a chilling notion dawned on me: There wasn't enough time to listen to them all.

I looked out the window at the sun slowly moving lower in the sky, turning from day to evening. I had less than two days left. Moments ago, it had felt like there was too much time. And now, there wasn't enough.

I picked up the first tape and read the words EARLY CHILDHOOD scrawled on its front. The next few were labeled in the same way, moving chronologically through her life. I skipped to the last tape, which was labeled with a single date: 7.24.82.

I looked over at Hess, who was still staring at the folded note in disbelief.

"Hess—"

"But she didn't tell me why . . ."

"Look at this—"

"Why write this note if she wasn't going to tell me why she killed herself?" she asked angrily.

"Hess!"

She stopped and looked at me wearily. "I'm sorry. What is it?"

I held up the tape. "She recorded this the day before she died. Maybe the answer is here."

Hess stared at it, then shook her head. "No. She didn't want me to listen. That's only for you."

I huffed. "Are you fucking kidding me? She's not here. She doesn't get to decide who knows what anymore. *I* decide." I studied the tape again, suddenly worried we'd have no way to play it. "Is there a tape player here?"

Hess stood up, and I heard things being thrown around in the next room. After a while, she came back out with an ancient player clutched in her hand. "I knew we had it somewhere around here." She set it down on the kitchen table and opened the slot, blowing the dust from its crevices.

I sat in the chair across from her and placed the tape inside. "Are you ready?" I asked.

She nodded. "I've been waiting almost thirty years for this."

I pressed the play button, and the wheels of the tape began to whir, and a voice like smoked honey filled the room, surrounding us with its music.

40

lulabelle

1982

ONE DAY LEFT

I have been to hell, and I ain't even dead yet.

In hell, there isn't just one man in a white suit—there are many, and some of them are women, too. They strap you down and leave you for hours at a time. They force medicine into your veins or down your throat. They make you eat terrible food and watch you relieve yourself and tell you when to fall asleep.

But the worst part of hell is there's no music.

The first night in the hospital, a group of men in white wrestled me into a room and strapped me to a bed. A bright bulb hung above me, searing into my eyeballs. I imagined it shattering and the little shards impaling my eye jelly.

I tried to tell the nurse who I was, but she just nodded like I was a lunatic. I didn't have an ID on me when they picked me up, and of course, I don't look like Belle Powers without the costume. Far as they were concerned, I was just another loony claiming to be Jesus.

While she examined me, the voice returned to my head.

She will give you too much medication, and you will choke on your own vomit.

I studied the nurse. She seemed competent enough.

He was just screwing with me. I wouldn't let him have the satisfaction.

He kept speaking, but I started to sing an old hymn, attempting to drown out the voice. The nurse told me to be quiet, but I kept singing. I couldn't let him win.

She warned me again, and when I refused, she put a needle in a glass vial and stuck it in my arm.

The voice stopped, but so did everything else in my brain. No sound at all. Not even silence. Just empty nothing.

They must have let me out of my restraints at some point, but I don't remember when. The next day was a stretch of bright haze, like walking down a fog-covered street in the middle of the afternoon.

They made me sit in the common area, and I watched the other patients slumped and drooling in their chairs like puffy slugs. Some jerked and twitched as if against their will.

We weren't allowed to play music because it excited the other patients too much, so the only sounds were their mumblings and screams, and an old television blaring gray words.

I talked with a doctor who told me I had something wrong with my brain. Whatever I was seeing or thinking wasn't real. It was all in my head. That's why the voices and the visions stopped when I was on the medicine.

I asked him how it happened, and he told me he wasn't certain, but many people thought it was the mother's fault. It could come from a mother who was overprotective, or one who rejected a child, or a combination of both. The child developed the illness in order to cope with the toxic environment created by the mother's delusional ideas.

I told him I never had a mother, and then he asked me a few questions about my aunt and determined that she was to blame—the combination of her rejection of me and her "extreme Christian beliefs" as he put it.

That got me thinking. I asked him if the bad mama was taken out of the equation early enough—say, when a child was five—if the damage could be undone. Could the child have a normal life?

He said, perhaps. As long as a more suitable mother was there to parent the child into adulthood.

We also talked about treatment options, and he said there were medications, some I'd already taken. I told him I hated those pills. They made me slow, and I couldn't feel anything.

And worst of all, I couldn't make music.

He said that was a common side effect. In order to quiet the bad, the good could be quieted as well. Once I got used to it, though, I wouldn't notice what I'd lost.

Hell I wouldn't.

You can be damn sure I got out of there as soon as I could.

Honestly, I don't know what to believe.

Part of me can look at all this and see the truth revealing itself. The medicine they gave me made the night songs and the visions stop. I still worried about the devil and my death, but the threat felt much less urgent.

Dope and booze changed my mind as well, made it easier for me to live with the curse. Does that mean it's all in my brain?

Or is this just a trick?

There is another part of me that still believes the curse is real, and this is the devil trying to gaslight me.

Either way, I know I can't be with you and Hess any longer. I can't let y'all see me take my own life. And I can't be a danger to my own child. I almost killed you by leaving you in that trunk. When the man in white showed up at the cabin, I thought I could protect you by locking you up and leading him away. I wasn't thinking straight, was I? What kind of mother could do that?

But I refuse to take those drugs or be strapped to a bed ever again. That is no kind of life. I'd never be able to make music again, never be able to think for myself. At least now I have my own thoughts, my music, my freedom.

If I do outlive this curse, I have to disappear, so you and Hess won't try to find me. You will think I'm gone, and that will protect you from whatever kind of evil's got a hold of me.

I don't want to make you sick like me, angel. Maybe if I leave now, you can still have a chance.

But if you're listening to this, then it means it didn't work. And I'm so sorry that this evil has found you. The last thing I ever wanted was to make you suffer.

Goes to show I was never cut out to be a mother. Here you are, in your time of need, and I can't protect or guide you.

I wish I could take all the pain away, to tell you how to make it better. But I don't have the answers. You will have to make your own decision about what to do next.

I love you, angel. Good luck.

41

rhea

2010

ONE DAY LEFT

"It's impossible," Hess whispered, her cheeks wet and raw.

I was speechless.

"Do you really think . . ." Hess paused, as if afraid to expose the thought to air. "Do you think she could still be alive?"

The tape hadn't been entirely coherent—some of it I was still parsing in my mind—but it seemed possible. She had made herself disappear, or at least she had planned to, all those years ago. She could still be out there somewhere.

I pulled out my laptop and searched for records of an Ernestine Arwood over the last sixty years. I found what had eluded me these past few months—her birth certificate, social security enrollment, some public assistance her aunt and uncle had taken for caring for her.

I went deeper, using databases I sometimes used for work. These hopped over firewalls to secure state records; most of the state systems were ancient at best, and it wasn't too hard to do if you knew the right code.

I got a hit on a '92 hospital stay in Arkansas, but the date of birth didn't match Belle's—born in '41, died in '93. The woman's race was identified as Black.

After combing through a few more dead ends, I finally found something.

A record of an Ernestine Arwood admitted to a state-run mental health facility in New Orleans in 2000.

Hess gasped behind my shoulder. "Could that be her?"

I flicked through the documents and found a date of birth: 10.29.49. "It's not the right date, but it's the right year. She might have lied to them." I searched for an accompanying photo, but the record was brief. Date of admittance and date of discharge. She'd stayed three months.

"We should call," I said, picking up my phone.

"They're not going to give you any information without verifying your identity in person. I had some issues when Martha was sick because I'm not a blood relative."

"Old Crone" from *The Cursed Woman* started to play in my head:

If I could be an old wom'n
I'd shimmy down to N'awlins
Make friends with the spirits
Sing to all who'd hear it
'Til my hair turn'd gray and broke
Like the Spanish moss hangin' from the oak

We drove all night on kudzu-lined highways and arrived in the city with the morning light. New Orleans felt lower to the land, like I was closer to the earth's pulsing, sentient core. People drank in the streets and bared themselves with abandon, as if this was a liminal place where the usual rules didn't apply. I felt safer here, like I could exist without constantly looking over my shoulder.

At the treatment facility, after proving my relationship to the patient, a case manager took us to his office where the walls were lined with file boxes and his computer looked older than me.

He handed us a thin file with the tab marked "Arwood, E" in fat black marker. "She spent a few months with us about ten years ago, before my time. I'm afraid there's no one on staff who was working then. We get a lot of turnover." He pulled out a VHS tape. "Her stay coincided with a grant geared toward making video records of patients." He tapped the tape. "This is her video file. I can't let you take it off the premises, but you can watch it here if you'd like."

Hess and I agreed, and he showed us how to work the ancient television in the corner of his office. He said he'd give us some privacy and walked out. I pulled the tape from its sleeve and pushed it gently into the player.

The screen suddenly illuminated in gray and yellow tones, and a blurred woman appeared with her back to the camera. A low sound came from the speakers, and I turned up the volume, so that the voice suddenly filled the room with its smoked honey.

The woman was singing.

Hess gasped and pressed her fingers to her lips. I leaned toward the screen.

A voice from behind the camera asked the woman to turn around, but she ignored them and kept on singing. It was hard to make out the exact words of the song, but the feeling of it was like hunching inside yourself and searching for comfort, music meant to soothe your own soul.

The camera moved toward the woman and then circled around so that she was finally facing the lens.

I had never imagined my mother as an old woman. She was perpetually frozen in her early thirties, her skin smooth and her eyes bright.

This woman's face was hollowed and rough, like the people I saw living on the street in Phoenix. But her eyes still blazed, the fire behind them untamed. She was not just older; she was more feral, a person left to her own devices and no longer afraid of what she might lose.

Hess stared at the screen, her eyes shining. She reached out, as if they might touch.

I didn't know how to react, except that I felt like a kaleidoscope. With each twist of reality, I was pulled apart and then reassembled into a new configuration.

The video ended, but neither of us moved or spoke. After a while, the case manager returned and handed Hess a Kleenex from the box on his desk. She dabbed her cheeks and asked, "What happened to her after she left?"

He frowned slightly. "We do everything we can to keep track of our patients, including assigning them a case manager. But this is a volatile, high-risk population, and they usually drop off the radar." He pulled the file back and studied it. "In this instance, the case manager lost track of her almost immediately, and she never resurfaced in our system."

After Hess asked a few more questions that led nowhere, we walked out into the parking lot, and the light stung my eyes. The air was too soupy to breathe. I took out my phone and looked at the time. It was almost six. According to my birth certificate, I was born at 9:03 p.m.

Three hours left.

When I stepped from the stairs, my shoe sank a few inches into the swamp of the asphalt before I yanked it back. I looked over at Hess, who was pacing back and forth on her phone in front of the building.

I tested the asphalt again, and it sucked my sneaker down like quicksand. I scanned around, mapping different routes away from the clinic that could avoid the asphalt-covered roads, but they surrounded us. There was no way out. I imagined staying in this same spot for the rest of my short life: sleeping, eating, peeing, dreaming on this hard, safe concrete stair.

I felt a hand on my shoulder and startled.

"Rhea? Are you all right?" Hess asked.

I was suddenly afraid that if I opened my mouth, my words wouldn't make sense, so I nodded and grimaced as if I was too overwhelmed to speak.

Hess nodded sympathetically. "I called a friend in the Nashville Police Department about filing a missing person's report. He said there are organizations we can contact to get the word out with her real name and a recent picture. If she's out there, we're going to find her."

There was something about Hess's face, the way she seemed so forceful and confident, that felt like she was acting out the part of a determined woman, like it was some elaborate performance.

I just couldn't believe it; none of it felt real. "We don't know that was her," I said before I could stop myself.

Hess's brow furrowed. "What are you talking about? Of course that was her."

"But how could she survive a plane crash? It doesn't make any sense."

Hess sighed. "I know it seems impossible, but I am certain that was her, honey. That was her voice. She even used her real name."

Her tone was patronizing, as if she'd already decided I was insane.

"Don't talk to me like I'm crazy," I snapped.

Hess paled. "I'm sorry, that was not my intention."

Even if it was her, I had no idea how she'd stopped the curse. "I just . . . I think I need to go for a walk. I need to clear my head."

She took a step toward me. "I know this is overwhelming—I'm still trying to wrap my mind around it myself." She took another step. "Why don't we go back to the rental? We should eat something anyway."

"No, I need to be alone."

"I don't think that's a good idea." She took another step, and I realized she could grab me if she reached out.

She's going to take you somewhere. Maybe even back into that facility. This is not safe.

I took a few steps back. "What are you trying to do? I can take a walk if I want."

Hess moved even closer. "Rhea, honey, I'm not trying to do anything. I'm with you. I'm on your side."

Lies.

"Why would I believe anything you say? You've been lying our entire relationship."

Go. Go now.

I turned to leave, and Hess grabbed my arm, pulling me back. "Wait, Rhea, please—" But I yanked it away, leaping onto the asphalt and streaking across the parking lot, the muck sticking to my shoes. I made it to the grass on the other side without getting stuck, and then through another short stretch of asphalt to the other side of the street.

I heard Hess call out my name from behind, and I took a sharp left into a maze of tourist-filled streets. A crowd staggered toward me clutching boozy slushies with stacks of glinting plastic beads around their necks. I tried to make myself invisible, flattening my body against the side of a decaying brick building, but I needn't have made the effort. Their eyes were glazed and unfocused as they passed.

Another mass headed my way, this one so large they were forcing other people into the street, and I ducked down a narrow alleyway to the right.

I followed the alleys for a while, enjoying the silence. Sewage smells mixed with the odors spilling from the backs of the restaurants I passed—fried dough, stewed shrimp, Cajun spice. I passed a building vibrating with the chaotic rhythms of jazz, and I put my hand up to the brick to feel the pulse.

If only it was possible to live this way, to creep along the backside of the world and be able to experience its pleasures, protected and unseen.

The alley spit me out into a small park surrounded by a black iron fence with thickets of bald cypress and a great, hulking live oak at its center. It looked like it'd been there for centuries, posed and waiting as the city rose up around it. Dark shapes huddled in the shadows of the park, but I found an open space at the base of the tree.

I sat down in the swampy heat, feeling the sweat trickle from beneath my wig, and I flung it off into the dirt. I wouldn't be needing that anymore.

A figure a few feet away pulled back their hood and studied me. Their eyes were wild and familiar, and I peered through the dim light to get a better look.

"What you starin' at?" the figure asked.

"I could ask you the same thing," I answered. At least I no longer had to pretend.

"You don't look like you belong here, angel. Maybe you should move along."

I hadn't felt this comfortable in months. I was exactly where I should be. "You'd be surprised."

"Suit yourself," the figure scoffed, and it turned into a husky cough. "You got a family, angel?"

"I used to."

"What happened to 'em?"

I imagined Micah right then, standing in the kitchen. Looking out the window and wondering where I was. The pain he must be in.

I shook my head, attempting to clear the image.

"I used to have a family, too," the figure said in response to my silence.

"What happened to yours?"

"I left 'em. It was better that way. I would have hurt 'em if I'd stayed."

"I know what you mean."

The figure threw off their first layer to reveal a woman draped in a surprisingly clean shawl with tarnished bangles on her wrists. Her hair was a silver cloud that in another context might have looked chic and bohemian. "Would you like me to tell your fortune?"

I laughed at this notion, and then quieted, afraid the woman would think I was laughing at her. "How much?"

The woman smiled and said, "For you, angel? No charge."

I nodded, and the woman closed her eyes and held her hands up. She sat frozen like that for a few minutes, and I started to regret this decision. These were precious moments I was sacrificing for meaningless whimsy. Then, the woman spoke.

"I see you in the mountains. There is a man with bright eyes, and a few women, but I can't make them out."

She paused for a moment, squinting into the future. "Ah, yes, and a child. A beautiful baby girl with the man's sparkling eyes, and your tall, strong frame."

Tears collected in my eyes, and I whispered for the woman to please stop.

But she kept rambling on about this cheap fantasy of a life, and I shouted for her to shut up. The woman quieted abruptly, stunned by my rudeness. She cursed and spat on the ground near my leg, then gathered up her various bags and waddled toward another part of the park.

I looked at my phone. Only one hour left.

Where did the time go? Did the woman bewitch me?

I opened my backpack and took out the sleeping pills I'd been prescribed by a psychiatrist my therapist had referred me to. Then I took out a glass bottle of Coca-Cola I'd bought at a gas station. I used the burner to pop off the cap like Micah had taught me on the trail fifteen years ago, and I remembered us drinking them when we stopped in a little town in Virginia.

I took a sip, and it didn't taste like the memory. It tasted like pennies and white sugar, and I thought, *Good, let it be ruined.*

A twig cracked nearby, and I jerked my head toward it. The silhouette of a man in a white suit, shining as if it had its own light source, appeared at the edge of the park, and stood, unmoving.

Watching.

Waiting.

My birthmark burned across my chest, and I imagined how I might escape. I could climb the fence behind me and run in the opposite direction. I saw myself getting lost in the throngs of revelers along Bourbon Street, finding a hotel, curling up in a bed. The man would appear once again in the corner of the room, or out on the balcony, or in the bathroom as I took a shower.

As soon as I was alone again, he would find me. It didn't matter where I went. I could not stop what was coming.

My only hope was to escape my own body—this fearful, shrinking, claustrophobic shell I'd been carting around for months.

All you have to do is swallow the pills and lie back. Do it. Do it now.

Another silhouette appeared a few feet away, but this one was different—both soft and statuesque in the moonlight. She glowed like a goddess in the murk.

"Oh, thank God," Hess wheezed. "I've been looking for you for hours."

"I'm sorry," I whispered, hiding the bottle of sleeping pills beneath my thigh.

"It's okay. I was just worried." Hess leaned against the tree and tried to catch her breath. "Are you all right? What happened?"

I eyed the man waiting at the edge of the park. I checked my phone. *Forty-five minutes left.*

I would tell her whatever was necessary to get her to leave.

"Yes, sorry. I needed to get some air after seeing that tape. But then I got lost and ended up here."

"Okay . . ."

"I can meet you back at the rental."

"But how will you find it?"

"I'll ask for directions."

"I'll just sit here with you. I'm in no rush."

"I told you—I need to be alone right now."

Hess didn't respond and instead sat down next to me. Before I could protest, she said, "I want to tell you about the day before your mother died. The last time I ever saw her."

"You already told me—"

"But not all the details. Please, humor me."

I checked my phone again.

Forty-four minutes.

Enough time for a story. Perhaps after she finished, I could get her to leave. I nodded.

Hess continued, "I remember it was a week after she disappeared. We hadn't left the cabin yet, because I wanted to be there in case she came back. I probably should have taken you somewhere else, but I wasn't thinking. I was so terrified something had happened to Lou; it was the only explanation that made sense. I knew she'd been struggling, but the woman I knew wasn't capable of abandoning you like that.

"Then, that morning, there was a knock at the door, and there she was, standing on the porch. She looked rough, like she hadn't slept or eaten, much less bathed, in days. I took a step forward, and she took a step back. I'd never seen her flinch from me like that.

"I said, 'Oh my God, Lou! Are you okay? What happened?'

"She didn't respond; she seemed out of it, and her eyes kept roving around. I tried to get her to come into the house, but she insisted on staying out on the porch.

"I told her, 'Lou, just tell me if you're okay. We can take you to the hospital if you're hurt. Then you can tell me what happened.'

"She said, 'No. No hospitals. I'm fine. I just needed to . . . clear my head.'

"I had been so convinced that something extraordinary had happened, that I couldn't fathom what she was saying.

"I asked her, 'What are you talking about? Where did you go?'

"And all she said was, 'Nowhere special.'

"I still couldn't grasp what was happening. I said, 'What do you mean? Why did you leave Rhea locked in a trunk?'

"Lou's face drained, and she asked, 'Is she okay?'

"I said, 'She's fine now. Hopefully she won't remember it. But she was so sick and scared when I found her. Do you know how dangerous that was? She could have died.'

"She glanced behind me at you napping on the couch, and I swear, this shadow passed over her features. She said, 'It's hard to explain.'

"Now I was furious. I said, 'Jesus Christ, Lou, what is going on?' I didn't know how to talk to this person in front of me. It was like someone else had taken over her body.

"She said, 'No matter what I say, you're not going to believe me. So maybe it's best if I say nothing at all.'

"I looked at her, searching for my Lou. She was so dirty and thin. She reminded me of the addicts that hung out in downtown Nashville. I thought, *Oh God, she relapsed.* I asked if she was on drugs, and I told her I would get her help. But then she almost smiled, and she said, 'I'm not on drugs. I wish I was on drugs. I wish it was that easy.'

"I thought back to when she broke up with me ten years earlier, and I wondered if maybe it was happening again. She'd decided she needed her freedom, and now she was leaving us.

"When she refused to give any explanation, I told her, 'Then we're not coming to California with you,' just to test her. We were about to go out there to prep for her first movie, and we'd already rented a house for the summer.

"She didn't even fight me. She said, 'I think that's for the best.' She looked upset, but not in a way that I'd ever seen her. I thought she must be feeling guilty, like she had the last time she left me, and I just couldn't believe it was happening again, after everything.

"She said it was time for her to go, and she went over to the couch, and she hovered there for a second, watching you. Finally, she sat down and laid a hand on your back. You didn't wake up. She closed her eyes and stroked your ear and the little wisps of hair that curled around it. She started to hum 'Lullaby for a Demon Child,' which I'd never seen her do before. We sang to you all the time, but never that song.

"Then she stood up, and for a moment it was like I could see her again. There was my Lou. She took both of my hands and squeezed them hard. She said, 'I won't tell you to take care of her, because I know you will.' She smiled, and her eyes went glassy. 'Thank you for saving me, and for this beautiful life, my love. I couldn't have had it without you.'

"I thought, She's really leaving us, isn't she? Shocked, I said, 'How dare you do this to us. After everything we've been through, you're just going to walk away? You promised you would never leave me again.'

"She looked upset again and released my hands, then headed to her car. I kept shouting at her, but she didn't turn around. I told her she was selfish, and a bad mother. I said I would never forgive her for this, no matter what she did.

"Then I watched her drive away, and she was gone.

"That was the last time I ever saw her." A few tears escaped down her cheeks.

I tried to remember the feeling of my mother's last touch. But I had been asleep.

Hess took a deep breath, wiping her eyes. "I will always regret not listening to her when she said something was wrong. For not fighting harder for her. I saw what I wanted to see." She broke again, then righted herself. "Even if she's still out there, in a way, she's already gone." She reached for my hands, and I let her take them. "But Rhea, you still have a chance. And yours is not the only life at stake here. Think of what your death will do to Micah. Or me."

I pulled my hands back. I knew this was bigger than me. Did she think I didn't know that? She had no idea what was at stake here.

I thought back to eight days before, to the morning before I left. I had woken up and realized my period was late, so I took a pregnancy test just to be sure.

When the double lines appeared, I threw up in the sink.

All I could think was, *Why now? Why now when I'm so close to the end?*

I imagined the life the baby would have led, if only I had figured out how to save us both.

They would have been different from every person who'd come before them. They would have been blameless, untainted, *uncursed.*

Or maybe they would have begun the cycle again, hurting themselves and others, hurtling toward the same painful, inevitable conclusion.

It was better to end it now, while I could still die on my terms. I had a few minutes left.

"I need you to leave," I said to Hess.

"I'm not leaving you."

"Fine, then I'll go." I tried to stand up, but Hess grabbed my arm and held me down.

"No."

I tried to twist out of her grip, but Hess was strong, and my body had become so weak.

"You know what I will never stop thinking about?" she asked.

I stilled.

"I should have told her that I would never leave her, no matter what." Hess's voice cracked, and I felt it as a pain in my left side. "I should have pulled her to me and not let her out of my sight until I knew she was okay. That she was safe."

The pain intensified, and I wished it would just stop. I didn't want to hurt anymore. I moaned and hunched forward, my body nearly spent. I was so tired. So tired I could feel my cells slackening and losing shape. I couldn't hold it together any longer.

"I'm pregnant."

Hess put her fingers to her lips. "Oh, God."

"I know."

"How far along?"

"Only a few weeks."

Hess exhaled and looked away with the back of her hand held up to her mouth. She did not let go of my arm.

"Why didn't you tell me you were my mother?" I asked suddenly. I didn't want to die not knowing.

She turned back to me with her brows knit together in shame. "Oh, honey." She closed her eyes, then opened them. "When Mr. Blau told me you didn't remember me, I figured it would be too overwhelming for you. You'd just found out Belle was your mother, and now I was going to drop another bomb? I had all this love for you, and it just seemed like too much to put on you. So I decided I would rebuild our relationship from scratch, and when the time was right, I would tell you the truth. But then so much time passed, and I was afraid it would hurt you and you'd cut me off again, and I just couldn't bear the thought of it." She exhaled. "I was also ashamed of having given you up, and of you finding out who I really am. Not that I think there is anything wrong with what Lou and I had, but when you grow up the way I did, it's hard not to feel like there's something wrong with you if you love another woman like that." She grimaced. "Basically, I was a coward. I'm so sorry."

As much as I wanted to hate her for it, I could feel the love in what she was saying, and I could understand what she'd done. Sometimes you held back, or you changed yourself, just so you wouldn't scare someone with the full force of your emotion. Sometimes you felt like a little tortured thing, a dirty, sad demon child, who didn't deserve real love.

I pulled out my phone with the other hand. 9:00 glowed from the screen. I gritted my teeth and leaned back against the tree trunk.

"Three more minutes," I said, eyeing the figure at the edge of the clearing. He was still there, watching. Waiting.

Hess squeezed my arm.

I had run out of time. I wouldn't be ending this on my own terms.

But at least I would not face it alone. I could not describe the relief, knowing that someone was there with me. Someone who loved me.

I felt the figure move closer, fear searing my insides, and I willed myself to be calm and collected when he arrived. I closed my eyes, and "Lullaby for a Demon Child" popped into my head. I knew it by heart, from listening to the album over and over again. And perhaps from even before then, when my mother sang it to me as a goodbye, and the melody of it penetrated my sleep and left a sad, elegant scar on my brain.

I started to hum the song, and Hess hummed with me. I sang the first round, and then Hess came in with hers, and then we came together, singing in harmony. There was Hess's ancient sound offering comfort, and my wispy sound offering a bit of my own fragility. And then, Lou's phantom voice rose above us both, offering a glimpse at the beauty to be had in this life. We were three women in a dark wood, singing comfort to a doomed girl:

Baby, don't be 'fraid
When it comes for you
Baby, don't be 'fraid
'Cause I'm there with you

As our singing tapered off and dissipated in the air like smoke from a thin candle, my phone screen glowed 9:03.

I braced for the man to approach me, to take his cold hands and pry open my mouth. Pour the pills down my throat.

I waited for a long time, but nothing came. When I opened my eyes, I saw only Hess sitting next to me.

9:33 glowed from the screen.

"It could still happen."

Hess didn't nod or protest. She just sat there with me, in the feeling.

"If this is all in my head, why does every woman in my family die at 33? How is that possible, if there isn't something else happening here? How do you explain it?"

Hess paused. "I don't know that everything can be explained."

"What about the man in white? And the dog?"

I had never told Hess about them, but she seemed to know. "When you were little, you were surrounded by Lou's music, including *The Cursed Woman* album. I think those images were put in your head at a very early age."

It was possible, but I could feel my mind resisting the notion. What about the other people online who had seen the man in white? It still felt like something larger. I traced my birthmark. "What about this mark?"

Hess studied it. "Your mother told me her birthmark came from what happened to her mother while she was still in the womb. And so it follows that yours would come from something that happened to your mother while you were still inside her." She smiled. "That looks exactly like the tree limb outside my bedroom window that Lou climbed to save me from my wedding."

I imagined the scene, and it was like watching a fairy tale unfold: a tiny, feral woman scales a tree to rescue her maiden from an unhappy life. *This* felt like truth—it didn't try to reason away the uncertainty. There was still something magical and elusive happening here, but perhaps not in the way I thought.

"I don't have all the answers. What I do know is that your mother didn't die at 33. We know that from the tape. And you don't have to die now. You can keep living for a long time, if that's your choice."

I imagined trudging through the next few years as I had the last six months. Even if Hess was right, and I could keep living like this, why would I? Who would choose to live in constant fear? It was painful and exhausting—it drained me every day, leaving me aching and empty. What kind of life was that? And how could I bring a child into it?

I must have looked hopeless, because Hess said, "I know it's going to be hard, and sometimes you might want to end it all. But we can find you the right help. And you'll have me. And Micah. And this baby, if you want to keep it. Think of what you'd be giving up." Hess took my hand in hers. "I'm saying that I believe this is real for you, and I want to help you live and thrive in that reality. It's what I should have told your mother years ago. If I had, maybe she'd be with us right now. Maybe we'd be going through this together. Or maybe not." She wiped away a tear. "But dammit, I'm here now."

I imagined the life the fortune teller had foretold, of the mountains and the women and the little girl. The man with bright eyes.

Micah's devastated face appeared in my mind. Would he ever forgive me for hurting him? For leaving? How could he still love me? I'd done things believing that I would never see him again.

And none of this changed the fact that he wanted to commit me against my will. I still refused to be locked up.

"What is it?"

"I'm afraid of seeing Micah. After what I've done. It all feels too broken. Like it would still be better if I just disappeared."

"But Rhea—"

"Think about what I've put him through. He must be in so much agony, not knowing where I am. How could he ever take me back? How could he ever love me after this?"

"Rhea, he knows where you are."

"What?"

"I've been updating him. He knows I'm with you, and I'm keeping you safe."

"But why would he let you do that, after he tried to check me into that facility—"

"I made a deal with him."

"But why—"

"I told you I wanted answers, too, of what happened to Lou and why. I wanted to go on this journey with you and see what you saw, and when you really needed me, I wanted to be there. *Really* there, in your world."

I thought back to the last few days, of having her on this strange quest with me. I had taken her presence for granted, even resented it at times, but I couldn't deny it had grounded me. She was the calming presence I'd tried to visualize in therapy—the person that tethered me to the world.

"I don't want to get locked up somewhere I can't leave."

"I promise you that won't happen." She took a deep breath. "I know it seems like a hill you can't climb. But if you're still the little girl I raised, I know you can do it. And you won't have to do it alone."

Something slid into place in my mind. Belle had wanted this. For Hess and me to be together. The thought was like a soft grunt in my throat, a great, shimmering rightness. My mother had led me here, where I might be saved.

And maybe even freed.

EPILOGUE

rhea

2011

ONE YEAR LATER

I woke to a soft cooing on my birthday. I was thirty-four.

And I was alive.

There was a part of me that still didn't believe it. I scanned around the cabin, attempting to verify its authenticity. Was this the real world? Was I in a dream? A simulation? Had there ever been a real world to begin with, or had it always been something else, something that couldn't be verified?

I took a deep breath and asked myself if it mattered. In this dimension, whatever it was made of, or whoever was pulling the strings, I had Eos, or E for short, who was lying against my chest in the rocker where we'd both fallen asleep after a three a.m. feeding. In this world, I had Micah. I looked over at the bed and watched his chest rise and fall, his sandy hair now threaded with silver.

And somewhere in the cabin was my mother. Likely already up and making a simple birthday breakfast in her cabin fleece and diamond necklace. Hess was often only a few feet away, having moved in with us to help out with the baby.

I carefully moved E to her crib, praying that she wouldn't wake. I watched her serene, unmarked form illuminated by dawn and tried not to think about what lay ahead of her, of what kind of curses she would battle in this life. Then I threw on my jacket and pulled on my boots. If she woke, Micah or Hess would feed her the pumped milk in the fridge.

I left through the back door and walked with my hands in my pockets toward my favorite trail heading north up to the nearest peak. I could feel the new heft of my body as the path steepened. I'd gained weight from the baby and my meds, but there was also a pervasive exhaustion that pulled me down like strong gravity. I told myself to power through. The air was crisp against my cheeks as I hiked uphill, listening to the birdsong.

Sometimes it still felt like a struggle to get out of bed, and I avoided most large gatherings if I could help it. But the medicine and the therapy helped curb the hallucinations, the delusions, and the anxiety. I could see now how I had gotten lost in a world my mother had seeded early in my life, that had then sprouted and become its own strange universe. Not everything could be explained, but I was okay with that. I could live in the in-between, and still keep my feet on the ground. I had found things to keep me tethered—our little family of me, Micah, E, and Hess. Living in this cabin, surrounded by the peace of this forest. And a special new project I'd been working on.

I'd listened to every one of Lou's tapes, and I'd learned how greatly they diverged from the stories the world told, many of them crafted by Lou herself, and how wrong, and in some cases, how right, I'd been about her. Now I was going through the process of transcribing them into a coherent, written form.

I wasn't planning to publish the stories; I would never violate her privacy like that. But maybe one day, when E was older, I would share my mother's story with her, and she would understand where she came from without being haunted by it.

My doctor had said there was a chance she could develop mental illness like me, and Lou, and the women before her, but it was not guaranteed. The environment she grew up in and the experiences she had were also thought to play a role, and so maybe there was a chance for her, with Micah, Hess, and me there to protect and guide her, and to be there to support her if she started to struggle.

In this way, perhaps the curse could finally be broken.

We hadn't found Lou yet. Given how rough she'd been living, she could have died and been buried as Jane Doe, the gravedigger having no idea he was piling dirt on top of a country icon.

Or she could still be out there, living in the woods like the beguiling witch she was. Free as she always wanted to be.

The truth was, we would probably never know, and wasn't that like her, in the end? Even after listening to hundreds of hours of her life story, Belle Powers remained a mystery.

When the light began to materialize around me, I knew it was time to go back.

I approached the cabin from the front this time, and I saw Hess sitting in a wooden rocker on the porch, looking out over the mountains with her mug of coffee. I sat in the chair beside her, and we watched the sun slowly peek over the ridge, making the fog glow like electric fluff.

E laughed as Micah played with her in the living room, the little sounds of life adding music to the light spreading over the horizon.

Hess and I looked at each other, and we both had tears in our eyes.

Somewhere out there, Lou was watching us, and she was saying, "Damn, that's beautiful."

ACKNOWLEDGMENTS

Thank you to my editor, Laura Brown, for helping me find the right version of this story, and to her assistant, Natalie Argentina, and the wonderful team at Atria.

Thank you, as always, to my agent, Alexandra Machinist, for your power and your heart, and to her assistant, Xanthe Coffman, and the team at CAA.

Thank you to the queens of country music for creating and living with such vibrance—y'all are truly an inspiration.

Thank you to the Country Music Hall of Fame Museum, the Ryman Auditorium Museum, Dollywood, and especially the Jefferson Street Sound Museum run by the inimitable Lorenzo Washington. Thank you to *The Tennessean* for your reporting on life in Nashville over the years. And thank you to Ken Burns for creating a documentary on the history of country music, and to PBS for releasing it.

Thank you to my early readers—Kate Ringo, Alex Addison, Lauren Billingsley—and to my ride or die writing group—Timothy Wojcik, Rosa del Duca, Jason Baum.

I wouldn't have written this book without the many years my brother, my dad, and I spent traveling to see my great-grandparents Dorothy and William Overton, known to us as Gan and Papa, in Hendersonville outside of Nashville. I remember following Papa to his rural Baptist church to watch him preach, still driving in his nineties and flying over the back roads.

Thank you to my friends and family, especially my mom, for the many trips to Dollywood and Pigeon Forge throughout my childhood, the research trip to Nashville, and the endless support. Thank you to my stepfather, Doug—your struggle helped me understand these characters in a way I never could have anticipated. We miss you.

Thank you to my husband, AJ.

And thank you to my daughter, Ripley. I rewrote this book with you hiccupping in my belly, and now you're wiggling in the crib next to me. Your early arrival only put me a few weeks behind deadline. We love you.

ABOUT THE AUTHOR

Alli Dyer was born in Tennessee and raised in the mountains of Virginia. She is also the author of *Strange Folk,* and for the last decade, she has worked in entertainment and book publishing. She currently lives in Los Angeles with her family.

Atria Books, an imprint of Simon & Schuster, fosters an open environment where ideas flourish, bestselling authors soar to new heights, and tomorrow's finest voices are discovered and nurtured. Since its launch in 2002, Atria has published hundreds of bestsellers and extraordinary books, which would not have been possible without the invaluable support and expertise of its team and publishing partners. Thank you to the Atria Books colleagues who collaborated on *Night Songs,* as well as to the hundreds of professionals in the Simon & Schuster advertising, audio, communications, design, ebook, finance, human resources, legal, marketing, operations, production, sales, supply chain, subsidiary rights, and warehouse departments who help Atria bring great books to light.

EDITORIAL
Laura Brown
Natalie Argentina

JACKET DESIGN
Kelli McAdams
James Iacobelli

MARKETING
Zakiya Jamal

MANAGING EDITORIAL
Paige Lytle
Shelby Pumphrey
Abby Borchers
Sofia Echeverry

PRODUCTION
Liz Byer
Vanessa Silverio
Crystal Watanabe
Yvonne Taylor

PUBLICITY
Alison Hinchcliffe
Jessica Laino

PUBLISHING OFFICE
Dana Trocker
Abby Velasco

SUBSIDIARY RIGHTS
Nicole Bond
Sara Bowne
Rebecca Justiniano